Reviews of *Wounded Tiger* by readers like you:

Wounded Tiger is one of the most amazing books I have ever read! I could hardly put the book down. It is a great story of love and redemption that I will never forget!

—Sherri Craig

If you liked *Unbroken*, you will love *Wounded Tiger*. No other book about WWII so clearly contrasts the differences between enemies and so powerfully shows how we are all the same.

—Timothy Serbin

This is a superb read. The author brilliantly takes apparently disparate stories then weaves them into a single theme that at no time seems the least bit disjointed. As an Army War College graduate and a student of military history, I was most impressed with the historical accuracy of this book. Although set mostly during WWII, this is not a war story per se. It is a story of God's love winning out through a most brutal and savage conflict.

—William Funderburg

Troubled about current events? This book is for you. The material and historical value of this book are inestimable. The narratives contained within it express the only solution to the human predicament and they do so against the backdrop of WWII. The characters and events are impossible not to believe and every reader is certain, in my judgment, to be amazed and humbled beyond all expectation. I heard an interview with the author conducted by James Dobson at the time of the 2016 anniversary of the Pearl Harbor attack. The story is so much more than anything I anticipated that I am compelled to recommend it.

—The Language Tester

I had trouble putting this book down. I loved following the true stories of several people throughout its pages. It brought a whole new perspective to my view of our war with Japan and how I should view others.

—The Baker Family

Words are not adequate to describe. Absolutely phenomenal! If you are a WWII history buff, this book needs to be on top of your list. Upon hitting the halfway mark of the book, it became extraordinary difficult to put it down. I think I ended up finishing it around 2 am on a weekend. I rarely read books a second time. This is a book I will need to read again to more fully absorb the awesomeness of the accounts that are told.

—SoCal1996

Most Honorable. Not since *The Hunger Games* have I felt so enthusiastic about a book. I really, really loved this book!! After the initial awe of the characters in this extraordinary tale, I found myself appreciating the way the book itself was written. In a day of shock value and vulgarity in the name of truth, this book took the higher road of honor and simplicity while never straying from the truth. Every word, every quote, timed precisely right! Maps were so helpful! I want to reassure other female readers that this is a story about people during the backdrop of war. The author did an excellent job keeping the war part simple and understandable. Looking forward to see how this will be portrayed on film.

—Snowlover

A Wonderful Story—and true. If this were purely fiction, it would be an inspiring story of war, hatred, cruelty, and redemption. That it is true makes it one of those stories that MUST be read. When I finished the book, I exhaled, said "Wow!", and woke up my wife to tell her that she HAD to read the book. Amazing. Simply amazing.

—Jim Kaucher

Great read! This is one of the best books that I have read in a long time. It had me captivated from the beginning and just kept getting more and more intriguing. Loved it! I plan to buy some copies as gifts.

—Amazon Customer

War, Love, Hate, and Redemption. As a history buff with a pretty fair knowledge of WWII, I was entranced to read about the Pacific front from the primary viewpoint of the Japanese who lived through it. Mr. Bennett, an incredibly persistent researcher, dug deep and traveled widely into the histories of all the primary characters on both sides of the war. He has brought them very much to life, delving deeply into their histories, characters, and especially their emotions. Weaving them all together is the subject of faith—or lack of it—and how love can overcome hatred and faith can bring one back from the edge of death. I cannot recommend this book highly enough.

—Cruising Lover

This story brilliantly weaves together the lives of the three main characters. *Wounded Tiger* is a sensational read! The depth of the characters, the complexity of the story, and the strength of the research makes this story jump off the pages. This story brilliantly weaves together the lives of the three main characters and reveals truth that is stranger than fiction. I was captivated from the beginning and was left wanting more. This is an excellent book, and I would highly recommend it!

—Kindle Customer

Amazing true story. If you like nonfiction, you will love this book. If you prefer fiction, you will love this book. The story is amazing.

—Yoshi

Wow, Wow, Wow! Enthralling story and a must-read. *Wounded Tiger* is a brilliantly woven true story about two men who while seeking revenge find redemption and how a woman's incredible gift of grace and forgiveness affects the outcome. I was impressed how the story in an indirect way reveals the values and causes which made this time period to be known by many as America's Greatest Generation . . . Martin Bennett, with much research and a commitment to excellence, has produced a story that needs to be told and what will someday be an epic film.

—B. Kelly Hamner

Untold Tales of Pearl Harbor. From dawn to dusk, never putting it down, I devoured this book in one satisfying sitting! Author T Martin Bennett masterfully recounts the astonishing story of Mitsuo Fuchida, Japanese pilot who led the infamous attack on Pearl Harbor. Not a war story, but character-driven nonfiction originally written as an epic screenplay, *Wounded Tiger* traces miraculous, but authentic transformation from revenge to redemption—this, through the providentially entwined lives of Mitsuo Fuchida with an American war prisoner and a girl Fuchida never met. Bennett weaves together meticulously documented, albeit stranger-than-fiction, largely-untold tales of unlikely characters whose respective life stories unfold magnificently. So compelling is this book, I featured it on my radio program, TRUTHTalk Beyond the Sound Bite. *Wounded Tiger* offers a gripping account of WWII as you've never heard it. Read it to believe it; and believe it you will!

—Debra Mullins

EXCELLENT BOOK!!!! This book is one of my favorite books. It is very interesting, and when I started it, I never wanted to stop reading it. The scenes seemed very real and addicting. Overall I enjoyed this, and I highly recommend taking time to read this book. If I could rate this ten stars I would!

—David Crouden

No Words to Describe It. I don't even have words adequate enough to say how much I loved this book. It was not easy to read by any means, but I loved it so much. I cannot imagine the research that was done to produce such a treasure, Martin. Having an uncle who was in Pearl Harbor made it even more interesting to me. The tapestry of interwoven lives was beautiful. Toward the end of the book, I began reading it v-e-r-y slowly, simply because I did not want the story to end. Thank you, Martin, for writing this book. When it does become a motion picture, it will be spectacular! Everyone needs to read this book. It is full of inspiration, faith, and forgiveness.

—countrygirl

My husband enjoyed *Wounded Tiger* so much that I decided to read it. Someone loaned *Wounded Tiger* to my husband along with his praise for the book. I immediately purchased it as a Christmas present for my son-in-law who likes history and war stories. War stories are not enticing to me, and I felt it was a man's book, but my husband enjoyed *Wounded Tiger* so much that I decided to read it before wrapping it in Christmas paper for my son-in-law. I could hardly put it down, and it clarified some WWII battles for me, especially why Japan would bomb Pearl Harbor, and each character in the book became a personal friend to me.

—Ruth E. Vincent

This is one of the best books I've read in a while! This true account follows several people's compelling stories, and in the end, weaves them together in an unbelievable conclusion. It's a great reminder of how one person's life can have such an impact on so many around them (think *It's a Wonderful Life,* only true). Inspiring and encouraging!

—Shelli

Powerful read. Couldn't put it down. The writing and research are incredible. Anyone who loves Japan and wants to understand the culture needs to read this book.

—Rizon

Inspirational and Compelling! One of the most inspirational and compelling nonfiction novels I have had the privilege of reading is *Wounded Tiger* by T. Martin Bennett . . . With vivid description T Martin Bennett brings to life a war that begins with an alliance between Germany, Italy and Japan and sweeps across Europe, encompassing nations in the Pacific . . . With the use of Japanese words, excepts from propaganda, and news reports the author builds realism into an epic drama that's often forgotten . . . I can't say enough about the power of this amazing story, in whose pages we see faith, victory, and hope.

—Believer

Riveting! This story is absolutely gripping, especially when you consider that it's true! Found myself in tears a number of times near the end.

—gcsdls

Novel conveyed dynamics in Japan during and following WWII. I bought this book for a friend of mine who spent twenty-four years in Japan, beginning in 1948. I asked her for her comments after she read the book and they follow: "I lived in Nagasaki from 1948–-1951 and experienced the postwar physical and spiritual devastation of the Japanese people as reflected in *Wounded Tiger*. I thought the three wartime stories followed in the book—Japanese military, Christian missionaries, American prisoners of war—was a fascinating way to deal not only with history but with the influences that created a new way of thinking and being in the Japanese." I had conversations with my friend as she was reading the book. She was moved to tears at some points and "couldn't put it down." I think it is a fine example of the way novelization of history can convey powerful truths.

—carolyn in brentwood

A True Story—Thrilling from Beginning to End. *Wounded Tiger* is both a modern day epic and authentic historical account during one of the most desperate times in our world's history: a true story of providence and the miraculous, beautifully crafted and told by T. Martin Bennett. Couldn't put it down, and didn't want it to end.

—Dana J Peinado

I could not put this book down! This nonfiction novel by T Martin Bennett is a phenomenal read. Every chapter is captivating as Bennett reweaves the tapestry for us of lives touched by war . . . and by God. If you enjoyed *Unbroken* by Laura Hillenbrand, *Wounded Tiger* is a MUST-READ. And with the times as they are now—with our soldiers over in Afghanistan and Iraq—this book has never been more timely in its arrival. Masterfully written and gut wrenching in its depiction of pain, hatred, loss, and forgiveness.

—Julie Kovacic

The Ultimate Redemption Story. "What man intends for evil, God intends for good." There's no better example of that biblical truth than the story of *Wounded Tiger*. A man who was proud to have led an attack that killed thousands has his hard heart turned inside out by an act of inexplicable compassion. We've all heard the expression, "a Hollywood screenwriter wouldn't even make this up." Clear your schedule for a day or two. You won't be able to put the book down.

—Dana Cooper

Beautiful. It's amazing that all of these seemingly impossible events actually took place. This true story helps me have faith that there is method to the madness. The accounts of the three interwoven lives are brutal but beautiful. Couldn't put it down once I started!

—Jessica

WOUNDED TIGER

WOUNDED TIGER

*The true story of Mitsuo Fuchida, the pilot who led the
attack on Pearl Harbor, whose life was changed by an
American prisoner and by a girl he never met.*

*The three strands of the extraordinary
lives of Mitsuo Fuchida, Jake DeShazer,
and the Covells that weave into one.*

A True Story

by

T MARTIN BENNETT

BROWN BOOKS
PUBLISHING GROUP

Wounded Tiger

First Edition, February 2014
Second Edition, December 2016

Front cover artwork: Faith Te, www.artisticrealism.com

Cover Japanese calligraphy: Bokuseki Ohwada

Back cover photo: ©Ludmila Yilmaz via iStock Images

Brown Books Publishing Group
16250 Knoll Trail Drive, Suite 205
Dallas, Texas 75248
www.BrownBooks.com
(972) 381-0009

A New Era in Publishing®

ISBN 978-0-9912290-4-8
LCCN 2016957597

Printed in the United States
10 9 8 7 6 5 4 3 2

To order this book directly, please go to:
WoundedTiger.com

Social Networks:
www.facebook.com/WoundedTigerStory
www.twitter.com/TMartinBennett
www.linkedin.com/in/TMartinBennett

Film investor information: Investors@WoundedTiger.com

Wounded Tiger Insider Updates for
Information on book and film development:
bitly.com/WTI-Updates

Dedicated to my wonderful mother,
Carolyn Onstad Bennett,
who seemed to always find something
nice to say when no one else could.

January 12, 1931—February 26, 2016

ACKNOWLEDGEMENTS

Though I wish it were possible, I can't acknowledge every person who made a contribution to this book in one form or another, as the number would be in the hundreds, but I remain extremely grateful to all for the time and effort they spent to give me input, advice, corrections, and suggestions. This book is better because of you.

SPECIAL THANKS

To Haruko Fuchida Overturf, for her critique of the manuscript, for opening her home to me, and for sharing valuable family photos.

To Carol Aiko DeShazer Dixon for access to the DeShazer letters and papers held at the University of Pittsburgh and to her personal collection of photographs and material.

And to Hajime Watanabe for his extensive notes on the Covell family and WWII history in the Philippines and for his family graciously hosting me while I did research in Japan.

HISTORICAL CONSULTANTS

Donald M. Goldstein, PhD, Professor Emeritus at the University of Pittsburgh, New York Times best-selling author of over sixty articles and twenty-two books including *At Dawn We Slept: The Untold Story of Pearl Harbor, Miracle at Midway, God's Samurai: Lead Pilot at Pearl Harbor, Dec. 7, 1941: The Day the Japanese Attacked Pearl Harbor, Return of the Raider: A Doolittle Raider's Story of War & Forgiveness,* and others.

Dan King, Pacific War historian, Japanese linguist, author of *The Last Zero Fighter* and *A Tomb Called Iwo Jima*, lover of squid sushi.

David H. Lippman, WWII historian, journalist, author of e-book *World War II Plus 75—The Road to War*.

Glenn McMaster, Pacific War historian

Jonathan Parshall, co-author of *Shattered Sword: The Untold Story of the Battle of Midway*, founder of the *Combined Fleet* website.

Haruo Tohmatsu, Ph.D., Professor, History of Japanese Politics and History, National Defense Academy of Japan, author of *A Gathering Darkness: The Coming of War to the Far East and the Pacific, 1921-1942.*

PAID EDITORS

John David Kudrick—Many thanks to your useful suggestions, good advice, and encouragement.

David Lambert, editorial director of The Somersault Group—You were certainly the most constructive editor on this manuscript, and I'm deeply grateful for the amount of time you gave to this project. I only wish I could have spent more time with you.

VOLUNTEER EDITORS

Space limits me to those whose work was more significant than that of others, but I thank *everyone* for their input. The following people were especially helpful in their editing suggestions. Thank you very, very much.

Timothy Boyle
Rachel E. Dewey, Keuka College
Ellen V. Fuller
Donald Gilleland

Ken Haron
Shingo Katayama
Hai-In Nelson
Sue Schley

PHOTOGRAPH / IMAGE CREDITS

Image credits acknowledge sources and do not necessarily denote copyright ownership unless accompanied by the © symbol. Images in the public domain or of unknown ownership are uncredited.

INDIVIDUALS

Leon Avila
Carol Aiko DeShazer Dixon
Elmo Familiaran
Matt Jones via Shipbucket
Trish Lai
Miyako Fuchida Overturf
Christian Zebley

COMPANIES, INSTITUTIONS, AND ORGANIZATIONS

Alamy Images
The American Baptist Historical Society (ABHS)
The Associated Press
Getty Images
Kanto Gakuin University
Keuka College
The National Archives of Australia
The National Geographic Society
Philippine Central University
Seattle Pacific University
The University of Maryland / The Gordon W. Prange Collection
The University of Pittsburgh Archives / The Goldstein Collection

INTRODUCTION

Every event and every scene in this nonfiction novel are based on facts and history. The authenticity of these stories stands on its own. I don't like stories purportedly to be "true" only to discover that they're mostly water and hardly any "juice." This story is 96 percent juice.

That said, to weave the stories together more seamlessly and to recreate conversations, artistic license had to be used. When possible, the dialogue is word-for-word accurate. I have read and reread thousands of pages of research and primary source documents, traveled across the United States and to Japan interviewing experts, authors, and professors; I have submitted my work to people as close to the stories as I could find, and I have made every effort to ensure accuracy and honesty to history, to culture, and to the individuals.

Simply stated, the essence of every scene in this story is true.

T Martin Bennett
December 31, 2013

NOTES ON THE SECOND EDITION

This edition contains thousands of edits, over ten thousand new words, the addition of new and updated information regarding names, dates, geography, and other material, and the inclusion of over 270 historical photos, maps, and images.

I encourage every reader to resist the temptation to flip ahead to explore the photos as you may spoil some of the adventure of reading this true story, which involves the unexpected.

T Martin Bennett
October 10, 2016

Are we not all children of the same Father?
Are we not all created by the same God?

—*Malachi 2:10*

Prelude

The Sacred Nod

Japan is a land of earthquakes. Unpredictable and devastating, sometimes the ground gently shudders, a last slipping of unseen forces deep below the surface. Rarely noticed by everyday people, such quivers can be passed off as the wind simply rustling the branches of a tree. This was such a day. Only those closest to the epicenter felt the tremor that would lead to a cataclysm unlike anything the world had ever seen.

December 1, 1941. The Imperial Palace. Tokyo, Japan.

The weight of seventy-three million souls rested on the shoulders of the forty-two-year-old Emperor Hirohito. The boyish leader with his sparse mustache and frameless glasses sat motionless on a raised platform backed by a gilded screen. Assembled before him were the chief leaders of Imperial Japan. He exuded unquestioned authority in his navy blue uniform, replete with medals, a gold shoulder braid, and a red sash across his chest. Without a hint of emotion, he contemplated the petitions of his nineteen most trusted officials, separated into military and civil at two extended tables facing one another. Floor-length burgundy fabric patterned with gold perfectly draped both tables.

From Hirohito's earliest memories he had been saturated with the understanding that he was born not only the military and political leader of Japan but their spiritual leader as well—a living god to whom his subjects owed absolute obedience. He watched intently as Prime Minister Major General Hideki Tojo rose from his seat, the silence pierced by the jangle of his medals and the squeak of his chair as it slid back on the parquet floor.

Tojo bowed deeply—then stood upright. Only a month earlier, his

Prime Minister Hideki Tojo, Nov. 3, 1941.

iconic visage appeared worldwide on the cover of *Time* magazine—bald head, broad mustache, and black, round-rimmed glasses. Officers and soldiers alike knew him as "The Razor" as much for his quick wit and decision making as for his brutal military prowess. He patted his forehead with a handkerchief and pushed back his glasses. "Your Majesty," he began in the stark silence, "you have heard the words of each of your advisors and commanders in this room. At the moment, our empire stands at the threshold of glory or oblivion. We tremble with fear in the presence of His Majesty."

The emperor knew well why Tojo perspired, for he, too was haunted by the recent report from their elite group of researchers who had delivered their unanimous conclusion: Japan could not sustain its war with China for more than five years and could *never* win an extended war with the United States, whose manufacturing capacity was twelve times that of Japan. Although he had dismissed the report and was supremely confident in Japan's military preeminence, the communiqué unsettled him. Beginning a chess match with merely two pieces would yield better odds than starting an all-out war with the United States of America. Their agreed strategy was solely to assault and cripple the Americans and quickly secure terms of mutual nonaggression, allowing Japan free reign in greater East Asia.

He clenched his fist, unable to shake from his mind the warnings of Fleet Commander Admiral Yamamoto, who said, "To fight the United States is like fighting the whole world. Tokyo will be burnt to the ground three times before it's over."

Tojo's eyes turned downward. "We subjects are keenly aware of the great responsibility we must assume from this point forward."

The break of eye contact released the emperor to look upwards at the dark-coffered ceiling that permeated his council chamber with the scent of ancient wood. A final decision had to be made, and he knew it was his alone to make. Once the diver left the cliff, there could be no return. He'd already turned loose their task force of aircraft carriers from Hitokappu Bay five days earlier and, as Tojo spoke, they steamed for Hawaii at battle speed. But even now, he knew only a word from him would instantly turn them home.

The outcome of a war with the Americans could be disastrous, yet the apple on the tree enticed him. Germany had swept across Europe in a blitzkrieg, virtually unopposed, and was now battering the doors of Moscow. Japan had allied itself with Germany and Italy and had no

Emperor Hirohito in his full dress uniform.

misgivings that the Germans would be the ultimate victors of a European war that was all but over. This wasn't the time to hesitate and get left behind. Negotiations to end the United States' embargoes of oil and scrap iron had broken down and they *needed* raw materials. Besides, accepting any terms from America would be seen as a sign of weakness by his people.

"Once His Majesty reaches a decision to commence hostilities," Tojo said, "we will all strive to repay our obligations to him . . ."

Hirohito tapped his fingers in succession against the end of his armrest. He and his leaders had been furiously constructing a colossal war machine while the United States sat on the sidelines, bogged down by internal dissent as its outdated military deteriorated under a poor economy and the indecision of Washington. His nation was in the best position it had ever been in, or perhaps would *ever* be in to establish its dominance over the Pacific and East Asia. Japan was at its strongest, and America at its weakest. The Empire of Japan was finally poised for conquest and to secure its place in history.

"... to bring the government and the military ever closer together, to resolve that the nation united will go to victory, to make an all-out effort to achieve our war aims, and to set His Majesty's mind at ease."

Tojo remained standing as all eyes in the chamber turned slowly toward the emperor—waiting—waiting.

At times Hirohito entered into the conversation, but at other times he restrained himself from uttering a single word during the entire meeting. Such was the case on this occasion. Ever so slightly, he nodded with a crooked smile—and his feet left the cliff as he fell weightlessly down to the water far below. The precarious question of victory remained, but the pursuit of the answer was undeniable: millions would perish.

December 8, 1941 (Japan time). Early a.m. before dawn. The Pacific Ocean 275 miles northwest of Oahu.

In the black of night, the Kido Butai smashed through heavy seas at full speed due south. The carrier battle group was the world's newest and most powerful naval fleet—6 carriers tightly packed with 414 attack aircraft, 2 battleships, 20 escort ships, and 23 submarines. The massive *Akagi,* equipped with two levels of hangars housing ninety-one planes, was the largest aircraft carrier the Imperial Japanese Navy had ever built and was the flagship of the First Air Fleet under the command of Vice Admiral Chuichi Nagumo—a meticulous planner, cautious to a fault.

Salt mist and the smell of aviation fuel hung in the air of the hangars as engineers in white jumpsuits feverishly unlashed aircraft from their moorings on the floor, unchocked the wheels of fighters and bombers, and began transferring planes to elevators to be raised to the dark flight deck. The steel hull gave a haunting screech as it twisted from the pounding waves. Engineers fastened eighteen-foot torpedoes and 1,760-pound armor-piercing bombs to the bellies of Nakajima B5Ns; fit Aichi D3A dive-bombers with 550-pound bombs; and fed thousands of rounds of ammunition to Zero fighters.

In an organized frenzy, men coaxed aircraft into position onto waiting elevators. Planes began to fill the wind-blown deck, each engine coughing clouds of smoke and snorting blue flames from their exhaust pipes, rumbling to join the deafening thunder of a storm about to break.

At the front of the low-ceilinged briefing room crammed with men anxious for a fight, stood the senior flight commander of the First Air Fleet, First Carrier Division, the pilot who would lead the historic attack— Commander Mitsuo Fuchida. Facing his eager airmen seated upright and standing before gray walls, Fuchida stood proudly, his hands behind his back in his dark brown jumpsuit trimmed with a fur collar and overlaid with a brown kapok-filled float vest. He had a narrow, dense mustache. Having anticipated this day for months, today his joy mixed with the fire in his eyes and the adrenaline in his veins.

"In the event we fail to destroy the aircraft on the ground," Fuchida announced, "or we lose the element of surprise, I will give the signal for the dive bombers to begin the attack. Otherwise, the torpedo bombers will initiate, as planned." He scanned the faces of his torpedo pilots who nodded. He had longed and *dreamed* of this day of vindication before the eyes of the world.

Off to his side stood his fleet commander, the rather stocky Vice

Admiral Nagumo, and beside him, Fuchida's long-time best friend and chief planner of the impending attack, Lieutenant Minoru Genda in his officer's uniform, strikingly handsome. A blackboard behind him displayed flight paths to islands, his last-minute details, and exhortations of: *"As the gods have given us victory in the past, so will they give us victory in the future!"* and *"Win or lose, you will fight and die for your country!"*

Lieutenant Commander Mitsuo Fuchida.

As the idling planes rumbled outside the door, and their ship rose and fell in the turbulent sea, Fuchida sensed a powerful mixture of fatherly pride and deep compassion for the 146 young airmen before him, men he knew by name, men he had personally trained, all of them impatient, restless, serious—some whose mothers would weep when the day was over. Under any other circumstances he would have forbidden his fliers from taking off in such stormy seas, but such was their destiny.

Lieutenant Commander Minoru Genda.

"Years of training and careful planning have brought us to this moment in time." He paused to let his eyes penetrate the hearts of his fliers, then snatched his soft leather flight helmet from the table, pulled it over his head, and adjusted the goggles above his forehead.

"Our duty is not only to protect the untarnished past of our ancestors but to annihilate the enemies of Japan and to establish a *new* order for the future, the *imperial* way!" Passion energized his body as he paced like a tiger eyeing an opening cage door. "*This* is our day, *today*, our opportunity to mark our place in

Vice Admiral Chūichi Nagumo in his full dress uniform.

history. The world will soon know that we are the *new* samurai. The Empire's fate depends on the result of this battle. Let every man do his utmost!" He snapped to attention and threw both arms to the sky as the men leaped to their feet, then led his warriors into a resounding cheer, "Tenno Heika, Banzai! Banzai! Banzai!"[1]

To the east, the dark blue morning sky glowed orange along the ocean horizon. Engineers sprinted between aircraft on the windblown deck while pilots and flight crews clambered into their idling planes.

Shuffling through a crowded passageway, Fuchida stared distantly at the floor as he fastened his chinstrap and scoured his mind for any details he may have overlooked. Glancing up, Genda's face woke him from his thoughts. Airmen eased past them toward the angry chorus of attack planes. Fuchida lowered his hands and gazed far into Genda's eyes. This was it. There was no turning back.

---

[1] Literally, "Heavenly sovereign, ten thousand years." Figuratively, "May the Emperor reign for ten thousand years."

Part I

The Clouds of War

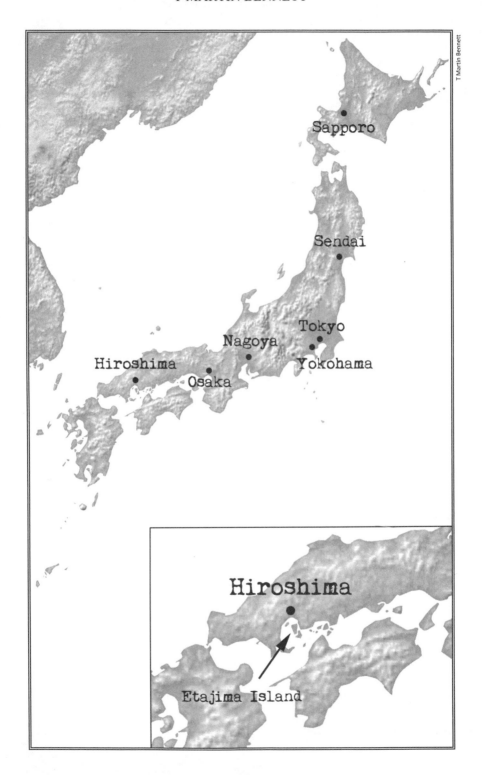

Chapter 1

Nineteen years earlier - Spring 1922. The
Imperial Japanese Naval Academy, Etajima Island,
Hiroshima, Japan.

Light burst through the morning clouds in a stunning array of
columns. It shone above a steep, densely green mountain ridge
behind the long, two-story red-brick building of the Imperial
Japanese Naval Academy. A rising sun flag flapped loosely out front in the
ocean breeze. Shirtless, barefoot cadets in white pants jogged past the
young, clean-shaven Fuchida and Genda in their blue uniforms on their way
to class.

Fuchida inhaled the morning hope. A new day. He studied the brick
structure and reflected on the strange fact that each brick had been
individually wrapped in paper and shipped 11,000 miles from their naval
mentor, Great Britain. Looking up, the startling sunburst in the morning
sky seemed strikingly similar to Japan's own naval flag.

"The sun rises on you, Fuchi," Genda said, staring at the sky.

Fuchida contemplated the golden sunlight piercing the clouds, then
looked back at Genda with a smirk. "It's only morning. Just wait until the
afternoon."

The two quickly converged with other cadets heading to class past
meticulously manicured pine trees up the stone steps into the brick
building.

The Imperial Japanese Naval Academy was for the elite—those being
groomed for leadership in the growing naval force of Japan. Fuchida was
exceptionally bright, if not a bit impulsive and cocky—a "hands on" type of
young man and, above all, passionate for his country. Genda possessed an
equally sharp intellect but leaned more to the strategic side of things. He

Miyako Fuchida Overturf

Mitsuo Fuchida with his Unebi Middle School Classmates (equivalent to high school elsewhere), second from the left, age 16, February 1919.

strove to do things better—better than anyone else.

Fuchida, aged nineteen, walked through the hallway among his classmates with a slight swagger that he'd earned. Mocked as a child by his classmates for his small size and shy demeanor, he had determined to prove them wrong. He didn't feel lucky—he'd worked hard for his place, a place even his own friends and family never thought he'd arrive. Despite failing both the physical and academic examinations on his first attempts, he spent hours swimming, studying late into the night and running—mercilessly disciplining himself to pass them both. And he did, gaining acceptance into the premier academy of the nation, an exclusive club. He'd bought his passage with sweat and sheer force of will and ranked among the top of his class.

Inside the schoolroom, cadets took notes, attentively cocking their heads to the words of their professor, Lieutenant Nakahama. Maps, charts, and ship illustrations adorned the walls; writing and diagrams filled the front blackboard.

"Submarines, destroyers, and now aircraft from our new carriers all lend their support to the heart of our fleet—our battleships." He smacked his pointer onto a large profile of Japan's newest battleship, the *Mutsu*. Fuchida had studied her well. She was less than a year old, armed with 8 massive guns which hurled one-ton shells over 23 miles—43,000 tons of modern military power, the pride of the Imperial Navy.

Lieutenant Nakahama gently laid the pointer across his desk and began to pace the perimeter of the classroom. "Continuing from yesterday, following the Great War in 1919, delegates from twenty-seven nations convened for the Paris Peace Conference to set terms for peace, and to form the League of Nations. For the first time, Japan was recognized and invited as one of the five major powers. But was the League truly an organization for world peace—or just another means for Anglo-Saxon nations to extend their own power and influence?"

Fuchida's eyes followed the professor to the side of the room as he adjusted the angle of the blinds.

"To clarify things, Japan offered the Racial Equality Proposal which simply declared all members be given equal and just treatment without regard to race or nationality. Despite the protests by some who declared that a colored person could never be equal to a white European, the proposal

The Red Brick Students Hall at the Etajima Naval Academy.

passed by a majority of votes—only to be set aside and defeated, when it was decided that an issue of this level had to be unanimous. Do you know who made that decision?"

Genda raised his hand, and the professor nodded. "Sir, wasn't that by President Woodrow Wilson?"

Professor Nakahama brought his hands behind his back. "Indeed. The chairman of the committee—President Wilson of the United States."

Fuchida glanced over at Genda with disgust as Lieutenant Nakahama completed his circuit to the front of the class.

"Japan was invited to dinner, yes, but then given no place to sit." He scanned across the faces of the cadets. "In the end, it was just as well that the proposal was defeated. The Yamato race has no equal on earth— unconquered for twenty-six hundred years." For a moment the professor and Fuchida caught eyes, connected, and exchanged the slightest of smiles.

The roaring engines of two gigantic idling flying boats nearly drowned out the instructions shouted by the officer as Fuchida, Genda, and the class of cadets huddled closely along the shoreline straining to listen.

Etajima sits about three miles due south of Hiroshima, a major city near the southwestern end of the main island of Honshu. The island spans roughly seven miles across at its widest and is nine-and-a-half miles long looking rather like a lobster with the area between its pinchers forming a wide inland bay—perfect for docking ships, boats, and seaplanes. Fuchida found himself the following morning with his classmates near the water's edge where the academy was built.

"These Felixstowe F-five biplanes were built in England," the instructor shouted, "and have a wingspan of over one hundred feet. Outfitted with two Rolls Royce engines, each engine produces three hundred forty-five horsepower."

Fuchida pressed nearer to the front and looked enviously at the pilot in the open cockpit.

The instructor shouted on. "Now, are there any among you who might aspire to become a—"

The British-built Felixstowe F.5 with Royal Air Force markings.

"Hai!" Fuchida shot up his hand without thinking. To overcome his innate shyness, he'd cultivated the habit to always raise his hand first and figure out what to do later. It had never crossed his mind to be a pilot, but the thrill of seeing the graceful aircraft taking off and landing in the bay sparked his desire for adventure.

"Fuchida! Hurry!" The instructor raised his hand motioning to Fuchida.

Genda gave him an encouraging swat on the back as he squeezed through the herd of cadets and an officer escorted him to the aircraft. After gingerly climbing up the side of the flying boat and plopping down in a back seat, one of the four places in the nose of the open-air cockpit, he clumsily strapped on a pair of goggles and buckled himself in. Attendants shoved the idling plane from the dock and Fuchida gave Genda a "thumbs-up," who responded with the same.

The propellers wound into a thunderous roar, the vibrations sending a chill of exhilaration through Fuchida's body, and the huge bird sped and skipped across the water as it accelerated, its engines straining until it skimmed off into the sky lifting him airborne for his very first time. Fuchida was in heaven.

Circling the island and passing over the academy, Fuchida waved wildly to the cadets below as he took in an expansive sight of the land he'd never experienced before. Between long views studying the ground, he examined every feature of the cockpit as if he'd just bought the plane and kept asking himself, "What do I need to do to be able to fly one of these?"

Afterwards, Fuchida and Genda discussed the day like little kids over a newfound toy. Fuchida beamed. "Maybe the navy is about ships, but one day I'm going to be a pilot. *That's* what I'm going to be!"

"I'll drink to that! On me!" Genda replied, who was equally enthralled with their new experience. "Aircraft are the future of the navy!"

Their paths had become one.

The Navy built the academy on Etajima for good reasons—near the shore naval base of Kure, which was home to massive shipyards, and near Hiroshima, a military center as well. But the school also wanted to keep the underclassmen and officers separated from society as much as possible to immerse them in military life. In celebration of their new dream of

becoming pilots, Fuchida invited Genda on a rare outing to Hiroshima. In the crisp evening air, they stood out from the crowds in their blue officer's uniforms as they strode down the busy sidewalks under wooden buildings plastered with signs and trimmed with gaudy lights.

"But we only had four battleships," Fuchida said, "and Russia had, I think eleven, so don't you think it was our *training* that led to victory at Tsushima?"

"We also had nearly

Fuchida's portrait while at the Etajima Naval Academy, 1920.

University of Pittsburgh

fifty cruisers and destroyers to their sixteen," Genda replied, "so that was a big factor. But Admiral Togo," Genda shook his head, "he's a naval genius. *He's* the one who really handed us that victory. Togo. A pure warrior."

The two came to a halt as Fuchida stared at a pair of attractive, young girls in kimonos who passed by from the opposite direction, chatting on, oblivious to the fixed gaze of their admirers.

After a slight pause, Genda asked, "So, Fuchi, what's more exciting, airplanes or girls?"

Fuchida took a long pull on his cigarette. "I suppose it depends on which I'm closest to. Pilots control planes, but then, girls control pilots . . ."

Genda smirked as they continued walking. "Let me take you to that bar I was talking about. They've got a drink with three flavors that'll set your tongue on fire."

As they made their way down the sidewalk, Fuchida paused to look up at a tall stone church, his eyes seeming to search for something in particular. "You know, that would be a perfect place for an enemy lookout. If I had my way, I'd tear those buildings down."

"You think so?"

"Westerners. Dividing our people's loyalty with their foreign god. Those people can't be trusted." He bristled with the intrusion of the beliefs of any other people than that of his homeland, especially Americans. Not particularly spiritual, but having been brought up with Buddhist and Shinto teachings, he was most offended by outsiders trespassing on his homeland. Foreigners and spies, he thought.

"No one should be called 'Great Master' but the emperor alone." Fuchida took a last puff of his cigarette while studying an elderly man gently escorting his wife up the stone steps to the church. "One day our empire will rise up while this old building, and everything it stands for will crumble to rubble and ash." He glanced over to Genda as he exhaled a cloud of smoke, then flicked his cigarette butt at the church, giving one last look up and down at the old stone structure, shook his head, and walked on.

Chapter 2

September 3, 1923. Kanto Gakuin School, Yokohama, Japan.

It had been a long day already, yet it had just begun. With sleeves rolled up and his hands on his hips, Jimmy Covell, a twenty-seven-year-old American, stood in disbelief before a smoldering heap of broken concrete and steel, once a school building. Clouds of smoke wafted by as two Japanese men trotted past with shovels and wooden buckets. He slid off his smudged, round, horn-rimmed glasses and rubbed them onto his sleeve, wiped his forehead with the back of his arm, and put his spectacles back on. Just from the way he carried his light frame, Jimmy made people feel he was the gentlest of men, and he was. "Has everyone been accounted for? Is anyone missing?" he inquired in English to the Japanese teacher beside him.

"We're still checking. Sasaki and Ohashi were killed by the collapse along with a helper named Kaneko."

Jimmy hung his head. He knew them all but felt there was no time for sorrow. He had to put it out of his mind for now.

"But I think all of the

The young and ambitious James Howard Covell, Kobe, Japan, 1920, age 24.

The middle school building following the earthquake.

students are OK. At least classes weren't in session," the teacher said.

Two days earlier the Great Kanto Earthquake had leveled the Tokyo-Yokohama area, killing nearly 150,000 people in violent tremors lasting almost 10 minutes. Out-of-control fires completed the devastation.

With both a Bachelor of Education degree from the University of Rochester and a Master of Theology from Brown University, Jimmy had volunteered to join the Baptist Overseas Missions Society three years earlier. They subsequently sent him as a teacher to the Kanto Gakuin School, founded in 1884 in downtown Yokohama, a sprawling industrial center south of Tokyo.

"How about Dr. Sakata's house? Is he all right?" Jimmy asked.

"We've still got some fires going. I'm not sure."

Jimmy slung his rucksack over his shoulder and clambered up the hill past others rescuing books from the rubble. As he approached, enormous flames and billowing smoke erupted just beyond the ridge. Dr. Sakata stood passively mesmerized by the blaze among a small group of onlookers, likewise helplessly watching the fire creep toward his wooden home. At thirty-two, he was young for a school president. His taut face was adorned with a shallow, broad mustache.

"Dr. Sakata, are you all right? Is your house OK?" Jimmy said.

Sakata shook his head. "I don't know. It's too hot to go in." He looked back at Jimmy head to toe. "How'd you get here from Tokyo? I thought the trains weren't running."

"They aren't. I walked." Jimmy slid his pack off his shoulder and dug through it. He was relatively athletic, and the half-day walk wasn't much to him. "I bought some rice balls in town, which wasn't easy to do." He pulled out a paper bag and an envelope with some money he'd sacrificially scraped together and held them out to Dr. Sakata, who appeared puzzled. Jimmy opened the envelope to reveal the currency inside.

"Oh, no, I'm sorry," Sakata said as he turned away. "I couldn't accept this from you. You'll need this for yourself."

Jimmy sighed at his American hospitality being blunted by Japanese propriety. "Now's not the time to be polite," Jimmy said. "Be practical." He forced the items into Dr. Sakata's hands. "The Mission asked me to help at the train station downtown, so I need to leave now to get there before nightfall." He left the gifts with Dr. Sakata who gave a short bow of thanks, then viewed the fire.

"We're going to figure how to hold classes in a few weeks, so stay in touch."

Dr. Sakata greets Jimmy Covell shortly after he arrived in 1920.

The collapsed main building at Kanto Gakuin.

Jimmy nodded, glanced up at the column of smoke, and turned away.

As he approached downtown Yokohama in the late afternoon under a smoke-ladened sky, the streets thronged with a river of people pouring out from the city, their backs strapped with what goods they could save. Most of the city had become a vast plane of smoldering black ash and rubble. Many tied makeshift masks or rags to their faces as they fled. Others carted the moaning wounded and the silent dead. Angry clouds of smoke and ash obscured the surreal view of the few stone and brick buildings left standing. Jimmy curiously eyed a four-story lone brick wall with empty window frames standing defiantly among the smoky ruins.

"Excuse me, please, do you have any water?" a woman said in Japanese.

Turning to the troubled voice, Jimmy spotted a young lady with a baby boy fastened to her back pleading to passersby, who only gave rude glances and pushed on with their exodus. "Please?! My husband is dead! Please, water, someone!"

Jostling through the mass of people, Jimmy made his way to the woman in her pink kimono, smudged with soot, and attempted his best Japanese, "I have water."

She began to turn with a smile, then was taken aback, not expecting to

see a westerner. Regaining herself, she smiled and gave a brief bow.

Jimmy reached into his bag and felt for his canteen and continued in his clumsy Japanese, "I have water. More water and food at train station." He prayed to God they had the water he'd heard about as he gave the canteen to the mother, who clutched it and gulped the water. Jimmy gently stroked the hair of the content, little boy on her back, oblivious to the surrounding devastation.

The woman bowed again and spoke while panting from the long drink. "Thank you so very much." She shyly turned her head to her son on her back. Jimmy smiled and brought the canteen to the little boy's puckered mouth as the young lady studied Jimmy's face. The boy was fascinatingly beautiful to him.

He screwed the cap back on and motioned for the woman to follow him as he navigated upstream against the tide of the fleeing masses. "I take you to station. Come."

One of the few structures to defy the odds of destruction, the Yokohama train station stood intact when Jimmy and the distraught mother finally arrived near sunset, the dusk closing the sky with a melancholy reddish brown. Having heard of food and water, thousands converged on the terminal lit by oil lamps. Uncooked bags of rice, sandwiches, and drinks of water were snatched up as fast as the volunteers could hand them out. Each table displayed folded paper signs in English and Japanese that read: *Courtesy of the American Baptist Mission Society.*

Jimmy escorted the mother and child through the crowd to a group ladling water into whatever containers people held out. "Water for you, and for beautiful child. Food, too. Sleep here tonight." He gave a short bow and

The woman peered up, clearly touched.

Jimmy smiled and rubbed baby boy on her back. "My wife and I have child coming. I understand." He, too, had to hold back his emotions.

She smiled, nodded, and looked into Jimmy's face one last time, then blended into the line waiting for water.

The volunteers consisted of a mix of Japanese and Americans, young and old, men and women. Despite the desperation of the circumstances, those seeking relief seemed to cooperate graciously. Jimmy felt overwhelmed by the immense needs of the people and the paltry goods the mission had for so vast a crowd. But he knew he should try to help however he could—at least, that's what he'd told his pregnant wife, Charma, two days earlier when he left her.

As he came behind a table, a petite American female worker greeted him. "Hey, Jimmy. Our house is nothing but a pile of sticks. The place was *completely* wrecked. I'm staying with friends now. How about you?"

Jimmy handed out two bags of rice to an old woman who smiled,

Survivors of the 1923 Kanto earthquake seek shelter outside the destroyed city.

nodded, and said, "Arigatou gozaimasu."[2]

"Oh, our house in Tokyo survived the quake all right, but not the fires," Jimmy said. "The house is gone. We just have our clothes and our lives. Three people at the school were killed, but the city—wow. It's unbelievable."

The crowds froze and looked up with anxiety as an aftershock rocked the station swaying the hanging oil lamps.

The worker spoke softer under her breath. "A lot of folks are spreading rumors that Korean workers set the fires and then went and poisoned the wells."

Jimmy shook his head and cautiously glanced around. He knew the Japanese wouldn't understand her English, but he wanted to see if anyone noticed.

She reached back and grabbed another tray of rice bags. "Vigilante groups rounded up Koreans, beat them, and killed them. Lots of them. Some say hundreds."

Jimmy stopped to look at her. "Who said that?"

She turned her back to the tables. "I saw it myself. Five or six Koreans tied to trees by a mob." Her voice trembled as she brought her hand to her

---

[2] Thank you very much.

mouth. "Their noses were cut off, eyes gouged out, covered in blood, still breathing."

"Good Lord! Where were the police?!"

Her eyes filled with tears. She looked back at Jimmy. "They were the ones beating them."

The next morning, filthy and exhausted, Jimmy hiked back to the home where friends hosted him and Charma, a place outside Tokyo on a narrow street lined with wooden homes packed together at the foot of a green mountain. The quake damaged some houses, but all remained relatively upright. Grateful for the fresh, smoke-free air, he noticed sheets on a clothesline fluttering in the wind as a dog barked at him. He glanced down at the wiry, yapping canine. "You have no idea, my friend."

After taking off his shoes inside the doorway, he collapsed into a chair at the kitchen table.

His very pregnant wife, Charma, brought a bowl of noodles, being careful not to spill it. "Where'd you stay last night? We were a bit worried."

"Oh, at the station downtown," Jimmy mumbled. "I was so tired I could've slept on a pile of bricks, and there were *lots* of piles of bricks to choose from. I made it to the school the day before. It's an incredible mess. Three people were killed in the collapse. I don't know exactly what happened." Jimmy blinked slowly. "But we're still going to open in a few weeks. I'm looking forward to teaching again."

"The soup's hot. Give it a minute to . . ." Charma winced in pain and turned her head.

Jimmy jumped up. "No, no, no! Let me get that. You have enough on your hands, honey."

Miriam, who owned the house with her husband, walked in with her chin up. "That's it, Charma. No guests serve themselves in my house. I've got that." Charma rolled her eyes as Jimmy helped her into a rather beaten-up easy chair. She took a deep breath and sighed.

"You're so sweet," Charma said. "Won't be long now. What do you think of 'Peggy'?"

"Well, Peggy's a fine name," Jimmy said as he squatted beside her and gently rubbed her belly, "but . . . I thought you were giving us a boy."

"Girls first. You know that."

Jimmy took her hand and melodramatically kissed it. "Yes, indeed. How could I forget? 'Peggy' it is."

Chapter 3

January 1926. San Francisco Bay.

The biting wind ruffled Fuchida and Genda's navy blue pants as they stood motionless in a crisp "at ease" posture with their hands behind their backs. The entire crew lined the rail, spaced evenly down the length of the cruiser *Yakumo*. Three American battleships escorted them and two other cruisers into the San Francisco Bay as seagulls called from above.

Fuchida studied the new, stark-white US battleships, guns proudly cocked into the sky at their maximum angle, then wistfully glanced at their own aging, turn-of-the-century Japanese cruisers breathing smoke from triple stacks.

Maintaining his posture, Fuchida whispered to Genda, "Look at us in

The 624-foot, 33,000-ton USS Maryland *in her lighter paint before the war, one of three Colorado-class battleships in America's new navy.*

The 25-year-old training cruiser Yakumo
came in at 434 feet and displaced 9,600 tons.

our old smoky rust buckets! And look at the *Maryland*, the pride of the American fleet. It's *humiliating!*"

Having successfully graduated from the naval academy at the top of their class, Fuchida and Genda proceeded on a final training mission that took them to one of Japan's allies, the United States. Despite building tensions, the two nations retained their relationship forged during the First World War.

"Relax," Genda whispered back, likewise unmoving. "You have to ride an ox before you can ride a horse." Genda grinned.

Fuchida smoldered.

After the captain had moored their cruiser on the same pier as their host battleship, *USS Maryland*, he briefed his cadets in the main mess area. "I'm sure you're looking forward to seeing the city and touring the American battleships. Just remember that America is still our ally. You represent the emperor and all of Japan . . ."

Under a sunny sky with a chilly bay breeze, Captain D. F. Sellers personally and proudly gave the tour to the eager Japanese cadets aboard his *USS Maryland*. Speaking with great gestures on the forward deck of the battleship beneath one of the mammoth gun turrets, he continued his impromptu speech. "... and can fire a twenty-two-hundred-pound shell up to forty thousand yards. That's twenty-two miles—considerably beyond the horizon." He ended with a smug smile.

A Japanese cadet nodded and turned to his classmates to translate into Japanese. "It will fire a shell that is, ah, one thousand kilos, a distance of twenty-two miles."

As the band plays, Admiral Wiley, commander in chief of the United States Fleet completes his visit on the flagship of Rear Admiral Hyakutake, commander of the Japanese Training Squadron in San Francisco, California, January 1926.

Fuchida whispered, "I know, I *know!* We have the same guns on our battleships, you idiot! Ask him about the planes in the back. That's what I'm interested in."

Later they stood beneath the two floatplanes mounted on a raised launch rail on the rear deck of the battleship: Vought UO-1 floatplanes— biplanes that were designed with a single large pontoon under the plane in the center with two smaller pontoons below the wingtips for stability. The aircraft were catapult launched for reconnaissance missions and then, when returning, would land in the water to be recovered by winch and hauled back onto the ship.

As the captain carried on, Fuchida elbowed Genda and whispered in Japanese, "They think of planes in terms of reconnaissance only. Why can't aircraft be used as attack vehicles? Why not?"

"I was just thinking the same thing," Genda whispered back. "No plane's really been developed that's capable of attacking a capital ship effectively. It's never been tried. It seems foolish that even our aircraft carriers only launch scouts and fighters to protect the battleships and cruisers and to communicate shellfire adjustment on targets."

"One day the *carriers* will rule the seas," Fuchida said, "attacking battleships that can never reach them." Glancing back at the enormous guns of the rear turret, he smiled and said, "These big guns will be useless."

Genda looked up at the floatplane and back at Fuchida with a glint in his eye.

The tour ended below decks in a cramped interior that exposed the inside hull of the ship. Captain Sellers crouched down and rapped the steel wall with his knuckles. "Using the latest advances we constructed a triple layer hull with thirteen and a half inches of steel at the waterline." He stood upright, adjusted his hat and put his hands on his hips. "Combined with watertight compartments, the *Maryland* is just about unsinkable."

As the translator spoke in Japanese, Genda leaned to Fuchida and whispered, "The clever hawk hides his talons."

"And who knows what the future holds?" Fuchida replied.

Captain Sellers glanced over at the whispering two, who quickly smiled and nodded.

Fuchida attempted his best English. "Very impressive!"

The following morning, the captain assigned Fuchida to escort a group

Vought floatplanes on the aft deck of USS Tennessee.

of Japanese civilians, mostly farmers, who came to tour the *Yakumo*. One of the highest concentrations of Japanese anywhere in North America was in San Francisco, and this was a rare opportunity for the immigrants to meet with some of their own countrymen. After following them up the gangplank of the aging gunboat, Fuchida in his navy blues led the party of simply-dressed commoners beside one of their rusting gun turrets layered with multiple coats of blistered paint.

As they stood listening to Fuchida's little speech about the ship, the visitors kept looking off at the stately, new *Maryland*, three times the size of the *Yakumo*.

One of the farmers pointed finally pointed to the ship on the other side of the pier. "Midshipman, are there any battleships like *that* in Japan?"

"Yes, of course, we have a very modern fleet with brand new battleships, just like the American battleships." Fuchida smiled, carefully concealing his own feelings.

"Then why didn't you bring one of *those* instead of *this*? It's so old it's embarrassing! It'll only create more prejudice against us."

"Well, you see, this is simply a training ship for young graduates." He paused. "What do you mean—*more* prejudice?"

Another man with a worn, cone-shaped straw hat pushed forward, "They've passed laws against the Japanese, preventing us from immigrating here or owning land. Now we've lost our farms."

Another blurted out, "And we can't even defend ourselves in court. We're not allowed to testify. It's not fair!"

Fuchida uncharacteristically spoke his thoughts, "Why would they do that?"

Still, another pulled out several newspapers and waved them in the air. "Look at this. See what they write about us!"

Fuchida took the papers and, with a shake, flattened them out. Having made a point of studying English, he could easily read the headlines that shouted: "*Japanese a Menace to American Women*" and "*The Yellow Peril— How Japanese Crowd Out the White Race*." A wave of shock, disgust, and even fear came over him as he scanned the papers. From behind, one of the men tapped Fuchida on the arm and held out a matchbox. Fuchida turned to look at the matchbox, then quizzically at the man's face. The man pointed at the wording on the box: *"White Men & Women—Patronize Your Own Race!"* Fuchida looked out across the bay. After coming to the shores of the great United States for the first time in his life, he felt like he had been slapped in the face.

The man with the straw hat continued. "We just want to farm and live our lives with our families, but I can't even bring my wife and children here to join me. It's as if they're saying that we're not welcome here, that we're not good enough, but why? We work hard. We don't bother anyone!"

"No one speaks up for you?" Fuchida asked.

"A few American businessmen and some churches, but can't you do something?"

The group all turned to look at Fuchida, ambushed by an ugly truth for which he had no response. His years of focused training at the naval academy had kept him from lifting his eyes to see the dark clouds gathering in the distance.

After the tour, Fuchida stood at the base of the gangplank as the small

In late 1927 the Navy promoted Fuchida (far right) to sublieutenant and gave him his long-awaited orders to join the Navy's flight training school at Kasumigaura.

company left, shaking the hand of each visitor and giving a slight bow; each likewise bowing in return.

As the farmers continued down the pier, three young American sailors in their white uniforms, black neckerchiefs, and round canvas hats cocked to just the right angle approached from the opposite direction, towering over the Japanese farmers. The sailors came to an abrupt halt, looked over the aging cruiser, then at the men.

"Hey, Chinaman! Ching chow yung pang!"

The Japanese men peered up at the sailor in confusion.

"You call that a ship? We use stuff like that for target practice!"

Another sailor made hand gestures of guns shooting, then tilted his arm like a sinking ship complete with sound effects. His buddies snickered and shook their heads.

Fuchida didn't hear every word, but he completely understood their message. The farmers looked back helplessly at Fuchida, his nostrils flaring like a caged animal being pelted with pebbles by ignorant, fearless children.

Chapter 4

January 7, 1931. The Kashihara Shrine complex,
twenty miles southeast of Osaka.

Filled with joy and anticipation, Mitsuo Fuchida stood proudly in his ceremonial blue dress uniform complete with sword beside Haruko Kitaoka, meticulously adorned in a red kimono that faded through gold into a scene of birds and flowers—her jet-black hair coifed and her face made up with traditional white rice powder. With her head humbly bowed, the two stood before a crowd of sixty guests in the Shinto shrine for their wedding ceremony. His promotion to lieutenant in December made the moment that much sweeter.

Having only been introduced to Haruko a month earlier, Fuchida found himself on a whirlwind adventure. His mother and father, concerned with him having no wife and family—an oversight of the busy pilot of twenty-nine—arranged a meeting with a qualified young lady, and Haruko appealed to him from the start. Although engagement was usually six months, knowing that his next tour at sea could last a year, this tiger was in no mood to wait. As was his manner, he set his goals and quickly moved forward.

The soft, traditional gagaku music drifted through the room while the priest poured sake into the third of three flat cups, lifted it, then presented it to Fuchida, who took three small sips and bowed returning the cup to the priest, who then held out the cup to Haruko.

Fuchida pushed from his mind his days and nights of flying and sailing and could see nothing and no one but his bride-to-be, who, likewise, took three sips and bowed to the priest. As she raised her head, he caught her eyes, and both attempted to restrain their smiles.

Music graced the air along with sumptuous food. Lots of it. With

Mitsuo (right) & Haruko (left) Fuchida.

months of hard work laying ahead, Fuchida made the most of every moment with Haruko, who now appeared beside Fuchida in a blue kimono, her first change of the night. He wanted the time to last knowing it would be over in the blink of an eye. To the delight of their guests, Fuchida picked up a piece of broiled fish with his chopsticks and brought it up to Haruko's mouth as she smiled and shook her head. Not satisfied, the guests shouted and cheered as Fuchida persisted. Finally, Haruko took a small bite of the meat to the applause of the guests and tried her best to chew while laughing.

Yes, he thought, she is indeed the one.

Chapter 5

Spring 1931. The Deschutes River, Central
Oregon.

Jacob "Jake" DeShazer, a lanky, blue-eyed boy of nineteen, stood fishing
for steelhead trout along the boulder-strewn riverbank in his long-
sleeved white shirt, suspenders, and a worn fedora. A few paces
upstream his mother fished in her typical simple dress draped over her
heavy frame and a straw sun hat. Green brush and craggy trees clung to the
rocky banks that gave way to steep, arid hills of dead grass and high-desert
scrub.

Though Jake loved the peaceful sound of the river and the distant
birds, inside he wrestled with what on earth he'd do after he graduated high
school. In his mind, he rehearsed how to fend off his stepfather's probing
questions and sorry suggestions he expected that evening.

A trout tugged his line, darting through the clear water as Jake pulled
back. The line went slack. Jake jerked up his pole in frustration. "That last
one was a good eighteen inches! Stupid fish!"

"But smart enough to get away from you." His mom smiled, then
paused. "Have you thought about that offer from Mr. Jennings at the
hardware store?"

There it was again. She was fishing for more than just fish. Jake's dad
died when he was two, and his mother had remarried soon after, taking her
second husband's name of Andrus. She was a tough woman, but not hard.
Her words were kind, her love and affection true to the bone, and when she
prayed at the table, Jake knew she meant it. To him, she was the epitome of
what came to mind when someone talked about baseball, apple pie, and
"Mom." But there came a time when she needed to let him be a man on his
own, and Jake felt that time was now.

Carol Aiko DeShazer Dixon

Little Jake and his family, around 1920. Top row: Julia DeShazer, mother Hulda DeShazer Andrus; second row: Jake DeShazer, Ruth DeShazer, step-father Hiram Andrus with Jake's half-sister Helen Andrus on his lap; on the bottom is Glen DeShazer.

"He doesn't pay anything. Not enough, anyway," he said. Jake liked his stepfather, a wheat farmer, but wasn't of the mind to be a farmer himself.

"Well, something's better than nothing, and we could use the help." Mrs. Andrus pushed aside a wiry bush and gingerly stepped over the rocks to reposition her line. Her pole yanked down, then up, as a trout churned the waters and splashed into the air. "But not smart enough to get away from me! This one's coming to dinner tonight!"

The western sky glowed purple to orange above a low ridge of mountains silhouetting the Andrus' 640-acre wheat ranch, a collection of wooden farm buildings and a spinning windpump in Madras, Oregon. Fenced pens and barns housed ten horses and a dozen dairy cows. The snort of a mare at the fence blended in with the warm sounds of family echoing from the glowing windows of their farmhouse.

Seasoned fish sizzled in an iron skillet tended by Helen, Jake's thirteen-year-old half-sister, as the family took their seats at the table—Ruth, Jake's big sister; Glen, just two years younger than him; and Hiram Andrus, his stepfather, who tucked a faded red and white checkered napkin into his collar and continued the press on Jake.

"What about Mr. McGregor's cattle ranch? You're good with horses, Jake."

"I suppose so. I can stop by there next week." Jake yanked the napkin from under his silverware, flapped it open, and laid it on his lap.

"Make way for the cornbread!" Mrs. Andrus announced as she raised a tray with potholders over their heads to the table.

"Right here!" Glen reached for a knife right when the tray thumped the table and filled the air with the warm scent of sweet corn.

Mrs. Andrus pulled off her mitts. "Well, we've got to celebrate Jakie's graduation tomorrow."

Glen sawed his knife across the cornbread. "You sure he's graduating?"

Mr. Andrus replied, "If he doesn't, we'll give him another try next year," and gave a wink at Jake, who punched Glen in the shoulder.

Mr. Andrus turned to Glen. "Don't you dare take a bite until your

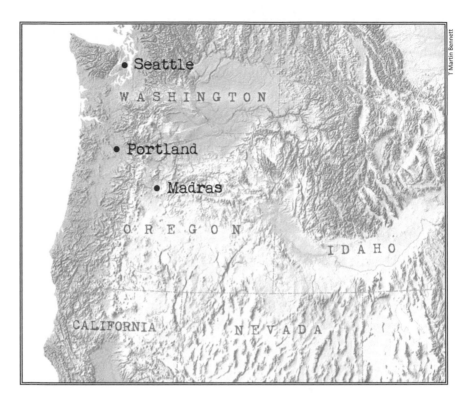

mother sits down and we give thanks."

Glen shouted, "Helen?! C'mon and sit down!" Helen proudly carried in the platter of sizzling fried fish on blue-and-white stoneware while Mrs. Andrus finally took a seat at the end of the table opposite her husband with a big sigh.

"OK! I think we're all ready!" she said.

Jake turned to his mom. "I want to save up and one day buy my own house, Ma. Maybe even build it. I want to build something that'll last. I just have to have the right job."

Ruth poured herself a glass of milk. "You couldn't build a chicken coop, so you can forget about a house."

"Oh, stop," Mrs. Andrus said. "You can do it, son. Now, let's hold hands." The commotion at the table turned still as they reached for one another's hands and bowed their heads.

Jake DeShazer on the top left of his high school graduating class of 1931.

The following afternoon, Jake and his classmates stood in their Sunday best on the steps of Madras High School for their class photo. The girls looked like they'd been waiting for this all year; the boys stood awkwardly as if they couldn't wait to get home to change.

Under his black drape, the photographer fumbled around. "Hold it . . . smile. OK. Got it." He ducked out from the cloth and stood up. "Now go out and change the world!"

Jake rolled his eyes as the proud parents broke out into a smattering of applause.

Jake's official high school portrait.

Chapter 6

Fall 1931. The Kanto Gakuin School, Yokohama, Japan.

The college campus stood empty, but the muted sound of singing flowed from the school gymnasium that featured a tall, square spire wrapped in ivy. Eight years after the devastating earthquake, the small college had been rebuilt and combined with another school. Inside, nearly 500 students sang a hymn in Japanese— "A Mighty Fortress Is Our God."

Although athletic, Jimmy was a pianist and sang with the best of them—a member of the glee club throughout his college years, but today he stood shoulder to shoulder with the students. Finishing the song accompanied by a simple organ, Jimmy sang out in Japanese with his whole heart. He didn't just sing the words, he meant them.

Let goods and kindred go, this mortal life also;
The body they may kill: God's truth abideth still,
His kingdom is forever.

At the podium, Dr. Sakata bent the squeaky gooseneck microphone. "Thank you so much. You are excused to classes."

That evening, Jimmy hunched at a small desk below a wall of books pecking away on a typewriter finishing his newsletter. Although his family of five lived in a small Japanese-style home with tatami mat flooring and sliding paper doors, they managed to squeeze in a couple pieces of Western-style furniture.

Jimmy barely heard his six-year-old son, David, screeching on his violin in another room, or saw Alice, almost five, finishing a glass of milk at the kitchen table beside Charma. Peggy, now eight, sat curled in a blue loveseat lost in a book. Jimmy continued at the typewriter, pausing now and then to adjust his glasses and roll up the sheet to read what he'd just typed.

Charma called from the kitchen, "How're your freshmen boys doing in English this year?"

Jimmy kept clacking away. "Better than I'm doing in Japanese."

Charma studied a magazine and slowly rose from the table, still reading. "Hey, you didn't tell me they published your article in the college paper."

"You didn't ask." Jimmy grinned without looking up.

Charma squeezed into the loveseat beside Peggy, who glanced up from her book. "Peggy, listen to what your father wrote: *Why do children work so hard in the fields at such a young age? Why do they work so hard in factories?*"

Jimmy stopped typing to listen.

"Why are women and children allowed to be taken advantage of in factories to earn big profits for corporations? And why do we stand by and ignore these things?"

Jimmy spun around in his chair pointing up an index finger with each hand. "That *reminds* me. I'm taking some students down to the settlement tomorrow morning."

Peggy jumped up. "I want to come! Can I come this time?"

Jimmy reached out and pulled her to his side. "Of course. Everyone can help."

The next day, Jimmy led his group of nine student volunteers and two teachers armed with backpacks, boxes, and food pots into the slums of Yokohama. Known as "the city of tunnels" because of its maze of buildings, shacks, and alleys, the towering smokestacks of the Japan Carbon Company overshadowed the area, layering the land in a film of soot, draining the color from everything in sight the same way it seemed to drain the life of its inhabitants. A den of drinking and brawling for the unemployed or under-employed, it smelled of industry and rotting garbage.

Children and adults in the Settlement playing their favorite sport!

Jimmy held Peggy's hand as he and the company of Japanese and Americans carefully plotted their steps on discarded planks that served as sidewalks through the muddy paths, trying to avoid the worst of the muck between the leaning wooden buildings.

He bent down to Peggy. "*These* are our brothers and sisters." They trudged on as Peggy gazed up at stoic onlookers with folded arms in filthy rags. What might have repulsed others, excited Jimmy. These were *his* people.

Jimmy had co-founded this little "Settlement," as he called it, two years earlier with school faculty and student volunteers through fund drives and donations. For him, faith meant nothing without works, and he diligently came to their little house in Yokohama every week, sometimes several times a week, with whatever people he could pull together. Rain or shine, summer or winter, he came. People from the shantytown often came to his home in town where he and Charma invited them in. When people realized that the Covells gave away food coupons, they'd line up at their door before sunrise.

The alleyway led to an opening where two Japanese students were already setting up tables in front of a new clapboard house displaying a sign in Japanese and English: *Kanto Gakuin Settlement House. All are Welcome Here.*

"Good morning!" Jimmy said as he settled his backpack onto the doorstep. "What are we doing first?" The others filed in behind him as the two students bowed.

"Good morning, Covell sensei. First, cleaning lice from hair, then math lessons, then Bible study. Night classes for the adults start again next week."

A curious band of grimy children began to surround the small party and jostled each other while holding out their hands for food. One had open sores on his arms.

Jimmy spoke in Japanese as he looked at the children. "Get your hair cleaned first, then you can have rice balls and pickles."

The children sprinted for the tables with the washing bowls shouting, "Me first!"

Some of the local adults stood at a distance with folded arms, but Jimmy and the volunteers had earned the trust of others, who were quite friendly. He knew it would take time, and it was paying off. A student picked up a giggling child and carried him over to the table.

Off to the side, Jimmy noticed a young girl about Peggy's age standing

Charma Covell in the upper right, Peggy showing off her dress on the lower left, and David on the lower right. Going to the Settlement was often a family affair.

*There was plenty of time for fun and time
for the serious things, too. Jimmy on the far right.*

with her head held low. Jimmy squatted down to her as Peggy came close and spoke in her best Japanese, "Would you like a pickle?" The little girl's eyes sparkled while she nodded.

Peggy reached out her hand and said, "Don't be afraid. Come on. Let's get your hair clean." The little girl looked up at Jimmy with concern, then to Peggy. Her face softened as she took Peggy's hand with a smile.

Chapter 7

Spring 1932. Yokosuka Naval Base, Tokyo Bay.

Fuchida's light-gray two-seat Mitsubishi B1M biplane sped over the glistening water unleashing its torpedo with a splash toward a barge marked with red flags. Fuchida directed his pilot to veer to the right, then circle back to the left so he could look down just as a small splash and smoke signal released from his torpedo marked a hit on the dead center of the barge. He smiled with satisfaction and gave his pilot a congratulatory pat on the shoulder.

On a shore platform among other observers, Genda, now also a lieutenant, peered through binoculars. He took down his field glasses and nodded with approval.

The Yokosuka Naval Base near Tokyo specialized in training pilots in bombing techniques of all methods, including horizontal, high-level bombing and dive bombing, but Fuchida focused on their specialty— torpedo bombing.

Seeing Japan strengthening its military power thrilled him as they expanded their empire, especially into the recently acquired Manchuria area of China, renamed Manchukuo. He knew they badly needed to secure raw materials and other resources with what he saw as their right as the leading nation of Asia and had no problem with their aggressive expansion.

In 1895, Japan wrested control of Korea from the Qing Empire of China and fully annexed it into the Japanese Empire in 1910, completing their piecemeal takeover of the nation through a series of shrewd "reforms" and the disarming of the Korean military. This victory only whetted the Japanese appetite for the prize of Manchuria, and in September of 1931, the Japanese Army overran and seized that area as well.

Fuchida's plane taxied down the airstrip beside a long row of biplanes boldly emblazoned with the blood red *Hinomaru* or "sun circle" on their wings and fuselages.

He wearily pushed up his goggles in his second seat as the pilot killed the engine and the prop sputtered to a stop. Mechanics in white rushed to grab the wings. Genda stood waiting with his hands on his hips, the binoculars still slung around his neck. Fuchida dropped to the ground from a small ladder and unbuckled his flight cap.

Genda stepped forward. "Well done, Fuchi! You're gaining a reputation."

"Genda! I heard you'd just begun teaching here! Congratulations."

Genda put his arm around him and squeezed his shoulder. "No, no, the congratulations go to the man who has taken a bride to preserve the Fuchida name."

Fuchida blushed and changed the subject. "So tell me, what's new?"

Genda cocked his head for Fuchida to follow. They approached a hangar where Genda nodded to a pair of soldiers who heaved open huge

Navy Type 13 carrier-borne attack aircraft, or
Mitsubishi B1M biplanes, lined up on a base protecting Tokyo Bay.

sliding doors.

Stepping inside Fuchida's jaw dropped. He'd heard about this plane but had never seen one. Before him sat a Mitsubishi 1MF10, the newest, fastest plane of a new generation of all-metal low-wing monoplanes. Mechanics attended to the aircraft like trainers of a thoroughbred racehorse.

"I've already taken this test model out, and she's much faster and more maneuverable than any biplane. We're still working out imperfections, but this is the future of naval aircraft."

"OK, so when do *I* get a chance?"

"As soon as possible, since you'll be training the pilots."

"Me?" Fuchida did his best to act humble in the Japanese tradition, but he knew he fooled no one.

"This is only the first of many superior aircraft that will be a part of the finest air division in the world. You're the best, and everyone knows it, *especially* you."

The following day, Fuchida and Genda found themselves in the same meeting room for the last session of the day. Seated in rows with their hats sitting on their desks facing forward, the two friends sat among a narrowing company of elite officers receiving the latest training from the best military minds in Japan.

The instructor's voice seemed to grow more intense as he swung his arm across a huge map of Asia. "The British colonized the subcontinent of India, the nation of Burma, Hong Kong, Singapore, and the Malay Peninsula; the Dutch have taken Indonesia with their rich supplies of oil and tin; the Australians occupy lands in New Guinea; and the Philippines are essentially a territory of the United States which has built major naval and air bases there."

Fuchida was engrossed. He'd never quite put it all together before in this way, but it rang true in his heart—conquer or be conquered. The teacher tilted his head down as his eyes scanned the room of officers.

"The rich, white Westerners are little more than proud colonists who subjugate native peoples. The money squeezed from Asian blood maintains these minorities in their wasteful lifestyles. Not only are they enslaving other nations and stealing their wealth, but they're doing it right in our own backyard to our own fellow Asians. I've been to Shanghai, a home to many westerners, where signs say, '*Dogs and Yellow People—No Entry!*'"

Fuchida squirmed uncomfortably. It was just the same in San Francisco, something he would never forget.

"Yet these very same Western nations have the *arrogance* to insist that only the white races have the right to colonize, that we, under the leadership of our august and divine emperor, have no right to improve the conditions of Asians in Manchukuo . . ." He slapped his hand flat on upper China. ". . . now a part of our growing empire, our rightful *destiny!*"

Fuchida's ears tingled and his heart beat with excitement as the veneer of the West was stripped away to expose them as the culprits they were.

"Our goal is to stabilize East Asia through cooperation between Japan, Manchukuo, and China for our common prosperity. Since China, however, has ignored our true motives and has mobilized her armies against us, we can only counter her step by force of arms. Soon, the nations will see the establishment of a new world order." He paused and looked over the room. "East Asia will come to know economic prosperity free from the grip of Western colonialism. We will cleanse Asia from Anglo-Saxon expansion. Under our leadership," he held his arms out wide, "the eight corners of the world will be brought together under one roof!" He finished by bringing his cupped hands together.

The eyes of Fuchida were riveted on the professor, unaware of anything except the words pouring from his heart. The professor stepped away from the map and walked close to the officers in the classroom—the future leaders of Japan and her empire.

"We never forget that our lives belong to the emperor. We yield it to no one else under any circumstances. A true Japanese cannot surrender as it is not in our nature to do so. There is no lower shame or contempt. If our enemies don't know this now, one day they will, and fear will grip their hearts. We bow to *no one* but to the emperor!"

The instructor stood tall and pulled his head back a bit. "The United States is our enemy, so we will patiently let them mock us and lecture us and insult us with cartoons in their newspapers . . . and as they become weaker in their misplaced self-confidence, we will continue to become stronger. Soon, we will have the most powerful navy on earth. We will continue our military preparations and wait for the right opportunity to take our proper place in the world as the leading nation of Asia."

Fuchida could feel the professor's anger beneath the surface.

"And *finally*, the West will be forced to give to the Yamato people what we have long deserved . . ."

Fuchida leaned to Genda and whispered, "Respect."

The instructor quickly turned to Fuchida, stared, then looked across the class and nodded his head.

"Yes, indeed. Respect."

Chapter 8

Spring 1932. Central Oregon.

Straw dust clung to Jake's sweaty face, the hay press chugged and clanked away against a weathered shed with a rusted corrugated roof as the sun descended in the west. Jake adjusted his cowboy hat with his gloved hands and rushed to twist the second strand of wire onto a finished hay bale as others forked hay into the feeder. Another young ranch hand worked the levers and belts on the single engine machine—sputtering unevenly, spitting puffs of smoke into the cloudy sky, now painted with faint streaks of red.

The potbellied foreman pulled on the brim of his hat, glanced down at his pocket watch, then up to the sun. "We're not lacing shoes, son—get a move on!"

"Yes, sir. Fingers gettin' a bit sore." Jake grabbed the wires right as the machine pushed another bale out and swung it onto a trailer half full of bales where another hand snatched it and bucked it up into place. Easy for a fat boss standing around to tell us to move faster, he thought. Jake made up his mind not to farm wheat, but helping ranch cattle wasn't much different. The

Jake with an armful of puppies!

dry climate and poor soil didn't lend itself to much other than *growing* grass or raising creatures that *ate* grass. That was about it for the area.

That night, Jake threw his hat on a chair, wiped his face with a towel, and crouched beside his bed to slide out an old coffee can from underneath—his "hope chest" for building his own house. He took it up and spilled his cash onto his dresser top. Pushing the coins and paper dollars around and counting under his breath, he glanced up at the May calendar advertising McFinney's Hardware Store—most days already crossed out. His eyes hopelessly roamed the room, "Oh, that's just *great!* In about a hundred years I'll be able to buy one shoe!" He fell back onto his faded patchwork bedspread and stared at the ceiling. "I might as well just be working for free!" He sighed heavily and whispered to himself, "I've gotta find another job."

Chapter 9

Summer 1932. The Kanto Gakuin School, Yokohama.

I t was a balmy summer evening when Jimmy joined a group of seventy-seven students in a cramped second-floor classroom festooned with sweeping hand-painted banners in Japanese that read *Christian Student Movement—International Goodwill Meeting.* Other posters declared *Peace, Our Greatest Gift for the Future,* and *Support Eternal Peace.* There were a few other staff in attendance. Hand-held fans fluttered throughout the audience like butterfly wings.

Jimmy Covell intently focused on the student leader, who spoke passionately. "We *can* create goodwill to mankind. Many of us want disarmament, but those who profit from selling the death machines of war *oppose* it." A small applause rose as the young man cleared his throat. "We can resist the great enemy of war itself by first disarming our minds and hearts of the hatred and national pride that leads to fighting in the first place."

A regular at these meetings, Jimmy's heart filled with joy at the courage of these young men to openly oppose the military ambitions of the nation. The Japanese way was to conform, but these rising students, the leaders of tomorrow, were declaring themselves their own persons. He loved it.

A student beside Jimmy leaned to him and whispered, "Why are they here?" tilting his head toward the back of the room.

Jimmy nonchalantly gave a quick glance to the back. Fear gripped him at the sight of four police officers with a Japanese man in a business suit standing silently beside them. He discreetly leaned to the student, "The Thought Police are here," he whispered. "The Tokkō. Just keep looking forward." He'd never seen the Tokkō here before. This was not a good development.

Kanto Gakuin University

The Covell family in front of their Yokohama home, 1932. Top row:
The ever-smiling Peggy and Charma; second row: Jimmy, Alice, and David.

The speaker saw the officers along the far wall but pressed ahead, his eyes darting across the audience.

Jimmy was quite aware that the Japanese made use of military police officers, called the *Kempeitai*, among the civilian population, but they also maintained the "Special Higher Police" or "Thought Police," the *Tokubetsu Kōtō Keisatsu* or just the *Tokkō* for short. Formed in 1911 in response to an anarchist group's plot in 1910 to kill Emperor Meiji (Hirohito's grandfather), they investigated political groups or anyone who were deemed a threat to the "essence of Japan," but in recent years their power had expanded rapidly—questioning, detaining, and arresting thousands for "subversive ideologies"—anything that opposed the officially approved philosophy of the government. The Thought Police had no uniform and spent most of their time in offices poring over documents, but they possessed power at the highest level.

The leader of the Tokkō had finally had enough. He nodded to the lead officer, who proceeded to stride to the front of the room with the other three policemen, waving his hands over his head, and interrupting the speaker mid-sentence. "This meeting is adjourned!" The speaker stopped as gasps trickled through the crowd. "This is an illegal meeting! All of you

Kanto Gakuin jr. high school students doing non-military field training.

know that anyone who organizes a group for the purpose of challenging the national essence of Japan will be sentenced to imprisonment. Everyone go back home! *Go!*"

The other police officers took hold of the speaker and his two friends beside him at the podium, yanked their arms behind their backs, and clasped them in handcuffs. By then, everyone was standing and muttering in hushed fear and shock.

As the police escorted the student leaders toward the back of the room, Jimmy called out in Japanese, "What have they done wrong?! They only want to help make the world a safer place! You should arrest me instead of them!

The lead officer paused to look Jimmy up and down. "You're just a stupid *gaijin!*"[3] Another officer pushed Jimmy aside as they made their way for the exit.

"They only want peace! What's wrong with that?"

The cuffed student leader stumbled forward with his head bowed. He glanced over at Jimmy who felt the fear of this young man facing an uncertain future. The unknown Japanese businessman in the back, certainly a member of the *Tokkō*, fixed his displeased eyes on Jimmy.

Some weeks later, briefcase in hand, Jimmy strode across the campus and checked his watch, then turned to the sound of plain-clothes students marching in step to the commands of an army officer. Jimmy's face darkened. He made an about-face and stormed off. This was the last straw.

Inside Dr. Sakata's office, Jimmy stood before his desk with his hands stretched wide and shouted in English, "What in the *world* is going on? I thought we'd all agreed not to accept military training here?"

Dr. Sakata looked up, restraining his emotions. "You know I don't like this any more than you do, but you need to understand that if we didn't accept training for the students now, their compulsory service in the army would be even longer. It's only because of my own military service that they allowed us to be the *last* Christian school in *all* Japan to accept this training.

---

[3] A foreigner or outsider, often used pejoratively.

Kanto Gakuin University

Dr. Hiroshi Sakata, president of the Kanto Gakuin School.

It doesn't mean we accept the idea of war."

"No? Then what does it mean? *What?*"

"If the government sees us as a threat they'll *shut us down*, and how will that serve our students?"

Jimmy walked away from the desk and turned around.

Dr. Sakata pulled open a desk drawer and dropped an envelope on the front of his desk facing Jimmy. "This is your stamp?" Sakata asked with a touch of annoyance. "You're stamping your letters with this?" he said tapping the envelope with his finger.

Jimmy stepped closer and peered down through his round-rimmed glasses at a canceled envelope, rubber-stamped with bright red letters reading, *Friendships not Battleships.* Jimmy's face lightened as he had had this stamp custom made for himself. He peered up and cocked his head. "Friendships *are* better than battleships," he said with a grin. "Don't you agree?"

Sakata looked away and back with frustration. "Have you used this before?"

"Many times."

Dr. Sakata exhaled angrily. "We have to be careful not to arouse *suspicion*. You need to stop stamping your mail like this!" Their eyes locked.

"I will." Jimmy paused. "When there are no more battleships." He cared deeply for Dr. Sakata and knew what a quandary he was in, but saw no easy path ahead for either of them. The president wiped his forehead with a handkerchief, stood up, and walked over to the window. Jimmy joined him observing the students marching in unison, sticks over their shoulders standing in for rifles.

"Have you registered?"

Jimmy looked at Dr. Sakata. "Registered?"

The school president continued gazing at the students through the window. "All foreigners must register with the Tokkō. I'm sorry, but we have to comply."

Chapter 10

Summer 1935. Near the California-Nevada Border, twenty miles east of Alturas, California.

Jake sat hunched over in the saddle and sighed. They were at a standstill—again. The air was rich with the scent of pine trees scattered across the low mountains. He pushed his hat high up on his forehead and twisted to check on the six mules strung together behind him on the mountain road, saddled with all manner of crates, canvas bags, and kegs. After two years at a dollar a day as a ranch hand, he jumped at the chance for this five-dollar-a-day job as a sheep tender delivering supplies to herdsmen. He thought of it as the biggest hotel in the world, sleeping under an open sky.

"Hey! In the back! Yeah, you!" Jake glared at the last mule in the train as it cocked its ears forward. "We're a team here. You know, mule *team?!* We all work *to - geth - er!* You, me, and . . ." The mule turned his lip up and pitched his head away.

"Hey! Don't you look away when I'm talking to you! Maybe you do that at home, but not with me, you don't! Now pick it up back there. Got it?" The mule shook the dust off his head and neck as if to say, "No."

"Well, at least I'm not working with jackasses . . ." Jake turned back around with a smirk and yanked down the brim of his hat. With a click of his tongue and a kick to his mule, the train lurched forward again, up the gradual mountain path. With few expenses, he was finally enjoying himself and saving up money.

Chapter 11

1936. Tokyo.

Fuchida cupped a crumpled ball of paper in both hands as he knelt on the floor across from his son, Yoshiya, now three years old, who held a thin plank in a fierce baseball stance. "And . . . the pitch!" He tossed the ball underhand, and Yoshiya whacked it across the room.

"Home run! I did it! I win!" Yoshiya ran wildly around his father who stood up, grabbed his son, and swung him onto his shoulders.

Haruko, his wife, beamed. "It's so nice to have you home. Your trips at sea seem to last so long." Fuchida plucked a cluster of grapes from a bowl on the table and popped a few into his mouth, then handed part of the cluster up to his son around his neck.

Fuchida and his three-year-old son, Yoshiya, at the Meiji Shrine, Tokyo.

"Well, I'll be home for a while now. I still can't believe they selected me." The Naval Staff College in Tokyo was the next step into the upper echelons of the Imperial Japanese Navy, but of the hundreds of applicants, only twenty-four were selected. He had worked hard to achieve entrance to the program and was excited by the opportunity to hone his knowledge and skills, not to mention the opportunity to gain a little prestige.

"I think you wouldn't have believed it if they *didn't* select you. And now my husband is even a lieutenant commander. Now all you need is a daughter . . ." Smiling,

Haruko looked down at her bulging belly and circled it with her hands.

Fuchida broke a small branch of grapes from his cluster and held them to Haruko's mouth. "Then feed the baby . . ."

The Naval Staff College, Tokyo.

The instructor strode back and forth at the front of the classroom as he continued before the group of officers.

"We are rapidly amassing heavy cruisers, destroyers, and submarines. As I speak, plans are underway to construct the largest, most powerful battleships the world has ever seen—*twice* the size of the biggest American battleships. With such power, we will be able to negotiate from a position of strength without having to fire a single shot."

Sitting at attention among fellow officers, Fuchida did his best to follow along but kept drifting off, thinking what he would say in counterarguments. He knew that the premise of *Kantai Kessen* or the "decisive victory" doctrine was based on the Japanese Navy's resounding success in defeating the Russian Navy in the Battle of Tsushima, but so much had changed since 1905. The strategy was to lure the enemy into the home waters of Japan, all the while picking off ships with submarines, then ambushing the worn fleet in a single, decisive battle, destroying the enemy and ending the war in one fell swoop of the sword. But Fuchida felt the naval command was preparing for the battles of the past, not the war of the future.

"If forced into war, we'll do the same with the United States as we did with the Russians." The instructor leaned onto his desk and looked over the room with authority. "We soundly defeated their navy by drawing them into one decisive battle. Our superior battleships and tactics will *crush* them. They'll never bother us again."

Fuchida downed a shot of sake in the smoke-filled officer's dining area that evening. "Ridiculous!" Sitting with Genda and friends, he continued. "What, are we going to hand the enemy our script and tell them to follow it? What if they don't do exactly what we expect?"

Genda gobbled the last noodles and broth from his bowl held to his mouth, then slammed it down. "Even if everything went according to plan, both navies would lose a lot of ships, and the United States has a much greater capacity to replace their ships than we do."

"To control the outcome, we *must* dominate the sky and focus on building more planes and aircraft carriers . . ."

". . . instead of battleships," Genda chimed in. "Better used as piers or scrap iron."

The fellow officers chuckled nervously.

Genda shook a cigarette out of his pack and lit it. "They live in the past, in the glory days of the big gunships ruling the seas."

The other officers at the table listened intently. Fuchida leaned forward and spoke more quietly, "Deputy Navy Minister Yamamoto agrees that we should prepare more aircraft carriers."

"Yes, but Vice Admiral Nagumo *dis*agrees."

One of the other officers wedged his way into the conversation. "Why don't you teach on this, Genda? It's a valid point."

Genda exhaled a cloud of smoke and smirked. "The admirals won't allow *fliers* to teach at their *naval* college. They don't understand. The world's changed—but they haven't."

Lt. Fuchida at the Naval Staff College in his formal naval dress uniform featuring a fore and aft hat.

Chapter 12

Spring 1937. The Kanto Gakuin School, Yokohama.

In a recreation shed among volleyball nets, baseball bats, and shelves of musty tarps and balls, Jimmy sat at a workbench rubbing oil on an old baseball mitt like a doctor with a wounded patient. A nineteen-year-old student stood beside him, looking impatiently outside through a dirty window at the rest of the students throwing baseballs and shouting to each other.

"So," Jimmy said in his best Japanese, "you think the students can take the staff in baseball, eh?"

The boy shrugged.

"We're not going to play easy, you know." Jimmy always made a point to try to connect in some personal way with his students and wasn't one to give up easily. The steady sound of bats cracking balls echoed outside.

The student observed Jimmy's meticulous oiling of the glove. "Mr. Covell . . . excuse me for asking . . . but why do the Western nations dislike the Japanese people?"

Jimmy pushed his glasses back up, poured more oil on his rag, and continued without looking up, not revealing his joy in the boy opening up. "This is a good question." The question troubled him deeply, one he'd long contemplated, written about, and spent a great deal of time working toward answering. "Why do the Japanese dislike the Koreans and the Chinese—and even the Burakumin, the Ainu people, and the Ryukyuans, all people of Japan?" He glanced up over his glasses. Jimmy's sensitivity to others led him to research these people within Japanese society, the Burakumin, Ainu, and Ryukyuans, who had endured centuries of outcast status due to occupation, the region they came from, or even their looks. People who were loyal citizens of Japan but with Korean or Chinese ancestry were equally shunned. He routinely suppressed his anger at the Japanese for loudly complaining about how the world treated them while they mistreated others in their own nation just as badly—or worse.

He looked up at the student who looked back intently. "It's easy to see the faults in others, but not so easy to see our own," he said, "isn't it?"

The student nodded.

Jimmy pulled the glove on and smacked his fist into the pocket. "We're all a little proud. We think we're better than others. But if everyone thinks they're better than everyone else, then doesn't that make us all the same?" He grinned realizing his impromptu logic.

The boy gave a confirming grin.

Pulling off the glove and handing it to the teen, Jimmy spoke with a glint in his eye. "We all have the same Father. We're made in his image. We're all brothers."

Jimmy stood up and tossed a baseball to the student who wasn't quite prepared to catch it. "Now," Jimmy said, "let's see who has the most team spirit, eh?" Seeing the boy's bashful grin, he patted him on the shoulder, pulled on a baseball cap, grabbed a few bats, and escorted him into the sun onto the grassy field.

Charma couldn't help herself from glancing over to Jimmy at the kitchen table as she dried plates and handed them to a Japanese helper who stacked them in the cupboard. He was huffing, sighing, and fidgeting as he flipped pages of a new book. Every now and then the children playing in the next room let out a squeal or a thump on the floor.

"New textbook?" Charma asked.

Jimmy didn't look up. "More like wholesale propaganda. But then, what would you expect from the Ministry of Education, Bureau of *Thought Control?!*" Jimmy removed his glasses and with the other hand reached across his forehead to massage his aching temples. How they got him to do their dirty work was beyond him and pushing him to his limits. When he peered up, he noticed the overcast afternoon sky darkening.

Restoring his round-rimmed glasses, he looked over at Charma and spoke in "full teacher" mode. "In 1870 Japan nationalized all the Shinto shrines which then came under state control. The office of the emperor was elevated to a position of, well, to more than just the national leader—the *spiritual* leader as well. In the last decade or so, *all* the outlets of communication have come under complete government control—you know, radio, newspapers, magazines, and, of course, education. So *this*," Jimmy held up the book, "is the new required reading for the schools."

Charma picked up another wet plate from the rack. "For which grades?"

"All college and upper-level students in the entire nation have to study it. Teachers, too. Every day. *Kokutai No Hongi - The Principles of the National Essence of Japan.*" He set the open book down on the table with a slight plop. "It's taken me a while to get the translation straight. It's kind of difficult in places, so bear with me."

Jimmy twisted his head and shrugged his shoulders. He was a fighter preparing to enter the ring. "Listen to this, quote: *'The unbroken line of emperors, receiving the . . . the oracle of the founder of the nation reigns over the Japanese Empire eternally.'*" He flipped forward a few pages and slid his finger down to his penciled notes. "Quote: *'His Majesty set forth the great policy of returning to the spirit of ancient times which had as its nucleus the emperor, who is a humanly manifested deity in keeping with the great significance of the "god-handed" founding of the Empire.'* Keep in mind this is a school textbook, of all things."

As he ruffled the pages to find another spot, Peggy, thirteen, crept up behind him, putting her arms around his shoulders, hugging him with her face pressed against his while clutching a bright, yellow-bordered *National Geographic.* "What're you reading, Daddy?"

Jimmy sat back and grasped her arm, his face lightening. "I've been promoted to a position in the ministry of propaganda. Isn't that great?"

Peggy wrinkled her brow. "Dad, you're being sarcastic again. Mom said you should just speak your mind or say nothing at all."

Charma grinned.

"OK. The government is trying to force teachers to spread their idea of the divinity of the emperor to tighten their grip on enforcing their military ambitions. Is that better?"

"What do you mean?"

"They, the government, that is, want total control of the people, so they're essentially conscripting the teachers to tighten that control. It's the last thing I'd *ever* want to do."

Peggy smiled and nodded. "Sorry, dad. You'll figure it out. You always do!" She gave a quick kiss on his cheek, stood up, and opened the magazine she'd been holding. "The 1936 Olympics were *marvelous* last year. Look at these pictures from Berlin!" She spread the magazine flat over his book and began flipping pages and pointing out photos. "The excitement of the crowds. Look at this stadium! The parades! So . . . in three years the Olympics will be in *Tokyo!*"

Jimmy knew *exactly* what was coming.

"Can we go?"

Glancing at Charma, Jimmy could only think of how tight their money was, yet he loved to please his children. "I think there *might* be a possi . . ."

"Oh, Daddy!" Peggy gave another hug to Jimmy, then jumped back to the color photos in the *National Geographic*. "Look at the pageantry on the boulevards! It'll be just like that here!" She opened to a spread of strikingly colorful pictures of throngs of people on streets decorated with national flags and dozens and dozens of huge red banners . . . emblazoned with swastikas.

A twinge of fear shot through his body. He'd read enough of Germany's repeated disregard of treaties by rearming and their massive buildup of weapons to know it could only lead to one place. He leaned back in his chair, gently closed the magazine, and handed it to Peggy with a disarming smile and a pat on her hand. "Let's talk about this more a little later, all right?"

Peggy looked at him with her innocent eyes, oblivious to the omens of death she had just seen. "OK, Dad. Thanks." She picked an apple from a bowl of fruit on the table and trotted off with her magazine.

After a few seconds to recompose himself, Jimmy sighed deeply and cleared his throat. He needed Charma to hear this. "All right," he continued. "Let me get to the heart of the matter. Quote: '*Loyalty means to revere the*

Lower photo: Wilhelm Tobien/National Geographic Creative

*Top: The 1936 Olympic Games open in Berlin as the torchbearer runs
up with fire carried from southern Greece. Bottom: Banners over Berlin
on Unter den Linden (street) with The Zeughaus (armory) on the right.
From the February 1937 issue of National Geographic Magazine.*

emperor and to follow him implicitly . . . The land of Japan stands high above the other nations of the world, and her people excel <u>all</u> the peoples of the world . . .."' Jimmy looked at Charma and raised his eyebrows.

Though holding a damp handful of utensils, she and their Japanese housekeeper stopped drying, and both appeared disturbed and frightened. Thunder shook the windows.

"Our imperial forces have a duty to make our national prestige greatly felt within and without our country, to preserve the peace of the Orient in the face of the world powers, and to preserve and enhance the happiness of mankind . . . It is when this harmonious spirit of our nation is spread abroad throughout the world to every race that true world peace and its progress and prosperity are realized . . ."

Jimmy rolled his eyes and sat back, lifting the book off the table. *"'The annexation of Korea and the efforts exerted in the founding of Manchukuo are one and all but expressions of the great august[4] will promoting the peace of the country and the advancement of the great task of love for the people, thus radiating the grace of the Imperial Throne.'"* Jimmy muttered under his breath. "Yeah. Try telling that to the Koreans."

Shaking his head, he flipped past a few more pages. "OK, OK, here it is. *'The warrior spirits work inseparably with the spirits of peace. It is in subduing those who refuse to conform to the magnificent influence of the emperor's virtues that the mission of our Imperial Military Forces lies.'"* Jimmy threw the book in the air and let it land on the table with a thump.

Charma winced.

"The emperor is divine, the people owe total loyalty to him alone, and the destiny of Japan is to expand and conquer," Jimmy said, then waited for some reaction from Charma. "They're using the schools to build a world-class military machine!" Jimmy jumped up from his chair and angrily swung around behind it. "I'm perfectly fine with people giving this kind of loyalty and obedience to God in the name of peace, but to a *man* in the name of *war*? *No one* should render unto Caesar what belongs to God alone!"

---

[4] Inspiring reverence or admiration; of supreme dignity or grandeur; majestic.

David, now twelve, and his Japanese companion suddenly invaded the room—both in white headbands furiously clacking wooden samurai swords. David twisted, quickly raising his sword, and chopped down at his friend who parried the swing with his own sword and an accompanying grunt. As David lifted his sword for a new swing, Jimmy reached out and grabbed the wooden blade mid-air. He looked into his son's smiling face, then over to Charma with dead seriousness. Glancing back at David, he gently eased the sword down from his son's hand. "Son, we don't do that in this family. Swords are for killing."

Jimmy slid the *hachimaki* off David's head and smiled, trying not to cause him to be afraid. "If you want to fight, why don't you boys go play some Shogi,[5] all right?" The boys darted back out of the room as fast as they'd come in. Thunder cracked outside as a hard rain began to fall. Jimmy stared into the backyard and spoke as if to himself. "I told the president I wouldn't be attending their ceremony tomorrow."

Putting the last cup away and closing the cupboard cabinet, Charma turned around. "What ceremony?"

Standing in a light drizzle, the entire student body of Kanto Gakuin lined both sides of the paved street from the school gate leading up to the main castle-like building, all at attention, evenly spaced, perfectly silent— the only sound being rain dripping between the leaves and an occasional cough.

Eventually, a superbly polished black sedan arrived at the gate and solemnly made its way to the front building, an ivy-covered tower, and came to a slow halt with a dull squeal of the brakes. An administrator at the curb dressed a crisp black suit and tie shouted out at the top of his voice, "Saikeirei!" literally, "profound bow," the deepest bow generally reserved for the emperor alone.

Another administrator in suit and tie opened the car door as all of the students bowed deeply and held their positions.

Dr. Sakata stepped out of the car holding a large, white, rectangular

---

[5] A traditional Japanese board game similar to chess.

box in his white gloves and regally made his way up the steps into the school's main hall followed by a small cadre of administrators in methodical procession.

Inside the most honored place at the school, Dr. Sakata meticulously unfolded the purple velvet inside the box, and, one at a time withdrew the imperial portraits of the emperor and empress, ceremoniously setting them inside a shrine-like wooden box adorned with purple curtains. The top of the small shrine displayed a golden chrysanthemum—crest, symbol of the imperial family. Stepping back while facing the shrine, he and the entourage bowed reverently in unison and held their posture.

The main entrance gate to Kanto Gakuin. Constructed in 1929.

Chapter 13

Spring 1937. Medford, Oregon.

An unending chorus of chirps from turkey chicks emanated from cardboard boxes stacked in a column inside the busy hardware and feed store. While a bearded man in a clerk's apron peered into an open box counting, Jake spoke excitedly on a wall phone with a mouthpiece that extended out like a black daffodil.

"Ma! You sitting down? I said, 'Are you sitting down?' You're not going to believe this. I saved up a thousand dollars. Yeah. Two years of work. Uh-huh. One *thousand* dollars!"

As the clerk folded up the top of the box and flipped his journal closed, he glanced at Jake. "Keep 'em warm, now. Cover 'em up good."

Jake looked back, distracted by his call, and waved. "Yeah, I know. Put 'em in the truck. Ma? I bought five hundred turkey chicks, and I'm gonna get 'em fat for the holidays and double my money. What do you think of that?!"

Six Months Later.

Standing in a snow-frosted duster and cowboy hat at the same phone, Jake dejectedly waited for the call to go through. Behind him, men wrestled with full-grown turkeys flapping and squawking in a cloud of feathers and stuffed them into cages.

"You're not gonna believe this, Ma. Too many turkeys this year. No market. I lost it all. Yeah. Nearly every penny. OK, I'll write later." Jake slammed the earpiece down and glared at his lost venture. He whispered to himself, "I should've just *fed* my money to the turkeys. A thousand bucks!"

Alturas, Cal.
Jan 25, 1937

Dear Folks:
Well how are you by this time. Guess your about froze up. I'm in the hospital here with a broken leg having a pretty good time in this cold weather. A horse fell down on my leg when he slipped on the ice. It didn't break in any joints and will heal up all right. Compensation pays all my expense and I get payed some of my wages too. It broke between the ankle

Apparently, even horses need extra traction in winter,
as Jake explains in a letter to his parents.

and my knee in six
places. I hop hobble
around on crutches now.
I haven't received any
letters from you yet
but there may be some
were I was working.
If you write you better
write there as I may
not be here more than
a week. Well I hope
everything is all right
with you and Grandma
stands the cold allright.
Well don't worry about
me as I get everything
I need here and had a good
doctor set my leg.
        lots of love
            Jake

Chapter 14

Early December 1937. Nanking, China.[6]

As his engine blared in the wind, the sunlight highlighted a streak on the half windshield at the front of Fuchida's open cockpit. He rubbed it off with the back of his left jacket sleeve, his right hand steady on the stick. Fuchida in his goggles patted the side wall of his Yokosuka B4Y biplane like a familiar dog as he led a squadron of twelve planes above China at 15,000 feet, the wind rushing past his smiling face.

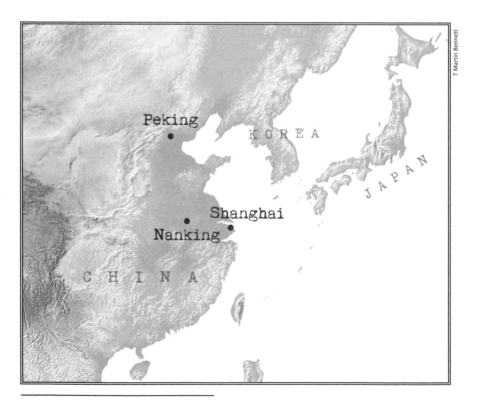

---

[6] Modern-day Nanjing, China.

The USS Panay *(River Gunboat PG45) in 1928.*

The aircraft carried three men with the navigator and radio operator/gunner behind Fuchida.

Although carriers primarily launched his attacks, this division of Imperial Navy bombers was working in conjunction with the Japanese Army in China. Like the rest of his nation, he beamed with pride over the headlines that read *Japanese Troops on Shanghai Front Capture Lotien* and thrilled to see their military theories becoming realities, but Fuchida's call away from the Naval Staff College to China stemmed from a bad turn of events.

Japan's war with China had begun in earnest earlier that year at the Marco Polo bridge where fighting broke out into full battle. In Nanking, navy pilots created a diplomatic crisis when they bombed an American gunboat in the Yangtze River, sinking it and killing three sailors along with scores of Chinese in junks traveling with the Western river boats.

The pilots had received orders from their own headquarters via an army request to attack all shipping in the Yangtze at Nanking. The Japanese officials referred to the event to as the "Panay Incident" after the name of the American ship, *USS Panay*, and called it an "incident" because Japan in no way wanted to be seen as being at war with China, which could have spurred United States and British intervention. For them, it was another part of bringing the eight corners of the world under one roof—*hakkō ichiu*.

Japanese diplomats apologized profusely to the Americans and the military called in Fuchida with others to put a clamp on poorly targeted bombing raids in the area some 175 miles west of Shanghai.

Locating the arms manufacturing area near the Yangtze River off to his left, Fuchida raised his hand in the air, tipped his wings, and led his group into their bombing run. They veered left, vectored in on their targets, and released their payloads.

On the ground, the Chinese anti-aircraft guns began firing away, but had swung into action too late—the bombs were already falling and Fuchida's group was peeling away, waiting and watching to see if they hit their marks.

Miyako Fuchida Overturf

Fuchida grinned with satisfaction as buildings erupted into a series of thundering explosions that cracked through the air blowing debris into the sky. He had little doubt that China would soon fold under the weight of the Japanese war machine.

After several months in China, Fuchida returned to Japan, stopping briefly to see his mother in Nara prefecture. Yazo, his father, had died the previous year. As a younger man, his father aspired to join the military, but his hopes were crushed by a baseball accident that robbed him of the sight in

Fuchida's mother, Shika, and father, Yazo Fuchida, as they appeared in 1920.

The torii entrance to the Grand Ise Shrine at sunrise as it appears today.

one eye. Still, he had been a respected teacher in the community and so deeply loved by his former students, they made a statue of him in his honor.

Fuchida loved hunting and fishing with his father. He was unprepared for how much he missed his presence and advice.

As he gazed from their porch to Mount Wakakusa in the east, the loss of his father weighed on his heart, and he wondered, "What am I living for? What am I willing to die for?" He was long overdue for a visit to another place. He smiled and nodded. "Perhaps," he thought, "perhaps I will renew myself there."

On his train ride back to the Naval Staff College in Tokyo to complete his studies, he took a detour to Ise City, the location of over 120 Shinto shrines. In the Shinto faith, all objects, animate or not, or features of nature, are respected for their *kami*, or spirits—some more than others.

Once at the main complex, he headed straight to Ise Jingū, or the Ise Grand Shrine, home to the shrine of Amaterasu-omikami, the goddess of the sun—the most sacred place in Japan.

In his khaki uniform, Fuchida stood pensively below the traditional entrance to all Shinto shrines, the torii—a pair of huge, wooden beams spanning between the tops of two cypress columns, the upper beam always being longer. He looked across the arched Uji Bridge over the Isuzu River—the demarcation separating the sacred from the worldly. "Just what I need," he thought.

Fuchida looked up and closed his eyes for a moment listening to the *hoh-hokekyo* chirp of the Japanese bush warbler and breathed in the spring air of the towering cypress trees. He needed to cleanse his mind from the impurities of war. The still of the forest and solitude of the sacred grounds revitalized his sense of gratitude and a feeling of favor. He recalled that the bridge faced east, that, on the day of the winter solstice, the sun would rise, shining straight down the bridge under the tori—fitting for a temple to the sun god.

Few worshipers attended the shrine that day which afforded him a measure of privacy that he relished as he crossed the wooden bridge, the planks giving an occasional creak. Certainly, Fuchida thought, there is nothing to compare with the sun itself. It brings light and causes all things to grow. Without it, there would be no life on earth.

He came to the Temizusha, an open-sided, roofed structure over a stone-walled pool of water and reached for one of the many long-handled bamboo ladles from the wooden grid that overlaid the basin. Fuchida felt

Wooden dippers have been in use at the Temizusha for centuries.

privileged. In the distant past, no one but the imperial family was allowed to worship there, but beginning in the twelfth century, the samurai warriors were given access, for the sun goddess was the god of victory. In time, the emperor granted access. Fuchida sensed a deep union with the samurai of old as he lifted the dipper and gently cascaded the cool water over his left hand, then switched hands and poured water over his right. He wondered what the old woman next to him thought she needed purification from.

The entrance to the main shrine of Naikū.

Though not particularly devout, his father taught him Buddhist verses as a boy, which he had brushed out onto rice paper and memorized. He'd also spent time in Shinto shrines. Today his mind seemed to drift off into a blend of thoughts and memories—*A pure, cloudless heart is a heart which finds life in the true way by dying to one's self and one's own ends . . .*

Following the path further through the lush forest, he began climbing the steep, stone steps leading to another wooden torii in front of a fenced sanctuary called Kōtai Jingū, founded 2,000 years ago and home to the sacred mirror believed to be the very one used to bring Amaterasu-omikami from her cave to deliver sunlight to the entire world. At the top of the steps, his heart pumping from the hike, Fuchida was awed to think that this kami was connected directly to the emperor of Japan—a spiritual descendant of the kami themselves.

Closing his eyes once again, he reverently bowed twice, clapped his hands twice, bowed again and remained bowed in silence. Opening his eyes and standing upright, he stepped back and bowed again. He wondered if he really believed it—but there was nothing like the awesome power of the sun itself. Certainly, the favor of the sun shone down onto his home of Japan, blessing their nation above all others.

Chapter 15

December 1938. Yokohama.

"*With their backs to the sanctuary of the Lord, they were facing east, bowing low to the ground, worshiping the sun.*" Jimmy read quietly in Japanese from the eighth chapter Ezekiel to the gathering of students and friends in his tatami-matted living room that evening. A few lamps cast a golden hue over the dim, silent room as Jimmy glanced up over the top of his glasses and scanned their earnest faces. He wondered how much of what he saw, they, too perceived. Peggy sat beside her father, almost leaning against him as he continued. "'*He said to me, "Have you seen this, son of man? Is it nothing . . . to do the detestable things they are doing here, leading the whole nation into violence, thumbing their noses at me, and rousing my fury against them? Therefore, I will deal with them in fury. I will neither pity nor spare them. And though they cry for mercy—I will not listen."*'" He gently laid down the Bible, removed his glasses, and blotted his eyes with his shirt sleeve.

A long-haired Japanese girl cocked her head and looked at Jimmy quizzically, as if to try to understand his reason for showing such emotion. He understood that few of them could fathom the depths of horror he feared might lie ahead if the nation didn't change its course. "Worshiping the sun," and "I will neither pity nor spare them" resonated in his mind.

One highlight of his time was spending time with students and friends crowded together with his wife and children inside their home, all sitting cross-legged or kneeling on the floor, some with open Bibles before them. Here he was free to speak his heart and mind, and so he did. Deeds were almost as important as beliefs to him, but beliefs *always* preceded deeds.

With a refreshing smile and inhaling deeply, he turned and pointed to

1939

J o y o u s

N e w

Y e a r

1938

M e r r y

C h r i s t m a s

Greetings from the Covells

73 Kanoedai, Naka-ku, Yokohama

The Covell family annual Christmas/New Year's photo card for their friends.
Top row: David, Charma, and Peggy; second row: Alice and Jimmy.

a framed poem on the wall, written in both Japanese and English. "This is my heart. This is my prayer." Reciting from memory in Japanese, he looked into each face around the room, one at a time, "*Lord, make me an instrument of your peace; where there is hatred, let me sow love; where there is injury, pardon; where there is doubt, faith; where there is despair, hope; where there is darkness, light; and where there is sadness, joy.*" He closed his eyes for a second while he spoke. "*O Divine Master, grant that I may not so much seek to be consoled as to console; to be understood, as to understand; to be loved, as to love others; for it is in giving that we receive, it is in pardoning that we are pardoned, and it is in dying that we are born to eternal life.*" He ended looking at Peggy, whose eyes glimmered with admiration.

The room fell silent as most looked downward in contemplation. Jimmy waited.

One student, a young man, ventured a word. "Mr. Covell, these things are difficult things to do."

"No, not difficult," Jimmy responded, "*impossible* to do—on our own. But with Almighty God, *all* things are possible."

The student gently nodded, then both connected in a soft smile.

On the crowded sidewalk along a street in downtown Yokohama, Jimmy held Peggy's arm through his, Jimmy's other hand clutching a basket of *hakusai* heads—Japanese nappa cabbage. He listened to her story unfold as a packed streetcar rumbled past.

"So I asked if I could try out for that part of the play and since they needed two more girls, they said, 'Sure! We'd love to have you.' Isn't that great dad?" They stopped walking as Peggy glanced up at her father's face.

He stared at a row of colorful posters being plastered over a wooden wall of older, peeling bills. The new, identical sheets featured an illustration of proud soldiers surrounded by cheering throngs of civilians, emblazoned with the words, *Asia is for Asians! Working together we bring prosperity to the world!* The cold chill he felt wasn't from the weather. Only a week earlier, with considerable curiosity, he'd watched several Tokkō in a drugstore meticulously go through stacks of magazines tearing out a single page from each one. This was all going nowhere good, and fast.

The workman pushed his brush to flatten out the wrinkles of the last poster, then plopped it back into a tray of paste at the feet of Jimmy and Peggy. Squinting through the smoke of the cigarette in his teeth, the unshaven worker slowly raised his eyes, stopping at Peggy's fearful face. He smiled with missing teeth, shook his head, and slapped the brush back against the advertisement, pasting it to the wall. Peggy pressed against Jimmy's side, reassured by her father's firm arm around her.

Japanese propaganda poster used in China: "With the cooperation of Japan, China, and Manchukuo, the world can be in peace."

Jimmy navigated past the workman and posters. "It's all right, Peggy," he whispered. "Not everyone here believes that."

Once again, Jimmy stood before the desk of Dr. Sakata, the school president, who sat with his head down and sighed nervously.

Dr. Sakata looked up. "I deeply regret that the school board has asked me to request your resignation by the end of this school year."

"Because I oppose Japan's march to war?" Jimmy wasn't actually offended. He knew it was coming sooner or later. He just wanted to hear the official reasons, if any.

Dr. Sakata stood up, his troubled posture intimating sympathy. "Many foreigners have been refused re-entry to Japan, many have been deported, and some have even been arrested. You know this." He walked to the window and gazed at the empty yard. "Last week the Tokkō confronted me and demanded I answer their question." He turned to Jimmy. "They shouted, 'Who is greater, the emperor or Jesus?'"

"What did you say?"

"I told them they couldn't be compared." Smiling, he continued, "Then I asked *them*, 'Which is better, white or silence?'"

Jimmy's face lit up. He pitied Dr. Sakata, who stood over the ever-widening gap between what the nation demanded of him, and what his conscience begged of him.

Dr. Sakata moved closer to Jimmy. "I've intervened to protect you, but I'm afraid I can't do so much longer. Your life's in danger." Walking to a map on the wall he put his hands behind his back. "Perhaps we can get you a transfer to a school in Tokyo."

"No. It's just a matter of time before they deport me. I've talked to the mission board, and I'd like to go to the Philippines to teach there. The Americans have a strong military presence so we'll be safe. It's not too far away, so when all this talk of war is over, I'll come back."

Dr. Sakata looked back over his shoulder and nodded. "The students love you. We look forward to having you here again in the future."

They shook hands and held for a moment.

With staff and students in front of their home in Japan, Jimmy in the upper right. Note David, Alice, and Peggy beside her father.

"Thanks for letting me serve here," Jimmy said. "It's been the greatest experience of my life. Truly."

June 8, 1939. Yokohama Bay.

Under a vanishing light rain, Jimmy set down his suitcases. "There she is," he said. He, Charma, Peggy, David, and Alice admired the 570-foot passenger liner *RMS Empress of Russia* towering above the waterfront of Yokohama, all three funnels pouring smoke into the blue-gray sky. A sea of people covered the dock with umbrellas and suitcases, most moving toward several gangplanks flowing onto the ship.

Jimmy both dreaded this moment and looked forward to it; the end of a wonderful time with his daughter, but the beginning of a new adventure for her. He expected it would be a long time before they were together again.

Charma and a Japanese woman embraced, who wiped the tears from her face as Peggy, likewise, hugged a Japanese girl her age. The family was surrounded by seventy or so well-wishers, all pressing in to say their last goodbyes in the rain.

After shaking hands with a Buddhist monk dressed in traditional gray,

The Empress of Russia *regularly traversed the Pacific Ocean after her launch in 1912 and could transport as many as 1184 passengers.*

a dear friend, Jimmy raised his hands for their attention and spoke in Japanese as the rain dripped from his fedora. "Our life here in Japan, our home for nearly twenty years, has overflowed with friendship, love, and wonderful memories. We're so grateful for all of our many, many friends." Charma blotted her eyes with a handkerchief. "This is only a short trip. We'll be coming back again, soon, I hope. Though we may be far away, our hearts will always be close to yours. Goodbye, my friends."

In perfect cue, the ship's steam whistle sounded with a fierce shout, jetting a white cloud into the air. The family gathered their belongings and shuffled toward the gangplank amid a unison of shouts from friends, "Covell sensei banzai! Covell sensei banzai!"

The rising warrior in 1938 with his wife, Haruko, daughter, Miyako, and son, Yoshiya in Zushi, Japan, not far from the Yokosuka Naval Base.

Chapter 16

November 1939. The open sea south of Tokyo Bay.

The aircraft carrier *Akagi* carved through the ocean under a brisk, overcast sky. From the air above, Fuchida, now with a narrow mustache, gazed down on the ship from his three-man Nakajima B5N torpedo bomber as they banked for their approach.

Yamamoto's got no guts, Fuchida reflected. He was displeased with the new commander in chief of the Combined Fleet, installed two and a half months earlier. He knew how much time Yamamoto had spent in the UK and in the United States, his two years at Harvard, and how friendly and comfortable he'd become with the West. Why did he oppose Japan's plans to move into a deeper partnership with Germany? He didn't seem like the bold commander Japan needed to take charge right now.

Fuchida's growing experience and skill brought him to the position of squadron commander on the biggest carrier in the Imperial Japanese Navy, the *Akagi*. Her 855-foot runway looked precariously small from the air as his pilot lined up for his landing approach, noting the steam trailing from the vent in the middle of the runway indicating wind direction.

In the tower, Vice Admiral Isoroku Yamamoto, clean-shaven head and face, observed the approach of Fuchida's plane through binoculars. He was already familiar with Fuchida, although they hadn't met, as, two years earlier, Yamamoto had had the unpleasant task as deputy Navy minister of being responsible for apologizing to the US ambassador for bombing *USS Panay* in China. He dropped the glasses to his chest while keeping his eyes on the aircraft, and leaned toward Captain Kusaka beside him. "Is that Fuchida, the squadron commander?"

"Yes, sir."

"Have him sent to my quarters."

"Yes, sir. Right away."

After Kusaka had given brief instructions on a phone to the flight deck, they both watched intently as Fuchida's aircraft approached, adjusted its wings like a goose, hit the wooden deck with a hard thump into the arresting cables, and jerked to a violent halt.

The pilot killed the engine as Fuchida pushed his canopy back to see an engineer in white waving both hands over his head to get his attention. Fuchida unbuckled his straps and looked down as the engineer pointed up to Yamamoto in the tower. Fuchida pulled his goggles up and nodded as he caught the gaze of Yamamoto. Fuchida smiled, then turned and twisted his head. Not him! Still, he was curious about the meeting.

After cleaning up and changing into his navy blue uniform, Fuchida arrived and an aide seated him at a glossy wooden table opposite Yamamoto. Detailed inlaid wood paneling richly adorned his quarters. Every piece of metal in sight was polished brass. Yamamoto's look was as straightforward as his mindset—no facial hair or glasses. His hair was close-cropped nearly to the skin. After the obligatory small talk, Yamamoto got to the point.

"I expected your squadron to do well in the night bombing practice exercises last month which I observed directly . . ." While staring at Fuchida, Yamamoto took a slow puff from his cigarette. "But I didn't expect all twenty-seven torpedoes to score hits, especially under tracer fire and with spotlights in your eyes."

Perhaps, Fuchida thought, he'd been too quick to judge Yamamoto. Superior officers were usually all too eager to criticize fliers. He looked downward, "Sir, we were only doing our job. A failure of one flier is a failure of all."

"But you proved your point, that a night attack on capital ships can be very successful."

Fuchida looked up.

"Tell me, what do you think of Hitler's blitzkrieg?"

He tried to restrain his delight as he was mesmerized by the news streaming from Germany and their unstoppable forces. "Admiral, I think

Vice Admiral Isoroku Yamamoto, late 1930s.

this is a brilliant strategy." Though usually relaxed, even Fuchida felt tense in the presence of Yamamoto and made a conscious effort not to glance at the Admiral's left hand, missing two fingers from his participation in the Battle of Tsushima, Japan's greatest naval victory to date. "Conquering a nation in six weeks? This required careful planning and perfect execution. They carried it out flawlessly. The Germans can't be stopped. The way to attack is swiftly and decisively."

"How's your work coming along here on the *Akagi*? Please speak freely. I want the truth." Yamamoto's eyes would accept nothing less. He tapped his cigarette in the ashtray.

Fuchida wasn't sure what would happen if he said what he *really* believed but knew he'd never have a better chance than this one. "Admiral," Fuchida repositioned himself, "the one question I'm repeatedly asked that tests my patience is, 'How many planes do we need to protect our battleships?' This is upside down!" Fuchida leaned forward. "Carriers shouldn't be thought of as *defensive* forces, but as *attack* forces. What I believe we should do is to gather all of our carriers with our aircraft into one, great air squadron with *massive* striking power and have the battleships, cruisers, and destroyers protect the carriers. Instead of separate commanders over each ship, all the ship's squadrons should be put under a *single* command. I believe this would be far more effective." Fuchida leaned back. "But if I ever spoke my mind freely around the old commanders, well, they'd hang me, so I just shut up."

Fuchida taking a stroll with his daughter, Miyako, 1939.

Yamamoto nodded. "No, I agree. I've been thinking along the same lines for some time now. I'm convinced that we've underestimated the tactical strength of air power."

Fuchida was relieved, but even more, he was surprised. He was beginning to like this new commander.

"Soon, we'll move in this direction." Yamamoto rose, as did Fuchida, and extended his hand. "We'll speak again."

Yamamoto's grip felt firm and warm.

Chapter 17

Summer 1940. McChord Field. Tacoma, Washington.

Jake stood in grease-smeared coveralls below the wing of a Douglas B-23 Dragon and handed a wrench up to the mechanic beneath the open cowling of one of its two engines. The smell of oil-soaked rags filled the air, and the new hangar rang with the click and ping of engineers working on the two other, brand-new, B-23s recently delivered to the McChord base.

It wasn't what Jake had planned on, but with Europe at war, he was an attractive candidate to the US Army Air Corps who were looking for men, and a steady paying job made the Army Air Corps equally attractive to him. To Jake, grease under his fingernails was better than turkey feathers under his collar. At least now he had money.

Chewing a wad of gum, a 30-ish mechanic with the bill of his cap flipped up stood on a short step latter and rattled on. "So, I wondered to myself, 'Why the heck am I fixing broken down cars for nothin', when I can work for Uncle Sam with better pay, all the benefits, and none of the bellyaching customers?' Get me?"

"Me and business don't seem to get along too well, either," Jake said. "I joined up to be a pilot, but they said I was too old." Jake didn't mind the mechanical work or even working for someone else, but being told he fly a plane took the wind out of his sails.

McChord Air Force Base entrance with Mt. Rainier in the distance.

*Only thirty-eight B-23 Dragons were ever constructed. It was soon
replaced with the superior North American B-25 Mitchell medium bomber.*

"Hand me a half-inch wrench, will ya?" The gum chewer twisted away
without looking back.

Jake opened a jangling drawer of tools and found what he was looking
for. "What do you think the Japs are up to? The papers say things are getting
hot." He handed off the wrench.

The mechanic ducked out from under the cowling, shook his head,
then pulled a rag from his back pocket and wiped the black grease from his
hands. "Don't you know? The Japs are a big joke. They can't fly 'cause they
can't see. Here, take your fingers and do this." He put two fingers at each
temple and stretched his face pulling his eyes into slits. Jake did the same,
making the pair appear like a couple of school kids goofing off. "How's it
look? All blurry huh?" He let go of his face, leaving greasy finger marks on
his temples and shook his head.

"Yeah. Yeah, you're right." Jake stood with his eyes pulled and gazed
around the hangar. It really *was* all blurry.

"See, that's why they all wear glasses." He grabbed a black hose and
pushed it onto a fitting. "And they don't have no balance, either. All them
Jap moms put their babies on their backs, and they rock all around. They
can't fly worth beans. If they ever get the idea to mess with the U.S.A. . . . ."
He looked down at Jake. "They'll be D.O.A. Get me?" He turned back, gave
a weird chuckle to himself and kept chewing his gum.

Jake nodded with a smile as if he'd been handed a pearl of wisdom.

Chapter 18

July 1940. Central Philippine University the city of Iloilo on the island of Panay, The Philippines.

Peggy thumped her tan leather suitcase down the stairs, dragging the over-stuffed bag to the front door of their concrete, tin-roofed staff quarters. Their home was a rather utilitarian place, but it sufficed. After having no occupants for a year, nature attempted to take it over, but the family banded together and drove out the rats and bats, swept it clean, and made it into a home. At least for the time being. The school campus consisted of white buildings with red tile roofs surrounded by coconut palms reaching to the sky.

"Here, Peg." Charma held out a magazine featuring a photo of Peggy at age eleven with her sister Alice, eight at the time, both in kimonos holding Japanese dolls. The article headline read *Foreign Girls Love Japan.* "Why don't you take this with you?"

"Oh, Mom, thanks." Peggy had forgotten about the magazine photo. The image raised feelings of longing for the only

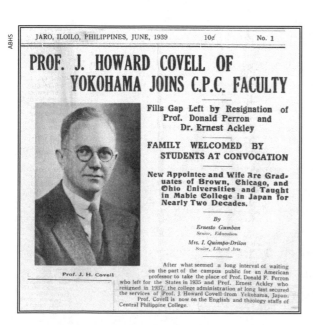

JARO, ILOILO, PHILIPPINES, JUNE, 1939   10¢   No. 1

PROF. J. HOWARD COVELL OF YOKOHAMA JOINS C.P.C. FACULTY

Fills Gap Left by Resignation of Prof. Donald Perron and Dr. Ernest Ackley

FAMILY WELCOMED BY STUDENTS AT CONVOCATION

New Appointee and Wife Are Graduates of Brown, Chicago, and Ohio Universities and Taught in Mabie College in Japan for Nearly Two Decades.

By
Ernesto Gumban
Senior, Education

Mrs. I. Quimpo-Drilon
Senior, Liberal Arts

Prof. J. H. Covell

After what seemed a long interval of waiting on the part of the campus public for an American professor to take the place of Prof. Donald F. Perron who left for the States in 1935 and Prof. Ernest Ackley who resigned in 1937, the college administration at long last secured the services of Prof. J. Howard Covell from Yokohama, Japan. Prof. Covell is now on the English and theology staffs of Central Philippine College.

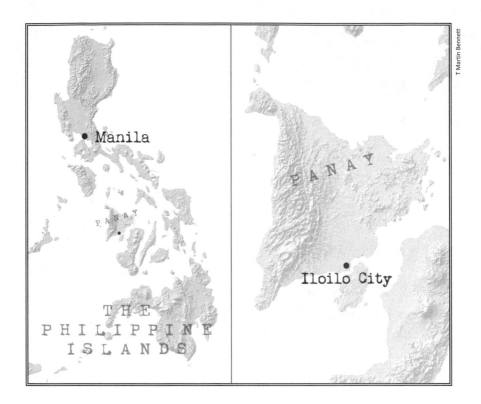

home she'd ever known—Japan.

Peggy breathed relief that they'd escaped the simmering trouble in Japan when her dad accepted the offer to teach English and Bible at the Central Philippine University, and they relocated to the Panay, a triangle-shaped tropical island in the middle of over 7,000 islands of the Philippines. Panay, covered with lush vegetation, palm trees, and wild orchids, measured about 100 miles wide by 120 miles long. The school hired her mom as a missions teacher, too, so she thought that was pretty great.

"I don't have much for the cold weather of New York," Peggy said to her mom, "so I'll have to get some winter clothes when I'm at college."

"Less to take with you on the ship and the trains. A ten-thousand-mile trip for a young lady like you? It'll be quite a journey." She ran her fingers through Peggy's hair.

Peggy smiled. Although not yet seventeen, she felt more like a woman, but to her mom, she knew she'd always be just a girl.

"Let me see your ticket," Jimmy said as he picked up her suitcase and impatiently motioned with his hand.

"*Dad*, I've got it." Peggy reached in her shoulder bag, pulled out her ticket, and waved it in front of him sarcastically. She hated being talked to like a kid, but crossing the Pacific Ocean and the continental United States by herself would be a challenge, a trip halfway around the world, but she was up for it. She loved adventures. Who knew what she might find?

The cogan-grass-roofed home of the Covell family while serving at Central Philippine University.

Keuka College for Women in upstate New York had accepted her application and she couldn't wait to start. But, now, surrounded by her mom, dad, sister and brother, she felt a twist in her stomach knowing she would soon miss them.

Jimmy ushered her toward the open doorway. "Kiss your brother and sister. We can't be late. Got to get to Manila early enough to make sure

The Covells in 1940. Left to right: Peggy, Charma, David, Jimmy, and Alice.

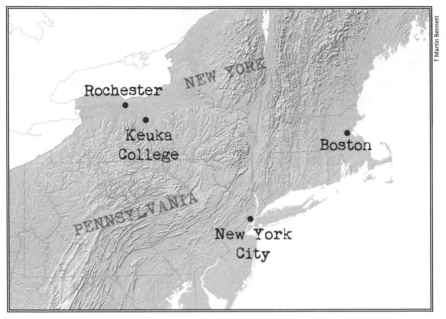

Keuka College lies beside Keuka Lake, within the
Finger Lakes Region southeast of Rochester, New York.

everything's set." He wiped his sleeve across the perspiration beaded over his forehead. "Don't want the steamer leaving without you. Then we'd be *stuck* with you!"

Peggy hugged her brother, David. "Well, it'll be a while before we're all back together again."

He smiled, then gave her a slight slug in the shoulder.

She reached to her younger sister, Alice, giving her a hug like the best friend she was. "I guess I'll see both of you sometime when you come to school in the States in not too long, OK?"

Alice's eyes filled with tears. She wrapped her arms around Peggy again, and they both held tightly.

Standing at the rail onboard their vessel in Manila Bay, Charma, Jimmy, and Peggy studied a crane hauling a cargo net of mailbags as it swung into the hold of their steamship, *The President Taft*. Jimmy turned to Peggy, placed his hands on her shoulders, and looked her up and down as if to regret her coming of age. "Look to serve others, Peggy. That's how you serve God." He reached out and pulled her to himself as passengers with bags pressed past them.

Charma wiped her eyes. "Your brother and sister will be going to California soon for school out there. Please, *please* be careful, dear."

"Don't you worry about me. I'm more worried about you and dad, with all this talk of war." Peggy felt safe leaving the Philippines, but couldn't help wondering what could happen in the islands. "I just don't understand it."

As seagulls called overhead in the fading afternoon light, the loudspeaker system blared, "All aboard for San Francisco! Last call. All aboard for San Francisco! Non-passengers, please disembark!"

Jimmy squeezed Peggy's shoulder and reassured her with his eyes. "Listen, General MacArthur's here with over one hundred thousand

PRESIDENT TAFT
Dollar Steamship Lines

Courtesy, Dollar Steamship Lines

A year after Peggy's voyage, the War Department requisitioned the President Taft *for a troop transport.*

Filipino and American soldiers. We're safe until things settle down, and then we can all go back to Japan. Besides," he said with a gentle stroke of her face, "I don't believe the Japanese really want war, anyway."

Chapter 19

October 8, 1940. Tokyo Bay.

Battleships, aircraft carriers, heavy cruisers, destroyers, and a host of warships—600,000 tons of them—blanketed the bay under a rumbling sky darkened by over 500 airplanes in the most muscular display of naval military power the world had ever seen.

Tens of thousands of cheering spectators lined the shores in the parks of Yokohama waving arms and flags from windows and trees, on rooftops, from buses, and on the beaches from one end to the other, erupting into deafening cheers and shouts of "Banzai! Banzai!"

Sailors in white perfectly lined the entire length of the deck of the aircraft carrier *Akagi*. In the tower, Fuchida and Capt. Kusaka shielded their eyes from the sun as they gazed upward in pride at the display of air power

The fast battleship Hiei *after significant retrofitting and upgrades during sea trials in December 1939.*

droning above.

On the deck of the battleship *Hiei* stood Admiral Yamamoto and the top military brass of the Imperial Japanese Navy—all in their impeccable navy blues replete with gold braids, colorful ribbons, and bright medals—facing Emperor Hirohito, seated on a raised platform, also in his military uniform.

The Imperial Japanese government declared 1940 as the 2,600[th] anniversary of the founding of the nation by their first emperor, Jimmu, in 660 B.C.—believed to be a direct descendent of the sun goddess, *Amaterasu*.

And this was only one of many national celebrations held throughout the country during the year. In April, the leaders of the city of Miyazaki on the southern island of Kyushu dedicated the *Hakko-Ichiu*[7] Monument towering 120 feet into the heavens on the very spot believed to be the location of Emperor Jimmu's palace.

Less than a month before the naval display, the Japanese Ambassador Kurusu had signed the Tripartite Pact with Adolf Hitler of Germany and the Italian foreign minister Ciano, securing Japan's position as one of the three Axis powers. Japan held Formosa, Korea, and Manchukuo—along with

Japanese citizens living abroad responded to appeals, shipping stones from all over the world to help construct the Hakko-Ichiu *Monument, which demonstrated the universal and eternal rule of the line of Japanese Emperors over the world.*

---

[7] Literally "eight cords, one roof," i.e., "All the world under one roof."

other portions of China. Virtually all of Europe had fallen under German or Soviet control, and the marauding German wolf pack submarines terrorized ships in the Atlantic, targeting military and civilian vessels alike.

On the battleship *Hiei*, as an officer shouted, "Salute!" all snapped their right hands up to their caps and a nearby battleship let loose her colossal guns with an ear-splitting concussion that reverberated through the harbor with an echoing shockwave.

The New World Order had begun.

Chapter 20

July 1941. Tacoma, Washington.

Benny Goodman's wild, upbeat "Sing! Sing! Sing!" blasted through tinny speakers in the smoky air of the off-base club, packed shoulder to shoulder with lusty servicemen and lovelorn gals. Jake slumped at the bar with a cheap date draped around his neck, his mind trying to think clearly through the fog of beer. "'You don't want my turkeys?' I said. 'You, you don't wanna buy my turkeys?'" He flicked the ash off his cigarette and took a long puff. Tired of work and tired of his life, it was his time to blow off a little steam.

"Aw, go on, Jake," his girl whined. "You said he *bought* your turkeys!"

"Yeah, yeah, he bought them all, but I lost, but I lost all my *money*." Jake raised his tall glass and polished off the last of it.

"Well, for crying out loud, Jake, how could you lose all your money if he *bought* them all!"

Jake slammed his glass on the counter and closed his eyes to concentrate. He had to nearly shout over the raucous music and laughter. "I had to, had to borrow some money to buy extra feed, and I had to, the price dropped, fourteen cents a pound and, but, but when . . ."

"Bartender!" Jake's girl waved a hand in the air. "One more beer for this one. Then he goes to bed! This fella's a funny one."

The bald bartender winked back.

Jake turned to the girl and blinked slowly. "Lillian, I . . ."

"Josephine. *Josephine!*"

"Josephine . . . don't let me ever buy baby turkeys again. No, not ever."

Chapter 21

August 1941. Kagoshima Air Base on the island of
Kyushu, the southernmost main island of Japan.

An Aichi D3A dive bomber touched down on the runway in the
morning sun and taxied past rows and rows of parked aircraft.
Inside a brick building, Fuchida, in his regular khaki-green
uniform before a classroom of young pilots, held out his hands palms down,
one slightly ahead of the other, and flew them like planes. ". . . and by a
shotai of five aircraft, if the release is timed properly, we can achieve an
accuracy rate of seventy percent—every time." He dropped his arms. The
blackboard behind him displayed various bombing trajectories on an x-y
axis. "So, for higher altitudes, we assemble a *chūtai* of nine aircraft grouped
in threes and, following the leader's signal, all release at the same time. With

this method, we can be assured of destroying our target about forty percent of the time. Tomorrow we'll let you try the three-plane *shotai* at low altitude. That is all. You are dismissed."

The students gathered their papers and made their way toward the door where an officer stood smiling back at Fuchida. Clapping his hands deliberately, he slowly walked to the front. "Well done, teacher. Well done."

Fuchida looked up as he closed his manuals. "Egusa! What gives me such an honor? Would the man Genda calls the number one dive bomber in all Japan like to be a student in my class?"

Egusa cocked his head. "Would you accept me?"

"No. You'd make me look bad."

Egusa pulled up a seat in front of Fuchida's desk, plunked down, took a drag on his cigarette, and quickly eyed the door to make sure the students were clear.

Fuchida sensed this was no ordinary call.

"What's really going on down here?" Egusa said. "No officer of your rank was ever kept a squadron commander. They keep moving you around to all these bases. Why?"

Fuchida reopened his folder to a rear pocket and plucked out a document on official letterhead and handed it to Egusa, who immediately began reading. "Not just a *squadron* commander," Fuchida said, "but *flight* commander of the First and Second Carrier Divisions—the entire air fleet."

Egusa stood and shook Fuchida's hand in genuine excitement. "Wow! Congratulations, commander!"

Fuchida took the paper and slid it back into his folder, flipping it shut. As a career military man, he obeyed his orders, but he didn't like working without a clear aim. He was uneasy. He leaned closer to Egusa. "All of the very best airmen have been brought together on these southern bases. So many swords being sharpened, but no plan for battle . . ."

September 5, 1941. The Imperial Palace, Tokyo.

In the evening, Emperor Hirohito held a final briefing in his office with General Sugiyama, his sixty-one-year-old Army chief of staff; Admiral

Nagano, chief of the Imperial Japanese Naval General Staff; and Prime Minister Konoe. With an impending Imperial Conference the next morning to discuss the decision of war with the United States, everyone wanted the clarity and unity beforehand.

The emperor in his impeccable black suit had been struggling the night before over what to do and the implications of every choice. He spoke to General Sugiyama. "In the event we must finally open hostilities, will our operations have a probability of victory?"

"Yes, Your Majesty, they will," he calmly replied while nodding his head downward.

"And can you carry out the southern operations as planned?"

"I believe so."

Hirohito's voice began to rise. "At the time of the Rokō Bridge Incident in China, the army told me that we could achieve peace *immediately* after dealing them one blow with three divisions, and that Chiang Kai-shek would give up right away. That was *four years* ago! *You* were army minister at that time!"

Holding his gaze downward, the old general replied, "Your Majesty,

The Nijūbashi Bridge spanning the moat that
leads to the main gate of the Imperial Palace on the left.

China is a vast area with many ways in and many ways out, and we met unexpectedly large difficu—"

"You say the interior of *China* is vast? Isn't the Pacific Ocean even bigger than China?! Didn't I caution you each time about those matters? Sugiyama, are you *lying* to me?!"

All were stunned at the extraordinary outbreak of emotion from the emperor, his face red with anger. He turned and paced away.

Lifting his head, Sugiyama responded, "If we waste time, let the days pass, and are forced to fight after it is too late, then we won't be able to do a thing about it."

The emperor collected himself as he stood near a tall window draped with burgundy curtains and sighed hard as he stared out into the unknown blackness. "All right. I understand." He knew his entire legacy would be based on this one, overwhelming decision.

Konoe raised his voice. "Your Majesty, shall I make changes in tomorrow's agenda? How would you like me to go about it?"

The emperor continued to stare into the night, his white-gloved hands behind his back. Konoe appeared weaker every day, leaning toward negotiations while the military leaders, Sugiyama and Nagano, continued to look stronger. Negotiate and wait? . . . Wait for what? Time was running out. "There is no need to change anything."

The following morning in the formal council chamber, the meeting of the cabinet went on as planned. Emperor Hirohito weighed the arguments while listening to a wide-ranging discussion on all of the possibilities and considerations of expanding the war into Southeast Asia, or the southern operation as it was called, the complications if the Soviet Union attacked from the north, and a possible war with the United States.

General Sugiyama held the floor. "The United States will not be able to be defeated; however, with success in the southern operation, Great Britain will be crushed, producing a great change in American public opinion. Therefore, a favorable conclusion to the war is not necessarily beyond hope. We must develop the rich resources of the southern area and utilize the economic power of the East Asian continent to establish a durable, self-sufficient economic position. We will continue to work with Germany and Italy to break up the unity of the United States and Britain. Linking the victories in Europe with our victories in Asia will produce an advantageous situation for us. In this way, we could hope to come out of the war somewhere even with the United States." The general, his chest covered with medals, bowed, then stood upright, and took his seat.

On his raised platform, the emperor held a report in his hands. "Regarding this *Outline for Carrying Out the National Policies of the Empire*, having listened to everything said today, I ask that you would continue to complete all preparations for war with the United States, Britain, and the Netherlands and to be prepared to come to a final decision on war by the end of October. At the same time, I want it to be clearly understood that I want full cooperation for diplomatic negotiations for a settlement, if it is at all possible."

Heads nodded around the room, but Hirohito knew most of their minds were made up. The emperor laid the sheet gently onto the desk before him and reached into his breast pocket to retrieve a small piece of worn paper which he carefully unfolded. It was a well-known *tanka*, an ancient form of Japanese poetry, written by Emperor Meiji in 1904 at the uncertain outset of the Russo-Japanese war, a war in which Japan was ultimately victorious. Emperor Meiji was Hirohito's grandfather. Adjusting his glasses, he read solemnly:

> *Across the four seas*
> *all are brothers.*
> *In such a world*
> *why do the waves rage,*
> *the winds roar?*

The room went dead silent. All wanted to confidently predict the future, and even more, to assure it, but Hirohito knew that these were things no one could possibly know, least of all, himself. He looked up with gravity, briefly glanced at a few faces, carefully folded the poem, and slowly slid it back into his pocket without a further word.

Chapter 22

Fall 1941. Keuka College, fifty miles southeast
of Rochester, New York.

With a cream colored sweater wrapped over her shoulders, sleeves tied across her chest, Peggy clutched her books as she crossed the grassy campus with her roommate, Jean, a slightly stout girl in a long, plaid skirt.

"Music major," Jean said. "Been playing piano since I was six. What about you?"

The changing leaves set off the terracotta brick of the main building behind them as they headed toward the lake in the autumn air. Peggy let her eyes wander across the clouded sky.

"Sociology—I *think*."

Keuka College before the snows of winter had arrived.

Keuka College

Peggy, in the white sweater,
served as secretary for her freshman class.

"Why's that? Sounds hard."

"I don't know. I guess I just like working with people."

A skein of Canadian geese drifted down and skimmed to a stop on the lake. Peggy studied the waterfowl bobbing their heads in the lake and stretching their wings. Peggy's face lightened. "Hey, good timing! I brought some bread to feed the geese. C'mon, let's go."

"The hunters'll *love* us for fattening up the geese."

Peggy looked back sternly. "Well, *these* geese are heading *south* for the winter."

Chapter 23

September 1941. Kagoshima Air Base. The island of Kyushu, southern Japan.

Three engineers in white struggled with an eighteen-foot Type 91 torpedo on its cart below a green Nakajima bomber as another plane taxied past a long line of aircraft.

In his office stacked with books and papers, Fuchida compared a textbook to his written notes in preparation for another class. An orderly tapped on his open door. Fuchida didn't look up.

"Sir? Lieutenant Commander Genda is here to see you."

Fuchida could hardly believe his old friend was at the Kanoya base and excitedly rose just as Genda entered, smiling broadly.

"Genda! Where've you been hiding? It's been too long, but I've been busy." They shook hands firmly with joy.

Genda tossed his hat on top of a filing cabinet. "So have I, but neither of us is as busy as we'll soon be."

All the months of training and the mysterious gathering of pilots had aroused a lot of curiosity among the fliers, but none more than Fuchida. He knew there were a lot of places they could be heading, from northern China to Indochina, but he was prepared and far more than merely curious. "I'm listening."

As he lit a match, Genda motioned for Fuchida to have a seat, then he put the flame to his cigarette and waved the match out. "I've been in nothing but meetings for the last few months." He strolled over to a sweeping map centered on the Pacific Ocean, taking his time to survey it from side to side, his hands on his hips. Various notes were pinned around the edges and small rising-sun flag pins marked territories of Japan as did Chinese and American flag pins in other places in East Asia and the Pacific.

Fuchida sensed this would be no ordinary conversation.

"When Germany conquered France, we gained free access to what was French Indochina here," Genda said pointing to a rising sun flag pinned on the coast below mainland China, ". . . putting us in a better position to fight the Chinese, to obtain rich supplies of rice, and enabling us to later drive south to Malaya giving us access to essential tin and rubber. The colony of Indochina will soon be reorganized to assure a steady flow of rice at controlled prices." He glanced at Fuchida to see he was following. "At the same time, the United States continues to give us ultimatums to abandon Manchukuo . . ." He swung his finger up north.

Lt. Commander Minoru Genda, chief planner of the Pearl Harbor Attack.

University of Pittsburgh

Fuchida rose and continued Genda's point, ". . . which is impossible. We need the natural resources, we've spent too many lives for it, and we'll never accept orders from another nation like America." It would be a national disgrace, after urging the nation onward year after year, to then give it all up and bow to the wishes of America. The demands were insulting.

Genda turned to Fuchida and continued. "The United States continues to strangle us. First, they cut off high-octane aviation fuel, then high-grade scrap iron, then all iron and copper, and then all oil. *Then*, they froze all assets. Until recently, they've been providing us eighty percent of all of our oil."

Fuchida folded his arms. He knew all this, but wasn't sure where Genda was going. "You don't need to tell *me*. I have a hard enough time getting gas for my own *car*."

"But—more oil could be available to us in the Dutch East Indies *if* we expanded further south." Genda took a long puff on his cigarette and looked at Fuchida from the side of his eyes. "You'd be interested to know that the Germans gave us captured mail from a steamer headed for Singapore. It included a letter from the British cabinet to the Singapore government, the bastion of military power in the area." Genda paused. "The British said they're *completely* unable to defend Singapore and can send *no* fleet to her aid. *None*. It's wide open."

Fuchida overseeing the training of flyers at the Kagoshima Air Base.

At this Fuchida raised his hand and shook his head. "But if we launch into the East Indies, the American fleet would *immediately* assemble to attack and cut us off using the Philippines as a base." The United States had been slowly building up strength in the Philippines for this very reason, and Fuchida knew it.

"So the best battle plan is to cut the sword from our enemy's belt before he can ever draw it." Genda looked at Fuchida's puzzled face for a moment, then plucked a rising sun flag pin from the edge of the map and planted it far across the map onto Oahu, Hawaii. Fuchida's eyes widened. "Yamamoto plans to attack Pearl Harbor. We will completely destroy the American fleet before it's ever deployed."

"*Pearl Harbor*? Are you out of your mind? That's the stronghold of the US fleet!"

"Exactly," Genda said as he calmly picked up a set of rising sun flags and began removing the flags of other nations following his explanation. "At the same time, we'll simultaneously attack Hong Kong, Indochina, Malaya, Singapore, the Philippines, Wake Island, and Guam, then seize the Dutch Indies with her oil, making them *all* a part of Greater East Asia. America will be paralyzed, and Australia and New Zealand will be isolated."

Fuchida's mind reeled as he ran his hands through his hair and studied the new layout. In all of his many imaginations, the thought of attacking Hawaii had never seriously crossed his mind.

"By combining the strength of six carriers into one attack group, we'll be able to launch a massive, coordinated aerial assault of hundreds of aircraft and overwhelm the Americans. They'd never expect such an air attack as it's never been done before."

Fuchida folded his arms. He could only stare in disbelief as he took it all in while searching for the weaknesses of the plan. His eyes penetrated every new flag on the map. "That would take *months* of preparation and planning."

"What do you think you've been doing down here all this time?" Genda plucked US flags from the Philippines, Wake Island, and Guam. "What do you think *I've* been doing all this time?" He plucked British flags from Hong Kong, Malaya, and Singapore; Dutch flags from the East Indies, Sumatra and Java; and the Australian flag from New Guinea, replacing them all with Japanese flags.

"From Japan to Hawaii and back? That's a round trip of over eight thousand miles,[8] beyond the limits of many of the ships needed in an attack like that. And besides, how could such a huge fleet travel so far, *completely* undetected by the Americans? It doesn't seem possible."

"We've been experimenting with refueling on the open seas and believe it will work." Reaching back to the map and leaning down he swept his hand below Hawaii. "The Americans are scouting south and west, so

---

[8] The Imperial Japanese Navy measured distance in nautical miles that they referred to as *kairi*. All nautical distances in this book are translated into statute miles throughout.

we'll approach from due north." He looked Fuchida in the eyes. "Admiral Yamamoto has insisted on the *absolute* need for a surprise aerial assault, and that we must act swiftly and decisively. The attack will be extremely difficult, but not impossible. I told Admiral Yamamoto that you had a strong fighting spirit and were a gifted leader with the ability to understand *any* given situation and to react to it quickly, which is why I recommended you to lead the attack, and Yamamoto himself agreed."

As much as Fuchida sometimes banged his own drum, he felt overwhelmed and humbled by Genda's words and wondered about his own abilities to lead such a challenge.

"He wants you to command the combined squadrons of the carrier fleet. The American battleships are Yamamoto's primary targets, but I want to take out as many carriers as we can find. With the Pacific Fleet out of the way, the Americans will be forced to negotiate terms favorable to Japan." Genda jabbed the British and American flags onto the fringe of the map.

"Does Yamamoto plan to take Hawaii?" Fuchida said.

"No." Genda strode from the map and stepped closer to Fuchida. "We wouldn't have the resources with the southern operation in full swing. The United States doesn't want war with Japan, and we don't want war with them. Hitler conquered America's old friends, and Roosevelt did nothing.

University of Pittsburgh

Yamamoto and Combined Fleet staff on his flagship
Nagato, *1941. Bottom row, 6th from the left is Admiral Yamamoto.*

We're willing to bleed and die for our emperor, but all they care about is baseball and jazz music." Both Genda and Fuchida smiled.

"Sink their fleet," Genda continued, "kill their men, and they'll be begging for peace. They'll give us anything we want. The war'll be over in a few months. They'll keep to themselves, and we'll retain all conquered territories, free from interference." Genda beamed.

"And the Germans," Fuchida said, "are pounding on the gates of Moscow."

"Our 1937 naval building program is complete," Genda said. "Japan has never been stronger, and America has never been weaker. This is our one, great chance. Success will guarantee our free reign in the Pacific and East Asia."

Fuchida studied Genda's impassioned face for a moment, then turned back to the map, his eyes fixed on Oahu. "So, success at Pearl Harbor is the key, then, isn't it?"

"That's the key."

Fuchida stood gazing over the map. "Yamamoto's betting everything on this one, isn't he?"

Genda likewise surveyed the expansive map. "We all are. He said that nothing less than a fatal blow will do. Understand that Yamamoto insists that diplomatic negotiations continue and that the strike force will remain fully prepared to turn back no matter what stage we're at, even if we're one day away from the attack."

Fuchida knew as well as Genda that "negotiations" between diplomats in Japan and Washington were little more than window dressing to justify the expansion of the war. The diplomats may have captured the front pages of the newspapers, but in reality, they had become irrelevant. The emperor's cabinet of war hawks had driven off any doves, and they felt that whatever they had the power to take, they had the *right* to take.

Fuchida inhaled deeply. "The negligence and arrogance of the Americans will be their undoing. If they're asleep . . . they deserve to be defeated."

A grin took over Fuchida's face as he turned to Genda. "I was born a boy at the right time."

Genda smiled back. "So was I."

Chapter 24

October 1941. High desert bombing range, Washington.

A twin-engine light bomber sped past in the open sky. Inside the Douglas A-20, Jake sat motionless peering through the bombsight with his fingers twisting control dials, oblivious to the deafening drone of the engines.

The instructor hunched over him with a hand gripping the fuselage frame, the other holding a stopwatch. He yelled over the din of the engines. "What altitude did you dial in?"

Jake yelled back without moving. "Fifty-three hundred feet, sir." To earn the position of bombardier, Jake studied long and hard to pass complex exams focusing on math—his favorite subject. It felt nice to know

The Douglas A-20 Havoc light bomber.

he was finally good at *something*. This was certainly more interesting than handing off tools to a mechanic or raising domestic fowl—and more exciting.

"True airspeed?"

"Two hundred and twenty knots, sir."

"When the target comes into view, release your payload just a half-second early to compensate for rack lag. Hit the outside second ring, and I'll buy you a beer. Don't worry—it takes a while to get the feel of it all."

"OK. OK. I see it coming up. OK, there it is. Bombs away!"

The instructor clicked his timer and stared at the dial. Jake looked up at his face, waiting.

On the ground a spotter in a tower watched the chalk target through binoculars. Seeing a small puff of smoke, he grabbed the radio. "That's a hit sir—inside the first ring."

The instructor reached his hand up to his headset. "The *first* ring? Copy that." He shook his head. "You got me for two beers, Jake. You're *killin'* me."

Jake bobbed his head with a glowing smirk.

Chapter 25

October 1941. Central Philippine University,
Iloilo City, Island of Panay, The Philippines.

T wo students in all white slung a baseball back and forth on the
campus yard in front of several stucco, two-story buildings, also
white, with beige striped awnings over the windows. Tall coconut
palms accented the school surrounded by dense, tropical foliage. In 1901, a
donation of $2,000 from John D. Rockefeller to the Baptist Church in the
Philippines was enough to found a Bible college which later became Central
Philippine University, a small school
with a growing reputation for Christian
excellence.

Standing before a blackboard of
scrawled notes, Jimmy in his white suit
adjusted his round-rimmed glasses and
held up his index finger as the class of
eighteen students filed past him toward
the door. "The quiz will cover the
timeline of the kings of Israel and Judah.
Tuesday."

Francis H. Rose, the school
president, a man with clear, blue eyes
and a head topped with thick, white
hair, stood just inside the doorway
tapping a folded newspaper against his
palm. A Renaissance man in the truest
sense, Francis had acquired five degrees,
yet he was as adept with a greasy wrench

ABHS

*Francis Rose's wife, Gertrude, said
they often had a difficult time
balancing their budget because
Francis was constantly giving to
the needs of so many others.*

ABHS

Students on the campus of Central Philippine University shortly before the war.

on an engine water pump as he was with a pen and parchment writing poetry.

After waiting for the tide of students to flow past, Francis walked up to Jimmy and plopped the open newspaper onto his desk. "Is it any wonder enrollment is down? *Way* down?"

Jimmy read the headlines: "*PHILIPPINES RUSH DEFENSE EFFORT, General MacArthur and Staff of American Officers Train Filipino Manpower.*" Jimmy studied the paper a moment and looked up, pushing back the wave of fear with his own strength of hope. Tapping the newspaper with his finger, he said, "The greatest concentration of American bombers anywhere in the world is right here in the Philippines." Jimmy was certain Francis knew it, too, but he didn't seem to have any confidence. "MacArthur says we've got hundreds of aircraft here, thousands of American and Filipino troops, and we can *easily* repel *any* attack from the Japanese."

Francis ignored Jimmy's bravado. "All the ROTC students and staff are on alert, and all able-bodied men are on notice. We need to start putting together some contingency plans."

For Jimmy, it was the same old saber rattling and jockeying he'd been enduring for years. At least, he kept telling himself that. "I have a hard time, a *very* hard time, believing the Japanese would ever try to invade the islands." He angrily snapped a rubber band around a bundle of papers.

"And if they do?"

Jimmy glanced away, then back at Francis—and blinked a couple of times.

By candlelight, Charma rested in her stuffed chair reading *Les Misérables*, while Jimmy sat in his rocker beside their boxy shortwave radio broadcasting the "Information Please" news program from San Francisco. Blackouts had become mandatory two months earlier to shroud the cities in darkness to make them more difficult bombing targets. Straining to hear through the crackle and sonic hum, Jimmy cocked his head toward the radio.

"Considering the recent movements reported by the War Department of the Japanese Army and Navy, particularly in the areas of China and

A staff portrait at CPU during more peaceful times, Jimmy in the front center.

Southeast Asia, the possibility of obtaining satisfactory results from negotiating with Japan is a fading hope. But US Ambassador Joseph Grew continues his unrelenting pursuit of a diplomatic solution to . . ."

Jimmy snapped off the radio and sat back and rocked, the creak of his chair the only sound in the room. He unconsciously stared into the distance and spoke as if to himself. "In 1901, the future president of the YMCA[9], John Mott, said America can send ten thousand missionaries to Japan now, or in forty years they'll have to send a hundred thousand soldiers." Jimmy kept rocking.

Charma eased her book down to her lap.

"That was exactly forty years ago." He stopped rocking and turned to Charma. "We need to think about getting off the island." The fear he'd held under the surface for so long was breaking through.

"We need to make some plans." Relieved that Peggy was in college in upstate New York, and David and Alice were in boarding school with friends in San Francisco, his concern was shifting to the welfare of his and Charma's lives. He gazed down at the cover of a worn *LIFE* magazine on the coffee table displaying Emperor Hirohito proudly atop a white horse, saluting. "Soon."

Emperor Hirohito inspecting his troops astride his Imperial stallion Shirayuki (White Snow).

---

[9] The Young Men's Christian Association, founded in 1844 with the goal to help develop "Muscular Christianity" —a commitment to spiritual devotion and physical health.

Chapter 26

October 1941. The aircraft carrier Akagi, Ariake
Sea, the island of Kyushu, southern Japan.

A shuttle boat puttered up beside the majestic *Akagi*, anchored
among the fleet of warships in the inland bay, her peaceful exterior
giving no hint of the frenzy of activity within.

In a planning room aboard the carrier, hazy with cigarette smoke,
Fuchida stood with his arms folded near Genda and a group of officers
staring down at two large tables displaying perfect models: One of Oahu and
the other of Pearl Harbor itself. The fine detail and accuracy of the replicas
amazed him. Much had taken place in preparation already, yet the immense
amount of planning and logistics facing him and the team felt
overwhelming. It still seemed like an impossible task. How could the entire
Combined Fleet enter American waters and then launch hundreds of planes

The pride of the Japanese carriers, the Akagi *in 1941.*

over hundreds of miles undetected *all the way to Pearl Harbor?* Surely, even if the fleet wasn't discovered, regular American patrol aircraft would discover them and every American aircraft on the island would be sent into the air to attack them. Were they all out of their minds?

Between Fuchida and Genda stood Rear Admiral Kusaka, formerly Fuchida's chief aboard the *Akagi*. "Genda has advised that to achieve a crushing blow to the American fleet, all possible resources should be combined for a massive aerial attack, like none ever attempted from the sea."

Genda spoke up. "If I may, Admiral? All six carriers will be employed and kept in a tight formation allowing the aircraft to group quickly. We should be able to put no fewer than three hundred fifty planes into action in two waves, and I recommend the attack be during daylight for maximum accuracy. We'll rely primarily on torpedoes to destroy the carriers and battleships."

Fuchida's mind was working. He knew they were waiting to hear his experienced opinion.

Vice Admiral Chuichi Nagumo, commander in chief of the First Air Fleet and the man with the primary responsibility for the entire operation, stood beside Fuchida. As a lifelong practitioner of *kendo*, the martial art of sword fighting with bamboo swords, he valued the careful assessment of an opponent before making a strike. He ran his hand over his balding head. "Lieutenant Fuchida, please be frank."

Fuchida shook his head. "The models are excellent, but where are the placements of the American ships?" Genda nodded to an assistant who unrolled a map with the last known locations of the ships in the harbor sketched in.

"A torpedo attack is essential," Genda said. "It'll do far greater damage than aerial bombs."

"What's the average depth of the harbor?"

Another assistant spoke up reading from papers. "Sir, the harbor's maximum depth is approximately fourteen meters." He looked at Fuchida, fearfully awaiting his response.

"*Fourteen meters?*" he said in disbelief. "We don't have any aerial torpedoes that'll run that shallow. They'll stick straight in the mud!" The commanders turned to Genda.

"Do it anyway!" Genda said. "We'll *find* a way to make it work."

Fuchida knew Genda well enough that sometimes his theories exceeded his practical knowledge, but set the concern aside for the present. Genda was a brilliant man. He also recognized they had resourceful engineers. "What about torpedo nets? I can't imagine the Americans won't have their nets up."

Genda casually lit a cigarette. "*You* think the harbor's too shallow for torpedoes." He looked Fuchida in the eyes. "The *Americans* think it's too shallow for torpedoes. Our reports show they're not using nets. If they are, our first torpedoes will blow holes right through them, and we'll drop more torpedoes down the same lines."

Fuchida waved his hand over the map. "Many of the ships are double-berthed. Torpedoes can't reach the inside positions. Aerial bombs are the only option."

"Dive bombers, then," Nagumo said.

Again, Fuchida shook his head. "Dive bombers can penetrate their carrier decks, but battleship deck armor is too heavy. Level bombers can do it, but we don't have aerial bombs powerful enough for the job."

Genda leaned in. "I've given a lot of thought to this. What about the sixteen-inch armor-piercing shells used for the guns of our battleships? What if we added fins and fastened them to your planes? Couldn't you use them successfully?"

Fuchida pondered. "That's never been done, either, but I'll talk to the engineers." Things were adding up in Fuchida's mind—so many untested systems, so many untried plans. He'd seen in the past how his commanders made finely tuned plans based on every variable being in their favor. But one problem, and the plan unraveled like an old tatami mat.

Ever cautious, Nagumo looked Fuchida in the face. "Is everything going to be OK?"

The eyes of all pressed into Fuchida. If there were ever a chance to call things off, or least call for a delay, now would be the time. His few seconds of hesitation felt like minutes. "I can't tell you at this time, sir. Success depends on our training from now on."

Nagumo nodded and glanced at Genda. "Very good. Very good. Get on with the training of the pilots, Fuchida, but not a word is to be mentioned about the objective. *Complete* secrecy must be maintained. None of the flyers are to know. Is that understood?"

"Yes, sir."

"I'm still concerned about detection." Nagumo sighed deeply.

Fuchida rubbed his face. "If we can achieve surprise, *total* surprise . . . the Pacific Fleet will be a memory." Still, it was a *very* unlikely scenario to him.

November 12, 1941.

Their months of planning and practice had come to an end. All prepared to depart to a staging point in the far north to launch their attack and Admiral Yamamoto called the commanders and leading officers of the Task Force Fleet to the *Akagi* for final instructions. The men stood motionless on the flight deck of the flagship *Akagi* in the noon sun. Distant mountains hemmed in the bay as Yamamoto, in his navy blue winter uniform, shouted so all could hear.

"Our opponent, this time, is not an easy one," Yamamoto said, the cold autumn air breezing over the deck. "Japan has faced many worthy opponents in her long history—but the United States is the most worthy of all. You must be prepared for great American resistance."

Fuchida could see the concern in his eyes that came from a man who had experienced war and studied it for a lifetime.

"Admiral Kimmel, commander in chief of the Pacific Fleet, is known to be farsighted and aggressive, so we can't count on surprise. You may have to fight your way to the target. The success or failure of the operation of this unit taking the first step in this battle will influence the success or failure of the entire Pacific operation. I'm praying for the best effort from all of us, and for our success." Yamamoto slowly scanned the faces of his men. "We await the emperor's decision."

Fuchida was confident but concerned. Everything was in place for success, but there would be no middle ground for the outcome of the attack.

Admiral Yamamoto turned to Vice Admiral Nagumo, shook his hand and nodded, then did the same with Rear Admiral Kusaka and Genda. Before leaving, he came to Fuchida and grasped his hand firmly and looked him soberly in the face.

Fuchida understood he would be the lead warrior in an event that could change the course of Japan's future, and perhaps the world itself. He was ready.

Chapter 27

November 26, 1941. Just off the Kuril Islands, Japan.

Under cover of night from a remote bay on one of the northernmost islands of Japan, the most powerful naval battle group that had ever been assembled set off eastward. Fuchida stood on the open flight deck of the *Akagi* in the dim starlight, his pant legs flapping in the icy wind, and took in the sight of the First Air Fleet of six aircraft carriers, two battleships and two dozen support ships—cruisers, oilers, and destroyers, plus twenty-eight submarines. The Japanese Navy gave their ships colorful names such as "Flying Dragon" (*Hiryu*) "Auspicious Crane" (*Zuikaku*) and "Red Castle" (*Akagi*)—the name of a

Fuchida on the Akagi, November 25, 1941, sitting to the right of the white post, at their farewell meeting in the wardroom.

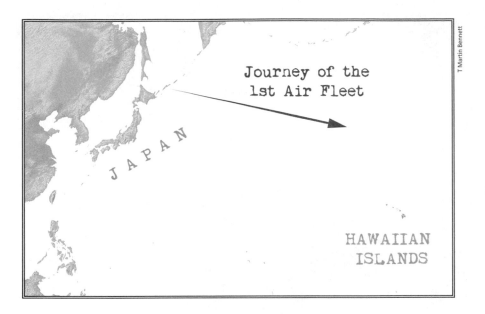

Journey of the
1st Air Fleet

JAPAN

HAWAIIAN
ISLANDS

T Martin Bennett

dormant volcano and home to the legends of gods.

He felt a personal closeness to the *Akagi*, the flagship of the fleet, like she was a long-trusted friend. He paced further down the deck. Over the previous months, he had shouted himself hoarse working with groups of fliers, giving instructions and encouraging the men at every opportunity to strive for excellence.

Now, with the frenzied training behind him, he enjoyed the brisk sea breeze and the slow pitch and yaw of the ship. He inhaled with relief and excitement for the coming fight.

December 1, 1941. The Imperial Palace, Tokyo, Japan.

Nineteen leaders sat stiffly in the imperial council chamber with only Tojo standing, having just completed his last words to the emperor. They all had spent countless hours over weeks and months discussing every conceivable plan and every possible outcome, and it had finally come down to this one, electrically-charged moment. All eyes were fixed on the emperor waiting nervously. Emperor Hirohito gently nodded his head. It would be war.

Shortly after departing from Japan, December, 1941.

Part II

Thunder and Lightning

Chapter 28

December 8, 1941 (Japan), December 7 (USA) before the dawn. The Pacific Ocean, 260 miles north of Oahu, Hawaii.

The carrier *Akagi* rose and fell on the high seas in the pre-dawn darkness, hurling great sheets of white water into the wind. In the ready room, having just poured out his heart to his fellow fliers, Fuchida in his full flight gear, came face to face with Genda in the passageway. Eighteen years of friendship and experiences flashed before him as their eyes locked onto each other. Danger or not, this was the course they had chosen and, having received their orders, there would be no

Fuchida the day before the attack. Because he knew his men would all face the imminent threat of death, he felt it was his responsibility to keep their spirits up.

University of Pittsburgh

*A Mitsubishi A6M Zero fighter sits beside the
tower of the* Akagi *on the day of the Pearl Harbor Attack.*

turning back. As planes rumbled outside and pilots shoved past them in the
corridor, Fuchida's serious gaze at Genda grew into a smile. Genda smiled
back. This would be the greatest day of their lives.

Ocean spray burst over the bow as the *Akagi* continued to pitch
through the frighteningly rough waters. Engineers wrestled against the
wings of over two dozen aircraft packing the deck attempting to keep the
idling planes in position. The pilots couldn't distinguish the distant water
from the border of the sky—something nearly essential for flying. Had this
been a drill, Fuchida would have quickly scrapped it, but this was war. First
to launch—the Zero escort fighters, who powered off the front of the *Akagi*,
took to the sky, and circled their ship.

Fuchida approached his own light-gray Nakajima bomber with its
distinctive red tail—striped with three horizontal yellow bars for his pilots
to easily identify him en route as their commander. He affectionately ran his
hand across the leading edge of the wing like a samurai examining his

Zero fighters prepare to launch from the carrier Shokaku.

katana[10]. Smiling, he turned to his engineer, Sub-lieutenant Kazuo Kanegasaki, a man taller than the rest, and shouted over the thundering engines and blowing wind, "Is my aircraft in order?" he said, knowing full well what the answer would be.

Kanegasaki bowed his head with a quick nod, "Sharpened to a keen edge, sir!" Despite the urgency of the moment, Kanegasaki, surrounded by other engineers in white, withdrew a long, white bandana from his pocket and held it in outstretched hands to Fuchida. "All the maintenance crew would like to go with you to Pearl Harbor. Since we can't, we want you to take this *hachimaki*[11] as a symbol that we are with you—in spirit." The crew gave a brief bow as Fuchida did likewise. He humbly accepted the hachimaki with both hands and tied it around his leather helmet, samurai style.

He gave Kanegasaki one, last smile, then clambered up the wing and into the center position of his aircraft. The plane seated three men: in the front sat Fuchida's pilot, Lt. Mutsuzaki; Fuchida took the middle as bombardier, navigator, and flight commander; and Petty Officer Mizuki

---

[10] A curved, slender sword of the samurai warrior.
[11] Literally, "helmet scarf." Traditionally worn as a symbol of courage and great effort, historically worn by samurai entering battle.

occupied the rear seat as radio operator/gunner. As General Commander of the entire operation, Fuchida had far more to focus on than flying as he was responsible for directing the attack as well as documenting the progress of the raid for later review. And their precious 1,760-pound armor-piercing bomb—the ultimate purpose of their aircraft—was his responsibility, too. After strapping in, he reached back and slid the canopy shut as his pilot wound up the engine and taxied into takeoff position.

Fuchida had accumulated over 3,000 hours in the air without a major incident, but he was quite conscious that even the slightest problem with his plane over the open ocean could mean death. Flying into hostile air and coming under fire greatly increased the risk, and their estimates had put the "acceptable loss" at nearly half their 360 aircraft. Japanese intelligence estimated there to be over 500 planes stationed near Pearl Harbor. He and his companions would be flying for eight hours where anything could happen. Should they have to ditch in the sea, rescue would be impossible.

Fuchida had purchased bright red underwear and undershirt for the attack. Should he return from the battle wounded, he hoped it would help prevent others from being discouraged at the sight of his blood. To attain the heightened state of mind that accepts life and death as inseparable, he

A rare photo showing Fuchida's actual Nakajima B5N2 with his striped tail.

practiced Zen, often stopping at the Engaku-ji Buddhist temple complex in Kamakura, to the south of Tokyo.

His aircraft nudged forward. Fuchida quashed his thoughts as there was no sense being concerned about what couldn't be changed. The successful execution of the attack was all he cared about now. Nothing else.

With the flagman's OK, his plane throttled up, pressing him back into his seat, and roared down the familiar wooden runway past the cheering engineers waving their caps and handkerchiefs and shouting for joy. As they cleared the end of the pitching ship and lifted into the dark dawn sky, Fuchida was once again filled with child-like elation, thrilled to see his first-wave attack aircraft forming into their flight groups. Once the first of 183 planes took to the air and were properly grouped, they headed south to Oahu.

Fuchida led the way for his band of forty-nine Nakajima B5N2 level bombers. To his right, at a slightly lower altitude were forty B5N2's equipped with torpedoes. To his left, flying a little higher, were fifty-one Aichi D3A dive bombers. Protecting the three groups were forty-three Mitsubishi A6M Zero fighters, who would also participate in strafing targets.

While Fuchida reviewed his plans, the horizon to the left caught his eye. Bursting through the cobalt morning sky over a cloud-covered sea, the rising sun beamed rays of bright light through the billows in a realization of their Rising Sun Flag which dated back to the days of the feudal warlords in Japan.

With boyhood excitement, he slid back his canopy and waved both hands in the air to his comrades, his white hachimaki trailing in the wind, and pointed to the sun. Nearby fliers likewise slid open their canopies and waved with enthusiasm. Now he was *certain* the gods were with them and that he was *born* to be a warrior of the Japanese Empire, *born* for this one, great day in history!

Twenty-five minutes before the Pearl Harbor Attack. Kota Bharu, British Malaya, 350 miles northwest of Singapore.

Japanese destroyers ferociously pummeled the sandy shore positions with barrages of artillery shells, their guns illuminating the darkness with brilliant flashes of light. Four columns of troop transports loaded with 5,300 infantry soldiers flooded the northern beaches at Kota Bharu and came under heavy small arms fire from the British Indian and Australian forces. The Japanese soldiers were the first of tens of thousands to follow in the

invasion of British Malaya on their way to seize Singapore, the crown jewel of British strength in Southeast Asia.

Five minutes before the attack. Oahu, Hawaii.

Flying above the volcanic mountains of Oahu draped with clouds, Fuchida never imagined they would remain undetected from Japan all the way to their destination. Clouds obscured most of the island, but he could see the southwest coastline of Oahu. He looked up and around his group of aircraft in disbelief. "Not a single patrol plane on watch!"

"Matsuzaki," Fuchida said to his pilot through his speaking tube, "it seems we can go ahead with the surprise attack."

"Yes, I also think it's a surprise attack."

Shoving back the canopy, he aimed his signal pistol downward and fired a single Black Dragon flare, trailing a black line of smoke in the sky signaling for the entire squadron to shift into their standby formation to prepare for an imminent attack.

Fuchida scanned his map, then peered through his binoculars to study the harbor ahead of them. There were the battleships! One, two, three . . . all eight, just as he'd hoped! "They're here!" he shouted. "They're all here!" The harbor was *exactly* as he expected, just like the model they'd been studying for months. He'd already found out two days earlier that there were no American carriers in port—a disappointment—but everyone had a fear that, perhaps, some or all, of the battleships could have left as well.

He reached for his speaker tube. "Mizuki, send the message to all pilots: All forces attack! Mutsuzaki, watch for interceptors!"

His B5N2, a high-level bomber, climbed while the torpedo bombers dropped lower. As the various aircraft took their well-rehearsed positions beginning their approach to assault the American fleet, Fuchida realized that they had done it. They had beaten all odds and caught their prey *completely* unaware!

It was time to notify the fleet. He looked back at the telegrapher. "Mizuki, we have achieved the complete surprise of our enemy. Send the message, 'Tora! Tora! Tora!'"[12]

"Yes, sir!" Mizuki began clicking away on his telegraphic key.

Back at the *Akagi*, Fuchida's engineer, Kanegasaki with the others in the empty hangar, stood below a PA speaker listening keenly: "Attention! Attention! Commander Fuchida has reported back from Hawaii the following message . . . 'Tora! Tora! Tora!'" The crew of the entire ship burst into ecstatic cheers and shouts of euphoria.

3:00 A.M., December 8. The Imperial Palace. Tokyo, Japan.

Quietly in his office, Emperor Hirohito, somewhat bleary-eyed having stayed up anxiously through the night, sat upright at his desk with four other nervous and weary officials seated in his office of red velvet and

---

[12] "Tiger! Tiger! Tiger!"

lacquered wood.

A messenger appeared at the door, bowed crisply, and entered. "Your Majesty, we have just received this communication from the combined fleet." He stepped to the emperor's desk and held out a note in outstretched hands with his head bowed.

The emperor took the note gingerly, scanned the message, sighed, nodded, and smiled. "Commander Fuchida sends this message." He paused for effect. "'*Tora, tora, tora.*'"

The officials beamed with relief, wiped the perspiration from their foreheads, and vigorously shook each other's hands.

The Battleship Nagato, Hashirajima Anchorage, Japan.

Aboard the *Nagato*, Admiral Yamamoto sat in the operations room with head down, eyes closed—walls plastered with maps of the Pacific Ocean, Indonesia, The Philippines, China, and more. On the center table sat

The battleship Nagato *at anchor, flagship of Admiral Isoroku Yamamoto at the time of the attack.*

a large globe and additional maps, charts, pencils, and notebooks. Other officers in the room sat equally silently and nervously.

To the side, a radio loudly transmitted communications from various aircraft in Morse code as an operator scrawled notes. He turned to see if Yamamoto heard. "Admiral! Sir! We have received the signal of 'Tora! Tora! Tora!'"

The room came to life.

Without emotion, Yamamoto opened his eyes. "I heard the code. Did you get that message directly from his aircraft?"

"Yes, sir, directly from Commander Fuchida's plane over Hawaii."

Smiles broke across the faces of the relieved officers. Yamamoto nodded, but wasn't quite prepared to celebrate, yet.

```
Pearl Harbor, Oahu, Hawaii.
3:18 a.m. Japanese Standard Time, December 8.
7:48 a.m. Hawaiian Time, December 7.
```

A remarkably clear photograph taken by a Japanese airman during the very beginning of the attack. The column of water is from a torpedo strike on the battleship USS Maryland.

Battleship Row as seen by a Japanese pilot at the time of the attack.

Fuchida brought his group into their bombing run toward battleship row and watched as dive bombers fell from the sky onto Hickam Field, the Army air base near the mouth of Pearl Harbor, dropping their payload onto tightly packed formations of parked aircraft. Zero fighters tore through the rows of planes in a spectacular display of explosions and flames. He knew this was perhaps the most crucial part of their plan, for if Hickam's B-17s and P-40s managed to take to the air and follow the Japanese back to their own fleet, it could prove disastrous.

Closing into the harbor like predators about to leap onto their unaware prey, Fuchida cautiously watched the torpedo bombers make their final approaches, each pilot on his own highly-planned course. They were the slowest and most vulnerable of all their attack planes. As the drone of the engines approached the idle ships, torpedoes splashed into the bay and swam silently to their targets as the next planes fell into position behind them. The first wave of torpedoes sped toward the moored battleships.

Two half-dressed American sailors at the rail of the battleship *USS Maryland* stared in amazement. "What the hell?!" A pair of massive concussions exploded columns of water 150 feet into the air.

Japanese bombs destroy the USS Shaw.

A rapid succession of blasts rocked battleship after battleship, one after another, which began filling the air with thick plumes of black smoke. Anti-aircraft fire began to pock the sky with black smoke blossoms as waves of Val dive bombers screamed down on the fleet, releasing their 550-pound payloads with merciless precision.

Fuchida peered down through binoculars assessing the organized chaos while his pilot took a pass over the ship they were targeting. As he finished counting the battleships in the harbor, an anti-aircraft shell exploded on their left, violently shaking their plane. He cursed under his breath. His pilot, Matsuzaki, checked his instruments and spoke to Fuchida through the speaking tube hanging from his neck, "Don't worry about that. We're all right, sir." A second shell burst even closer on the right, convulsing the plane and sending bits of shrapnel through the aircraft.

Everything having gone so well so far, Fuchida wanted to get on with their business and hopefully make it back to their carrier alive. "Let's get a good sighting, drop our bomb, then circle out wider," he ordered. The pilot nodded and led his level bombing run over the battleships as Fuchida's *chūtai* of five bombers formed into their unusual formation composed just for this attack—three in front, two behind, just like they'd practiced dozens of times before.

Taking aim through his bombsight at his target through the growing clouds of smoke, he waited until the exact moment, then released his 1,760-pound armor-piercing bomb onto *USS Maryland* below. With the many planes dropping so many bombs, he couldn't tell which of the planes in his group hit the target; but could see two explosions on the ship below and knew their group had accomplished their goal.

His plane shuddered from another hellacious explosion, this one from the harbor far below. As he looked out, a thundering red fireball wrapped in smoke rose a thousand meters skyward from a battleship. He grinned and nodded. The hateful, mean-looking red flame was the telltale mark of a direct hit on the powder magazine.[13] His airmen were performing

Pearl Harbor at the height of the attack with anti-aircraft flak filling the sky.

---

[13] This was the *USS Arizona*.

terrifically, and the Americans were foolish to leave their fleet utterly unprotected.

Fuchida's plane banked away as he studied the ships below, keeling over into the flaming waters under shrouds of billowing, black smoke. The mission was unfolding as an astounding success. His heart blazed with joy.

10:50 a.m. Pacific Time. McChord Field, Tacoma, Washington.

An olive-green fuel truck rumbled past an open hangar housing two B-17 bombers. Inside the mess hall kitchen, Jake sat peeling potatoes huddled around a huge pot with five others in white aprons, listening to the Giants-Dodgers football game booming over the radio.

"Are you crazy?" Jake said. "Tuffy Leemans is a freight train when they hand him the ball. He's gonna take the Giants to the playoffs— *again*." Jake lobbed his peeled potato into the aluminum tub and grabbed another.

New York Giants'
Alphonse "Tuffy" Leemans.

"The Giants didn't make the playoffs last year, idiot," another piped in. "Tuffy couldn't pull a caboose compared to Pug Manders, Brooklyn's *three-time* Pro Bowl fullback who averaged over *forty* yards a game!"

"Wise guy," Jake answered. "The Giants made the playoffs in '38 and '39, and *Tuffy's* averaging forty-*seven* yards a game. And you probably didn't know that today, *today*, is 'Tuffy Leemans Day' at the ballpark. You got a 'Pug Manders Day'? No, of *course* you don't!"

The crew stopped at the sound of a commotion rumbling from behind a pair of double doors, which burst open as airmen flew in. "The Japs hit Pearl! The Japs just bombed Pearl Harbor! They're all over Hawaii!"

The room erupted into curses of astonishment. Jake leaped up and hurled a potato against the wall. "You Jap bastards are gonna *pay* for this! *No one* does that to the U.S.A. and gets away with it! *No one!*"

2:10 p.m. Eastern Standard Time. Keuka College outside Rochester, New York.

An American flag flapped atop the flagpole over the vacant campus grounds. In a small staff break room, female students and teachers packed together and overflowed into the hallway listening frozen to a radio report from a floor-standing console. Some girls stifled sobs, others held handkerchiefs to their faces.

Peggy listened stoically beside the window. She had long-feared and half-expected to hear news like this.

The radio announcer continued through crackling static: *"There's*

*Ball Hall, the main building on the
Keuka College campus, as it was in 1941.*

chaos on Oahu and great loss of life as information continues to come in on the Japanese attack. The American fleet at Pearl Harbor is completely engulfed in smoke and flames, and there are now reports of a full-scale invasion by the Japanese. American troops are being put on alert as . . ."

"Oh God! Oh God, no!" one of the girls blurted out as she broke down into uncontrollable sobs.

Peggy turned to the window and stared as a chill spread over her skin. She spoke under her breath, "Dad . . ." The Japanese would be invading the Philippines.

Chapter 29

Just past noon. The aircraft carrier Akagi.

F uchida's bomber touched down into the arresting cables and jolted to a stop, the last plane back from both the first and second attack waves. Fuchida had taken it upon himself to make sure no stragglers were left behind, and the skies were clear. Genda approached the aircraft as Fuchida struggled out and stretched his arms and legs, then dropped to the deck.

"How many did we lose?" Fuchida asked.

"Still waiting on the other reports, but it looks to be about thirty."

Fuchida paused, wondering which of his men were killed, loosened the

Fighters warm up on the windy deck of the Akagi *for the second attack wave.*

hachimaki from his head, pulled off his sweaty cap and goggles, and began unbuckling his parachute harness as they walked toward the tower. "That's it. There's no one else."

In front of a briefing room full of exhausted airmen, Fuchida carefully drew marks of hits on a blackboard displaying the harbor. He labeled the ships as A, B, C and so on with long arrows showing torpedo strikes, round dots marking 800 kilogram aerial bomb hits, and X's marking 250 kilogram dive-bombing hits. He looked over his shoulder. "Shirakata?"

A pilot stood and smartly bowed his head. "Sir. Successful torpedo strike on Colorado class battleship, position D."

As Fuchida chalked a line up to the ship, Kanegasaki, Fuchida's mechanic, appeared at the doorway wiping grease from his hands and gave a quick bow. "Please excuse me, commander, but I thought you should see this. It's important."

Slightly perturbed, Fuchida glanced up at Kanegasaki, then turned to the pilots. "Remain as you are. I will return shortly." He followed his engineer down the stairs to the upper flight deck where mechanics and engineers made quick repairs and rearmed and refueled aircraft. In the event the fleet came under attack, or if the American carriers were found close enough for a strike, they needed to be prepared. Fuchida didn't like being taken away in the middle of debriefing but knew his personal engineer wouldn't have called him for something insignificant.

Typical damage inflicted on planes by anti-aircraft fire with explosive shells.

Kanegasaki escorted him below decks to his B5N2—pocked with shrapnel holes on the port side. He ran his hand over the wing of Fuchida's aircraft and pressed his fingers into a hole. "Here are the hits from the anti-aircraft fire that struck your plane. Had any punctured your fuel tank, of course, we wouldn't be speaking right now. I counted twenty-one holes from the American flak, including this . . ." He leaned down and lifted a hatch in the fuselage revealing a half-frayed control wire held together by a whisker-thin metal thread. He tugged it with his finger and said soberly, "Your elevator cable."

Fuchida knew that the loss of this one cable would have resulted in the immediate loss of control and the certain destruction of his aircraft.

Kanegasaki stood upright and looked thoughtfully at Fuchida for a moment as his face lightened. "Commander—the gods smile on you."

The day's attack left 8 battlships lost, sunk, or damaged, 11 other ships sunk or damaged, 350 aircraft destroyed or damaged, and 3,500 people killed or wounded.

Chapter 30

December 7, three hours after the attack on
Pearl Harbor. McChord Field, Tacoma, Washington.

Jake clenched the telephone handset to his face inside the glass and wood phone booth, one of many along a wall in a room packed with cursing soldiers. With one hand covering his ear, he shouted into the receiver, "I'm telling you, Ma, those . . . I said I'm telling you, those little Japs are gonna wish they'd never done what they did!"

Jake's mother stood in the kitchen in her apron, smudges of flour on her face and hands, clenching the phone with both hands. Helen winced as Mr. Andrus watched and listened with his arms folded. "Now son, we're all upset about this, but you mustn't— "

"They just murdered a bunch of Americans in cold blood!"

Jake's mother glanced over to her husband. She spoke gently but firmly. "Well son, you know I'm all right with war. After all, David killed Goliath, but you should never pay back evil with evil, but to do good to— "

"Don't tell me, Ma! Let's see, God tells us to forgive our enemies, but he burns all his up! Do I have it right, Ma?! *Well, do I?!*"

"Son, I— "

"As far as I'm concerned, I'd be happy if we wiped every last Jap off the face of the earth! They want a fight? Well, now they got one!" Jake slammed the phone down and struggled to push the folding glass door open and squeezed out as another fuming soldier headed in.

Five hours after the attack. Central Philippines University.

Jimmy stood in Francis's office in his bare feet—his shirt half untucked, his hair wild. The sun peeked over the mountains and flooded through the windows. "There's nothing as *stupid* as war!" He jerked his head around and paced to the wall and back. "Well, we shouldn't let this setback change what we need to do here—*at all!* I say we stay the course and keep classes open. If the Japanese invade, MacArthur'll push 'em back off the islands, and then we can get on with business."

"Well . . ." Francis stood up from his desk, walked over to a globe, and gave it a gentle spin. "We'll give it a try and see how things go."

"The territory of Hawaii? Pearl Harbor?! What were they thinking?" Jimmy squinted into the unwelcome daylight.

"Listen, Jimmy, I'll do what I can to run the university 'business as usual,' but you need to be ready for anything."

Jimmy turned back as the globe slowly come to a stop, then rested his hand on it like the head of a child. He spoke softer, "I just can't believe they've done this."

Six hours after the attack. Kai Tak Airport, Hong Kong.

One after another, 34 single-engine Ki-32 light bombers released their explosives onto the British aircraft below, obliterating the few on the ground, followed by Ki-97 fighters that decimated what the bombers missed in an endless barrage of bullets. On the outskirts of Hong Kong, 40,000 Japanese troops with heavy artillery amassed to overwhelm the city.

Six hours after the attack. Tokyo, Japan.

Kneeling beside a radio on a low table, Fuchida's wife, Haruko, and their two children gave full attention to the announcement: "*. . . being forced to cross swords with the Americans against our will, our airmen made a daring attack this morning in a dazzling victory for His Majesty the emperor. In our efforts to stabilize East Asia and to defend our empire against Western aggression, our warriors . . .*"

"Children, they're talking about your father. He is a great man." Yoshiya, their son of eight, looked up at his mother and smiled.

Eight hours after the attack on Pearl Harbor. Clark Air Base, about forty miles northwest of Manila, Philippines.

"Hey, not so fast. One American cigarette equals *three* Filipino cigarettes—or vice versa, get it? You calling or raising?"

Under the shade of an enormous hangar, three aircraft mechanics played a fast game of poker on shipping crates while finishing ham sandwiches and Coca-Cola. The smooth harmonies of *Chattanooga Choo Choo* echoed over the radio. Behind them, engineers wheeled bombs beneath the open bomb bay doors of two B-17s.

The first mechanic studied his cards and raised an eyebrow to a second who rolled his eyes. The first pushed in six Filipino cigarettes. "I'm seeing ya."

Outside beside the runway, a pilot sat in the cockpit of his parked fighter drinking coffee. Open fields of razor-sharp cogon grass surrounded the base which housed a row of hangars—home to twenty-four P-40 fighters, ten B-18 medium bombers, and nineteen B-17 heavy bombers. Servicemen fueled up and loaded aircraft with weapons for a counterstrike on Formosa,[14] occupied by Japan and a key base for several divisions of attack aircraft.

One engineer behind the poker players in the hangar yelled out, "Hey, we ain't got all day! We got some special delivery for the Japs coming up! You better be ready!"

"Yeah, yeah, keep your shirt on!" The first player snapped his hand of cards shut and grabbed a swig of Coke.

Midway through the song the announcer broke in over the radio: "*We interrupt this broadcast to bring you this bulletin. Japanese bombers have been sighted attacking Clark Air Base. I repeat, Japanese bombers have . . .*"

One of the most widely employed Allied aircraft, the Curtiss P-40 Warhawk played an essential role throughout the war.

---

[14] Modern Taiwan.

"Hey, fellas! That's us!" the second player blurted out.

The first player discarded as the third player dealt him two cards without a flinch.

"Hey genius, if we were under attack, don't you think we'd know about it?! We've got a hundred and fifty thousand boots on the ground and bases loaded with bombers. The Japs aren't so stupid that . . ."

Everyone in the hangar froze and looked up as they heard the distant whistling of falling bombs. Outside, the air raid siren began to howl. The plane behind them exploded with a thunderous blast.

A group of Mitsubishi G3M Type 96 attack aircraft approach their destination.

A succession of bombs burst down the runway and hangars, shaking the ground with bone-rattling concussions, blowing parked planes to bits and igniting a fuel depot into an inferno of flames. Men scattered across the taxiways and grass shoulders, diving into ditches as forty-six Type 96 twin-engine bombers pounded the base and thirty-four Zero fighters followed by strafing the leftovers.

Prepared for a tough fight, the Japanese never imagined such a pathetic lack of opposition.

A handful of soldiers struggled to load anti-aircraft guns, none of which had ever been fired before or even tested.

Chapter 31

December 10, 1941. The Imperial Palace.

Wearing a dark gray overcoat in the cool morning, Emperor Hirohito shuffled along on a covered wooden walkway observing his gardens, his hands behind his back.

An attendant in black, a few steps behind, read the morning newspaper to him: "The Hawaiian debacle and the sweeping victories being scored by the Imperial Japanese Army and Naval forces on all fronts have swept away a good deal of the braggadocio spirit of the American people. Only a few weeks ago they were boasting that the United States could finish off Japan in three months."

The emperor stopped, reached for a branch and bent it down, snapping off a small, dead twig. "Please continue," he said.

"Today these same Americans are trembling in their shoes, and they have every reason for doing so. The British will soon be cursing Roosevelt as 'That blasted idiot.' We hate to think what his own people will be calling the 'Would-be Lord High Protector of the Universe' when they awaken to the full realization of what he got them into. Once the boast of America and the envy of decrepit Britannia, the Pacific Fleet has vanished from the seas while only a few battered hulks remain. With her battle fleet annihilated in the most humiliating disaster in all history, the United States has been reduced at one stroke to a third-rate naval power." The attendant folded the paper to display a political cartoon and bowed, handing it with both hands to the emperor.

Hirohito took the paper and examined the cartoon which displayed a huge, powerful fist labeled "*Japan*" punching down three distraught figures grasping an oversized rifle: Uncle Sam of America, John Bull of Great

Britain, and Chiang Kai-shek of China, all falling backward. Hirohito looked up at the attendant with a smile and handed the newspaper back, pleased to see cartoons mocking the Americans instead of the other way around. He turned to gaze at his garden of rocks, bushes, and trees and inhaled deeply. "Such a beautiful day."

December 23, 1941. Kagoshima Air Base.

Fuchida sighed with relief as he piloted his plane back to his air base from the *Akagi*. The journey of the fleet back into their home waters had been long and treacherous as fears abounded of an American reprisal strike from their carriers—none of which were in Pearl Harbor during the attack. They also had to stop and refuel on the open seas knowing that American submarines could be nearby. And a severe storm had swept a few of their precious sailors to their deaths. But now he was at ease with the mission behind him—more successful than anyone had ever imagined.

The military made no announcement to the public of the return of the pilots from the carrier to the base, but as planes began appearing, word trickled out that these were the airmen of the magnificent Pearl Harbor attack and the townspeople rushed to catch a glimpse of their triumphant warriors. Normally off-limits to civilians, the base made an exception for the jubilant crowds to welcome their new national heroes.

By the time Fuchida arrived, the last one from his group, he could see a mass of citizens waving flags near the hangars, something he hadn't expected in the least.

After taxiing beside the crowd, cutting his engine, and throwing back his canopy, the people greeted him with a surge of ecstatic cheering and the waving of flags and handkerchiefs. In the months leading up to the attack, many of the townspeople had been annoyed and even angered by the constant flight training over their city, often loudly buzzing no more than thirty feet over their homes. Now that they understood why, they were thrilled.

Pushing up his goggles, Fuchida jumped down to the tarmac as the mayor of Kagoshima City stepped forward in his black suit and top hat, who bowed and shook Fuchida's hand vigorously. He watched with delight as parents brought their children who pressed around him. A young lady with a charming smile presented him with a bouquet. Fuchida admired her just a bit too long as he drank the victor's wine down to the dregs.

With the bouquet in his left hand, he raised his right and signaled for quiet. He shouted so all could hear. "Thank you for your wonderful welcome. I'm sorry, but for security reasons, I cannot give you an account of our operation." The crowd burst into cheering that dissolved into a chant of "Fuchida! Fuchida! Fuchida!" He smiled with many nods of the head, then gave another long, admiring look at the young lady.

That evening, the governor and city officials honored the fliers at an

An extraordinary gathering of the top leaders of the Imperial Japanese Navy, after the Pearl Harbor Attack aboard the Akagi, *December 1942.*

Of note—*Bottom row center (with braid over shoulder): Admiral Osami Nagano, chief of Navy General Staff; 2nd to his left, Vice Admiral Chūichi Nagumo, commander of the First Naval Fleet; to Nagano's right, Admiral Isoroku Yamamoto, commander in chief of the Combined Fleet. Top row: 6th from the right, Lieutenant Minoru Genda. Second row: far right, Lieutenant Mitsuo Fuchida.*

Admiral Osami Nagano.

exclusive restaurant. Over a sumptuous dinner of *tai*, a fish reserved for New Year's or a wedding celebration, Fuchida and officers laughed, recounted stories, and indulged in the beer and *sake* of conquering warriors.

The following afternoon, the top brass of the Imperial Japanese Navy hosted him and Shigeharu Murata, Japan's undisputed torpedo ace, for a luncheon back on the *Akagi* featuring the Chief of the Naval General Staff Admiral Osami Nagano, along with many of his top officers; Admiral Yamamoto with his own Chief of Staff; and Rear Admiral Matome Ugaki with his cadre of staff members.

The officers proffered Fuchida and Murata the seats of honor at the head of the table where each admiral, in order of rank from the highest first, passed his sake cup to the two heroes in congratulations and the applause of the usually subdued group of distinguished officers. The honor overwhelmed Fuchida.

Rising from his seat, Admiral Yamamoto raised his white-gloved hand motioning for quiet while grasping a scroll in the other. A hush came over the room as he turned to Fuchida. "I listened on the radio during the entire attack," he said. "I heard your order, 'All forces attack.' When I heard that, I needed no report to tell me that the attack would be successful. And, yes, I heard your signal that you had achieved surprise—Tora! Tora! Tora!"

The admiral then unrolled a vertical scroll known as a *kakejiku* painted with shodo calligraphy. "On the very day of the strike," he said, glancing at Fuchida, "I felt inspired to write this for you."

The honor petrified Fuchida.

Yamamoto delivered his poem with feeling:

"Message of 'Attack!' reaches my ears
from more than three thousand miles away
—a message from Hawaii.
Thinking of flight leader Fuchida's brilliant action
on the early morning of December 8.
So writes Isoroku Yamamoto."

The officers burst into applause and cheers as Yamamoto rolled up the kakejiku and formally handed it to Fuchida with outstretched arms and a bow.

In near disbelief, Fuchida, likewise, rose to his feet, bowed, and received the prized gift from the man he most admired in the entire Imperial Navy. As the room of officers continued their strong applause, when Fuchida thought things couldn't possibly get any better, Yamamoto also clapping his hands, leaned close to him and whispered, "The emperor requests an audience with you as well."

Certainly, the sun had risen on him in all of its beaming glory.

December 26, 1941. The Imperial Palace.

Inside an imperial meeting room, no larger than sixteen feet on a side, Fuchida stood stiffly before the emperor beside three of his fellow officers. Emperor Hirohito, outfitted in his full military dress, sword at his side, was seated on a raised platform along one of the walls. In the center of the room sat a large, low table, neatly arranged with charts, maps, and twelve glossy aerial photographs of the Pearl Harbor mission. Unmoving, Fuchida glanced at the officers who stood before the emperor: Vice Admiral Nagano, chief of the Imperial Japanese Naval General Staff; Commander Shimazaki, the leader of the second wave of aircraft in the Pearl Harbor attack; and Vice Admiral Nagumo, commander in chief of the First Air Fleet who was finishing his remarks. All were in their full dress uniforms with braids and medals. Such power in such a small room, he thought.

The aroma of incense drifted through the air from a censer that had been paraded through the room earlier by an imperial aide. Fuchida had always thought himself a strong person, and his recent exploits only boosted that sentiment, but now he found his heart trembling and his fingers twitching as he stood before the Imperial Emperor of Japan, the leader whom the entire nation served as one man. Few had ever seen him in person. His voice had never been heard by the public. Fuchida never imagined that leading the Pearl Harbor attack would be easier than explaining it now to the emperor himself.

Vice Admiral Nagumo continued his account, "The auspicious weather, the enemy's failure to detect the task force, the clouds that first hid the attack, then miraculously parted at the perfect moment—such a combination of circumstances was proof of divine power, through the

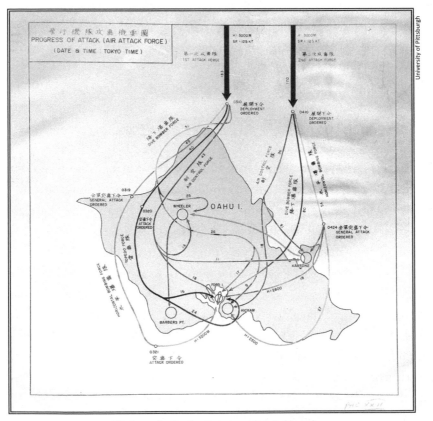

Flight paths for the first wave (top left) and
second wave (top right) for the Pearl Harbor Attack.
Fuchida's path seen on the far left and lower left.

Photos taken by Japanese airmen during the attack on Pearl Harbor.

instrument of the emperor."

Nagumo bowed deeply, and Fuchida was introduced. The emperor turned his head to Fuchida. An aide nodded to Fuchida who bowed, took a breath to compose himself, and began his explanation of the attack using the photos and a special map he had personally drawn for the emperor displaying the placement of American ships in the harbor and the record of torpedo and aerial bombing hits.

"Your Majesty, our mission was favored from the start and ordained for success." He swallowed hard, then transitioned into the teacher he

Following page: Damage Assessment
Map drawn by Fuchida and presented to the emperor.

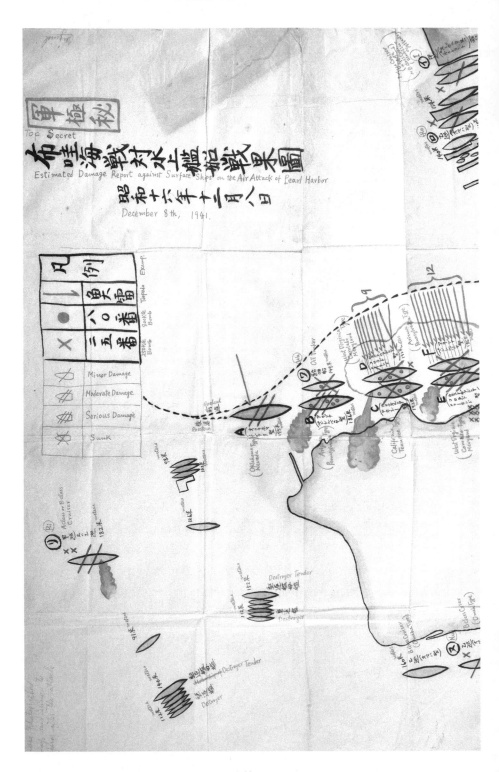

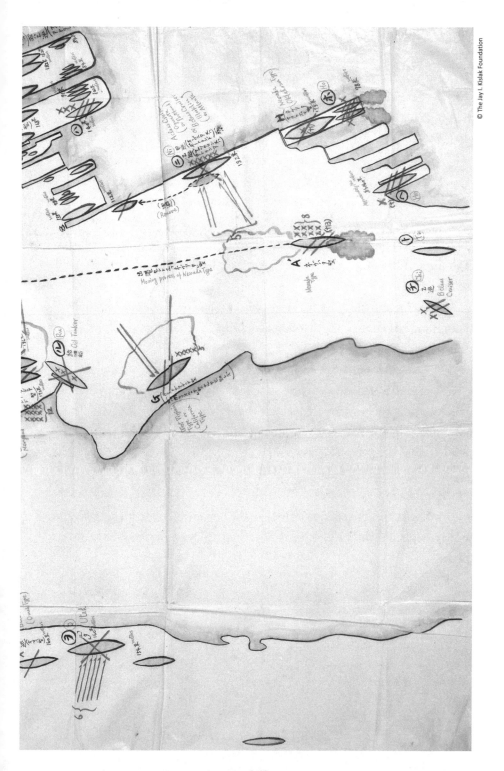

always was, outlining each detail of the attack, growing more enthusiastic as he spoke.

An aide handed Fuchida's map to the emperor for examination.

As he neared the end of his presentation, the emperor said, "We note that fifteen enemy planes were shot down. Were any of these civilian planes?"

"Your Majesty, three or four aircraft hit were unarmed training planes. One green aircraft was shot down, which might have been civilian."

"I hope it wasn't." The emperor looked down for a moment. "What was the initial reaction of the Americans?"

"Two minutes after our first bombs were dropped, we received heavy anti-aircraft fire. In truth, we were surprised the Americans could respond so quickly."

The emperor shuffled the large photographs in his hands, carefully examining each one. "Was any damage inflicted other than on ships, planes, and airfields?"

"The airmen were careful to strike only military targets."

The emperor nodded to him in such a way that Fuchida knew his presentation time was concluded. Fuchida bowed deeply.

The emperor's attendant bowed to indicate the end of the audience, but Hirohito turned to Nagano one last time. "We would like to have the pictures remain in the palace, as we wish to show them to Her Imperial Majesty the empress."

Fuchida and the officers bowed as the emperor rose from his seat and slowly stepped from the platform and exited. Things could not have gone better.

Chapter 32

Late December 1941. Central Philippines
University.

Jimmy and Charma Covell stood against a wall along Lopez Jaena Street, choked with people and bicycles under furious clouds of black smoke that darkened the sky with the sooty smell of war. It was worse than he had imagined. Much worse. Jimmy kept stroking his unshaven cheeks and chin.

About a mile and a half away, explosions continued to rock the harbor. Intermittent car horns, crying children, and barking dogs were the only sounds rising from the street. No one talked. Two Japanese warplanes roared overhead, frighteningly low. Jimmy watched blankly as cars and people flowed past—strapped and packed with as many goods as they could carry, fleeing west and north from Iloilo City. Two American jeeps and three troop trucks honked and navigated their way through the crowds.

Jimmy turned to Charma. "I guess the Christmas break'll be extra-long this year." He could see she wasn't amused. She was scared. He put his arm around her, then squeezed her shoulder. "Francis said we'll be traveling north about fifty miles, somewhere up near the mountains where we can stay with some families in Katipunan." He didn't have much to comfort Charma with, but it was all he had to give. Anyway, he was sure it wouldn't be like this for long. "The Americans will get things back to normal again. You'll see."

Outside the Covell home, Francis pulled up in his black '34 Ford Tudor, a wooden chest precariously rope-tied to the back. He honked as Jimmy dragged a steamer trunk and Charma lugged two suitcases from their front door.

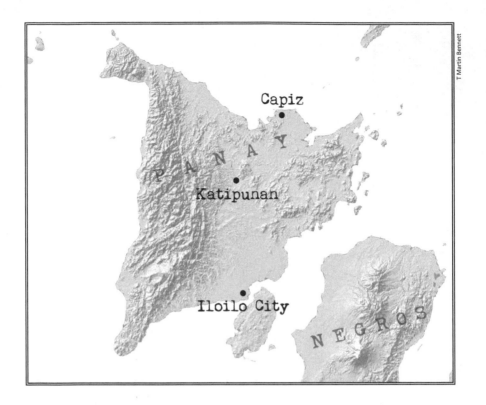

Besides teaching French, German, and higher mathematics, Gertrude hosted hundreds of people as dinner guests in her home with Francis, with over 400 staying the night.

"You OK? You got that?" Jimmy glanced back as he walked out.

"I'm all right. Just keep moving," Charma said.

Cars puttered past, equally crammed full of personal goods from phonographs to mattresses. Two students rode by on bicycles. Boxes and crates littered every yard.

Francis leaned over his wife, Gertrude, in the passenger seat, and shouted out the window, "See you in the village. It's about a ninety-minute drive. You know where you're goin'?"

"Yeah, yeah," Charma said as she hauled

her luggage to their own car. "Thanks, Francis."

Bouncing a basketball, Jimmy strolled up to Francis's side of the Ford. "You got room for this?"

"No problem. I'll send my chauffeur to pick it up along with a box of toothpicks I left behind." Francis put the car in gear and let it lurch forward.

"I take that as a 'no.' You're no fun."

"See you there."

As Francis pulled away, Jimmy spun the basketball on one finger and quietly sang out the end of an old Negro spiritual, but without conviction: *"He's got the whole world in his hands."*

Chapter 33

January 22, 1942. Rabaul, New Guinea.

L eading a formation of ninety navy fighters and bombers, Fuchida alternately looked out both sides of his cockpit observing each element of his attack force taking positions and gently descending toward the circular harbor in the distance. The ground remained blackish-gray from the 1937 eruption of a nearby volcano.

Royal Australian Air Force Headquarters (RAAF), Telecommunication Unit, Melbourne, Australia.

The steady clacking of electric teletype machines rattled the offices of the RAAF as uniformed secretaries added to the orchestra of noise with their manual typewriters while telephones rang beyond. Three sat at a bank of teletype machines, reading, typing, and furiously taking notes as an officer stood carefully observing. He leaned over an operator, focusing intently on the message appearing on one of the machines.

The operator shook his head, tore off the sheet, and spun around in his swivel chair to hand it to the waiting officer. "From Rabaul, sir."

The officer put on his glasses and read it out loud, stumbling through the words: "*Nos morituri te salutamus.*" Yanking off his glasses, he said, "What the bloody hell do they mean by that?"

The operator looked at the officer in seriousness and spoke the Latin fluidly, "*Nos morituri te salutamus . . .* We who are about to die salute you. A saying from the gladiators." He paused for a moment. "Sir, they've only got eight operable aircraft."

The officer's face fell as he crumpled the paper in his fist. "Lord, help them."

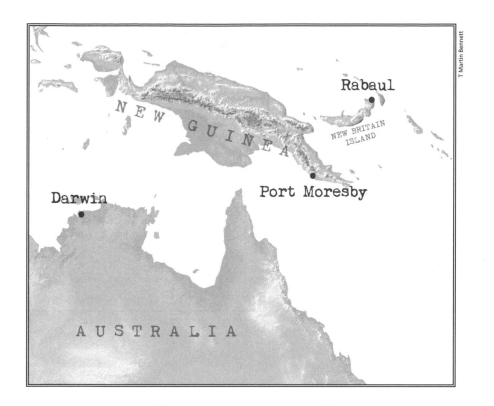

Rabaul, New Britain Island.

Machine-guns from fighter planes ripped through the few parked airplanes as terrified airmen fled for cover and dove into ditches. In the harbor, ships were pounded into the sea in a blanket of geysers and fiery explosions.

Fuchida chuckled to himself as his carrier-launched attack force approached virtually unopposed upon the Australian air base on the northeastern tip of the Australian territory of New Britain Island. The natural harbor that usually gave safe haven to its flying boats, critical for surveillance, was an open shooting gallery and was shown no mercy. Offshore, 7,500 troops proceeded on their way to land and develop the strategically important Rabaul harbor as a major naval and air base for Japan.

Fuchida reached forward and patted his pilot's shoulder. "We're wasting our resources. Too easy. Like fishing in a koi pond."

February 19, 1942. Darwin, Australia.

Two young boys in straw hats sat fishing at the end of a harbor pier in the morning sunlight. No luck so far. One sighed as the other nudged him and motioned with his head to the sky. Near the horizon, they could see what appeared to be a large group of birds. As they stared they began to hear the drone of airplanes. They chucked their poles into the water and took off running down the pier.

Leading an even larger wave of 188 attack aircraft, Fuchida looked carefully around him in the sunny skies, disgusted. "No air cover. No air cover at *all*." The Japanese Combined Fleet had received reports that the harbor city of Darwin was amassing ships and reinforcements to which they felt compelled to respond. Fuchida picked up the speaking tube from his neck and told his radioman to send the signal, "Take positions. Commence attack!" The pilot wagged his wings signaling the formation to prepare to attack.

In the undefended harbor below, bombers took their pick of the wide assortment of targets, from oil storage tanks to freighters and troop

Oil tanks blaze during the siege against Darwin, Australia.

transports to *USS Peary*, an American destroyer, and tore into the helpless prey, filling the bay with echoing explosions and the sky with clouds of jet black smoke. Fuchida aimed his bombsight while ordering his pilot to drift right or left until he was on target, then released his payload onto a freighter, blowing it into a million fragments.

Looking below, despite the overwhelming success of his raid, he shook his head, feeling that Japan was wasting valuable time on objectives of little consequence while ignoring their *real* enemy, the United States. He feared that while they were busy snatching a fan from a geisha, the United States was forging swords.

ABHS

A nipa hut dwelling on Panay in the 1940s.

Chapter 34

February 1942. Katipunan, Panay, the Philippines.

A barefoot Filipino, head to toe in white, led a carabao[15] pulling his creaking cart packed with sacks of rice and crates of clucking chickens throwing off feathers. The dirt road passed through a small town of mud-plastered homes and businesses constructed primarily of bamboo. Tall palm trees stood in the near distance. Several trunks and boxes leaned beside the doorway of one particular house filled with guests.

"President Roosevelt's pledged to send reinforcements," Francis said, sitting on an empty wooden crate in a living room jammed with furniture and suitcases. "He wouldn't say that if he didn't mean it." Francis flapped his shirt in and out to dry the sweat.

Eating a banana, Jimmy spoke with his mouth full. "But when? The Japanese have overrun Manila, and they're moving south. Fast." He peeled his banana down a bit. "People are getting angry and tired of waiting. They say this isn't their fight, it's *America's* fight, so *America* needs to send help."

Gertrude, Francis's wife, fanning herself with a magazine, added, "If the Japanese come to Panay, some people are saying they'll just turn themselves in, go to internment camps, and wait it out."

Charma jumped in, "Oh, I hope it doesn't come to that!"

"I'd rather hide out in the jungle," Jimmy said, "and take my chances than go to a camp." He popped the last of the banana into his mouth. "No telling what'll happen in a camp. One thing I know about Japanese culture for certain, the Japanese don't look too highly on people who surrender."

Francis nodded. "Yeah, I think a hideaway camp's the best bet." He

---

[15] Water buffalo of the Philippines.

A girl rides a carabao across a shallow river flowing from the mountains of Panay.

looked down, shook his head, and stood up. "I can't even believe we're saying these things. A few months ago I was president of a college, now I'm practically a hobo."

"True enough, but you have good friends—and bananas." Jimmy held out a banana. "Have one."

Chapter 35

February 1942. Columbia Army Air Base. Columbia, South Carolina.

Jake leaned against the edge of the entrance of a gray hangar beside a group of fliers, proudly wearing their cordovan leather flying jackets. They stood drinking coffee and puffing cigarettes while observing a flagman wave a twin-engine North American B-25 Mitchell bomber into its parking spot on the apron off the taxiway. The engines revved up as the plane finished the turn, then powered down. Lieutenant Bill Farrow, a six-foot, six-inch, lanky, blue-eyed pilot stood beside Jake and began whistling *Green Eyes* by Tommy Dorsey.

The city had constructed the base two years earlier as a civilian airport, but the day after the Pearl Harbor raid the military took control. Most of the buildings were little more than plywood covered with tar paper, but it had what the Army Air Corps needed for training—runways and hangars—which was what brought Jake and other fliers there.

Blowing the steam off his coffee, Jake took a few steps to a free-standing blackboard when a jeep pulled up to a squeaky halt.

A graduate of the University of South Carolina, Bill Farrow won a gold Bulova watch from his aunt by keeping his promise not to smoke or drink before his twenty-first birthday.

Test flight of an early B-25 Mitchell bomber.

The courier yelled, "Hey, Jake. Captain wants to see ya! On the double."

"Well, what's the captain got against me?" Jake mumbled as he looked back at the eyes of all gazing at him.

Bill couldn't resist and spoke with his South Carolina drawl, "Oooo. Sounds like the raccoon got caught sneaking in late again."

"Damn!" Jake took a last puff off his cigarette and threw the butt into his coffee.

"Kitchen patrol, here you come," Bill chided.

Jake, the shortest guy on the base, looked up at Bill, snorted the smoke out of his nostrils, handed him his paper coffee, and hopped into the jeep.

As Jake entered the office, the sight of twenty-four other enlisted men lined up against the wall caught him off guard. He discreetly tried to take his place at the end, being the last one in the room. The captain wasn't upset, but he was all business and spoke tersely as he paced.

"I've assembled you men because we're putting together a dangerous mission and we need volunteers. Some of you fellas are gonna get killed." He studied their faces as he paused, searching for the scent of fear.

One of the men spoke up. "Uh, captain, sir, can we know some of the details?"

"Negative. Even if you volunteer, you won't know until after you're on your way. Simply put, the mission is dead serious and will be extremely hazardous." He slowly looked across their attentive faces. "Now, how many of you want to sign up?"

Jake felt he was just as patriotic as the next guy and equally mad at the Japanese and Germans, but he didn't think there was any use volunteering for *that* job. *Some of you fellas are going to get killed.* No thanks. He had *nooooooo* desire to get in on anything like that.

The captain started at the far end opposite Jake and walked up to the first soldier. "Will you go?"

He quickly nodded. "Yes, sir. Yeah, I'll go."

He stepped to the next. "Soldier, will you?"

"Yes, sir. I'll go."

Jake knew that sooner or later, one or two would bow out, and that would be his cue to do likewise. He wasn't going. He had to stop himself from shaking his head "no" before someone noticed.

A B-25 bomber stationed in the Pacific in 1942 displaying nose art and giving a good view of the bombardier's position and aircraft guns.

After twenty-four "yes" answers, the captain stepped in front of Jake. "And will *you* go, soldier?"

"Yes, sir. You can count on me, sir." He couldn't believe the words coming out of his own mouth. He realized he was going wherever they were going, doing whatever they were going to do, and might never be coming back. Great.

Chapter 36

March 5, 1942. The southern coast of Java in the
Dutch East Indies.[16]

F uchida's group of 180 aircraft headed toward the port city of
Tjilatjap.[17] The objective of the battle was to capture the harbor,
preventing the Allied forces from retreating to Australia by sea. He
scanned the anchorage for his targets, but there were few left.

THE
PHILIPPINES

Singapore

DUTCH EAST INDIES

Rabaul

JAVA

NEW GUINEA

Tjilatjap

AUSTRALIA

T Martin Bennett

---

[16] Modern Indonesia.
[17] Modern Cilacap, Indonesia.

The Akagi *traversing the seas, part of the powerful*
First Air Fleet's group of five IJN aircraft carriers in March 1942.

Only a few days earlier the Japanese landed 35,000 troops at three separate points on the northern side of the island, quickly overwhelming the poorly organized troops of the Dutch, British, Australians, and Americans. The Japanese Navy sank four Allied ships with no losses of their own.

Fuchida knew the importance of securing the prize of Java, as the island was the fourth largest exporter of oil in the world. Without this island firmly under their control, along with its precious lifeblood of petroleum, Japan would never survive.

The lopsided odds in their favor continued to surprise him. Nothing could be easier. Using the bombing techniques he had honed for years, he positioned his shotai of three planes and set his bombsight on a freighter. The bombardiers of the other two planes fixed their eyes on Fuchida's plane to release the moment he did. He let loose his payload on the doomed ship below. "Release—perfect!"

As the plane passed the target, he looked back in time to see the ship impacted by a horrific blast that shook his plane—a pleasurable sign of success. No doubt, they'd have all the oil they'd ever need.

Chapter 37

March 1942. Eglin Air Base, Florida.

Jake's B-25 thundered over a riverbed at 165 miles an hour, so low, off to the side he looked straight into the dried mud banks whizzing past. As bombardier, Jake sat right up front in the nose, composed of twenty-five panels of Plexiglas, which gave him a breathtaking view of the ground speeding below his feet. He gripped the inside struts of the airframe with exhilaration.

Bill yelled out over the intercom, "Woohah! Let's give these critters a buzz!" He pulled the plane up and veered over a herd of scattering cattle. Their training required low-level flying and the crew couldn't get enough of it—one time even hooking a piece of brush on the fuselage, dragging it in the wind all the way back to the base.

Bill brought the plane into a high, banked turn. "Let's bring 'er on home, boys. That's enough for today."

Peering over the landscape with wide eyes, Jake felt like a kid on a roller coaster.

In the base meeting room, Jake sat among a sea of 160 khaki shirts and black ties, all captivated by Lieutenant Colonel Jimmy Doolittle, a reactivated officer briefing them on what was being called the "Special B-25 Project."

"I know it's low for a bombing run, but you'll have better accuracy on your targets at fifteen hundred feet, and you'll be less likely to be hit by anti-aircraft fire. No need to practice at any other height," Doolittle said.

At a stocky five feet, four inches, Jimmy Doolittle wasn't an imposing man to Jake, but he towered above all in specialty aviation. With a reputation for daredevil flying stunts and a doctoral degree in aeronautic engineering from MIT, he was a strange mix of renegade and scholar—perfect for this mission. Jake noticed Jimmy's slightly irregular nose, a bit bent from his boxing days and perhaps a plane crash or two.

Doolittle pointed to someone beside Jake with a raised hand. "Yes?"

George Barr, the red-haired navigator on Jake's crew, lowered his hand. He had a wide, thin mustache and a heavy Brooklyn accent. "Hey, boss, I understand

Jimmy Doolittle after he was promoted to the rank of Lt. General, mastermind of the raid.

you can't tell us where we're going, but we all know with these extra fuel tanks and all, well, it's gonna be over the river and through the woods, so to speak. And, honestly sir, I . . . I just don't know if these planes are up to it."

Another airman jumped in. "Colonel, our carburetors are *all* out of whack."

"And the exhaust pipes are breaking right off!" from another.

Jake turned toward the gum-chewing Harry Spatz, a blonde-haired, blue-eyed gunner from Kansas on his plane, who spoke with exasperation. "Sir, after five rounds my machine gun jams. Every time. I might as well be throwing rocks."

"Mine, too," another said.

"And our extra fuel tank leaks like a sieve."

As the room turned into a chorus of complaints, Jimmy motioned with his hands for quiet. "All right, all right. Pipe down. The planes are brand new and untested. I can assure you, we're working on all these things. Remember, I'm flying one of these birds just like you. We've got two weeks left, and— "

"You gotta be kidding," someone muttered.

"… and I'm going to see to it that we get 'em all worked out. Now listen, you boys know not a word of this mission is to be spoken to *anyone*. Not your wife, not your friends, or even your dog. Doing so could jeopardize the mission, many lives, and even get the FBI on your backs. I've said it before, but I need to say it again: If anyone wants to drop out, he can. No questions asked."

Jake never wanted to be on this mission in the first place, but now, with the anticipation and excitement of the unknown, the whole idea pulled him in. He grinned at the thought. This was going to be really *something*.

Madras, Oregon.

A red 1933 Ford pickup pulled up to the front porch of the ranch house in a cloud of dust illuminated by the afternoon sun. Mrs. Andrus, cradling a black-and-white cat in her arms, walked onto the porch letting the screen door smack against the frame behind her.

Shutting the truck door, Mr. Andrus stepped around the Ford and handed her a rather beaten up package and a few letters.

She looked puzzled. "I sent these over two weeks ago to Jake. Why'd they come back?"

Mr. Andrus took off his faded, greasy John Deere cap and wiped his forehead with a handkerchief.

Still holding the cat, she slowly read aloud the handwritten red lettering on the top of the box. "*'Location classified. Return to sender.'* He must have been transferred." She gave the box a shake to hear a muffled rattle inside and looked down at the cat with a grin. "Well, I suppose his brother won't mind eating Jake's cookies, then."

Chapter 38

April 1, 1942. San Francisco Harbor. The carrier
USS Hornet.

*B*at Out of Hell, Jake's B-25, hung high above the docks, suspended mid-air as a crane carefully swung it onto the aircraft carrier *USS Hornet*. Standing on the dock below, Jake and the crew shielded their eyes from the brilliant sun as they watched.

The dock reverberated with trucks unloading supplies, officers barking orders, and the ship's complement of nearly 3,000 sailors preparing to set out. A steam whistle from a harbor ship echoed in the distance.

USS Hornet *shortly after commissioning in late 1941.*

George, their navigator from New York, squinted with one eye shut. "You know, I don't remember the part about landing on an aircraft carrier. Any of you boys remember that part?"

Jake said, "You can forget about those round-trip tickets," still looking up as their plane moved toward the carrier. "This is gonna be a one-way trip."

Their copilot from Texas, Bob Hite, spoke with a cigarette pinched in his teeth. "Yeah, but where to? I don't get it."

Harry, the gunner, chomped his gum with his mouth wide open. "Some say we're taking the long road to Germany."

Bill, the pilot and leader of the pack, took off his hat and scratched his head and spoke with his refined twang, "Well, whatever it is, we're gonna be r-i-i-i-ght in the middle of it."

Jake turned out of the glaring sun toward Bill. "You said you got a girl waitin' for ya?"

Without looking, Bill nodded. "Lib Sims. A fine lady. We're gettin' married as soon as we're all back home from this thing. I told her June—just two months away."

Harry looked at his buddies. "Ah, today's April Fool's Day. You don't suppose . . . ?"

George shook his red-haired head. "The most expensive prank in American history? Uncle Sam's too cheap for that."

"You know," Bill said, "I had guys waving hundred-dollar bills at me to take my place a couple days ago."

"And . . . ?" Jake said.

Bill turned to Jake and grabbed his shoulder. "I told him, 'Not a chance, pal. I wouldn't miss this for a million bucks!'"

The following foggy morning, as *USS Hornet* slid beneath the Golden Gate Bridge escorted by two cruisers, four destroyers, and an oiler, Jake looked off the back of the carrier. He stood on the deck beside his plane in the #16 position and eyed the tail hanging over the churning foam below—the last plane in the back.

He gazed high above at the underside of the impressive, brand-new,

The bombers of the Doolittle Raid tied down to the rear deck of
USS Hornet. *The* "Bat Out of Hell" *plane #16 is in the far left corner.*

red bridge, nearly two miles wide, both ends fading into the gray mist, then
reached out and pulled on one of the tie downs on his Mitchell bomber. He
slid his hand over the engine cowling, covered by a black tarp to protect it
from the highly corrosive salty air.

Examining the nose art of *Bat Out of Hell,* Jake wondered, really, what
the hell he had gotten himself into—an adventure or a death wish? His pilot
had never launched from a carrier before. They'd been practicing short
take-offs for a while, without knowing why. Now he knew, but no one had
ever even *tried* to launch a B-25 from a carrier before, and his plane would
be fully loaded with fuel and *extra* fuel, not to mention four 500-pound
bombs.

Jake checked a bug spot on his Plexiglas windshield, spit on it, and
rubbed it off with his thumbnail. His mom back home didn't have any idea

where he was, and she wouldn't know until the mission was complete, or he was dead. Maybe she'd never know.

Shoulder to shoulder in a noisy, packed galley for lunch, Jake jabbed his fork into a piece of chicken, then dabbed it into his potatoes and gravy. With his mouth open, just as he was about to take a bite, the PA system crackled into the room.

"Attention all crew members of *USS Hornet*." The room quickly fell silent. Jake felt like his heart stopped beating. "Captain Mitscher would like to inform you that this task force is bound . . . for Tokyo."

The room erupted into deafening cheers and shouts. Harry, the gunner, looked at Jake, "Holy mackerel, Andy! *Tokyo!*"

Jake grabbed his glass of milk and held it out for a toast, "Here's to payback, *American style!*" His four other crew members reached for their glasses, clinked them together, and drank down their milk as shouts of men blended into a repeating chant: "*Hi ho, hi ho, it's off to Tokyo, we'll bomb and blast and come back fast, hi ho, hi ho hi ho hi ho . . . !*" Jake jumped up and pounded his chest with his fists. "Tokyo! We're comin' to get you!" Perhaps for the first time in his life, Jake knew *exactly* what he was doing and where he was going.

Lieutenant Colonel Jimmy Doolittle stood before the fliers in the dimly lit briefing room, an eight-foot-wide map of Japan behind him marked with flight routes to several cities, as an officer passed out manila envelopes to the pilots.

Jake noticed the real hornet's nest on a branch behind Doolittle, something a crew member brought aboard, and now a reminder of the pain they'd soon inflict on their enemy.

An officer held up an envelope marked "Classified" and called out, "Farrow? Lieutenant William Farrow?" Bill raised his hand and reached for his flight instructions.

Doolittle continued, waving papers as he spoke. "Thirteen crews are assigned to attack the greater Tokyo area, two will hit Nagoya, and one'll hit Kobe. Your flight plans have it all spelled out."

Jake leaned into Bill beside him who riffled through his papers and whispered back, "Nagoya."

Jake nodded and leaned to George, the navigator on his other side. "Nagoya."

Doolittle looked to his right. "Lieutenant Commander Jurika, here is our intelligence officer who spent the last two years in Japan locating and pinpointing industries, refineries, aircraft plants and other military objectives. He'll brief you on your particular targets, including areas of anti-aircraft installments to avoid." He tossed the papers onto a small table to the side.

Lieutenant Commander Stephen Jurika was born in Los Angeles, California, but grew up in the Philippines and Japan, eventually serving as a naval attaché at the American Embassy in Tokyo before the war.

"Soon we'll be joined by Halsey's task force with the carrier *Enterprise* for air protection while we're en route. As we head into Japanese waters, we'll be on alert. We could be hit at any time by enemy subs. If a Jap carrier sends aircraft against us, we'll have to shove all the B-25s overboard to put our fighters in the air to protect the ships."

Jake turned to Bill and raised his eyebrows thinking that it'd be a shame coming all that way for nothing.

Doolittle pointed back to the huge map and raised his voice. "The Japs have been telling their people that they're safe, that we can't hit 'em." He smirked, dropping his hand. "As some of you may have heard, a radio report in English was picked up from Tokyo the other day stating, and I quote, *'that it's absolutely impossible for enemy bombers to get within five hundred miles of Tokyo.'*" Chuckles rippled through the ranks. "Our job is to let 'em know that we can. The Japanese are a proud people, and more than bringing down their cities, we want to bring down their pride."

He began rapping the back of one hand into the palm of the other.

"Look for targets of opportunity to inflict the *maximum* damage with your bomb load—manufacturing plants, fuel depots—anything that looks like it'll burn. If we can get a few fires going in their cities of paper and wood, they'll never put 'em out. The low-level training we did was to keep you under their air cover and for better accuracy, but they'll still be firing at you from the ground, and there'll be interceptors after us for sure. After the attacks, you'll fly to designated airfields in China where they'll be ready to recover your aircraft."

With his hands on his hips, Doolittle spoke like a father to his sons. "I want every crew to get this clear—you're to bomb only military targets. I don't want any of you hotshots getting ideas about bombing the Imperial Palace. It's not worth a plane factory, a shipyard, or an oil refinery, so leave it alone. There's nothing that would unite their nation more than bombing the emperor's home. It's not a military target. Got it?"

Jake's heart pounded. He couldn't wait.

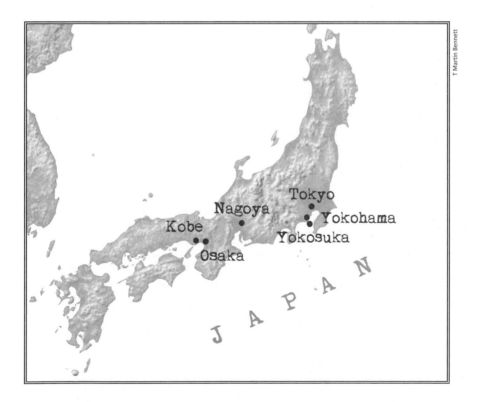

Chapter 39

Early April 1942. The open sea, east of
Singapore. The Akagi.

Cigar smoke curled through the air of Nagumo's brass-appointed
personal quarters as Fuchida paced before his desk. So much
success, he thought, can breed a false sense of confidence. Nagumo
listened to him, but he wasn't sure he actually *heard* him.

The admiral leaned back in his desk chair, rolled the cigar between his
fingers, took a slow, confident puff, and blew the smoke to the side. "We've
just sunk two destroyers, two cruisers, and the British carrier *Hermes*,"
Nagumo recounted, "all by air power, and we haven't lost a single ship or
even suffered a scratch of paint. How can you *possibly* complain?" He drew
in another puff of his cigar.

Nagumo's muscular strike force of five carriers, four battleships and
twenty-five various vessels traversed the sea heading northeast on their way
back to Japan. Their mission to cut off British supplies to Burma and to seek
out and destroy British fleet units in the Indian Ocean was yet another
distinguished success.

Like Nagumo, Fuchida was equally amazed at how quickly they had
annihilated the British, their former partner who had ruled the seas for
centuries, and even felt a measure of sadness at their demise, but he couldn't
shake his uneasiness.

"Admiral," Fuchida said, "I agree that we have been more than
successful in what we have been attempting to accomplish. I'm sorry I must
say this, but I see a big problem here."

Nagumo raised an eyebrow.

"The Americans remain our number one enemy, but we're spending
our valuable time and resources on the southern operation while leaving

other resources completely unused." He momentarily leaned on Nagumo's desktop. "What's the difference between their *sunken* battleships on the bottom of the Pearl Harbor, and our *anchored* battleships at Hiroshima Bay?"

Fuchida pushed off the desk and stood upright. "Respectfully, admiral, I don't think they're being properly utilized. I believe we should be attacking our real enemy, the United States," he said as he pointed east.

An unusual rear gunner's view of the Akagi, *April 1942.*

Nagumo calmly leaned forward and tapped off the ashes of his cigar. "You know that the southern operation is essential to secure resources for our empire. All the commanders are in agreement on this. Our Zeroes are unmatched in the skies, our torpedo bombers can dispatch capital ships in minutes, and the confidence and experience of our men are without equal. We have nothing to be afraid of, and I'm surprised that you would doubt our strength."

"Admiral, I don't doubt our power. Our men have performed superbly, but if we fail to destroy the American carriers while they have even the *least* ability to fight, they'll have hope. That hope must be destroyed. I believe we must go east as soon as possible." Fuchida glanced out through a porthole. "Even as we speak, the Americans are gathering strength."

Part III

The Eagle's Talons

Chapter 40

April 12, 1942. USS Hornet. The Pacific Ocean.

"Gimme two," Jake said. With his sleeves rolled up and a cigarette dangling from his lips, Jake snapped down two cards onto the table of a four-man poker game scattered with red, yellow, blue, and white poker chips. The sun beamed in through the smoke-filled room of pilots and sailors killing time.

The dealer had a pack of cigarettes rolled up in the sleeve of his t-shirt. He squinted and flicked two cards that Jake snatched up.

"Those weren't the two I was thinking of."

Whistling *Green Eyes* again, Bill walked up behind Jake and shook his head as Jake looked back abruptly.

"Now, Bill, don't go letting everyone know how bad my hand is. I'm gonna bluff, all right?"

"Perfect." Bill put his hand on Jake's shoulder. "Any of you boys gonna join us upstairs in a bit for the chapel service?"

Great, Jake thought. We got a holy Joe in the poker room. Jake liked Bill, all right, but he had to draw the line somewhere. No one moved. The dealer spun out three cards to another player. Jake didn't look back. "I'm here to kill Japs and maybe make a couple of bucks along the way, but, ah, put in a good word for me. I could use some help right about now."

"Sure. I understand." Bill smiled with a nod and a grin while not completely hiding his disappointment. "See you guys at dinner."

"Well, make your bet!" Jake said.

The crew of plane #16, Bat Out of Hell, *left to right:*
Lt. Robert Hite, copilot; Lt. William Farrow, pilot; Sgt. Harold Spatz,
engineer/gunner; Cpl. George Barr, navigator; Cpl. Jacob DeShazer, bombardier.

Chapter 41

Evening patrons crowded the popular restaurant of Nagoya, dimly lit by white hanging paper lanterns, but Tomiko Fujimoto, a sturdy, young lady of nineteen, could see no one but her fiancé across the table where they knelt. Her red and white kimono complimented her dark red lipstick and fair skin. As Kenji Saito slurped his noodles, Tomiko glanced around embarrassingly, then looked back into Kenji's eyes while trying to restrain her smile. She never believed she could compete with the more beautiful, petite girls, yet luck had shown her favor.

Kenji's broad shoulders and height set him apart from others his age. Being well known and well-liked by his peers made him a desired prize by many young ladies. He set down his bowl and chopsticks and picked up his tea. "Three more months."

"Three months," she said. They gazed at each other half smiling as only young lovers can do. "I've never known the time to go so slowly." Tomiko picked up a piece of tempura with her chopsticks. Relieved they could *finally* be together unaccompanied by family, Tomiko savored the moment but was getting impatient.

"Is your grandfather able to come to the wedding?"

"He says he will. I'm so happy he's able to come. It's a long trip for him, and he hasn't been well."

Kenji cast his eyes around cautiously, then reached out and placed his strong hand on top of Tomiko's. "If you're happy, I'm happy."

April 18, 1942. Nagoya. Early morning.

With an aluminum bento box slung over his shoulder by a leather strap, Kenji trudged down the narrow, wood-paved alley in the early morning wearing white coveralls, a pair of leather gloves tucked under his belt. Coming to a doorway, he glanced around and gently tapped on the wooden doorframe and whispered, "Tomiko?" He listened for an answer. "Tomiko." He turned his head as a man rode by on a rickety bicycle with a bundle on his back.

On the matted floor inside her room, Tomiko rolled over, sleeping soundly.

Kenji peered down at his watch, looked around, then knocked on the frame again, this time, harder. He spoke in a loud whisper, "Tomiko. I've got to go to work. I'll see you tonight."

With her eyes barely open, Tomiko stared for a few seconds, then realized that what she thought she was only half dreaming wasn't a dream.

She grasped her kimono and threw it on, slid her bedroom door open, and quickly tip-toed to the front door being careful to not arouse her parents. Creaking it open, to her surprise, she saw no one but an old woman walking by with a basket of vegetables. She leaned out further and looked up and down the alley both ways. Her long, black hair fell across her face as her eyes drifted toward the ground. She couldn't believe she'd missed him.

As she receded into the house, a glimmer of red caught her eye. Catching the sunlight was a red origami crane with her name written on it squeezed into the edge of the doorframe. Carefully plucking it out, she looked back down the empty street with a smile. "Thank you, Kenji," she said.

Chapter 42

April 18, 1942. The Pacific Ocean 700 miles east of Japan.

The massive *USS Hornet* turned into the wind and powered up to full speed, rising and falling on the churning white-capped seas as sixteen B-25 bombers waited in launch position with their engines rumbling. In the #1 plane sat Jimmy Doolittle with his men. The eyes of every sailor in the overloaded tower and on the packed deck stared intently as he went through the last check of his ailerons, rudder, and elevator.

Spinning propellers on the crammed deck of the Hornet left little room for error.

Jake stood beside the crew members of *Bat out of Hell* as apprehensively as the rest, his mouth hanging open a bit. Doolittle had the shortest runway of any plane because of the 15 bombers behind him—leaving him exactly 467 feet, which was less than half the distance the aircraft was designed to need to get airborne. Engineers modified every B-25 for the mission with three extra fuel tanks and every plane was given ten

One of the first American naval aviators, Captain Marc Mitscher (in the white cap) anxiously observed the launch of the first Raider along with the crew.

five-gallon cans of gas, nearly doubling the range, but also adding 4,000 pounds to the total weight—putting it at the extreme limits of still being airworthy. At least that was Doolittle's calculated assumption. Instead of three football fields of runway to get into the sky, they had one and a half. But they did have a good headwind.

Every time Bill, Bob, and Jake had paced off the distance in the preceding days, Bill kept shaking his head. If you didn't get into the air by the end, you'd just fall into the sea. Probably upside down.

Jake leaned to Bill and shouted over the drone of the engines. "Well, if he can't make it, no one can." The entire mission hinged on this one plane successfully making it into the air.

"He's Doolittle. He'll make it," Bill shouted back.

While holding the brakes, Doolittle revved up both engines full throttle vibrating the wingtips, waiting for the right timing to the rise and fall of the ship. The flagman dropped his checkered flag; the engineer yanked the wheel chocks, and Doolittle released his B-25, roaring down the runway into the misty wind. Jake clenched his fists on the opening of his jacket. The plane approached the end of the deck and dropped . . . then struggled into the gray sky. The crew broke into cheers, flapping their hats in the air as flight teams began scrambling to their aircraft.

Doolittle planned to launch the aircraft 400 nautical miles off the coast of Japan in the early evening hours of the 19th for a night raid, but the discovery of a Japanese fishing boat, suspected of being part of an early warning radio picket line, forced the immediate launch of all planes from over 700 miles out a day early. The cruiser USS Nashville quickly blew the Japanese vessel out of the water, but not before it had apparently sent out a radio signal that the Americans picked up. From this launching location, it would be impossible for any of the aircraft to reach their designated landing points in China. They'd also be attacking in broad daylight and, if Tokyo received the radio signal from the fishing boat, the Japanese military might well be waiting and fully prepared for the meager attack of sixteen unescorted bombers. The operation was now in jeopardy of being a complete disaster.

The #2 plane inched into position as other engines revved into roars behind him. The flagman waved the next B-25 off down the deck as Bill Farrow, in the #16 position, warmed up the engines of the Bat Out of Hell. A sudden gust of wind whipped into the aircraft, lifting the nose in the air and tipping the back down toward the water below. Jake dropped his bag and lunged for the nose wheel and grabbed hold as other sailors pulled on tie-down ropes, straining to bring the bucking animal under control, but not before one rope pulled a sailor toward the whirling propeller.

Bill stared in horror from his pilot's seat and screamed through the open window, "Look out!" The sailor slid into their left propeller, instantly severing his left arm and flinging him to the deck as the nose wheel smashed back down to the deck. Jake, Harry, and two others bolted over, pressed a jacket to the man's shoulder gushing blood, and carried him off to the side. Stunned but conscious, the sailor with his striking blue eyes, blood oozing onto the rain-soaked deck, gazed up at the men. "Give 'em hell, Jake. Do it for me, will ya?"

"You got it, pal." He would never forget those crystal blue eyes. Never.

Jimmy Doolittle's #1 plane successfully lofting into the sky from USS Hornet.

Things were looking like they could have been a catastrophe before they even left. Jake's heart was pounding. Besides a man nearly being killed, their plane had almost tumbled backward into the sea.

The #15 plane in front of them, *TNT*, revved up and moved ahead. "Get moving number sixteen!" a crewman yelled. Jake ran back to his plane, threw his bag up into the hatch, climbed aboard, and pulled the hatch shut. Inside, the roar of the engines was nearly as loud as outside. Bill taxied forward as Jake shimmied on his belly through a narrow passageway to his nose position. Crawling out of the square tube, a gust of damp wind greeted him, pouring in through a jagged, foot-wide hole in the Plexiglas—just to the right of his machine gun. "Hell no!" He stared.

It must have happened during the confusion when the plane was being thrown around by the wind, he figured, and somehow grazed the tail of the aircraft ahead of them. This could make for a miserable thirteen-hour flight and could even jeopardize their mission as the added drag would certainly cut down their range.

Jake yanked on his headset and strapped his throat microphone around his neck to notify Bill while the plane inched forward. Maybe they just shouldn't go. He watched the wooden deck planking roll under him through his nose windshield, then glanced at the rows of eyes outside fixed on his plane. Some men gave him a "thumbs up." There were only seconds for him to decide. Telling Bill about the gaping hole in the nose could easily get their mission scrubbed, a mission he *still* wasn't completely sure about.

He put his hand on his throat microphone and blinked a few times as he watched the flagman motioning the plane into takeoff position. The plane came to a halt as the engines began to ramp up. Jake swallowed hard, then shoved his arms into the seat harness and buckled in.

With the flagman's release and the plane throttling up to full power, the acceleration pressed Jake into his seat with thundering vibrations. The runway sped past him and disappeared into the white-capped ocean below. The plane climbed and banked wide left, circling to join two other planes in their group of three. Jake looked down to see the ships turning in unison toward the west, giving him a chill with a new thought—the next safe place they could land was 2,400 miles away.

Having his bearings, Bill dropped to a height of a hundred feet above the ocean to duck under any possible enemy radar. When Jake told Bill about the hole, he sent the copilot, Bob to shimmy up front to see if he could help fix it. He and Jake tried plugging it with a jacket, but it just kept blowing in. Eventually, the drag made them drop behind of the two other B-25s in their formation, and they lost sight of them. They were alone over the Pacific Ocean.

About an hour in, Bill broke the "silence" of the head-numbing drone of the two 14-cylinder Wright R-2600 engines. "Hey, Jake," Bill shouted over his headset.

"Yeah?"

"That fella who fell into the prop. You know him?"

Jake glanced to his left at the whirring propeller, spinning only a few inches from his window, speckles of dried blood still stuck to the Plexiglas, then at the endless horizon of the ocean ahead. "Bob. Bob Wall. He beat me out of twenty-seven bucks."

Bill looked at his copilot who shook his head. "That's a cryin' shame. Hope he pulls through."

"Yeah. Me, too. Just hope all the worst is behind us, now." Keeping his headset on to dull the oppressive drone, Jake pulled his jacket over his chest, kicked up his feet, wedged his head into the corner, and sighed as the rushing wind engulfed him. One thing was certain, there was no turning back.

Chapter 43

April 18, 1942. The open seas, southwest of Japan.
The aircraft carrier Akagi.

Fuchida sat alone in the flight standby room flipping through an aircraft parts folder when an orderly barged in.

"Sir, Commander Genda requests you immediately in operations!"

Arriving at the room, he saw Genda, Vice Admiral Nagumo, and a number of officers hunched over the map table. "What's going on?"

Genda looked up at Fuchida with a smile and handed him a report. "Well, Fuchi, they've come at last!" He took a triumphant puff of his cigarette.

Fuchida snatched the paper of the last transmissions of the patrol boat *Nittō Maru*:

06:30 Sighted what appear to be 3 enemy carrier-borne aircraft
06:45 Sighted 1 enemy carrier
06:50 Sighted 3 enemy carriers
07:30 Large enemy formation

A chill of joy and fear ran through his body as he took it in—*the Americans were going to attack Japan.* It seemed unbelievable. So early in the war, the Americans were setting out to attack? Japan would crush them in a textbook battle, just like his instructors had predicted. The chance to destroy the American carriers exhilarated him. *This is our real enemy—The US Navy!*

"The patrol boat hasn't been heard from since," Genda said, "but they

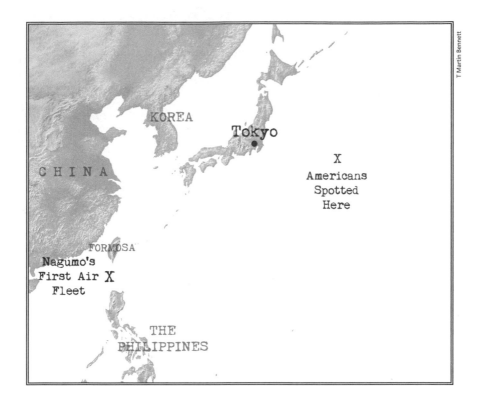

managed to let us know of the approach of the Americans and their location. Headquarters has ordered Tactical Method Number Three." Genda paused. "We're to intercept and engage the enemy."

Genda turned back down to the map as Fuchida squeezed into the group.

Nagumo thumped his finger between Formosa[18] and the Philippines. "Here. We are right here." He slid his hand to the right of Japan out into the open ocean and thumped his finger again. "And here is where the formation was spotted." He removed his hand, stood upright and said to Fuchida. "Six hundred fifty miles from Japan. This is *just* what we had hoped for."

Fuchida smiled. "And they'll need to be within three hundred miles of Japan before they can even *begin* to launch aircraft for an attack. That'll leave us with about a day to meet them head to head." He squinted with skepticism. "What could they possibly hope to accomplish?"

---

[18] Modern Taiwan.

Nagumo grinned. "Admiral Yamamoto has ordered the carriers *Soryu* and *Hiryu* to speed to the coast as well. We'll have our air defense on full alert tomorrow, and our carriers will be prepared to annihilate the Americans as soon as they arrive." He turned back to Fuchida and clapped his hands together. "We've got them *right* where we want them."

Chapter 44

The same day. The island of Panay, The Philippine Islands.

Fire blazed from the windows and through the wooden roofs of the buildings of Central Philippine University—stark, white-plaster structures pouring out brilliant flames and jet-black smoke. Japanese soldiers with bayoneted rifles swarmed the campus.

American forces had previously occupied the buildings as a temporary base shortly after the bombing of Iloilo, but with the landing of Japanese troops at three locations on Panay a few days earlier, expedience had forced the soldiers to retreat to the mountains and scatter into the jungle at hidden locations where food and weapons had been stored for a guerrilla-style warfare. With the orders to leave nothing behind for the Japanese, they torched the university.

Pushing through the leaves burdened with his overstuffed backpack, Jimmy slapped a mosquito on his sweaty neck and came to a halt. If it wasn't his feet that hurt, it was something else, but at least they were getting closer to their safe destination. Fearing the deeper penetration of Japanese forces, Jimmy thought it best to move further inland. The rest agreed, so they all banded together and hiked up into the overgrown mountains of Panay—a combination of forest and jungle.

Reverend Delfin Dianala led the muddy uphill procession, a typically thin Filipino, his jet-black hair glistening in the sun. He said with his Filipino accent, "The bats eat millions of mosquitoes around here, but that still leaves a few billion." He chuckled through a toothy smile.

Jimmy and Charma trekked up the steep, slick path in the tropical mountains beside Francis and Gertrude Rose, a dozen or so teachers, parents with children, and a handful of gold miners with their families. The miners fled from the IXL goldmine on the neighboring island of Masbate, only barely escaping the Japanese who had overwhelmed their island in January. Bringing up the rear, a young boy led a nanny goat and her kid.

Despite the fear of the Japanese among the locals, Rev. Dianala found *cargadores*, laborers who regularly helped transport goods over jungle paths they knew well. They brought six of their own carabao, Philippine water buffaloes, dragging wooden sleds over clay trails—strapped high with sacks, crates, suitcases, and the Rose's beloved pump organ, without which no self-respecting Baptist believed any church service could be held. The displaced teachers pushed ahead through a barrage of dark green, glossy-leafed foliage, and, as they came nearer to the mountains, towering shorea trees, palm trees, banana trees, and stands of bamboo.

Rev. Dianala wiped the grime-streaked sweat from his face with a handkerchief. "We're almost there," he said between his labored breaths. "Just up over the hill we'll come to a ridge, then down into a narrow valley. You'll see." Rev. Dianala, a native Filipino, led a church in the village of Katipunan, about two miles away. Some students and staff from the

A carabao pulling a conga sled, 1940s.

© Elmo Familiaran

Rev. Delfin and Beatriz Dianala with their family shortly after the war.

university fled to the village, but only the Filipinos felt relatively safe from the Japanese. All Caucasians or those deemed "American" in any way were being told to surrender. As an orphan, an American family at the university in Iloilo had befriended him, took him in, and raised Dianala as their own, covering all of his expenses for a full college education at their school. He took risks for the Americans no one else would take, as he knew how much others had risked to take him in off the streets. He felt compelled to do no less for the fleeing caravan of refugees.

When Jimmy finally broke through the heavier vegetation, he and the group entered into a clearing near the top of the mountain beside a gorge surrounded by steep, rocky walls. He looked up at the sun piercing the leafy, branched canopy in dozens of columns of light. Majestic mahogany trees lifted their branches to the heavens, alive with birds and families of macaque monkeys who swung buoyantly through the branches and vines, chattering with curiosity. Two tents stood in a small clearing below high-arching trees.

Jimmy gazed in awe at the wild orchids, a fascinating display of pink, white, and yellow. A brilliant red-bellied pitta sang its low-whistle song from a nearby branch and flitted away toward a trickling brook that wove its way through a rocky opening in the distance. He closed his eyes and breathed in the sweet scents of heaven on earth.

Panting, Francis Rose spread out his arms. "Well, this is it. I scouted this out a while back with Rev. Dianala. There are about twenty local families in the area, a creek nearby, and . . . we're pretty far from the main roads. Kind of a secret hideout. What do you think?"

Charma kept looking around in wonder and shook her head. "It's so beautiful! So peaceful."

"My kind of place," Jimmy added. "Amazing. Really."

"We'll put up a few more tents for now," Rev. Dianala said, "and the locals will help you build some bamboo nipa huts in a couple of weeks. We can help provide food for you, too. In time, you should be able to have a few gardens, maybe some chickens, and be somewhat self-sufficient."

Jack Treat, a sturdy, six-foot-two American in a khaki jungle hat swung the trunk he was carrying to the ground but kept his machine gun over his shoulder. Jack, a miner from Masbate, was one of many American civilians who had linked up with the Filipino guerrillas in recent weeks. A muscular man in his fifties, he seamlessly moved from worker to warrior. "We're in some of the most remote parts of the mountains. No one'll find you here—unless you owe 'em money. Then they'll find you."

"Isn't that the truth," Jimmy replied. Though a staunch pacifist, still, he took comfort in his armed escort.

The distant drone of two planes far above turned the heads of all skyward. "Japanese medium bombers," Jack said. "Probably transporting officers."

The rest of the hikers looked at each other uncomfortably.

"Well!" Francis said, standing proudly with his hands on his hips. "I've named it Hopevale: Valley of Hope."

"Hopevale," Jimmy said. "I like the name. I like everything about this place."

Francis smiled and slapped Jimmy on the shoulder. "Maybe God'll bring something good out of this after all, eh?"

Chapter 45

The same day. The Pacific Ocean, east of Nagoya, Japan.

As the *Bat Out of Hell* skimmed 100 feet over the ocean at 230 miles an hour, George, the navigator, examined his charts making measurements. He tapped the pilot on the shoulder. "Hey Bill, it's been over three and a half hours, now. We should see the coast soon."

"Roger that," Bill said.

Jake leaned forward in the nose straining to see. "Yeah, baby! There it is!"

Bill asked over the intercom, "Harry, you awake back there?"

In his top Plexiglas gun turret, Harry rubbed his eyes. "Yeah, yeah."

"Keep your eyes peeled for Zeroes. We're the last of the bunch. They gotta know we're comin'."

Harry cocked his two machine guns. "I'm all eyes back here." He squinted into the sky, unwrapped a piece of gum, and folded it into his mouth as the pilot eased the plane up to 1,500 feet for their bombing run.

Kenji stepped through an array of parallel pipes beside a row of six huge white cylindrical tanks—each forty feet tall. Two nearby workers in white gripped a large, steel valve wheel.

"Turn the first valve three revolutions to the left," Kenji said while pointing, "then wait for about five seconds." He watched and waited while the workers turned the wheel and looked back at Kenji. "That's right. Now do the same for the second."

Another worker called out from fifty feet away. "Kenji! Come look at this control box!"

"I'll be right back," he said as he pulled off his gloves.

Jake's point of view from his nose position inside their B-25 bomber.

The B-25 thundered over houses and buildings, startling people in the streets who looked up.

Bill yelled over the intercom, "Comin' up Jake! The refinery!"

Jake pushed hard on the floor lever to swing open the bomb bay doors and flipped toggle switches on the control panel from "Safe" to "Arm." He shut one eye as he took aim down the bombsight and watched the target gradually come into view through his Plexiglas nose. The simple, handmade sights were designed especially for this one, low-level mission.

"I got it. I see the fuel tanks." He poised his left thumb over the switch to release two incendiary bombs. Anti-aircraft fire began bursting from the ground, shaking their plane. Staring down the bombsight, Jake flipped the switch, accidently sending three bombs instead of two. "Sayonara!"

Kenji froze as he and the others gazed up to the sound of pounding anti-aircraft fire and the approaching aircraft. The bomber roared overhead followed by a concussion that erupted into gigantic fireballs of exploding fuel.

"Kenji!" two workers screamed in unison from across the way as others leaped for cover. Kenji sprinted and stumbled from the wicked inferno as the flames erupted behind him and quickly consumed him.

The plane banked into a high left turn to head for the next target. Jake gazed back at the boiling flashes of brilliant orange wrapped in clouds of jet-black smoke. "Oh, yeah! Now see how it feels!" To his right in the distance, he saw more columns of smoke from the bombing strike of the #14 plane just before they arrived.

"Heads up, Jake," Bill said. "Aircraft factory coming up."

Jake took aim again and waited for the buildings to align with the point of his bombsight. Anti-aircraft fire once again from the ground burst into the sky in front of him.

"Jake, let's go! We're getting some heat and need to move out!"

"OK . . . OK . . . Bombs away!" He selected his fourth bomb and pushed the release switch as they passed over a long industrial building—ripping it into a flaming explosion. Ground fire tracers shot past the plane from multiple angles. "Hey! They're shooting at us!"

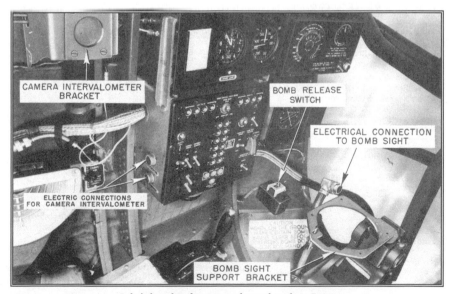

Jake's bombardier control panel in their B-25.

"Yeah. I don't think they like us." Bill pulled the plane into a steep right turn and headed back toward the ocean. Jake looked back at the blazing building with satisfaction. "Now that's *American* style barbecue!"

Departing the coastline, Bill dropped the plane back down to 100 feet above the water and headed southwest along the coast.

Jake spotted a fishing boat in the distance and grabbed his 30-caliber machine gun in the nose, gave it a hard rack and swung it onto the target. The fishermen, far from the explosions and expecting only to see friendly aircraft over their waters, smiled, jumped up, and began waving their arms at the approaching airplane.

"Greetings from the U.S.A.," Jake said, and let loose twenty-five rounds at the helpless fishermen, pocking the water, and splintering wood across their boat.

"Cut it out, Jake!" Bill yelled over the intercom. "Military targets only!"

Jake let out a sigh and stroked the gun like a pet dog as the gunsmoke swirled around him.

The fishermen looked at each other in shock and confusion, baffled but unhurt, as the sound of the B-25 roared over them and faded into the distance.

Jake's heartbeat finally began to slow down. He took an extra-big breath and exhaled. Mission accomplished. Now they were heading toward China, the night, and the unknown.

Chapter 46

Somewhere over China.

Night swallowed day as Jake and the crew made it across the East China Sea into China, over 1,000 miles from Nagoya. Jake had abandoned his post at the nose earlier and took a seat next to George, the navigator, behind the pilots. Over China, the plane soared above dark satin clouds, eerily illuminated by a crescent moon hung low in the sky.

George ran his finger across a flight map under a dim light bulb.

Bill came in over the intercom. "We're in a tough situation, fellas. In this weather, we can't find our rendezvous point to land, and I can't drop below the clouds because we might bump into something—like a mountain. So I'm gonna keep on a southwest course to see if we can run out of this weather and make a landing somewhere in free China."

"Hey, Bill," George piped in. "I say we head due west for fifty minutes, *then* head south and bail when we run out of fuel. At least that way we'll be out of Jap territory."

"Can't do that, George. It's all mountains to the west, and I wanna get this plane on the ground in one piece." George glanced at Jake beside him and shook his head.

An hour later, George couldn't wait any longer. "Bill, we *gotta* find the airfields soon if we're gonna land on wheels and not on our own two feet in a rice paddy. Bob, how much fuel we got left?"

Bob scanned the fuel gauges, then looked down at his notepad with his calculations.

"I figure, another fifteen minutes or so, but I wouldn't count on it. We've been in the air over thirteen hours."

"Any radio contact with our airfields?"

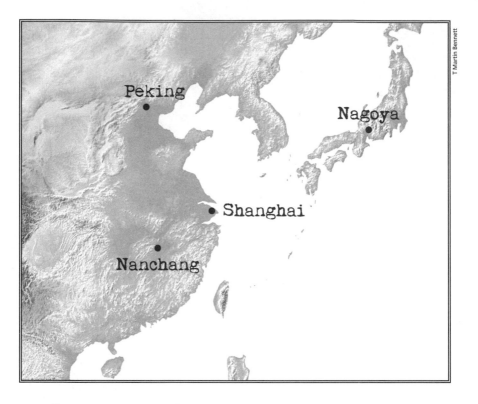

"No response on any frequencies. Where are we, George?"

George glanced over his chart. "Best I can calculate, just southwest of Nanchang. Jap territory."

Jake clearly read the faces of all. It wasn't looking good. In the hands of the enemies they'd just bombed wouldn't be a very good prospect.

A buzzer rang out as a red light flashed on Bob's panel. He reached over and flipped off the buzzer, but the light kept flashing.

Bill looked around. "That's all she wrote, boys. Let's just hope this is *un*occupied China, or we're in a *mess* of trouble. Everybody out. If we get out fast enough, maybe we can regroup on the ground."

One last time Jake checked his parachute straps, felt for his .45 pistol and flashlight, then dug through his duffle bag he'd be leaving behind. Chocolate—a good find. He slipped it into a pocket. He bumped into a book, his unread Bible and gazed for a second. No room and no time for that.

George released the floor hatch into the rushing wind and blackness below, hung his legs out, and took one last, serious look into the faces of his mates. "See ya in China!" He dropped through the hole and disappeared.

For the first time in Jake's life, the fact that he wasn't ready to die gripped him. But he resigned himself to the thought that this is the way he'd lived . . . and this is the way he'd die. No changing it now. He sat down and dropped his feet into the racing wind, which whipped hard against his legs. Bracing his hands on the frame, he pushed himself down and fell out into the darkness as the plane shrieked away.

Jake gave a firm yank on his rip cord and the parachute blossomed open giving him a hard jerk. As the drone of his plane faded into the clouds, he found himself drifting in total quiet for the first time in what was the longest, noisiest, most exhilarating day of his life. Enveloped by the mystical night, he saw nothing in the darkness and fog and could barely even feel the wind as he floated down with the rain. Swinging from side to side, he felt strangely alone.

Nearly 3,000 miles away, at the same moment in Madras, Oregon, Mrs. Andrus woke from her sleep. She blinked groggily and rolled toward her husband and whispered loudly. "Hiram. Hiram?" He groaned. She pulled the covers down and sat up. "I had this dream, a dreadful feeling, like I was dropping down, down, down."

"Mmmmm. Go to sleep."

"No, something's happened," she said. "I've got to pray for Jake." She leaned to the nightstand, yanked the chain on the light, got up, and put on her rose-patterned, quilted robe. Facing a chair next to the window, she grasped the seat and lowered herself to the floor onto her knees. Resting her forehead on her folded hands, she poured out her heart to the God of heaven to please, *please* help her son, wherever he was.

Early a.m., China.

Jake still couldn't see anything as he stared down through the rain, prepared for the worst, and wondered where he'd land—in a rice paddy? On a rooftop? In the trees? On the pavement? Suddenly the ground rose up below him, and he crumpled into the mud with a hard thump as his chute drifted down beside him.

He got up onto his hands and knees and rubbed his ribs, which he'd somehow banged a bit on the landing, then hugged a mound of damp soil next to him in relief. "Ahhh, dirt!" Unhooking his parachute in the dim fog and drizzle, he saw he was surrounded by dozens of square white posts with oriental writing on them. A Chinese graveyard. "Whoa!" He looked around a little surprised. "I hope I'm not joining you guys anytime soon."

The steady pelting of rain surrounded him. He stood up, drew his M1911 .45 and cocked it, slowly peered in all directions, then held it high in the air and fired off one round and waited for an answer. Nothing. Nothing but the sound of rain. He realized his luck to have landed on the mound of graves as flooded rice paddies surrounded him. He fired off two more rounds and waited again. Nothing.

Holstering his weapon and pulling out his knife, he crouched down and cut off a strip of parachute silk, wrapped it around his head and tied it in a knot in the back to keep the water off, then trudged off down a muddy path looking for shelter for the night.

After some time, he came upon what appeared to be a small brick shrine, just big enough for him to sit in and keep out of the rain. It was good enough, and he was beat, so he squeezed in and got as comfortable as he could. In his utter exhaustion, he soon nodded off to sleep to the soothing hiss of rainfall.

The dawn sun poked through the gray and white clouds on the horizon and hit Jake squarely in the face, nudging him from his sleep. Squinting, he rubbed his eyes and struggled to free himself from his small quarters and stumbled out. Standing upright and stretching, he took a long look around for people and for any kind of road. Not seeing either, he yanked off his parachute cap and headed in the direction that seemed to make the most sense. He needed first to find out if he was safely in Chinese territory or in occupied territory, but what he *really* wanted was to just find his buddies. He pushed around in his bag for that chocolate bar he stashed.

Jake came to more paddies of rice and found a path, which he followed for over an hour, then started to come upon some people in their houses that looked more like shacks to him. A woman hanging laundry beside some squawking chickens glanced at him for a second but paid no attention. He passed a couple of men on the road who weren't even suspicious. It seemed strange. If they didn't feel his being there was unusual, it must be a good sign that he was in unoccupied China.

Finally getting up the nerve, he stopped an older man pulling a small cart loaded with baskets. Jake pointed to himself. "American. Me American. You Chinese?" The man smiled and nodded his head without speaking and walked on. Not much help. Coming to a kind of feed store, he wrote a note to the clerk in English "Me American. Are you Chinese?" The clerk smiled as well but couldn't read the note. What he thought should be a pretty simple task was proving to be rather difficult. Who were the good guys?

After another hour of walking, Jake eventually came to a main road with telephone lines—civilization. He was confident of finding help soon, but knew he had to be cautious. As Jake continued, he came to a series of houses with soldiers a ways off the road. Some men were washing laundry in a rocky creek. Chinese? Japanese? He felt it was safer to just keep on walking.

Further down he came to a house and stopped. He could hear people inside. He needed to determine where he was and *had* to find some people who could help him. He slowly drew his .45, racked it to put a bullet in the chamber, then reholstered it with the hammer cocked, leaving his hand on his pistol. Taking a deep breath, he carefully approached the open front door and peered in. He saw two young soldiers in green khaki uniforms playing with some children. The soldiers had gold stars sewn onto their caps. He had absolutely no idea which force they belonged to.

Jake poked his head in. Everyone stopped and stared, but in a friendly way. He motioned to himself with his left hand while keeping his right on his weapon. "America." He pointed to one of the soldiers. "China or Japan?"

One soldier smiled and looked to the other soldier, then back to Jake. "China! We China!" It appeared they knew some English, but he wasn't convinced, so he kept his hand on his gun.

The soldiers came up to him and made motions of eating and pointed to Jake's mouth. "Food? Food?"

Jake smiled and nodded.

"Come!" The soldier looped his arm into Jake's, and the two walked him up the road back toward the encampment. As they walked, one soldier pointed to Jake's .45 and shook his head. "No gun. No gun."

Jake patted his holstered weapon. "The gun stays right there. OK, pal?"

The soldier smiled. "OK, OK. Come! Come!"

Arriving at another dwelling, nearby soldiers watched curiously as Jake entered a nicer, but equally tiny house—a sort of headquarters, Jake figured. They sat him at a small table and promptly brought out some vegetables and meat, none of which Jake could quite identify, except for the tea and the rice. He began wolfing it all down, glancing around cautiously between bites. The two soldiers stood before Jake with their arms folded, smiling and nodding. Suddenly, Jake felt a sharp pain in his back. With his mouth packed with food, he looked over his shoulder. five soldiers had their bayoneted rifles pointed at his back.

An officer in tall black riding boots slowly approached Jake, smiling. "You seem to be a long way from home." The officer casually removed Jake's .45 pistol. "Welcome to the Empire of Japan."

Jake turned forward, angry. "Y'know, they always told me all you guys looked the same. I shoulda known."

Chapter 47

April 19, 1942. Nagoya, Japan.

Workmen in white wrestled fire hoses in the morning light, spraying great arcs of water onto the smoldering, twisted steel of what was left of the destroyed refinery. Scorched holding tanks hissed and breathed out clouds of black smoke above flickering tongues of fire.

Five workers stood or squatted around a partially burned body, half covered in a white sheet. Other bodies under sheets lay behind them.

Kneeling beside the corpse, bowed almost to the ground, Tomiko in her pink kimono wept uncontrollably, heaving with near-silent sobs. She came running when she heard the news early that morning. It didn't seem real to her. It couldn't be real.

The men glanced impatiently at each other.

Collecting herself, trembling, and wiping her face with both sleeves, she sat upright. She nodded to the man with the clipboard. "It's Kenji," she said, then crumpled again to the ground and burst into pulsating sobs.

The leader jotted a note onto his clipboard and motioned to the others who pulled the cover over Kenji's head.

Tomiko sat up with her hands to her face and let out a shriek of grief, and collapsed again in tears, this time letting herself wail without restraint, her long, black hair cascading across the lifeless body. She knew would never see him again. Ever.

Chapter 48

April 19, 1942. The aircraft carrier Akagi. East
of mainland Japan.

A flagman guided a Zero fighter as he descended to the deck for a
landing. In the operations room, Fuchida, Vice Admiral Nagumo,
Genda, and other officers hunched over the map table. At a large,
lacquered conference table nearby, other officers studied papers and maps.

Fuchida shook his head and pointed to a tiny island. "No, even
Midway is too far for the B-25, and Alaska is impossible as well. They were
medium bombers. That's far outside their range." By this time, the news had
hit the American newspapers and shot around the world. Fuchida was
disgusted that the Japanese newspapers announced that the army shot down
nine planes, when *none* were shot down. Propaganda like that only backfires
when people learn the truth, he thought.

Nagumo asked, "And how did they penetrate our defenses? Even
though they arrived a day early, we were still on alert."

Genda answered, "Since our fighters patrol at three thousand meters[19]
they came in at thirty to sixty meters[20] above the ground—dangerously low,
but nearly invisible to our pilots at that height."

Another officer pointed to the map east of Japan. "We know they were
spotted out here."

Fuchida shook his head. "But you can't launch land-based medium
bombers from a carrier. It's just not possible."

"So few planes, so little damage." Nagumo exhaled the smoke of his
cigar. "In the end, it was a wasted attack. Even our newspapers are calling

---

[19] 10,000 feet.
[20] 100 to 200 feet.

TOKYO BOMBED, JAPS SAY; ADMIT DAMAGE IS HEAVY

U.S.-French War Feared to Be Near

Gift of Fleet to Germany Predicted—America Refuses to Deal With Laval

What Is Tokyo?

Heart of Nation of 96 Million People Who Hope to Rule the World

Radio Tells of Casualties to Civilians

No Hint Given as to Where Bombers Came From—Washington Keeps Silent

TOKYO: FULL PAGE OF PICTURES ON PAGE 8

---

the Doolittle Raid the 'Do-*nothing* Raid.'"

Fuchida collected himself and stood upright. "Respectfully, sir, I must disagree. They've exposed the weakness of our home defenses—in broad daylight."

Nagumo's face darkened.

"Never before has anyone been able to bomb our homeland."

Perturbed, Nagumo looked at the map and back at Fuchida. "Then, where *did* they come from?"

Fuchida took a long drag from his cigarette to buy time and scanned the map again. "I don't know . . . but I do know this: The Americans had no fear flying straight into the heart of Japan. We failed to shoot down a single plane." Nodding with admiration, he looked Nagumo in the eyes. "Whoever these Americans were . . . they had guts."

Chapter 49

April 20, 1942. Nanchang, China.

Jake and the four other members of his crew stood stoically on concrete steps leading up to stone columns of a granite block building. Eight Japanese officers in their dress uniforms proudly surrounded them as a photographer stared down into the viewfinder of his camera while holding his hand in the air motioning the men to be still. Other photographers stood off to the side in front of a growing group of civilian and military spectators.

Captured and put on display, the crew of plane #16 stands in the back.
Left to right: Jake DeShazer, Harry Spatz, Bob Hite, Bill Farrow, and George Barr.

The officers stood erect. Jake did his best to hide a scowl. He felt like a chained monkey in a circus. He was happy to see his lost buddies, who all made it safely to the ground—but not happy at all that they'd fallen into Japanese hands. After they had bailed out, one by one, Japanese soldiers tracked them down, arrested them, and interrogated them with threats of death. Jake was tight-lipped but knew his prospects of making it back home were thin to nothing.

After a few shots, the photographer repositioned only the five captured fliers in the front row. Harry nonchalantly puffed on a cigarette he'd bummed off a soldier.

With the publicity shots done, the officers blindfolded the fliers, tied their hands together in front of them, and shoved them into the back of a 1938 Ford pickup truck along with guards. Then they hauled them off to an airport and loaded the prisoners into a passenger plane—where to, Jake didn't know. The idea of taking over the aircraft was out of the question as there were four guards assigned to each prisoner who was blindfolded and handcuffed to his seat.

Although they'd been questioned, amazingly, no one among the Japanese connected them to the Tokyo raid. Not yet.

Chapter 50

Late April 1942. The battleship Yamato.
Hashirajima Bay, twenty-five miles due south of
Hiroshima.

"We've achieved our objectives far more quickly than we ever imagined, and that with only insignificant Japanese losses," Genda said to the roomful of high-ranking officers. "What's left of the American fleet remains paralyzed. General MacArthur deserted his men in the heat of battle, leaving them behind in the Philippines. And Singapore, the stronghold of the British Empire, fell in a week, resulting in the largest surrender of British-led forces in history, giving us the added prize of a cache of Johnny Walker Black Label, which you are now enjoying."

The officers chuckled and nodded, blew smoke, and raised their drinks while surveying the faces of their peers. Curls of smoke drifted up from cigarettes. Fuchida, who had personally experienced the exhilaration of uncontested victories, likewise beamed and took a victorious sip of his own whiskey.

Lieutenant Commander Genda gave his remarks on behalf of Vice Admiral Chūichi Nagumo before Yamamoto presented his newest strategy. Fuchida sat beside Genda's empty chair, listening attentively.

Isoroku Yamamoto, the highly-respected admiral of the Combined Fleet, had gathered his top commanders and their select staff to his flagship, the battleship *Yamato*. She and her sister ship, *Musashi*, were the most powerful and massive battleships ever to ply the seas, displacing 78,200 metric tons—50 percent heavier than the biggest and newest Colorado class battleships of the US Navy. A single gun turret of the *Yamato* weighed more than the largest American destroyer. Yet the *Yamato* was so luxuriously appointed that sailors began calling it "the Yamato Hotel"—a compliment and an insult. Still, she was the pride of the Imperial Japanese Navy.

Along both sides of the long table sat the leading commanders of the navy in their dark blue uniforms trimmed with gold braids. Their combined forces had attained the objectives of securing new lands rich with oil, rice, rubber, and resources needed by their empire—quickly, and with minimal losses. The Japanese had hurled the Americans to the floor before the eyes of the world, dealt the British Indian fleet a humiliating defeat, and had completely overrun the Dutch forces. Never had they imagined achieving so much so soon, and they found themselves in the unexpected position of needing to choose their next conquest as a stunned world sat and watched.

"All have exemplified outstanding Bushido spirit in the service of our august emperor," Genda continued. "The sun has finally set on the British Empire—as it rises on our own."

Genda bowed briefly to applause and headed to his seat as Yamamoto rose from his position at the head of the table. When Genda returned to his place, Fuchida looked up with a smile and nod of approval. But Fuchida was more interested in hearing Yamamoto, as there had been rumblings among

The mighty battleship Yamato *shortly before completion, late 1941.*

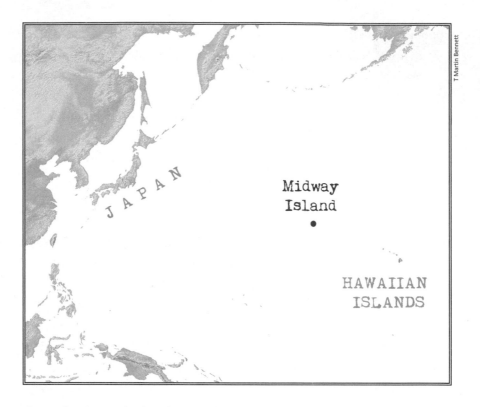

the ranks about whether the IJN should first head east to deal with the Americans or head south first, *then* deal with the Americans. Both groups believed that the aircraft carriers of the American fleet had to be destroyed but disagreed on how and when to do so.

The southern operation, as it had come to be known, was favored by many. They were concerned that the Allies would use Australia as a staging area to attack the Japanese and retake lost territory, so it remained a weak point on their perimeter. They wanted to concentrate their forces in order to occupy it and cut it off from Allied support. But Fuchida felt this was simply wasting time and taking resources from what he saw as the primary goal: destroying the remaining American carriers as quickly as possible, then bringing the conflict to a resolution through negotiations.

"Gentlemen," Yamamoto began, "we have reached an agreement with the Naval General Staff in Yokosuka on the next plan of operations. The Americans have done us a favor by their foolish air raid. They say, 'A bungling attack is better than the most skillful defense.' True enough, but they've made clear to us that their carriers must be destroyed, immediately. This was our missed objective in the Pearl Harbor operation, but we will not fail this time."

Fuchida began to smile as he leaned forward.

"In their weakened position and low morale, they won't venture a serious attack, so we will carry out Imperial General Headquarters Navy Order Number Eighteen—the seizure and occupation of Midway Island."

Several admirals nodded with approval. Fuchida immediately looked down and exhaled abruptly.

"Midway is a strategic island they cannot afford to lose, yet, at over one thousand miles from Oahu, it's beyond the reach of their land-based fighters. They'll be forced to send their carriers and whatever remaining strength to come to its defense, where we'll be waiting with the overwhelming force to *crush* them." Yamamoto's eyes gleamed. The Midway Atoll was a tiny, but significant, piece of real estate, virtually equidistant from Asia and North America, which housed a Naval Air Station, served as a refueling center for ships, and as a submarine base.

Vice Admiral Nagumo cleared his throat. "Admiral, when do you propose launching this attack?"

"There will be a full moon on June first. As close as possible to this date."

Murmurs filtered through the room. Fuchida's mind swirled. He couldn't fathom launching such a colossal attack in only *five weeks*. The Pearl Harbor attack had taken *months* of planning, practice, and tremendous organization of resources—and that was against an unprepared enemy. This time, the Americans would most likely be ready, or at least watchful, and the battle would require *far* greater resources.

Yamamoto looked out with authority. "Much later and we won't have adequate moonlight for night maneuvers on the beaches. Time is not in our favor. The balance of power will shift to the Americans if they're allowed to rebuild while retaining their surviving carriers." He turned to Nagumo. "You will command our six aircraft carriers, with Fuchida initiating the air attack on Midway. You will destroy their aircraft both on the ground and in the air to prepare for the occupation of the island. Then your fleet will provide air protection for the main fleet of seven battleships, their support ships, and troop carriers when they arrive for the landing of five thousand infantrymen on Midway two days later."

Fuchida tried not to sigh. It seemed like too much too soon.

"The Americans cannot react in fewer than three days from the time we begin. With over two hundred ships amassed for this battle, we will overwhelm and destroy *any* force the Americans could possibly respond with. Hawaii and the entire West Coast of the United States will be exposed and unprotected. After two months of continued operations in the southeast Pacific, we will take the territory of Hawaii, and they will be forced to the bargaining table. They'll be left with little choice but to negotiate terms for peace favorable to Japan."

As a junior officer, Fuchida was pushing things to venture any comments in such a setting, but he felt compelled to speak. He inhaled cautiously. "Admiral, please excuse me for speaking, but as you are well aware, Admiral Nagumo and the First Air Fleet have completed four months of demanding service covering over fifty thousand nautical miles. Our ships and aircraft are in need of repair, and the pilots may require time to recuperate to perform at their best before such a significant –"

"Out of the question. We must act *now*. This will be the decisive battle in the Pacific. Then we will have an impenetrable defensive perimeter to prevent another attack against our homeland." He leaned on the table and pounded his fist. "I am determined to *never* again allow American bombers over Tokyo to threaten our emperor!"

Chapter 51

Late April 1942. The Imperial Palace.

Emperor Hirohito reclined in a stuffed sable-brown leather chair, alone in a darkened room, the smoke of his cigarette illuminated by a movie projector clattering behind his right shoulder. He gazed without expression at Donald Duck hopelessly trying to free himself from a folding beach chair in the Disney film *Donald's Vacation*. A servant arrived with tea on an inlaid wooden tray. Without turning his eyes, the emperor inquired, "Where did you say they found this again?"

"Guam, Your Majesty. When we took the island in December."

The emperor picked up the teacup from the tray and looked back at the screen. "It's very funny," he said plainly.

"Yes, Your Majesty. May I get you anything else?"

He gave no answer as he sipped his tea and studied an angry, frustrated Donald Duck, trapped in his misfolded chair, quacking curses at a string of chipmunks stealing his food. A smile crept across the emperor's lips. "You see?" He glanced at the servant, then pointed at the screen. "Even the big duck is trapped by his love of luxury and easily defeated by a group of smaller creatures with fighting spirit."

Chapter 52

Grasping his bamboo sword with both hands beside his head, Fuchida lunged at Genda who parried off the glance. "This is nonsense!" Fuchida exclaimed. "Of *course* Tokyo will be bombed again."

Below deck in a cleared out storage area of scuffed walls, Fuchida and Genda, both barefoot, traded blows with shinai[21] in the martial art of kendo on the matted floor. They wore traditional broad, black pants, and full protective gear—black canvas helmets with wide flaps and ribbed metal masks, padded gauntlets, and black leather breastplates.

"Move the emperor to Kyoto or Nara," Fuchida said angrily, "but we shouldn't be taking a defensive posture!" He lunged again with a strike toward Genda's head.

Genda quickly deflected it with a crack and countered with a strike at Fuchida.

"A samurai carries no shield!" Fuchida said.

With the outlawing of the samurai class in the nineteenth century, they faded from their prior position of status, but the age-old martial art of kendo, "the way of the sword," found its place in the early twentieth century. The sport grew in popularity, eventually being performed before the emperor himself. Along with restoring the values of Bushido—"the way of the warrior," the samurai code of conduct,[22] kendo honed the mind and body as a classical fighter.

---

[21] Bamboo practice sword.

[22] Based on the seven virtues of rectitude (or integrity), courage, benevolence, respect, honesty, honor, and loyalty.

"If we can draw out their carriers, we'll defeat them," Genda said between breaths. "The Americans have little left to fight with. It would be nearly impossible for them to put up much fight at all."

Fuchida lowered his shinai and stepped up to Genda. "What a nonsensical operation! Our battleships will be three hundred miles behind us. What the hell can they do with those guns back there? At least if they were ahead of us, they could help defend our carriers! That's where we need them." Fuchida angrily jerked his shinai up into a defensive posture and stepped back. Genda leaped forward with a series of violent swings that Fuchida fended off.

"I don't think we'll need them," Genda said.

Fuchida stood erect and gestured with his free hand. "And why would the Americans risk their remaining carriers to defend a tiny island? What if they don't come out at all? When we take the island, how will we defend it from four thousand miles away?" Fuchida crouched again and circled to his right raising his shinai. "If we cut off Australia from American support by attacking Fiji and Samoa . . ." he lunged forward and struck Genda on the shoulder, "... then launch another full-scale attack on Pearl Harbor, *that*

Kendo fencing practice in the 1920s.

will bring out their fleet."

Panting, Genda pushed up his helmet to reveal his sweaty head wrapped in cotton cloth. "The plan is decided." He pulled off his helmet and unwrapped his head, as did Fuchida, who wiped the sweat from his face with the cloth. Genda continued, panting, "But then, you knew that . . . from the beginning. Once Yamamoto made up his mind . . . he had set his course." The two retired to a storage closet.

Fuchida said, "We're rushing into a plan without the ability to prepare."

Genda untied the straps of his gauntlets and tossed them on a shelf one at a time. "By the way, we've recovered some of the American B-25s in China. They ran out of fuel and crashed."

Fuchida looked at Genda with keen interest, the sweat dripping down his cheeks.

"They were medium bombers fitted with extra fuel tanks for a one-way long-range attack, we now think from a carrier. They were to land in China from the start. That's how they did it."

Unfastening his breastplate, Fuchida paused, then nodded. "Yankee ingenuity." He picked up a pack of cigarettes, shook one out, and raised it to his lips. "Very clever."

Chapter 53

Late April 1942. Madras, Oregon.

Mrs. Andrus dumped a scoop of grain into a pail as hungry horses in their stalls anxiously leaned out and pawed the sawdust. As she dug the scoop into the barrel of grain, her red merle Australian Shepherd let out a howl and a string of barks. She turned to see two black sedans pull up to the barn and skid to a stop. Four men in brown suits stumbled out with notepads. She knew it was good news or bad news about Jake and feared the worst.

"Excuse me, ma'am," the first one shouted as he trotted up and tipped his fedora. "Are you Mrs. Andrus, the mother of Jacob DeShazer?"

"That I am," she said politely.

"We're from the *Oregon Journal*."

"And *The Oregonian*," another declared.

"And would just like to get some details, and maybe a picture of your son, Jake."

"He's a hero," a third reporter chimed in.

Goosebumps skimmed over her back and arms. She'd read about Jake's adventure like everyone else, but with the joy only a mother could understand. Now the press wanted to know more.

The Doolittle Raid brought a boost to US morale across the country, but in the tiny town of Madras where wheat prices and weather were big news, word that one of their own was part of the bold attack on Japan was *sensational*.

"That's Jake all over," Mrs. Andrus said proudly. "He's daring—would never do anything that looked like a sissy."

The reporters scrawled furiously.

"From the first he wanted to get into the fight. Said he'd like to go over

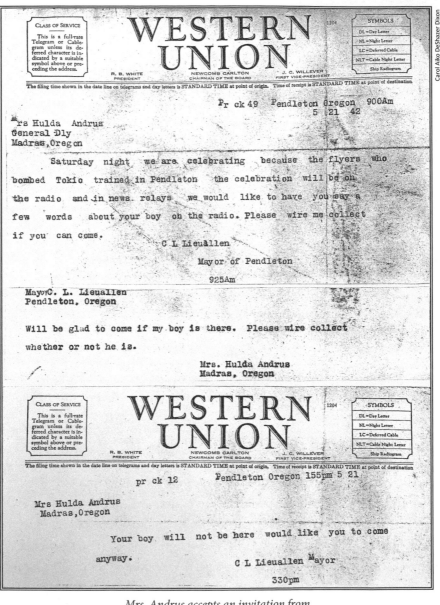

WESTERN UNION

CLASS OF SERVICE
This is a full-rate Telegram or Cablegram unless its deferred character is indicated by a suitable symbol above or preceding the address.

R. B. WHITE
PRESIDENT

NEWCOMB CARLTON
CHAIRMAN OF THE BOARD

J. C. WILLEVER
FIRST VICE-PRESIDENT

SYMBOLS
DL = Day Letter
NL = Night Letter
LC = Deferred Cable
NLT = Cable Night Letter
Ship Radiogram

The filing time shown in the date line on telegrams and day letters is STANDARD TIME at point of origin. Time of receipt is STANDARD TIME at point of destination.

Pr ck 49   Pendleton Oregon   900Am
5 21 42

Mrs Hulda Andrus
General Dly
Madras, Oregon

    Saturday night we are celebrating because the flyers who
bombed Tokio trained in Pendleton the celebration will be on
the radio and in news relays we would like to have you say a
few words about your boy on the radio. Please wire me collect
if you can come.

            C L Lieuallen

              Mayor of Pendleton

               925Am

Mayor C. L. Lieuallen
Pendleton, Oregon

Will be glad to come if my boy is there. Please wire collect
whether or not he is.

            Mrs. Hulda Andrus
            Madras, Oregon

WESTERN UNION

CLASS OF SERVICE
This is a full-rate Telegram or Cablegram unless its deferred character is indicated by a suitable symbol above or preceding the address.

R. B. WHITE
PRESIDENT

NEWCOMB CARLTON
CHAIRMAN OF THE BOARD

J. C. WILLEVER
FIRST VICE-PRESIDENT

SYMBOLS
DL = Day Letter
NL = Night Letter
LC = Deferred Cable
NLT = Cable Night Letter
Ship Radiogram

The filing time shown in the date line on telegrams and day letters is STANDARD TIME at point of origin. Time of receipt is STANDARD TIME at point of destination.

pr ck 12   Pendleton Oregon 155pm 5 21

Mrs Hulda Andrus
Madras, Oregon

    Your boy will not be here would like you to come
anyway.

          C L Lieuallen Mayor

          330pm

*Mrs. Andrus accepts an invitation from
the mayor of Pendleton—with one condition.*

and help lick the Japs."

"Are you concerned about him?" the first reporter asked.

Mrs. Andrus dumped another scoop of grain into the pail. She looked at the reporters with a smile. "The last note he sent me said, 'Don't worry about me, Mom, I'm in no danger.'" She carried the pail and leaned over the stall fence and dumped the grain into a bucket hanging beside a black horse.

The fourth reporter in a tan herringbone suit spoke up. "You know, he hasn't been located yet. If he falls into Jap hands, can he take the torture they dish out?"

Mrs. Andrus stopped and turned to the reporter and looked him in the eye, her gentle smile turning into a hard glare. "I said he's no sissy."

WAR DEPARTMENT

WASHINGTON

May 22, 1942

Mrs. Hulda Andrus
General Delivery
Madras, Oregon

Dear Mrs. Andrus:

I am extremely sorry to have to bring you bad news. It is not, however, absolutely reliable. The latest information we are able to get is that you son landed near Japanese occupied territory and that two of the crew members are missing and three have been taken prisoner by the Japanese. We are unable to definitely authenticate this report, and are also unable to determine which of the crew members are missing and which captured. An attempt is being made today, through the American Red Cross, to obtain more definite information. As fast as we obtain any additional information you may depend on my passing it on to you.

I am sincerely sorry that I am obliged to give you such an unfortunate report. I do want to point out however that your son comported himself with conspicuous bravery and distinction. He was awarded the Distinguished Flying Cross for gallantry in action and also was decorated by the Chinese Government.

I am proud to have served with Jacob, and hope that I may have an opportunity to serve with him again soon.

Very sincerely yours,

J. H. DOOLITTLE
Brigadier General, U. S. Army

P.S. As the above information is of military significance, it is requested that it be kept in the strictest confidence.

*A personal letter written by General Doolittle brought
little consolation and raised as many questions as it answered.*

Chapter 54

Late April 1942. Nanking,[23] China.

Blindfolded, unshaven, and filthy, Jake sat in a darkened room at a small table with his wrists cuffed together on his lap. He had had little to eat the past few days and even less sleep. He had no idea where he actually was and had completely lost track of time. His wrists ached.

A Japanese officer sat across from him at the table lit by a single hanging lamp. Three soldiers stood near a wall to the side, curiously observing. The officer snarled in English, "Who sent you on this mission?"

Jake gave no reply.

"Where did you fly from?"

Jake remained steadfast.

"Where - did - you - fly - from?!"

Jake knew what he was supposed to do. "My name is Jacob DeShazer, corporal, US Army Air Corps, serial number zero-six-five-eight— "

"Idiot! Don't you know what we can do to you?! We'll torture you and then we'll *shoot* you!" The interrogator stood up abruptly, knocking his own chair back onto the floor with a crack. He walked up beside Jake, leaned down, and spoke softly. "Did you know we have bombed San Francisco?" He moved right up to Jake's face. "We now occupy the city. Right now, our emperor is riding his white horse down the streets of your city." He paused a moment, then burst into cackling laugh.

He turned to one of the soldiers and blurted out in Japanese. "Take him to Kuroyama!" Two soldiers clenched his arms, hoisted him to his feet,

---

[23] Modern Nanjing, China.

and dragged him out the door.

In his darkness, Jake could tell they led him up a couple of flights of stairs, then they shoved him into another room where a soldier finally untied his black blindfold. Jake squinted and blinked as he stood in the harsh, incandescent light staring at a short, stocky officer puffing on a cigar on the other side of a table scattered with papers. Several other soldiers surrounded him. Now what?

The officer rubbed his hands together, then plucked the cigar from his mouth. "I wish you to know that I want to treat you good," the officer said with a British accent. He pointed at Jake. "*Very* good. I have the reputation of being the kindest judge in *all* of China. You know this? You're lucky to have me question you. You answer my questions, and I'll get you a glass of milk." He once again sucked the smoke from his stogie.

Jake looked around the room at his captors when a soldier from behind yelled something in Japanese and forced him down into a chair. The officer carefully slid some papers in front of Jake, all the while staring into his eyes. The water-stained sheets of paper were burned along one edge. The hair stood up on Jake's neck. It was a roster of the entire list of men on the Doolittle Raid retrieved from one of the wrecked B-25s. Jake pretended not to care. The records should have been destroyed by the crews before ditching the aircraft. Fools.

The officer confidently blew a cloud of smoke. "You and your friends, eh?" He waited for an answer. "Do you know this Doolittle?"

Jake stared at the wall. "I've heard of him. I think he's a stunt pilot." He swallowed hard with a dry throat. Man, was he thirsty.

The officer pounded his fist on the table, "*Look* at me when you answer!"

Jarred, but retaining his composure, Jake stared again into the officer's eyes, who quickly diverted his own away.

The officer paced and came back to the table. "Where are the Chinese hiding their gasoline?"

Jake knew that, as a prisoner of war, he was only required to give his name, rank, and serial number, but he also knew that, although the Japanese signed the Geneva Convention, they never ratified it and didn't have such a good reputation when it came to Chinese prisoners of war. But all that didn't even matter now since he really *didn't* know.

"Where is it?!" the officer said.

Again Jake looked up into the officer's face. "I don't know, and if I did, I wouldn't say."

Perturbed, the officer glanced over to the other soldiers, then back to Jake. He spoke with an air of confidence, "What does H-O-R-N-E-T spell?"

"Hornet."

"And what is that?"

Jake thought for a second. "It's a bug." He raised his cuffed hands and gestured with his fingers. "A kind of wasp that— "

The officer slapped his hand on the papers. "That is the name of the aircraft carrier you flew from to bomb Japan! Isn't it?!"

Jake stared at the officer's hand flat against the papers, then looked him back in the eyes. "I wouldn't know. I'm not in the navy. I'm in the Army Air Corps."

"And Doolittle was your commanding officer. Right?!"

"You know I can't answer that question."

Slowly walking to Jake's side of the table the officer drew his sword from its scabbard and, with both hands, suspended it above Jake's head. "It's considered a great honor for a judge to cut off the head of a prisoner! Tomorrow at sunrise I will have this honor!" He lowered his sword while staring at Jake, then slowly sheathed it. "What do you think about *that?*" He crossed his arms firmly.

Jake sat stoically gazing at the wall in front of him. "I think it would be a great honor for me to have the kindest judge in all of China cut off my head."

The room burst into chuckles, and the officer smiled and nodded. Jake showed no emotion. "Takeshita," the officer said staring at Jake with admiration, "go get him a glass of milk."

Early the next morning, Jake stood before an aging concrete wall— handcuffed and blindfolded. He'd barely slept the previous night while still handcuffed on a bare wooden floor with no blankets, and he hadn't eaten in a day, other than the cup of milk he accidentally won. Nothing seemed to matter to him now, and it showed in his hunched posture. He could hear the men speaking among themselves and discerned clicking of sticks of some kind. From what he'd been told, you didn't really feel a thing when they cut off your head. They used pretty sharp swords. They even made a game of it sometimes. Would his mom ever know what happened, or why? He wasn't sure why himself. He tried to swallow.

"Are you ready?" one soldier said to another in Japanese.

"I'm ready."

A soldier exclaimed in English "Prisoner, stand up straight."

Jake straightened up a bit. He was as ready as he'd ever be.

"OK, go ahead."

Someone slid off Jake's blindfold and he strained his eyes in the daylight sun. Another soldier unlocked his handcuffs.

Jake looked for the officer with the sword, but only saw a group of soldiers around a camera on a tripod. He was confused and, in a strange way, almost disappointed. "You want me to smile or something?" Jake said.

"Be still!" A shutter clicked. The photographer wound the film forward, then clicked again.

"Take him to the airport with the others," the photographer said motioning to a soldier. "Put the blindfold and handcuffs back on."

Chapter 55

May 1, 1942. Midway War Games on the Battleship Yamato. Hashirajima Anchoring Area, twenty-five miles south of Hiroshima.

The late afternoon sun shimmered over the peaceful waves as the fleet sat at rest in the bay. Inside the *Yamato*, it was war. Admiral Yamamoto and a crowd of elite officers anxiously stared down on a map table big enough to park a car on, watching an aide push markers across the chart for their war games. His guts were taut. The turning of the entire Pacific War could hinge on this single battle—a plan of his own making.

A "runner" strode up to Vice Admiral Nagumo, saluted, and held out a note with his other hand. This was day one of the war games and Nagumo's forces were engaging Midway by aerial assault, just like he'd done at Pearl Harbor.

"Sir, Red Team sends carrier attack aircraft against the Carrier Strike Force."

Yamamoto watched Genda shake his head and unconsciously roll his lit cigarette between his fingers as a scorekeeper placed a set of tiny red aircraft to the flank of

The master strategist, Admiral Yamamoto pores over a naval map.

University of Pittburgh

Rear Admiral Matome Ugaki,
chief of staff of the Combined Fleet
directly under Admiral Yamamoto.

Nagumo's fleet. The operation depended on surprise. Everyone knew that anything less could be disastrous. This was a bad start for the games, which would last for four days.

Ugaki, the judge, announced, "Two Red Team carrier air groups attack the Nagumo Force. Carriers *Shokaku, Kaga*, and *Soryu* are under attack."

The map displayed Japan, part of Russia, the Aleutian Islands, and the Hawaiian Islands—an area comprising over 15,000,000 square miles. Just southeast of the center of the map stood a red pin marking the nearly invisible and previously unimportant Midway Atoll, a tiny barrier reef with a few sand islets at the far northwestern tip of the Hawaiian island chain. Yamamoto had hoped the defense of this atoll would be the bait to draw the Americans into their trap. Nagumo's main body of the Combined Fleet was approaching from the northwest of Midway Island.

Every high-ranking officer of the Imperial Japanese Navy surrounded the table and intently peered down on the clusters of miniature blue wooden warships representing the various Japanese strike and occupation forces. Red miniatures represented the American surface forces.

With the advent of the Doolittle Raid, Yamamoto had finally won the battle with headquarters to gain approval of his plan to attack the Americans at Midway, but they mandated the plan be tested by the sharpest minds on his staff. They insisted Yamamoto put all doubts to rest before engaging in battle.

War games were serious business. Yamamoto, a keen poker player, knew that even the slightest error could result in disaster, and the "chips" he was playing with was over 200 naval vessels. It was in this gambling den that the commanders had to predict the unpredictable and expect the unexpected. The capture of Midway and the destruction of the American carriers were only a part of an ambitious and complex second phase of the war. Faltering here could be catastrophic, and Yamamoto knew it more than any of them.

For these war game exercises, Combined Chief of Staff Rear Admiral Ugaki acted both as commander in chief of the Blue Japanese Forces and as a judge. The commanders of the Red American Forces directed their navies from two other rooms.

Yamamoto's plan was for Vice Admiral Nagumo, leader of the Pearl Harbor attack, to once again lead the critical Carrier Strike Force, this time

The Midway Atoll, a distant member
of the Hawaiian island chain, November 1941.

against Midway. Genda stood beside him, both literally and figuratively. Admiral Yamamoto, the highest-ranking officer in the room, would lead the main force of the Combined Fleet, 600 miles to the rear of Nagumo's forces to keep himself hidden from the Americans. By the time the US forces came to defend their island, they would be ambushed by the overwhelming combined force of Nagumo's attack carriers and of Yamamoto's battleships in a later wave to clean up what would be left of the American fleet. At least, that's what he'd planned and hoped for.

After capturing Midway and destroying the American fleet, he would send his forces down to the northeast of Australia to take New Caledonia and Fiji to establish further bases and cut off the Americans from Australia. Finally, within two months of the Midway invasion, Yamamoto would send the full force of the Combined Fleet to attack and occupy Hawaii. The war would be over. America would have to accept Japanese terms.

The war games weren't intended to evaluate Yamamoto's chances or to alter the overall plan, but to anticipate potential problems and to correct them with appropriate tactics. He expected that only one bloody-fisted fighter would be left standing in this high stakes "winner take all" death match, but he was impatient and anxious to be done with the games and to get underway into battle. The games were perfunctory to him, simply to please headquarters.

An umpire with a black cup in his hand containing one die stood motionless waiting for Yamamoto, hunched over the edge of the map leaning on his outstretched arms. He was torn between wanting success and fearing compromising the very purpose of the games. After a few, long seconds, Yamamoto looked up from the top of his eyes at the umpire and nodded.

The murmuring in the room dissolved into the hollow rattling of the die in the black cup held against the officer's hand. He slapped the cup onto the table and slowly raised it revealing a three. "*Shokaku* three hits." The cup slapped again, "*Kaga* six hits." And once more, "*Soryu* takes two hits."

The officers sucked air through their teeth. Nagumo folded his arms and glared at Genda. Yamamoto's jaw tightened.

"Eleven enemy hits on Blue Team carriers," the umpire declared stiffly. "*Kaga* is destroyed. *Shokaku* and *Soryu* are badly damaged and out of operation." A scorekeeper leaned out placing black markers on the three carriers in the deadly quiet room.

Yamamoto rubbed his cheek hard. An enemy arrow had found the chink in his armor. His eyes moved to read Nagumo's face. He saw fear.

Ugaki frowned. "Such tactics are impossible on such short notice! An air attack from a carrier could only be from forces positioned and fully prepared for such a strike. Restore the carriers to undamaged condition and continue the exercise!"

The scorekeeper froze.

Yamamoto stood upright as the scorekeeper briefly glanced at him before removing the black markers from the carriers. Yamamoto turned toward Nagumo. "If your aircraft were occupied with the attack on Midway, what would you do if an enemy force appeared on your flank?"

Nagumo swallowed hard and sighed, biding for time. Although he was the commander of the attack force, he was an old-school battleship commander who lacked the expertise of air tactics that Genda had developed, who promptly responded on his behalf, "No matter where or when we meet the Americans, we will prevail. We have more aircraft, we have better aircraft, and we have far more experience. We're simply *better* than they are. We'll wipe them out!"

Yamamoto nodded, but without the confidence he had shown in the past. The games were fanning the embers of doubts he had hoped would have been doused by now.

Captain Miwa spoke up, "Admiral, this matter is of small concern. Our Navy has accumulated an unrivaled string of victories against all adversaries in the Pacific and we're bringing superior forces to this battle. As Commander Genda has stated, our experience is unparalleled. The Americans are mere beginners. Our defensive powers are unbreakable."

Yamamoto spoke quietly, "The American carriers have been showing up unexpectedly."

Ugaki said, "It is unlikely that such a marginal tactic would interfere with the exercise, but it is also true that greater consideration must be given to this possibility." He addressed Genda, "What provisions will you make to guard against an enemy carrier ambush?"

Genda was silent for a moment as he considered, then replied, "During our operations in the Indian Ocean we kept half our aircraft in reserve in case of unexpected developments. We could do so here as well, as six carriers should be sufficient to neutralize Midway in one attack."

Yamamoto faced Nagumo. "Very well. I want constant air protection by Zero fighters, and I want *half* of the bombers held in reserve and equipped with torpedoes for a quick counterstrike against surface units. We *must* be prepared for enemy carriers if they're discovered earlier than we've anticipated!"

Nagumo nodded.

"I'm counting on Fuchida to lead this attack." Yamamoto's piercing eyes spoke louder than his words as he then looked from face to face around the room seeking traces of fear. He felt the gnats of fear pestering his own mind as he peered back down, focusing on the tiny red aircraft on the table. He had gambled big at Hawaii and won against all odds. One last bet to win it all—or lose it all. He sighed heavily, slowly lifting his eyes to a porthole, and gazed out to the ocean horizon in the fading light beyond.

"Sir," Nagumo said confidently, "there is no better pilot in the Imperial Navy. We will succeed!"

Chapter 56

Early May 1942. Hopevale, the island of Panay,
The Philippine Islands.

Precariously perched on the upper frame of his new bamboo hut in progress, Jimmy yanked off his straw hat and smeared the sweat of his forehead off onto his equally sweaty arm. It was like a sauna, only with cockroaches, giant monitor lizards, scorpions, and the biggest centipedes he'd ever seen. Fred had killed an eleven-foot python in their camp. At least he was off the ground, for now.

Local Filipinos pitched in to show Jimmy and the others how to build their own nipa huts on stilts off the damp ground and away from the rats. Split bamboo woven with grass made up the floors, which were sturdy and let the air flow through from the cooler earth below. Men fastened premade walls of woven nipa palms with openings for windows shuttered by tilt-out covers held by sticks.

Traditional construction of a nipa hut on stilts as they've been built for hundreds of years.

He was glad to get a "home" built, even though he knew they'd only need it for a few months—six or so, he figured—until the Americans came to liberate the island from the

Dr. Fred Meyer, a Yale graduate and doctor at Emmanuel Hospital in Capiz for twenty-three years, he and his wife chose to stay on Panay to help.

Japanese. Jimmy looked down at Charma lugging a sheaf of cogon grass on her back for the roof. "Faster. I can't do this all by myself, you know."

"That's real funny." She heaved the load onto the ground. "Let's switch when you get tired of sitting up there."

Jimmy tipped his hat, then went back to strapping the bamboo beams to each other with split strands of banban.

Others kindled a fire to boil rice for lunch as a local woman led a pig on a rope leash into a makeshift pen. In little over a month, the band of refugee faculty members, missionaries, and teachers had begun to establish themselves in the lush, deeply forested mountains.

Francis Rose couldn't resist opening up the portable Estey reed organ Jimmy and Charma had lugged all the way from Japan to Iloilo and was dying to give it an airing under the leafy

Their faithful organ in use in Japan at a mountain retreat. Jimmy Covell seated at the rear resting his head on his hands.

awning. He brushed off the dirt and unlatched the cover as Signe Erickson, with a brilliant pink orchid pinned above her right ear, began assembling her flute. With several Filipino men hacking at bamboo behind him, Fred, now sitting on a suitcase before the organ, looked at Signe and nodded. He closed his eyes and, taking a deep breath, started pumping the pedals to commence Bach's Prelude No. 1 in C major. On cue, Signe released the fluid melody of Charles Gounod's Ave Maria, which mingled perfectly with the fresh mountain air, harmonizing with the peaceful atmosphere of Hopevale.

Born in Pennsylvania to Swedish immigrant parents, Signe Erickson double-majored in Theology and Missions before volunteering to serve in the Philippines.

As the music filtered through the jungle, all paused to enjoy the serenity of their safe haven. Even the monkeys stopped swinging between branches to listen.

Miss Adams, a nurse who'd long worked beside Dr. Meyer at the hospital, looked up to listen as she hand-fed cooked rice to a small parrot perched on her hand, a Philippine Hanging Parrot, a bright green, red-beaked bird splashed with red, orange, and yellow. She didn't tame the bird—it simply had no fear of people and ate freely from her open palm.

The ambiance of the music enveloped Jimmy as well. Despite fleeing from his home in Japan and again being driven from the city on Panay, he was filled with gratitude for their new home. Every need was met, and now he was living in a surreal paradise, a haven of peace in a world of war.

ABHS

Rev. Erle Round, with his wife Louise, his older son, Donald, and little Erle. Donald and his brother, Richard, had been attending school in Baguio on Luzon when the Japanese invaded and interned them at the Santo Tomas Prison Camp in Manila.

The next day, Francis found a high-walled gorge about 150 feet wide and extending for 400 feet. Moss, vines, flowering orchids, and bushes sprouted over much of the steep, rocky walls and huge shorea trees on the floor, some hundreds of years old, rose to the sky, upholding a canopy so thick, you could only catch glimpses of the heavens above.

A clearing at the base of the biggest tree gave Francis an idea, and he began stacking rocks near the mossy foot of the largest tree to form an altar for an open-air church. Jack, the miner, carried in some reddish rocks that he placed in rows as seats in rows opposite each other facing a center aisle.

Francis built two, neatly stacked "tables" on either side of the front as reading tables. For the altar, he bound two straight branches with strands of banban to make a crude cross, which he securely positioned at the top.

Erle Rounds, an eight-year-old whose parents were also helping with the construction, struggled to lift a small boulder. Jack watched in amusement.

"Jack! Jack, help me!"

Jack came up behind the boy, reached his muscular arms around him, and the two of them grasped the, flat-topped rock and stacked it on a base with a thud.

As he stood upright, Francis squinted while twisting his back to stretch a bit, then pointed to the front. "I want clear a spot over there for the organ and we can fill the entire front with fresh flowers. We've got an endless supply in here, ya know. Well? What do you think, Jack?"

Jack looked up at the vine-covered walls, listened to the chirps of wild birds, the occasional chatter of monkeys, and the distant sound of Jimmy and Signe on organ and flute and took a deep breath of the highland air. "It's nice. Real nice." He slumped down onto one of the stone seats. "You see, you can't quite fall asleep in this kind of chair, no matter how boring the message is." Jack pulled Earl onto his lap. "How many people do you want to accommodate?"

Francis scanned the area. "Enough for seventy-five or so." He peered down at his watch. "Oh yeah," he said while tapping his wrist, "they've got the radio working again, and we're gonna tune in to the report at two o'clock."

Jimmy stood outside his nearly finished hut, adjusting the dial of their battery-operated radio sitting on his porch to minimize the sonic squeal while the silent group of about twenty-five listened in, some with hands to their faces, others with arms folded and heads cocked in anticipation of the news report.

"Good evening everyone, everywhere. This is the Voice of Freedom broadcasting from somewhere in the Philippines. Bataan has fallen!"

Charma gasped.

"The Philippine-American troops on this war-ravaged and bloodstained peninsula have laid down their arms. With heads bloody but unbowed, they have yielded to the superior force and numbers of the enemy. The world will long remember the epic struggle that Filipino and American soldiers put up in the jungle fastness and along the . . ."

Jimmy's entire posture fell as the weight of the defeat sank in. The breathless clan stared at each other in disbelief with the sober realization that their hopes were crushed. There would be no rescue or quick victory.

Chapter 57

May 27, 1942. One week before the battle.

F uchida stared up dejectedly at Genda from his hospital bed, clenching his teeth and shutting his eyes between spasms.

"You picked a fine time for appendicitis," Genda said, turning his head to cough to the back of his hand. Next to Fuchida's bedside in the all-white infirmary room stood Vice Admiral Nagumo and Rear Admiral Kusaka—respectively commander in chief and chief of staff of the First Air Fleet.

The doctor yanked Fuchida's shirt back over his abdomen. "He needs to be transferred to a destroyer and taken to Beppu, the nearest military hospital for surgery," he said. "Immediately."

"No!" Fuchida opened his eyes widely and peered up at the doctor. He couldn't believe his bad luck. Not him. Not here. Not now. The pain was blinding, but he struggled to speak. "The *Akagi* serves as the task force surgical center and is . . . perfectly capable of performing an appendectomy."

"Fuchida," Genda pleaded, "you need to go." Genda coughed and hacked some more.

Fuchida shook his head.

The doctor looked to Nagumo for some sort of response, then at Fuchida. "We'll have to put you under general anesthesia. You'll need to— "

"No! Just use local anesthesia." Fuchida squinted again through the pain. "Even if I can't fly, I can at least be on hand for . . . consultation. I need to be in my right mind. And I'm *not* . . . leaving the *Akagi*!"

The doctor shook his head and spoke to Nagumo. "He *must* stay in bed for at *least* a week. He won't be able to fly for some time. Two weeks after surgery, at least."

Nagumo nodded to the doctor, then let out an angry sigh. "Two of our six carriers have failed to join the fleet because of damage from the battle in the Coral Sea." He rubbed the back of his neck and scanned Fuchida head to toe, then threw his arm out. "Now this!" He turned and stormed out of the room followed by Kusaka.

"You look lousy, pal," Genda said.

"You don't look so good yourself." Fuchida looked up helplessly at Genda. "Lieutenant Tomonaga on . . . on the *Hiryu* will lead. He's a very capable pilot."

Genda gazed back gravely and blinked hard.

Fuchida's eyes said it all: their chances for victory were slipping away.

Part IV

Blood in the Water

Chapter 58

June 4, 1942, 3:00 a.m. The aircraft carrier
Akagi. 250 miles northwest of Midway Island.

Nineteen oil-fired Kampon boilers generating one hundred thirty-two thousand horsepower drove the *Akagi* through the calm morning darkness at battle speed three—full speed. In the control bridge wrapped in four-foot high glass windows, Vice Admiral Nagumo looked down on the idling aircraft on the deck outlined by dim running lights. The captain gradually brought the enormous 850-foot floating runway into the wind. Pilots impatiently idled the thunderous engines of their fighters, white and blue flames flaring from their exhaust pipes in the morning darkness.

In his hospital bed far below decks, Fuchida awoke with a start, the distant rumble of aircraft engines calling him like the voice of an old friend. Doctor's orders or not, nothing could or *should* stop him—the chief flight commanding officer—from making his way to the deck to see his men off. He wasn't going to lie there like a dying animal on the greatest day of the Imperial Navy! Two other patients in beds beside him seemed asleep, so Fuchida eased himself up, but immediately fell back from the pain of his surgical wound.

He pulled up his gown to examine his incision for a second, then yanked it back down. It looked OK to him. Who cared what the surgeon said? With childlike enthusiasm, he tossed off his blanket and rolled onto his side, carefully slid from his bed, and threw on a robe.

"Commander," one of the patients whispered. "Should you be getting out of bed?"

Fuchida stopped for a moment and responded boyishly, "I can't bear to hear the sound of the engines and stay in sick bay." He paused. "You understand."

The patient smiled and nodded. No need for any explanation.

The captain ordered all doors sealed for battle conditions, so Fuchida twisted the large crank of the manhole cover in the center of the door to let himself through, wincing with needles of pain. He felt light-headed and faint as he stepped through and retightened the hatch. Grasping the handrail, he squatted in the passageway to catch his breath. He repeated the ordeal over ten times through a maze of hatches and ladders to finally make it to his bunk where his sweaty body collapsed with quivering pain. But the shuddering roar of each revving engine relentlessly drew him to the deck above. Collecting himself, he quickly wiped off with a washcloth, shaved, dressed in his uniform, and emerged in the lower aircraft hangar.

Under incandescent lights, dozens of engineers in their white jumpsuits fueled the carrier's reserve group of seventeen Type 97 aircraft and armed them with torpedoes in keeping with Yamamoto's instructions, should an American carrier be unexpectedly sighted. If the morning search

Zeroes on the deck of the Akagi *prepare to launch.*

proved negative, the planes could be switched over to bomb armament for a second attack on Midway.

Fuchida made his way through the packed configuration of olive-green aircraft, the paint randomly flaked off the aluminum skin by the salt air and constant service, each tied down over its own white outline for position. The familiar smell of grease, fuel and paint; the clatter of ratchets; and shouts of team members below and the rumble of aircraft above deck invigorated him. He'd walked this deck a hundred times before, but this time, each detail vividly struck him. The blood surged through his veins. He loved his ship. He loved his crew. He couldn't wait to get to the flight deck.

"Commander! Are you all right?" Kanegasaki, Fuchida's engineer from the Pearl Harbor attack, was overseeing four men jack up a 1,841-pound Type 91 torpedo under a Nakajima B5N bomber when he noticed the commander.

"Kanegasaki! I'm fine. Anyway," he said with a shrug, "I can't be in bed under circumstances like these." With a broad smile and a nod, Fuchida kept his posture and stride, never giving a hint of his pain.

The eastern horizon lightened from the dawn when he finally arrived on the flight deck of thirty-one idling aircraft, humming in a deafening chorus. Physically drained by his obstacle course, Fuchida leaned against the sandbagged-encased tower or "island" on the port side of the carrier.

"Are you all right?" a busy air officer shouted out as he trotted past.

Fuchida nodded and waved, put his hands on his knees and slowly lowered himself to lie down on the deck beside the tower. A nearby engineer kindly slid a parachute under Fuchida's head as he strained to watch his men. He was a proud father, even though sidelined.

The *Akagi* flashed a message to the other three carriers from her signal lamp that all was ready, and they flashed back that they were prepared. From the bridge crowded with officers, Vice Admiral Nagumo gave the command, "Launch the air attack force!"

The air officer on the deck blew his whistle and swung his green lantern in a huge circle, signaling the first pilot to take to the air. A flagman waved a white flag toward the front of the ship. Crewmen cheered, waving their white caps as the first fighter let loose his full throttle and roared down the flight deck out over the ocean.

The first few fighters from each carrier spread out around the fleet as part of the combat air patrol to guard against possible attack. One by one, the rest of the fighters and bombers from the four carriers—the *Akagi*, the *Soryu*, the *Hiryu*, and the *Kaga* –formed into groups orbiting their carriers, then joined up into one large formation and headed off to Midway Island. Nagumo mandated radio silence, so no one on board would know anything until the attack was nearly complete and the results had been sent back via radiotelegraph. All was now in the hands of Fuchida's pilots.

As soon as the last plane took off, *Akagi's* elevators whined back into use, bringing up half of the reserve Type 97 bombers armed with torpedoes to the flight deck and once lashed down, began their pre-flight checks. If the American fleet was spotted, they would be ready to strike as quickly as possible.

5:31 a.m.

Vice Admiral Nagumo stood on the bridge peering through a pair of long-range pedestal-mounted binoculars steadily scanning the horizon, now clearly outlined by the glowing orange sky as the sun began to break through. Messages crackled over the ship's intercom in the background. Seeing nothing, he stepped back and looked head to toe at Genda standing beside him looking through the window—in his pajamas: a white, kimono-style robe. He looked terrible. "I thought you were in sick bay with pneumonia."

Genda forced a smile. "Sir, they don't know I'm up here."

Nagumo turned to a newly arrived aide. "What's the report on the first launch?"

The aide saluted. "Admiral, seventy-one attack aircraft with thirty-six escort fighters en route to Midway. One of *Hiryu's* aircraft aborted with a mechanical failure. Eleven combat air patrol fighters over the fleet."

Nagumo returned to his binoculars. "Any sighting of the American fleet from our reconnaissance aircraft?"

"None, sir. We're still waiting for communication from our scouts."

Giving a perturbed glance at Genda, then back to the dawn sky, he exclaimed, "Get in uniform, will you?!"

"Yes, sir," Genda replied sheepishly. He saluted and exited in haste.

Nagumo's air fleet possessed cruisers fitted with floatplanes with the sole task of searching for enemy warships by radiating out from the fleet to about 300 miles, making a dogleg left for 25 miles, then returning back in a pattern like the petals of a daisy. Seven of these scout planes had been launched at the same time as the attack aircraft, around 4:30 a.m.

With perfectly clear visibility, this would have been thin coverage, but under the day's cloudy conditions, they were woefully inadequate to cover their assigned sectors. In addition, the Japanese Navy didn't generally train their seaplane crews as well as their carrier pilots, their aircraft were less reliable, and difficulties in launching that day delayed some scouts as much as half an hour. Aware of these shortcomings, Nagumo considered it unnecessary to alter the standard search pattern—confident that no American carriers were nearby.

University of Pittsburgh

"Sir?!" Rear Admiral Kusaka dialed in the focus of his binoculars. "It appears the cruiser *Nagara* is beginning to lay down a smoke screen up ahead."

"Their lookouts may have spotted enemy aircraft," Genda added.

"Now the *Kirishima* is also laying down smoke," Kusaka continued.

Nagumo remained unperturbed. "Reinforce the air control units from the reserve wave fighters if necessary."

A specialist in naval aviation, Rear Admiral Ryunosuke Kusaka served as chief of staff of the First Air Fleet under Admiral Chūichi Nagumo.

6:20 a.m., Midway Island.

In a sky pocked with hundreds of black bursts of anti-aircraft fire, Japanese dive bombers dropped into their bombing runs at steep angles, engines screaming, and released their explosives, engulfing the tiny island in flames and smoke. Nimble Zero fighters, too quick for the gunners to track, strafed buildings and aircraft hangars as a fuel storage tank erupted into a billowing fireball. Two dozen American fighters engaged the attacking formation of seventy-two bombers escorted by thirty-six Zero fighters and managed to down six or seven Japanese aircraft until, one by one, the more experienced opponents in their superior Zeroes hunted them down. Sixteen American fighters streaked into the sea before the surviving American fighters scattered, unable to protect the island.

7:05 a.m.

The *Akagi* cut through the ocean into a brilliant sunrise when a messenger approached Nagumo, bowed and held out a note from the telegraph office.

Midway Island under siege.

Nagumo plucked the note and quickly scanned it, shook his head and looked back out at the horizon as he spoke to Genda. "Air Commander Tomonaga requests a second attack wave to finish the job at Midway."

All were hoping the first wave from the four carriers would do the job, but Nagumo was also prepared to hear that the defenses of Midway had not been fully disabled as he was denied the attack aircraft of two carriers that were supposed to have joined his fleet. To successfully land the invasion required overcoming the American defenses, especially their ability to launch aircraft.

"Sir," Genda said hesitantly, "Excuse me, but . . . we recognize that Admiral Yamamoto specifically ordered the reserves to be equipped with torpedoes for naval combat in the event we discover the American fleet. It could take as long as two hours to dismount and rearm our aircraft with land bombs, and then we wouldn't be prepared to attack the Americans if they appear. But, I recommend that, if the scouts report nothing soon, we rearm for the heaviest strike possible on Midway. "

Nagumo nodded, "I agree," and looked away.

7:10 a.m.

Lying on the deck below the tower in the ocean breeze, Fuchida jotted notes on a piece of scrap paper. A team of twelve men pushed a light-gray Zero off the elevator onto the grease stained deck, spotting it with the group for the next launch. As the new fighters warmed their roaring engines, Fuchida began to feel somewhat better and slowly got to his feet. Not so bad. Ignoring the ache in his belly, he walked to the front of the tower and looked far to his left, then to his right at the other carriers also sending fighters into the air for protection. He wondered if there'd been any word back on the attack at Midway. Just as he was about to make his way up to the bridge, he heard shouting from a lookout above him.

"Two groups of enemy aircraft approaching from the southeast!"

Fuchida shielded the sun from his eyes and strained to see the aircraft that appeared like small dots just above the horizon, dead ahead. Lacking radar, the fleet relied on keen-eyed lookouts for early detection of the enemy.

From the bridge, Captain Aoki shouted into the speaking tube, "Flank speed! Hard to port!" which threw the ship into a huge, left-handed turn, making the *Akagi* a more difficult target while also giving her battery of anti-aircraft guns full aim at the approaching assailants.

In the air above, Fuchida saw Zeroes falling swiftly toward the advancing American bandits—six TBF Avengers armed with torpedoes comprised the first group. These slow-moving, low-flying aircraft needed to get within close range to have any chance of success and had somehow been separated from their fighter escorts. The lethal Zeroes made easy work of the doomed aircraft and riddled them with machine gun and cannon fire, downing them one by one in eruptions of streaking fireballs that fell twisting into the sea ending in plumes of white ocean mist. But TBF Avengers featured powerful rear-facing .50 caliber guns, whose fire managed to send a Zero tumbling in flames into the sea.

Despite the lashing, Fuchida watched intently as several American bombers managed to drop their deadly fish toward their targets before breaking off under heavy fire from both fighters and the ear-splitting anti-aircraft guns, peppering the sky with exploding shells and tracers as the bombers turned away.

As the huge *Akagi* circled again in the opposite direction, Fuchida scrambled to the port side of the deck in time to see several torpedoes bubble past in the distance. He looked across the water to their sister carrier *Hiryu,* as she also managed to steer clear of approaching torpedoes. No hits.

Fuchida smirked. The Americans were foolish to try an unescorted attack, he thought. They seemed so inexperienced. Just then, four more enemy aircraft came into view, and he could see they were twin-engine bombers, approaching at a speed so fast the fighters had trouble keeping them in their line of attack as they opened fire from above. He trotted back to the tower.

Because the *Akagi* was twisting and turning in a giant figure eight, Genda and Nagumo on the bridge had a hard time keeping track of where the enemy was approaching from, but on the open deck, Fuchida could clearly follow the planes as he watched the converging anti-aircraft fire being thrown up by every ship into the sky.

A fireball shot out from the engine of one of the approaching bombers, sending the plane down, trailing black smoke all the way until it crashed into the ocean. Just as quickly, a Japanese fighter took a hit and spiraled downward ending in a splash of mist.

In the midst of hellacious fire from all sides, all three remaining twin-engine B-26 Marauders splashed their torpedoes into the sea toward the *Akagi*. Taking full advantage of its flight path, one of the Marauders unloaded its machine guns at the *Akagi*, panging the ship with bullets and sending Fuchida leaping behind a huge electric winch for protection. Two gunners on the *Akagi* were not as lucky.

After the plane had roared past, Nagumo breathed a sigh of relief, but as the ship continued in a hard right turn to avoid the incoming torpedoes, an officer on the far right of the bridge turned to Nagumo.

"Admiral?!"

Genda, Nagumo, and the entire group of nearly a dozen bridge officers instantly looked right and stared in disbelief as the last B-26 hurtled directly toward their control tower in an apparent suicide run through a furious crossfire of anti-aircraft rounds pounding the sky.

Standing on the deck below, Fuchida fixed his eyes on the crazed plane

Capable of delivering 4,000 lbs. of bombs, this Pacific-based B-26 Marauder was fitted with the Mark XIII aerial torpedo with 600 lbs. of explosives.

as a bolt of fear shot through his spine for the first time in the battle. If the plane crashed into the tower, it would cripple the carrier as well as wipe out their top officers. Hundreds of rounds of deafening anti-aircraft fire streamed into the air but were failing to stop the Marauder as it bore down on the helpless ship, rapidly approaching closer and closer.

The eyes of all inside the bridge tower grew wide.

Fuchida couldn't believe that Americans had this kind of bravery and zeal for their country to launch a suicide attack. In a matter of seconds, the tower could be pulverized.

The officers instinctively ducked as the plane roared past, missing the tower by mere feet, cartwheeling into flaming shreds into the ocean. A curtain of white spray slowly drifted down to the sea over the sinking wreckage.

"*Enough!*" Nagumo shouted. "Midway's air base *must* be neutralized! Rearm all reserve bombers with land bombs for a second wave. *Immediately!*"

In the hangar below, Kanegasaki and his sweaty aircrew held onto an airplane to keep their balance in another hard turn when the intercom blared out, "Attention, prepare to carry out second assault. Reequip reserve aircraft with land bombs."

Kanegasaki looked at his men with dismay. Switching over a Type 97 bomber from a 17-foot torpedo to a 9-foot land bomb was far easier said than done. Their 5-man crew would have to lower the 1,760-pound torpedo onto a cart, unbolt the mounting bracket, and install a completely different bracket on each plane before they could begin to attach the land bombs—a thirty-minute procedure—and they had only enough carts to do half the squadron at a time. On a normal, rolling sea it was difficult. During evasive maneuvers, it was downright dangerous.

Sighing hard, Kanegasaki waved a mechanic over to wheel an empty cart for a torpedo secured to one of the bellies of the seventeen aircraft in his group. Nagumo gave the same instructions to the carriers *Kaga, Hiryu,* and *Soryu* and the dive bombers on the carriers were also to switch to land bombs. About eighty aircraft in all would have to be systematically switched over.

Two hundred miles east of Nagumo's carriers, a light-gray Aichi E13A long-range reconnaissance seaplane droned through the sky.

As the observer routinely looked down through patchy clouds, he saw what appeared to be foam trails and wakes on the ocean surface reflecting the morning sunlight. He fumbled for his binoculars and focused in.

7:53 a.m.

In the bridge of the *Akagi*, Genda smiled as he received a note from a courier. "Admiral, the battle group reports not a single hit on any fleet vessels."

Nagumo nodded.

An officer peering through one of the mounted, long-range binoculars inside the tower called out, "Admiral—the battleship *Kirishima* is laying down smoke."

On the deck below, Fuchida knew this meant another wave of attack aircraft was approaching their fleet, and this was *bad* timing. Only twenty minutes earlier they had thirty-three Zero fighters in the air protecting the fleet. Now they had merely thirteen since most of the fighters were being refueled and rearmed. But Fuchida doubted that unskilled Americans could penetrate even a moderate defense from their experienced Japanese fighters. He waited to see.

Another officer on the observation deck above the tower looking in the opposite direction through his binoculars sighted the aircraft and announced over the intercom, "Sir, fourteen, no, sixteen aircraft approaching from the southwest. Heading toward the carrier *Hiryu*."

Like patient hawks, the Japanese combat air patrol gathered and descended on the squadron of dive bombers, blazing their guns with relentless precision upon their prey. In seconds, six American planes tumbled in flames to the sea. As the remaining 10 bombers approached the *Hiryu* at a shallow angle, black puffs of flak from *Hiryu's* 5-inch guns began pummeling the formation, then their dozen or so 25mm guns threw up a tapestry of white anti-aircraft fire converging on the ever-approaching bombers.

Wanting to know more of what was going on, Fuchida headed up to the bridge. Arriving, Fuchida's ears tingled as Genda read out the latest radiotelegraph sent back by the No. 4 scout plane from the cruiser *Tone*.

"Sight what appears to be ten enemy surface units—in position bearing ten degrees, distance two hundred forty miles from Midway."

Nagumo glanced at Genda as Fuchida and several other officers rushed to the map table behind them and hunched over.

Genda continued, *"Course one hundred fifty degrees, speed twenty knots."* He handed the telegraph to Nagumo.

"Here!" Fuchida pointed.

"Sir," another officer at the map table said, "enemy position is approximately two hundred miles from our fleet, within striking distance."

"Surface units?!" Nagumo snorted. "What kind? Carriers?" He held on as the *Akagi* heaved into a starboard turn. "That location makes no sense!"

Fuchida agreed. The search arc of the No. 1 scout plane from the *Chikuma* should have spotted the group an hour earlier. The position *didn't* make sense. Not only that, but he knew they couldn't waste their resources on worthless targets like oilers and destroyers. They'd come to take the island and engage the carriers—*period*. Fuchida nervously tapped his finger

Over 1,400 of the Aichi E13A floatplanes were produced,
the most important aircraft of its kind in the Imperial Japanese Navy.

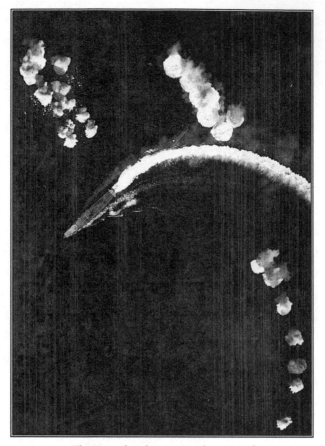

The Hiryu *barely escaping three sets of*
bombs dropped by American B-17 bombers.

on the map. Since the engineers on their carriers were now halfway through the process of rearming the reserve planes for land bombs they'd be unable to quickly attack if they found American carriers, and they didn't have time to waste in making a decision. Fuchida glanced at Genda. They couldn't be fully prepared for a naval attack *and* a land attack at the same time, but which *should* they be prepared for?

Nagumo's patience running thin, he shoved the note back to the messenger. "Have them ascertain what *kind* of ships!"

The bridge officers watched intently as the American dive bombers in the distance which made it through dropped their bombs on the *Hiryu*, each one exploding in columns of gray-white water in the sea. No hits. Smiling again, Fuchida shook his head at the foolishness of attempting such an attack with no fighter support and at such a poor angle, yet he still realized the fleet was lucky to have suffered no damage.

Another courier arrived at the bridge and saluted Vice Admiral Nagumo. "Sir, lookouts report high-level bombers approaching from the northwest. Five groups of three B-17 bombers at approximately twenty thousand feet."

Nagumo nodded almost with a shrug.

Nor did it concern Fuchida. The Japanese defense was performing flawlessly. At twenty thousand feet, any ship would have nearly thirty seconds to change course and evade bombs after they were released. This seemed to him like a desperation run. The Americans had simply run out of options.

With a pair of binoculars in hand, Fuchida stepped out onto the observation platform and looked far up into the sky until he located the group of bombers and followed various planes as they made their runs over their carrier. The five-inch guns of the *Akagi* pounded the sky, but the bombers were out of range. More Zeroes took to the air off the flight deck below him as one group of American bombers released their payload high above, and the *Akagi* went into yet another hard turn to port. After watching the bombs fall for twenty-five seconds, he saw dozens of shells explode in a chain of massive plumes in the sea, hundreds of yards from the ship.

Fuchida smiled. "High-level bombers. Useless."

8:09 a.m.

Nagumo proudly read aloud a fresh transcript from a scouting aircraft. *"The enemy is composed of five cruisers and five destroyers."* He looked around at Genda, Fuchida, and the others as a deep sense of relief settled in among the staff. "Just as I thought. Not an immediate threat." The word spread quickly.

Fuchida knew they had hardly been prepared for a confrontation with the American vessels, anyway. The Japanese fleet could effectively deal with their naval opponents later. Since the base at Midway had sent out all they could muster and would have few aircraft left for another wave for a good while, it was up to the Japanese to get their own second wave off to make an end of Midway's ability to attack the fleet. Hoping for the best, he leaned over the map table and wrote with a grease pencil next to the found American group: "*No carriers.*"

Another courier from the radiotelegraph office entered and handed Genda a note.

"Admiral," Genda said studying the note, "Tomonaga's attack force from Midway requests permission to be immediately recovered." Nagumo listened attentively. "Several aircraft damaged and others low on fuel."

Nagumo looked at Genda while bracing against a window frame, glanced down at the tilted deck as the *Akagi* pitched into a hard turn, and looked back at Genda. Obviously, no one would be landing until they were no longer under attack and could hold a steady course into the wind. Nagumo said, "Prepare for recovery operations. Signal first division to launch all its available fighters now so we don't have to reinforce air patrol while we recover our aircraft."

8:30 a.m.

Panting, a messenger arrived at the bridge and rushed before the admiral with a quick salute and blurted out, "Sir! From *Tone* number four scout. Enemy force accompanied by what appears to be an aircraft carrier." The bridge command reeled from the shockwave. Fuchida could think of only one thing—if they were close enough to strike the American carriers, then the Americans were close enough to strike them.

In frustration, Nagumo shot a glance at Genda as their plans crumbled before them, then faced the bow. "Prepare to carry out attacks on enemy fleet units. Leave torpedoes on those attack planes which have not yet been changed to bombs."

Below decks beneath a tied down bomber, Kanegasaki wiped the sweat from his brow, tightening the last bolt of a land bomb to the belly of a Nakajima B5N when the intercom echoed out once again, "Attention!

Suspend rearming operations immediately! Prepare weapons for attack against enemy ships!" His crew, bracing against a torpedo on its cart, stared at each other incredulously. Even with brakes on the cart, they strained to keep it from shifting as the *Akagi* continued its drastic evasive actions.

Another breathless courier arrived on the bridge, saluted the admiral, and read his message, "Sir! Admiral Yamaguchi of the *Hiryu* sends this message, 'Consider it advisable to launch attack force immediately!'"

Nagumo pursed his lips in frustration as he watched the last of *Akagi's* available fighters running down the flight deck on its takeoff run.

Admiral Kusaka shook his head, "Admiral, the scout should have identified a *Yorktown* or *Lexington*-class carrier by now. They said only that something which *appears* to be a carrier is following—most likely a small converted carrier providing air defense, like the *Hōshō.*"

Fuchida could see the wheels turning in his Nagumo's head. He could launch the dive bombers from the carriers *Hiryu* and *Soryu* which were already rearmed with anti-ship bombs, but only some of the level bombers on the *Akagi* and *Kaga,* which were in a state of confusion due to the suspension order. Also, there were few Zeroes able to escort the assault. Without their protection, Nagumo's attack aircraft could easily undergo the same fate that the Americans had just suffered in their futile offensives. Last of all, the circling attack planes returning from Midway were running low on fuel and had to be landed soon, or they'd be crashing into the sea. But if it meant the difference between victory and defeat, the aircraft could be fetched from the ocean by escorts while the strike was launched.

The eyes of the officers were fixed on Nagumo's face. He was on the horns of dilemma—launch now and get in the first strike and perhaps land a lethal blow against the Americans, but risk suffering heavy losses, including many returning aircraft, *or* wait and launch a combined attack with fighter escorts for an overwhelming assault while running the risk of allowing a possible American attack that could cripple his fleet.

He turned to his officers. "We will prepare to recover Tomonaga's strike force, then make preparations to launch a combined attack against the American carrier. We should be able to begin launching an air strike no later than ten o'clock." He ordered the messenger, "Have our fleet notified that after recovering all aircraft, we are to proceed north to engage and destroy the enemy task force."

8:40 a.m.

The next message received from the *Tone* No. 4 scout located a second group of American warships nearby to the first. No additional carrier had been confirmed but the possibility of an enemy fleet carrier was increased, and the opportunity to sink so many ships was now too great to ignore.

Nagumo ordered, "The American group is probably a surface force with a small carrier for protection. As our first attack proved insufficient because it used only half our strength, we will use all our aircraft for our next attack. We are to strike with all of our strength delivered in one massive blow. Then our battlecruisers can finish the enemy fleet while we turn and attack Midway with another such attack before nightfall."

Genda looked over at Fuchida. This was *exactly* what the war games scenario predicted, but the timing couldn't have been worse.

Chapter 59

8:50 a.m.

With the last of the returning bombers dropping to the flight deck and bouncing to a halt in the arresting wire, reports filtered up to the bridge about how the assault on Midway had progressed.

Fuchida read off a message to the officers. "Commander Tomonaga reports: *Midway Island heavily defended. Anti-aircraft fire fiercer than expected. Few aircraft at base making the attack of limited effectiveness.*"

As the bridge officers looked on, Genda prodded, "Casualty report?"

Fuchida shifted papers. "*Eleven aircraft lost. Fourteen seriously damaged. Twenty-nine aircraft in need of repair.*"

He folded the papers and looked up soberly. Fuchida wondered—if this is what they had lost on the first strike, what could they expect on the second? Why was such a tiny island so strongly defended?

But that was another concern. Now he only wanted to see his men get aloft as soon as possible to give a punishing blow to the American carrier and send it to the bottom. He knew that Japanese forces had sunk two American carriers just weeks earlier at the Battle of the Coral Sea and that a third American carrier was under repair in California. That left only two American carriers in the entire Pacific, and they had found one. Despite their loss of aircraft, with four Japanese carriers of highly experienced pilots, Fuchida was sure they'd have the upper hand. They *had* to finish the job.

8:55 a.m. The battleship Yamato.

Three hundred miles west of Nagumo's striking force, at the bridge of the mighty battleship *Yamato*, Admiral Yamamoto stood staring through

Yamamoto's flagship, the Yamato, *on the open sea.*

the windows over two huge gun turrets into the endless sea when a courier from the radiotelegraph office appeared.

"Admiral, sir, Vice Admiral Nagumo relays this message: '*Enemy composed of one carrier, five cruisers, and five destroyers sighted at zero eight hundred in position bearing ten degrees, distance two hundred forty miles from Midway. We're heading for it.*'"

Yamamoto nodded nonchalantly and turned to the ship's captain. "Do you think we should order Nagumo to attack the US carrier force at once?" He paused. "I think we had better do so."

The captain gave a slight grin. "Sir, Nagumo has reserved half his air force to attack enemy ships and is certainly preparing for an immediate strike."

Yamamoto grunted, nodded, and allowed himself a small grin as well. "Of course."

8:55 a.m. The carrier Akagi.

"Sir," an officer addressed Nagumo in the *Akagi* bridge, "*Tone* scout number four acknowledges your orders to remain in his area. He also communicates that ten enemy torpedo bombers are heading toward you, about twenty-five minutes out." The courier cautiously looked for a reaction.

Fuchida felt flush. Not only were the Americans going to get in the next punch before they could get their strike force aloft, but it would also delay their ability to spot their aircraft on deck.

Nagumo barked to his chief of staff, Admiral Kusaka, "Reinforce the air control units with fighters returned from Midway."

Kusaka nodded and replied, "Sir, the Midway fighters are in the process of recovery for refueling. Three from each carrier will be held back to escort the strike and the rest will join the patrol."

"Be *quick*, then!" Nagumo said. "And find out when we'll be prepared to launch our attack against the Americans!"

A few minutes later, Kusaka returned to the bridge. Fuchida could tell by his face that it wasn't going to be good news.

"Sir, the torpedo planes will not be ready for launch on the *Kaga* and *Akagi* until ten-thirty and the second division reports theirs may be as late as eleven. Evasive maneuvers will make the operation even more difficult. The crews are temporarily storing the dismounted weapons in the hangers to speed things along. Our dive bombers back from Midway will have time to join in the attack. I will issue instructions."

Nagumo cocked his head back, jutted out his chin, and looked down to his lower right at the deck of the *Akagi* as a Zero fighter came to a stop on the deck.

Fuchida could see in his eyes the bitter disappointment of having to endure another onslaught of American bombers before being able to launch their own strike force. They'd been lucky so far, but no one knew if that luck could last. This was getting ridiculous. They absolutely had to get into the fight. *Quickly.*

9:18 a.m.

The four Japanese carriers had just finished recovering their aircraft and would soon turn northeast to close the distance on their quarry. Kanegasaki, in the hangar below, urged on his perspiring men as they detached a 1,760 lb. bomb from a Nakajima B5N2 and laid it to the side of the hanger in a growing heap of munitions. Despite the chaos, discipline was holding. Out of his sight in the forward hanger, the *Akagi* had recovered its fighters and lowered them into the hangars for rearming and refueling. The lethal Zero fighters had done marvelously, but they had an acute weakness: although they carried 500 rounds of 7.7 mm ammunition for each of their two machine guns, they were often ineffective against the heavily armored American planes. Their 20 mm explosive cannon rounds were deadly, fired from two other guns in their wings, but each fighter carried only sixty rounds per gun or *seven seconds* of cannon fire.

Kanegasaki shook his head. It seemed to him it might have been better just to send the strike armed as it was rather than try to rearm in the constantly shifting hangar from the zigzagging evasive maneuvers of the *Akagi*. And moving the heavily loaded aircraft with torpedoes into takeoff position would be equally dangerous. The sooner the planes with their deadly contents were launched, the happier he would be.

An officer on the bridge peering through binoculars alerted, "*Tone* and *Chikuma* laying down smoke!"

A topside lookout shouted, "Sixteen bombers approaching! Twenty-five miles out!"

All three long-range binoculars in the bridge swung to the horizon.

"Fifteen or sixteen bombers," a bridge officer rattled off as he studied the group. "Appear to be torpedo bombers. No escort fighters in view. Approximately ten minutes to arrival."

The captain yelled into the speaking tube to the ship's pilot below, "Prepare to launch fighters!" and the great carrier turned gracefully into the southeast wind.

Fuchida anxiously looked down onto the deck where five idling Zeroes prepared to take off. Just thirty minutes earlier there had been thirty-six fighters in the air. Now they had only eighteen, but among them were some of the most skilled fighter pilots in the Imperial Japanese Navy. And they were waiting for the Americans.

The agile Mitsubishi A6M Zero fighters were nearly three times as fast as their lumbering prey that approached in a wide, V formation. The Zeroes gathered from above and concentrated on the slow, low-flying TBD Devastator torpedo bombers, then swooped down from all directions, opening their machine guns and cannons with cruel precision. Exploding into flames, two and three at a time, the American bombers collapsed into the ocean, streaking black smoke into the blue sea. Disregarding the relentless defensive machine gun fire from the rear gunners in the Devastators, the Zeroes remained undeterred and tore into the formation again and again until only a few of the original fifteen bombers continued heading toward the carriers *Soryu* and *Akagi*.

The last of the five fighters on the deck of the *Akagi* soared into the air among cheers of the aircrew.

Genda and Fuchida strained to follow the fate of the last three torpedo bombers who seemed to have made it through. Again, the combat air patrol fired down on the planes, blasting one into the water while another, torpedo still attached and the pilot shot dead, lazily drifted near to *Akagi* and passed beyond to crash. One lone plane droned on toward the *Soryu*, his rear gunner silent. His torpedo splashed into the sea and headed toward the port bow of the *Soryu* as the pilot turned his aircraft sharply to flee, only to be chased down by the five newly launched Zeroes from the *Akagi*. They quickly shredded his aircraft into a flaming wreck, where he joined his comrades in the sea below.

From the bridge, Fuchida watched the *Soryu* react. He held his breath and then, with no explosion following, let out a deep sigh. They'd survived yet another attack—unscathed.

9:38 a.m.

Fuchida reached inside his shirt with his left hand and gently felt his sweaty wound on his lower right abdomen. His pumping adrenaline had made him forget the throbbing pain of his operation, and now he began to feel faint.

Over the intercom, word came from the tower lookout, "Enemy aircraft approaching from the south. Appear to be two groups, roughly thirty miles out. Close to the horizon. No fighter escorts in sight."

Looking out the left side of the bridge to the south, Fuchida couldn't see them yet, but he was sure they were coming. The fleet now had more fighters in the air, but they were grouped to the east side of the fleet from their previous encounter, and would take time reach the new intruders.

As the two sections of American aircraft approached the outside of the fleet, anti-aircraft fire greeted them from the screening destroyers and cruisers. But the Americans continued through the flak bursts toward the closest carrier, the *Kaga*, just a few miles west of the *Akagi*.

On the platform outside the bridge, Fuchida looked up into the sky. No sign of his fighters. They were still too far away. Stepping to one of the mounted binoculars, he watched as the groups of approaching bombers continued to diverge. Finally, friendly fighters arrived and began attacking one of the groups.

One after another, three rearmed Zeroes accelerated off the deck of the *Akagi* joining the battle as the first group of American bombers approached the *Kaga*. The Japanese fighters amassed on the determined bombers and riddled the band of aircraft with machine-gun and cannon fire. Five bombers dropped in flames to the sea one by one, but the last two released their torpedoes toward the *Kaga*, which, again, maneuvered hard to starboard, evading both.

On the bridge of the *Akagi*, Fuchida stood up and looked down with a smile at the sailors on the deck below, who were shouting with cheers of joy, waving their white caps in euphoria.

Vice Admiral Nagumo pulled off his officer's cap, wiped his perspiring face with a handkerchief, replaced his cap, and exhaled with a sense of subdued pride. "*Kaga* is fighting well."

Genda pivoted to Nagumo, "Admiral, *Akagi's* first chūtai has rearmed with torpedoes. Work is proceeding on the second group now. The last of the available fighters have been launched to reinforce the air patrol and those remaining aboard *Akagi* are reserved for strike escort. We have no need to launch aircraft for quite some time. I recommend we commence spotting our rearmed bombers now to speed launch preparations. We can park them at the bow to continue to recover planes while the second chūtai's armament is completed. The elevators are a delay so it is advantageous to clear our hangers of the armed aircraft."

Nagumo nodded in agreement, "Issue orders to the striking force to speed preparations for launch."

Fuchida leaned over bracing his hands on his knees to rest. He blinked hard from his abdominal pain and the pressure of the assaults and shook his head. It had been an *unbelievably* brutal three hours of nearly non-stop attacks by over eighty enemy aircraft. During the course of the morning, at Midway and among the fleet, the Japanese had downed sixty-one American planes at a loss of only fifteen of their own. They had run the gauntlet, and the Americans had failed.

He eased himself back up and looked down as the first rearmed torpedo bomber on the flight deck as handlers pushed it towards the holding area at the bow. Soon they'd be sending off their *own* devastating strike against the Americans!

Chapter 60

10:00 a.m. The battleship Yamato.

A courier saluted Admiral Yamamoto in the bridge of his fleet flagship.

"Sir, message from Vice Admiral Nagumo." The courier snapped a sheet of paper between his white-gloved hands. *"Carried out attack of Midway at 0630. Many shore-based planes attacked us subsequent to 0715. We have suffered no damages."*

Yamamoto looked at Captain Kuroshima with a confident sparkle in his eye.

"After destroying enemy forces spotted at 0728, composed of one carrier, seven cruisers and five destroyers, we will resume our attack on Midway Island."

"You're excused," Yamamoto said to the courier. He turned his eyes toward the window and patted his hand on the sill, and smiled.

10:10 a.m. The carrier Akagi.

Fuchida ventured back down to the flight deck of the *Akagi* where he enthusiastically watched a fighter touch down and catch the arrester hook. The deck handlers quickly moved it to the elevator where it would descend into the hanger for rearming. A torpedo-equipped Nakajima B5N2 rose from another elevator. The spot for launch had begun

Fuchida whispered under his breath, "Now it's our turn."

In the bridge, the intercom alerted Genda.

"Combat Air Patrol reports twelve-plane torpedo squadron from the southeast accompanied by six fighter escorts."

"There *must* be another carrier in the area!" Genda uttered.

Again, urgently over the intercom, "Contact! Twelve torpedo planes bearing one-seventy port. Range: twenty-eight miles!"

Fuchida heard the message. Snatching the binoculars from another officer, he looked to the southeast. Sure enough, another squadron was approaching! And just as surely, the Japanese fighters descended once again, dozens of them with machine guns blazing. The Americans fought back furiously with a handful of their fighters and with the rear-facing machine guns of the Douglas TBD Devastator torpedo bombers. Swirling dogfights broke out as they exchanged blows—Zeroes and torpedo bombers alternately bursting into flames and falling from the skies, trailing black smoke, twisting into the sea in final, white columns of ocean spray.

The expert Zeroes dominated, shredding seven of the twelve bombers as the remaining five continued to barrel forward toward the Japanese carriers through a hail of flak from naval anti-aircraft guns firing as fast as sailors could load them.

Fuchida stared in awe as the few remaining bombers unexpectedly droned past the *Akagi* to release their torpedoes toward the carrier *Hiryu* as fighters relentlessly ripped into the planes sending several more down in flames. The agile carrier heaved hard to port, then reversed back to starboard, evading every incoming torpedo.

Fuchida sighed heavily as men on the deck, once again, cheered with relief. Although he reveled in their skilled victory, he felt a twinge of sympathy and a sense of admiration for the Americans who courageously attacked and fell to their deaths into the sea. His opponents earned his respect.

In the bridge, Genda looked out to his left as an officer announced over the intercom, "Enemy dive bombers approaching the carrier *Kaga* from the south!"

Genda saw the group high above the *Kaga*, dropping into a steep angle, one after the other—and this time with no interference from Japanese fighters which were nowhere to be seen. He held his breath, hoping they were just as unskilled as all the previous attackers. Three explosions in succession shot columns of water hundreds of feet into the air around the

Kaga, but the fourth detonation ripped through the rear deck, hurling debris and flames in a smoky explosion. Two more columns of water blasted skyward, then the bridge tower of the *Kaga* exploded into a thousand fragments as a massive fireball rolled up into the sky.

An SBD Dauntless dive bomber releases its payload.

"*Damn* it!" Genda yelled.

Down on the deck, Fuchida cursed under his breath and shook his head. Lookouts suddenly pointed above and screamed, "Dive bombers!"

Fuchida looked up. Several anti-aircraft guns swung into action, pounding away, filling the sky with scattered puffs of black as three planes lined up, one behind the other, and bore down on the *Akagi*. He'd never been on the receiving end of a bombing before and now had a strange, helpless feeling as he stared as the first dive bomber screamed straight toward his own ship, dive flaps flared, almost in slow motion, his bomb magically detaching and drifting downward, directly at him.

He dove for the deck beside the winch, clasping his hands behind his head. The first bomb hit the water thirty feet to the left of the tower with a concussive blast that jolted the ship, exploding a tower of water one-hundred feet into the air, dousing him and the deck with a shower of sooty-black seawater.

He looked up again, fixing his sight on the next falling bomb. This one looked to be a perfect hit. With a blinding flash, another horrific shock wave tore through the center of the deck, blasting smoke and splintering the wooden deck into the sky while flinging planes off the deck into the sea. Then a third bomb exploded in the water to the rear, sending a shudder through the huge ship from stern to bow and sending up another towering geyser of water.

Then, just as suddenly, they were gone, leaving behind the rumbling flames in the hangar below, the distant drone of fleeing aircraft, and the idling bombers on the deck. Fuchida got to his feet and ran to see the damage. Planes sat upended, their tails to the sky. He looked down into the open center elevator, now fallen to the bottom and bent like molten glass as clouds of black smoke poured out and were blown by the wind. One hit, he thought, they could survive.

Under dangling twisted steel in the hangar below, Kanegasaki and his crew wrestled hoses from racks and began spraying foam through the billowing smoke onto a wrecked bomber engulfed in flames. As he fought one fire, he saw thousands of gallons of aviation fuel cascading across the lower hangar deck, advancing the flames beneath another fully loaded aircraft. Soon, a dozen men were spraying foam. Kanegasaki craned his neck upward. Fuel pipes leading to the flight deck were fractured, dribbling more gasoline down the side of the hangar.

On the flight deck, an overturned plane flashed into flames as it threw off more clouds of heavy smoke, its blazing fuel trickling across the wooden deck. Fuchida followed sailors carrying the wounded into the briefing room, who laid them across tables.

"Why aren't these men being taken down to sick bay?" Fuchida yelled.

"Sir," a sailor said, "the ship's on fire below. No one can get past."

Bolting from the briefing room, Fuchida scrambled down a smoky ladder toward his personal quarters to fetch his notes and other items, but the dense smoke drove him back. A terrific explosion rocked the passageway, throwing him against the wall. Fuchida yanked his shirt over his nose and mouth and stumbled back to the ladder. Half-way up he paused as a thought shot through his mind: There were thirty-three others in sick bay with him that morning. If he had followed the doctor's orders, he would have been among them now—trapped.

As he struggled up to the raging deck, he raised his arm to shield his face from the vicious heat. He flinched as another concussion from a parked aircraft's exploding bomb in the hangar below ripped through the deck, hurling a plane onto its back and shooting flaming debris high into the air.

Wondering about the fate of the other ships, he gazed out and froze. Massive plumes of thick smoke poured from the *Kaga*. He turned to look in the opposite direction. His heart fell. There was the carrier *Soryu*, likewise a burning wreck.

He stood in disbelief. In merely five minutes, three of their mighty carriers were reduced to self-destructive burning hulls. Shocked and bewildered, Fuchida strained to hurry back up to the bridge. More explosions rocked the vessel. Arriving, he could see there were no words for anyone to say. Vice Admiral Nagumo looked forward, immovable.

Genda and Fuchida caught eye to eye. Genda's slightly parted lips revealed his clenched teeth as he muttered under his breath, "We should have known better!"[24]

Nagumo continued gazing straight ahead as flames swept across the deck, black clouds momentarily blocking the view from the bridge every few seconds. The *Akagi* had become a volcano of death, consuming itself into the sea.

Rear Admiral Kusaka urged gently, "Admiral." The bridge trembled from another explosion from deep within the ship. "I believe we must transfer your flag to the cruiser *Nagara*."

Nagumo remained calm. "We are all right," he said.

Fuchida saw the pain in the admiral's face. He didn't want to abandon his men at their worst moment. He wanted to believe there was some way to salvage his ship, which was hopelessly blowing to pieces before their eyes. The officers in the bridge and all aboard the *Akagi* were now being held hostage by the pride of an admiral who could not bring himself to give the fateful command to abandon ship.

Huddled behind a beam in the hangar with three others, Kanegasaki shielded his face from the blistering heat and wicked flames devouring the aircraft, the steel structure moaning and popping in the conflagration. "Back! We need to move further back!" But there was no place left for them to go.

Two more bombs burst out the side of the ship with a thunderous

---

[24] "Shimatta!" しまった, used as an expression of extreme disappointment or frustration.

blast, igniting a fuel storage tank and sending a colossal orange-black fireball churning into the sky.

On the bridge, Captain Aoki bowed toward Nagumo. "Admiral, you and your staff can do nothing more here. As the ship's captain, I will take care of this ship with all its responsibility. Please—transfer your flag immediately."

Nagumo stared. "It's not time yet," he said softly.

Fuchida looked down at the deck to his right. Crackling flames fully engulfed a fighter plane and began sweeping up the side of the tower.

Rear Admiral Kusaka spoke firmly, "Admiral! The ship is ablaze and dead in the water. The radios are out. You cannot direct the battle from here. The carrier *Hiryu* is still intact. You owe it to our remaining men to carry out your duties there. Please!"

Tears began pooling around the edges of Nagumo's eyes. He tightened his mouth. With labored breathing, he reluctantly lowered his head and nodded.

Fuel-fed flames now blocked the stairway. Fuchida peered out the port window to the water eighty feet below—a near fatal distance to jump. Impossible.

A mortally wounded Japanese carrier sits dead in the water at Midway.

Genda grabbed a metal stool, smashed out a side window, and threw a rope down to an anti-aircraft gun platform fourteen feet below. One at a time, each officer clambered through the opening and shimmied down the rope as flames randomly licked at their heels near the bottom.

The last man out, Fuchida grasped the sooty rope, and swung outside the bridge into the smoke, wincing from his wound. As he began his descent, another bomb on deck exploded with a thunderous blast, breaking his grip and dropping him past the platform to the flight deck twenty feet down. Sprawled on the fiery deck, pain wracked his body, but he remained conscious. Fighting to get back on his feet, splitting pain shot up through his legs and he collapsed to his chest. He knew both his ankles were broken.

Another two blasts shook the deck as swirling clouds of acrid gasoline smoke shrouded him, stinging his eyes and searing his lungs. With trembling arms, he strained himself into a crawl. Great drops of sweat washed black soot from his face and dripped onto the wooden deck. His uniform smoldered from the flaming fuel beside him as it crept ever closer. He had imagined a more glorious end to his life, but felt the ropes of death tighten around him dragging him down to his fate. His sight dimmed as he crumpled to the deck and breathed out, "If this is the way I am to die . . . then I'm ready." Waves of blistering smoke engulfed him.

Emerging from the billowing blackness, apparitions in white appeared through the veil of smoke—two sailors who had braved the inferno reached out and clutched Fuchida's arms, dragged him from the flames, laid him on a bamboo stretcher, and whisked him to the bow. Only half-conscious, from there they lowered him in a net sling and placed him into a large rowboat with the other officers from the bridge.

Fuchida laid his blackened head against a life preserver as six sailors silently rowed the crowded launch to a nearby cruiser while he regained his senses. He listened to the lap of the oars in the water and watched his beloved *Akagi* continue to rumble and cough in the throes of death—his hopes for the battle shattered, his dream of defeating the Americans, crushed. Blinking slowly, he gazed wistfully at the once majestic carrier, his eyes following the smoke of incense as it drifted up to the defeated gods of Japan.

Chapter 61

June 1942. The island of Panay, the Philippines.

Jimmy took in the lush greenery of the jungle camp of Hopevale as the melodies of songbirds unknown blended with the hum of cicadas. Columns of forest sunlight fell through the canopy onto a cascade of pink and white orchids hugging the crevassed wall, their sweet scent flowing through the tropical air. The astounding beauty and life of nature overwhelmed him. Everything seemed a perfect work of the Creator.

Three bamboo huts stood in small clearings as a small, crackling fire sent a light smoke drifting upwards. Jimmy and the group of two dozen adults and a handful of children assembled in front of one of the huts not far from the towering trees as Francis made his announcement.

"As you all know," he began, "the word around the island is that the Japanese want everyone to turn themselves in."

Several armed miners-turned-guerrillas stood off to the side. Little Earl, who had helped to stack rocks with Jack, reached up curiously to feel the wooden stock of Jack's submachine gun. Jack smiled down, and

Jennie Adams left her home in Nebraska to be with the people of the Philippines as a missionary and nurse working beside Dr. Fred Meyer in Emmanual Hospital.

motioned like he was going to hand the gun to Earl, who giggled. The clothes of all were dull with age, and most everyone stood barefoot, except for the miners in boots. Charma filled a speckled-blue ceramic cup with water trickling from a bamboo pipe and walked up beside Jimmy.

Despite the heat and humidity, Jimmy put his arm around Charma. They'd long believed that this would all be over quickly. That hope was fast fading. Jimmy seriously wondered if he'd made the wrong move by coming to Hopevale in the first place, or maybe by just staying on the island too long. Too late to change that now.

"We've received a letter from some of the university staff who are now imprisoned downtown at Iloilo." Francis held up the letter for all to see. "They say the Japanese are giving any Americans on the island four months to turn themselves in." He paused. "After that, anyone discovered will be killed. It's as simple as that. Surrender or be killed."

Jack spit. "Or surrender *and* be killed. No one trusts the Japs."

"We each have to decide what we want to do," Francis continued. "After four months, that's it."

Jimmy piped in, "We're no threat to them. They don't even know we're here. We're three miles from the closest road. If they ever found us, the worst that could happen is that they'd send us off to a camp." Most in the

A common band of resistance fighters in the Philippines.

band promptly nodded. "I think we need to just keep to ourselves and mind our own business. Just sit things out until all this passes over, like a bad storm."

Jennie, the nurse, added, "The local people need me here, and I see how much they've been encouraged by the church services we have here each week. I love these people, and I'm not going to leave them. Not now. I'm fine staying put."

Jack loudly clanked open his Zippo lighter and lit a cigarette,

参 降 投

SURRENDER CARD

Any Filipino or American soldier and their friends will received special consideration by presenting this card to the Imperial Japanese Forces.

本投降券持參者に對しては特別の考慮を與へられ度

One of many forms of propagnada and literature distributed by the Japanese as they sought to expand their East Asia Co-Prosperity Sphere.

leaving it dangling between his lips. "Get a load of this." He unfolded a worn color comic book whose cover displayed smiling Asian men locked arm in arm waving flags. "Courtesy of the Japanese department of propaganda." He exhaled the smoke through his nostrils and read aloud with a decidedly sarcastic pitch. "*We of Greater East Asia will combine our power and will become friends with the good countries of the world.*" He looked around. "Now ain't that sweet?" He read on. "*Together we will spread our splendid culture throughout the Philippines.*" Jack rolled his eyes and flipped to another page of smiling characters working on roads. "*The more we work, the more we study, we will achieve happiness. Then the people of Greater East Asia shall become prosperous. Let's become friendly like brothers.*" Jack abruptly folded the comic book, stuffed it in his shirt pocket, and yanked the cigarette from his mouth. "Anyone buying this bullshit?"

A few ladies looked down in embarrassment at his language. The men stared.

"There were at least eight thousand American and Filipino soldiers stationed on this island. Just under two thousand turned themselves in. The rest, well, they just disappeared into the jungle. Me and the boys from the mines have thrown in our lot with them. If the Japs want me, they're gonna have to come and get me. No *way* I'm gonna lay down for the Japs. They're all a bunch of liars."

Francis nodded politely. "Yes, well, Jack, we're not all of the same inclination, but I think we see your point."

The hospital surgeon, Fred, adjusted his gold, wire-rimmed glasses. "I can't say it's safe here, but I can't say it's safe to go to a prison camp either. I've done surgery on children for years in the city. Now I have patients all over the jungle barrios." He clasped his wife's hand. "Ruth and I have decided we're staying here."

Jimmy looked at Charma and caught her looking back at him. He raised his eyebrows in the slightest way. Charma inhaled, blinked slowly, and nodded.

"Francis," Jimmy said, "we know we're supposed to stay here. We're not going anywhere."

"Anyone else have anything to say?" Francis asked.

The people glanced around curiously.

"Then all those in favor of staying, raise your hand."

All hands went up and, again, everyone looked around.

"Well, from this day forward, for better or for worse, we're all in this together."

The arms came back down.

Francis scanned the group with dead seriousness. "Until death do us part."

Jimmy and Francis led their wives through the nearby jungle, pushing aside huge, shimmering leaves and arching ferns.

"It's pretty muddy," Jimmy said as he held a branch back for Charma. "Just don't twist your ankle on a rock or something."

Charma pulled her dress up a bit and stepped carefully as Francis led them to a vine-covered wall and drew some of the overhang aside revealing a small cave.

"If we get an alert from a lookout," Francis said, "that the Japanese are somewhere nearby, this is where we'll go. The other families have their spots, too. Some have hideouts in the ground with camouflaged roofs. You can be right in front of them and can't see 'em."

Jimmy ducked down and entered the rock hollow as the ladies tentatively followed. Francis came in and let the vines drape back over the entrance.

"So," Ruth said, "Does this make us cavemen?"

"That's cave*woman* to you," Francis replied.

Jimmy hunched a bit, scratched his armpits, and grunted like an ape.

Chapter 62

June 1942. Tokyo.

Kempei[25] officer in his olive-green uniform, sharply dressed in black riding boots, leather waist belt, and a white armband on his left sleeve, drew back and slapped Jake across the face. "How long was the flight deck of the *Hornet*?!"

Blindfolded, Jake knelt on a concrete floor with his hands tied behind his back and a three-inch diameter stick of bamboo wedged behind the crook of his knees. Having not shaved or bathed in nearly two months, sweat and dirt-matted his hair and beard. He reeked with an awful stench, but he hardly noticed as the screaming pain of his legs fogged his mind almost to the point of unconsciousness.

His bruised head wobbled. "Seven hundred . . . eight hundred . . . I . . . I . . . seven hundred . . ."

The officer nodded to a soldier who walked up to Jake and stomped his boot onto Jake's thigh. Jake screamed out with what little energy he had left, his knees feeling like they'd explode. The two weeks he'd been in Tokyo melded into a blur of interrogations, beatings, meals of watery rice, and nights of being perpetually

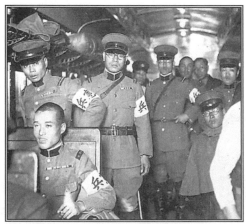

A group of Kempei shortly before the start of the war.

---

[25] Military police.

awakened by guards who prodded him with poles into his cell. He felt he was drifting in a dark, surreal hell.

"Seven hundred?" Jake twisted his head. "Eight hundred? . . . Eight hundred." He nodded unconvincingly and panted for air. "Eight hundred feet . . . Eight hundred feet." The pain throbbed through his knees, back, shoulders, and his neck. He just wanted it to end. *God*, he wanted it to just *stop*.

The officer turned to two other soldiers standing beside a wall. "Bring me a different one. Now!"

In another room, Jake's pilot, Bill Farrow, lay on his stomach completely drenched on a sopping wet wooden floor—blindfolded with his hands bound behind his back and his ankles tied together. A Kempei officer stood silently as soldiers rolled Bill onto his back with a wet flop. One soldier then sat on his legs and a second one sat on his stomach, crushing Bill's hands underneath as he screamed through clenched teeth. A third knelt at his head bracing it between his knees and proceeded to throw a coarse, wet cloth over his face. The officer motioned to a nearby soldier with a bucket who then poured a steady trickle of water over Bill's face as he grunted and twisted, gasping for air. After arching his back several times while choking in gurgles, his body went limp.

Two guards dragged Jake, now barely able to walk, down a decrepit, dark hallway lit by a few bare bulbs and shoved him into a six-foot by eight-foot wooden cell with a putrid "benjo hole" in the corner of the floor.

"Sit only!" the guard barked in English. "No lie down!"

Jake struggled to move his throbbing legs in front of him as the door shut him into further darkness and the bolt locked. A tiny rectangle of yellow light fell onto his chest. As the echo of footsteps faded away down the hall, Jake slowly bent to the side, then collapsed to the floor.

The next morning, a jangle of keys and a clank of the deadbolt awoke Jake into semi-consciousness as the door squeaked open.

"I said no lie down!" The guard pulled at Jake's sprawled body as he tried to sit upright. A second guard followed behind. Momentarily blocking the light to his cell Jake saw it was Harry, his gunner, his wrists in irons like his own. He looked like hell.

"No talking! Quiet!" the guard shouted in Japanese. Jake could figure out what he meant even if he didn't understand the words.

The bedraggled gunner limped to the cell wall and grimaced as he slid down into a sitting position. After the guards had locked the door behind them, they clopped off, and Jake and Harry stared at each other pensively. With one eye nearly shut from bruising, Harry raised his shackled hands a few inches and gave a thumbs-up with a smirk. Jake grinned back. They didn't break him.

Though the stench was nauseating, and his joints flashed with pain, the joy of seeing his partner still alive flooded the cell with a subtle triumph. They spoke in the quietest of whispers.

"They've got three others, too," Harry said.

"Who?"

"From Hallmark's plane, *The Green Hornet*: Hallmark, Meder, and Nielson."

"What about the other two of their crew?"

"Their plane hit the water. They drowned."

Jake cautiously glanced up at the small peephole beaming dim light. "They gonna kill us, you think?"

"Probably," Harry whispered back. "The information they're squeezing out now is all nonsense anyway. They know it." Harry tried to swallow. "They know they can get away with it, too."

"Why?" Jake whispered. "Aren't we at least pawns worth keeping for making bargains or something?"

"Nah. They don't care about that. From all the talk, I think our little raid got under their skin. They lost face. The Japs hate that. Now someone's gotta pay. Probably gonna be us."

"They gotta know one day America's gonna come over and kick their asses all to hell."

Harry blinked slowly with a nod.

"Well." Jake paused. "If I can just take down one more Jap on my way out, I'll be satisfied."

Harry smiled. Jake felt it deep inside. Nice to have a friend.

A Kempei officer sat behind an interrogation table while a soldier motioned for Jake to sit in the chair on the opposite side. In handcuffs, Jake still wore the same soiled shirt and pants he'd put on the morning of the raid. He sighed and took his seat.

The officer leaned forward and laid a pen and a small stack of papers before him. They were all in Japanese with a blank line at the bottom of each page.

Jake looked at the papers quizzically and peered up at the officer. "What is it?"

The officer blew cigarette smoke up toward the ceiling. "A confessional."

Jake pushed the papers away. "Sorry, pal. No way that—"

A soldier slapped him across the face. "You sign!"

By now, everything seemed to make no sense to Jake. Half of what he and the others had told the interrogators over the last two weeks they simply made up to try to stop the torture. Now they wanted his signature on a document everyone knew he couldn't even read. So what difference did it make, anyway?

Jake reached for the pen with his cuffed hands, looked up at the triumphant officer one last time with a form of defiant submission, and signed.

The officer smiled and puffed his cigarette.

Chapter 63

June 1942. Imperial General Headquarters, Tokyo.

Outside the imposing brick building clad in ivy and fitted with a white-columned entrance, Chief of the Imperial Japanese Army General Staff Sugiyama strode beside the bespectacled Tojo, Prime Minister and Army Minister of Japan.

Sugiyama came to a halt and rammed two fingers into his open palm. "They're *war criminals* and as such should be executed without delay!"

"It's not clear at this time if they are war criminals or prisoners of war," Tojo replied. "If only prisoners, we both know they can't be executed for an act of war. This has now become an international event. All the world knows we have them."

"And we have their confessions! They have clearly admitted to strafing schools and killing civilians, which amounts to murder! They're *war* criminals. We *must* teach the Americans a lesson. If they ever attempt such an act again, they will *all* suffer the same fate!"

Hideki Tojo.

Tojo paced again and brought his hands behind his back. "And what would be the fate of the Japanese interned in camps in the United States? We have eight of their men, they have thousands of our people. We cannot afford the chance for such unfavorable consequences."

Snorting, Sugiyama looked away.

Tojo continued, "Our best legal minds are looking into the rules of international law regarding this case. Even if they're found to be prisoners, I am inclined to create a law to impose the death penalty to execute them if they are found guilty of crimes."

"Ex post facto?"[26]

Tojo nodded.

"Tried in a military court, then?"

"Yes. In Shanghai by the Thirteenth Army under Lieutenant General Shimomura. I will send them back to where they were captured."

"Shanghai, then." Sugiyama gazed up with a smile at a carefully pruned Japanese black pine. "Good."

---

[26] Latin for "after the action," a legal term for a retroactive law, prohibited in most countries.

Chapter 64

June 1942. Tokyo.

J apanese soldiers paraded the eight American prisoners through the
streets like rats dragged from a sewer, prodding them with rifle butts
through a growing crowd of jubilant, shouting onlookers. Jake
narrowed his eyes in the rare sunlight beaming onto his filthy head as he
shuffled along, both hands and both feet in irons. He couldn't understand a
single word of the enraged, screaming Japanese, but then, he didn't need to.
He also happened to note the lack of younger and middle-aged men—now
all off to war.

*Japanese officers escort "Bat out of Hell" copilot Bob
Hite from their newly arrived transport plane in Tokyo, Japan.*

"Move! *Move!*" A soldier shoved Jake forward with his seven other comrades as rifled soldiers in front made a pathway through the pressing mass. Since they'd just been driven a short way by a couple of cars and unloaded, Jake wasn't sure where they were heading, but as they made their way toward a train platform, it was clear they were being moved somewhere far away. Where, he didn't know, or why.

Several women with raised hands wept and shouted out, "Oh! Kawai so ni! Kawai so ni!"[27]

Jake felt a warm breeze of compassion from the ladies in an otherwise icy, hateful crowd.

"What?!" an enraged officer yelled in Japanese as he approached. "Shut up! *All* of you!" He signaled for two soldiers. "They must be spies! Arrest them!"

Soldiers strong-armed the women away among further shrieks of sorrow.

Jake's feelings of warmth soon dissolved into cold fear as he wondered what would become of these women.

On the rolling train, Jake sat silently between his guard and the window, the "click-clack" of the rails gently thumping his head as he rested against the frame. The smoke of the locomotive blew through the open windows, coating his face with a film of soot. Japanese passengers peered in from the preceding coach and briefly stared at the odd cargo of American prisoners.

Jake forgot the aches of the tight shackles on his wrists and ankles when he and the others were given the first real food of their captivity: rice, white radishes, soybean pods, and shredded cabbage. Jake wolfed down the food fearing it might just as quickly be taken away.

The thought that they could have been killed and seemed to have been spared was marginally encouraging, but his treatment didn't give him any ideas his situation was likely to improve. Where were they going? How long would the war last? Could he make it out alive? All Jake had were questions, but no answers.

---

[27] "Oh, those poor boys!"

After several pain-filled, sleepless days and nights of trains, ferries, cramped cells, and a wretched berth on a freight ship, the eight prisoners finally arrived at the Bridge House Jail. Kempeitai housed them in the basement of a seven-story former British apartment complex in the heart of Shanghai that they'd taken over as a Japanese headquarters and jail facility, which housed nearly 600 lost souls. Guards corralled the Raiders into a ten-foot by fifteen-foot windowless room, a makeshift cell, and shoved them in with over twenty others: a mix of Chinese boys, men, women, and a Russian. A wooden bucket in the corner of the room overflowed with waste and an emaciated, old man laid on the floor—motionless. Jake wasn't sure if he was dead or alive. He wasn't sure how long he'd be alive, either. At over ninety degrees, the sweat and smell were overwhelming. The only way to rest was to take turns squatting against the wall or to curl up in a ball on the floor. Lice crawled over people's faces.

As a guard pushed the heavy wooden door of vertical wooden bars into its latch, the combination of heat and stench was too much for Harry, who vomited. Jake cringed and looked at Bill who closed his eyes.

Every one of the Americans was bruised, lame in some degree, and covered with sores, scabs and open wounds from their many beatings. Although bedbugs incessantly gnawed at their withering flesh, Jake was grateful for one thing: for the first time, he was among the seven other fliers in one place and able to talk freely.

After each took his turn to unwind his tale of where he grew up, what he wanted to do, who he wanted to marry, and, most importantly, what food he missed most—from biscuits and gravy to rhubarb pie with vanilla ice cream—the conversation gravitated to the inevitable.

"How long," Jake queried Bill, "how long can this last? What do you think'll happen to us?"

After a long pause, Bill replied with his refined drawl, "Well, these Japs been fighting the Chinese for five years already, and they've been gearing up for a war with us for a while. The word is, they've got five million men on the ground. We don't even have a million soldiers in the entire U.S. of A."

"We gonna win it?"

Bill nodded. "Oh, yeah. We'll rain fire on 'em, but we'll all be dead by then."

There was a long, uncomfortable silence.

"Yeah, but dead from what?" George added. With his six-foot-two-inch frame and his straggly hair and beard of red, he was a one-man freak show the guards frequently came to gawk at. They'd never seen red hair before.

"Take your pick," Bill answered. "Starvation, disease, torture, firing squad, decapitation . . ."

The men looked down at a rat darting between their bare feet.

". . . rat bites."

"Don't they need to keep us to trade or something?" Bob, the copilot asked. "They've got to."

"Maybe. Maybe not," Bill replied. "If they're losing, they'll most likely just shoot us all. They've broke every rule there is. We talk, and they'll be court-martialed and hung high. Dead men don't talk."

"Quiet!" Jake whispered. "Here they come."

Two guards approached with a bucket and soon, one began ladling yellowed, watery rice mixed with dirt and debris and an occasional fish head into pans as the other passed them in. As a woman squeezed forward, she lost her footing, slipped, and thumped her head against the wall and shrieked as she fell to the floor. Both guards burst out in laughter. One of them reached for a baton attached to his keys. "Too sick? You're too sick to stand up? I'll make you sick if you want to be sick." He reached between the bars and beat the woman on the head with his baton, who howled and crumbled under the blows.

Jake winced in disbelief. He was an enemy soldier and had attacked Japan. He was sure he'd killed people as well. But even if this Chinese woman had done something wrong, he couldn't fathom treating a frail woman like an animal and wondered why these Japanese seemed so different from Americans. There was bad in America, sure, but not like this. You don't beat a woman like that, especially if she's sick. He recoiled at the brash wickedness.

Two weeks later. Naval Prisoner of War Camp,
Kiangwan Road, Shanghai, China.

The eight prisoners stood at attention as best they could on the dirt
courtyard of the prison complex in the morning sun. Beyond the walls, Jake
heard the voices and shuffling of many others, but could see no one. He
knew they were "special" prisoners because of their raid, but he was getting
used to "special" treatment. He didn't know what was up this time. A squad
of armed soldiers stood at attention to the side as a short, black-booted
Army officer with his sword at his side proudly strode across the yard
toward a small step stool in front of the men. He turned abruptly to face the
prisoners, then stepped up to address his captive audience. Much to his
dismay, despite his step stool, he found himself still having to look up into
the eyes of Bill Farrow who stood directly before him—Jake's pilot who
towered over all the rest at six feet, four inches. Jake did his best to hide his
glee at the officer's disappointment.

"The domination of the white race in Asia is *over*!" the officer shouted
in surprisingly good English. "You are an inferior, *worthless* race, who owe
your lives to the benevolence of our emperor." He slowly scanned the gaunt,
bedraggled row of airmen. "Although we have cut off fifty heads this
morning—I regret that I cannot do the same to you, for the spirit of
Bushido prevents me. However, violation of a single command will result in
instant execution!" He inhaled deeply, slowly breathed out, and narrowed
his eyes. "You will be forever subjects of Imperial Japan!"

Jake was getting tired of all the speeches of superiority and was
beginning to not care if he lived or died. The officer was a little man to Jake,
in every way. A nothing.

Chapter 65

June 1942. Madras, Oregon.

M r. Andrus looked up from his tractor as his wife ran from their house toward him waving her hands over her head. He killed the engine, letting it sputter to a halt, and dismounted as a cloud of dust drifted over him in the late afternoon sun. Chickens squealed and flapped as Mrs. Andrus ran through the flock, panting with a letter in one hand and a ripped open envelope in the other.

"They still don't know where Jake is," she let out, breathing hard. She handed the sheet of official letterhead to her husband. "It's from Congressman Pierce."

Mr. Andrus pushed his straw hat back a bit and studied the note.

"They don't know if he's being held prisoner, or if . . . if he's . . ."

As she put her hand to her mouth, he reached his arm around her shoulders and grasped her with his weathered hand.

"They'll find him," he said firmly. He watched the tears roll down her cheeks leaving streaks in the dust on her face and felt her muffled sobs as her back heaved. He looked out to the setting sun over the mountains. Giving her a gentle squeeze, he whispered again, "Don't you worry. They'll find him."

WALTER M. PIERCE
2D CONGRESSIONAL DISTRICT
OREGON

HOME ADDRESS:
LA GRANDE, OREGON
R. D. No. 1

MEMBER COMMITTEE ON
AGRICULTURE

Congress of the United States
House of Representatives
Washington, D. C.

June 16, 1942   AIR MAIL

Mrs. Huld M. Andrus
Madras
Oregon

My dear Mrs. Andrus:

I feel very much troubled to be obliged to say
to you that I cannot learn anything about your son. They
assure me in the War Department that if he had actually lost
his life you would have had word but the very fact that you
have had no word means that he must be among the prisoners.
They are months getting these names because they go through
the Red Cross at Geneva and there is no way of hurrying them.

It seemed to me incredible that General Doolittle
would not have knowledge about the men who were with him, but
that is the case. They tell me that the chances are that
he is alive and that he is being cared for just as are great
numbers of other military prisoners of Japan. The only ones
who can be sent home or considered for exchange are the civilians
who did not bear arms.

They feel that we must be very careful in this
country about our attitude toward the Japanese so that they will
not visit any punishment upon our prisoners, and we are exceedingly careful. Please let us know just as soon as you hear
anything and we will check from day to day and let you hear.

My counsel is to believe your son alive and well.
The weeks of agony will be so hard on you, and can do him no
good, and so many hundreds of people have had that experience.
I am led to believe it will come to you also.

Very sincerely yours,

Walter M. Pierce

Walter M. Pierce, M.C.

*having the
missing
refound*

- 306 -

Chapter 66

July 1942. Yokosuka Base Hospital, Tokyo Bay.

A military hospital truck rumbled past armed guards in front of the broad, concrete steps of the brick hospital building.

Fuchida sat up in his hospital bed with a couple of pillows propped behind him. His feet, both in casts, protruded from under the sheets. Refolding his newspaper and laying it flat, he turned to his roommate, Egusa, his old flying friend and fellow casualty from Midway.

"Who else?" Fuchida said. "What about Kanegasaki, my flight mechanic? Did they ever find him? Was he picked up by another ship?"

Both of Egusa's arms and hands were wrapped in gauze, and the side of his face was distorted from burns. He shook his head. "They told me they rescued over a thousand from the *Akagi*, but not him. We lost three thousand of our best men along with all four carriers. And they said that the Americans had *three* carriers in the area, not two. It seems like they knew we were coming."

Fuchida picked up the newspaper again and stared at the wall, absorbed in thought. Friends he felt he had just spoken with yesterday, laughed with, ate with, now gone, and for what? He didn't see any way they could ever recover from their losses, and the United States was now building like madmen. The Japanese Navy would eventually be overrun. Anyone could see that. By several strokes of luck, somehow, he'd managed to survive. He shook the newspaper to flatten it, tried to read and then pulled it down. "I still can't believe they're doing this to us! No phone calls, no letters, no visitors? This is ridiculous!"

"You've seen the newspapers: 'Our Imperial Navy Smashes the Americans.'" Egusa grinned. "They can't have you go around talking and spoiling all their good news, can they?"

The stifling grip of the Japanese government censors on all media outlets ensured a consistently positive picture to the public, who remained ignorant throughout the war, except for those who were involved in the war and saw for themselves what was taking place.

The Public Security Preservation Law of 1925 essentially gave the government carte blanche to outlaw anything that contradicted the *kokutai*, or the "national essence" of Japan. News of the successful Pearl Harbor Attack blanketed the nation, but the miserable defeat at Midway remained hidden from view.

Fuchida angrily tossed the paper onto a metal tray table. "What's the point? Do they think the Americans are going to hide the truth from their people, too? Sooner or later it will all come out, and then the people will know they've been lied to." He looked away. "They should just tell the truth and own up to it." After a long pause, Fuchida uncomfortably shifted about. "I think it's time we just do what we've been planning."

"Now?" Egusa said. "AWOL?[28] We could be court-martialed."

"I'm tired of lying here." Fuchida sighed and looked at Egusa. "I'm calling a taxi and sneaking out. Are you coming or not?"

Egusa raised his eyebrows ambiguously.

"You have to come," Fuchida said. "I can't leave without you. You're carrying me out." He knew he could depend on his old friend.

Breaking into a grin, Egusa nodded with resignation.

Fuchida smeared his artist's brush on the pallet blending the green with a touch of white, then brought it to the canvas of a roughly painted bonsai tree, paused, and daubed the green onto a branch.

Miyako, now five, gazed in amazement. "Daddy, make it greener. The other branch."

He turned to his daughter beside his wheelchair. "I am. Be patient, little one."

Haruko set a cup of tea on a small stand beside him and rested her

---

[28] Absence Without Official Leave.

hand on his shoulder. Balsawood and paper airplanes dangled from the ceiling, slowly turning from the breeze of an open window. Some were painted shades of olive green; others were simply raw paper and wood.

"Well," Fuchida said as he swished his brush in water and wrapped a rag around it, "that's all for today." Even though his family lived only five miles from the base, they hadn't seen him since he left for Midway, though they knew he made it back to the hospital. Fuchida knew Haruko would be relieved to know his injuries weren't crippling and elated just to see him alive and well. He was glad to enjoy his family and breathe the fresh air of

Recuperating with his family after Midway,
Haruko's brother-in-law in the upper right.

ordinary life, even if he knew it wouldn't last for long.

"Daddy," Yoshiya, now nine, tugged his father's sleeve. "Can you help me build a two-engine bomber? That's what I want to make next."

He spun his chair around to face his son, who held up a magazine photo of a Type 1 land-based attack aircraft, his eyes just peering over the top. Fuchida took a sip of his tea. "We'll get plans tomorrow, OK?"

"OK. Can we paint this one?"

"Sure. That'll set off the Hinomaru[29] nicely."

As Yoshiya and Miyako happily trotted off, Haruko wheeled Fuchida near his favorite window overlooking the ocean.

"Are you relieved?" Haruko asked.

"More like surprised. No reprimand from the base. They're going to give me a desk job until I recover." He knew he was too valuable to be severely reprimanded for his escape shenanigans. He'd get a slap on the wrist, that's all. He reached for her hand. "You'll be able to visit me in the new hospital I'll be staying at in Ito City, too. They want to keep me away from the Yokosuka base. They're afraid I'll talk too much and confuse people with the facts."

Fuchida unconsciously let go of her hand as his eyes followed a distant plane. "I feel for Yamamoto. He took full responsibility for our defeat at Midway. A lesser man wouldn't have done so. I did my best to explain to him that we still have a strong fleet, that if we can only focus on bringing *air* power to the forefront, we could have a fighting chance." He felt a bit of guilt, demanding honesty from headquarters about the battle while, perhaps, being a little disingenuous to Yamamoto. Their chances of even a draw were slim at best.

Haruko rubbed his shoulders and shyly ventured a question, "What do you think is going to happen?"

He thought for a moment. "We have to learn from our mistakes and bring our strengths together. If we can clinch a key battle . . ." He hesitated. "I really don't know."

---

[29] Red sun circle.

Chapter 67

August 1942. Hopevale, the Philippines.

"I haven't done this in a while, but I'll do my best," Fred said holding up a scalpel that glistened in the sun. The group sat together on a large grass mat beneath the trees in the mid-afternoon.

Jimmy looked on with unease. This was unpleasant.

"You'll only have one chance," Ruth said, "so you'll have to do it right."

The surrounding locals had been good to the beleaguered strangers in their hideaway, but life was still hard in the wilderness.

The people looked at Fred, then down at the center of the mat.

"It's our last chicken," Ruth said.

The paltry meal for twelve was an overcooked, lean bird and a handful of wild bananas.

Fred began slicing the meat and queried, "So . . . who wants the wishbone?"

Soberly, everyone raised their hand.

Chapter 68

Peggy dropped her books with a thud on her dorm table, fell back onto her bed, and kicked off her two-tone saddle shoes. "That's it, Jean, I can't study another word. My mind's all blurry. I've gotta give my brain a rest."

Jean sat on the edge of her bed brushing her black, wavy hair. "Me, too. I'm beat."

"You'd think the professors would give us a break or something to start off the year, but instead, they're piling it on."

"You can say that again." Jean looked out through the curtains at the

A dorm room at the all-girls school in New York at the time Peggy attended.

cold, orange sky, then back at
Peggy. "Hey! *Mrs. Miniver* with
Greer Carson is showing down at
the Belvedere. What do you say we
get the girls and drive down to the
theater?"

Leaning up on her elbow,
Peggy pulled open the desk
drawer, took out her coin purse
and gave it a shake, jingling a few
coins. Movies weren't a part of her
tight budget, and she'd always
respected her parents' warnings
against letting herself be
influenced by bad entertainment,
but she'd heard good things about
Mrs. Miniver and wanted a break.

She smiled, "Sure, I'm game."

A gaggle of girls in long, plaid skirts pressed around the box office glass
under the incandescent glow of dozens of bulbs lining the theater marquis
and the entranceway. Inside, a cartoon had already begun as the ladies made
their way through a row, bumping knees and spilling popcorn.

Peggy plopped down beside Jean and began watching the cartoon
parody entitled *The Ducktators* featuring ducks as ridiculous caricatures of
Hitler, Mussolini, and with Tojo as a buck-toothed, dopey duck speaking
Japanese gibberish. Scattered chuckles in the audience didn't surprise Peggy.
Asians in upstate New York were a rare sight, and anti-Japanese sentiment
ran high in America.

After an Allied turtle repeatedly whomped the cartoon "Jap" duck with
a mallet, a hefty man behind Peggy grunted to a friend, "Damn Japs. Like
Halsey[30] says, 'The only good Jap is a dead Jap.'" His buddy replied, "Old
man Halsey says that one day, Japanese'll only be spoken in hell. Hee, hee!"

---

[30] William "Bull" Halsey, outspoken American fleet admiral, US Navy.

A chill ran over her skin, like when she was in Japan with her father and felt the contempt of the Japanese man putting up the propaganda posters against non-Asians. She closed her eyes to block out her surroundings.

Jean crunched a mouthful of popcorn and leaned the box to Peggy. "Hey, Peg, you want . . . are you OK? You feeling sick or something?"

Peggy opened her eyes and did her best to smile. "Yeah. Yeah, I guess you could say that. Listen, I think I'm going to take a short walk, then wait in the lobby for a bit. Don't worry about me. I'll be back. You have fun, OK?"

"I can come with you," Jean said.

"No, that's all right. I'll be all right. I just need a little time."

Peggy excused herself, walked up the carpet in the darkened theater, pushed out through the glass doorway, and drifted in thought down the sidewalk. With her arms folded across her chest, pulling her coat tightly, trying to keep out a coldness she still felt from inside the theater, she shuddered at the thought of the cruelty of mankind. Weren't we all the same inside? And how was this war going to end? She remembered her childhood friends in Japan and wondered how they were. Why did people want to kill each other so badly? Glancing up at the bright, crescent moon she whispered aloud, "Dear God, what's *wrong* with this world?"

Chapter 69

August 28, 1942. Shanghai, China.

As the spectacled Japanese judge rustled a sheet of paper between his hands, Jake cocked his head and sighed impatiently. Guards had summoned him and the seven other prisoners that morning, handcuffed them, and trucked them to a new location—some type of military prison camp—and shoved into a small courtroom packed with armed guards and officers. Looking at the Japanese dressed in their crisp, clean uniforms, he sighed and shook his head as he reflected on the fact that, in the last four months, he'd taken only *one* bath, and his hair and beard had been shaved only once. Like the others, he was still draped in the worn, smelly clothes he put on the morning they took to the air on April 18th. He was braced for the worst. The fact that no Japanese would look him in the eye added to the foreboding atmosphere.

Five judges in black robes sat behind a set of tables on a raised platform. The presiding judge in the center held a sheet of paper—Major General Shoji Ito, chief justice officer of the Japanese Thirteenth Army Military Court at Shanghai.

To Jake, the judges looked like utter fools in their black wigs, yet they retained an air of dignity, making them appear even sillier.

Dean Hallmark, pilot of *The Green Hornet*, laid still on a stretcher on the floor, too weak to stand. He appeared to drift in and out of consciousness, sometimes speaking nonsense. A big man, the rest of the guys referred to him as "Jungle Jim," but the starvation diet, beatings, heat, and disease had gotten the best of him. Flies buzzed over his body, but he lacked even the strength to wave them off. George Barr, the redhead, nearly collapsed and was given a seat. The six others stood at a wobbly attention.

To Jake, it was obvious that this was a perfunctory exercise and that whatever decision would be handed down from this "trial" had been made long ago and probably somewhere far away. Officers had already asked each of the captives to tell his life story in miniature as the judges yawned and looked away.

It had now come to the moment of truth, but, like all other official business, it, too, was given in Japanese. The judge adjusted the reading glasses on the end of his nose. *"On April 18, 1942, the defendants, motivated by their sporting instincts and sense of glory freely volunteered to attack Japan. Over their assigned targets, the defendants showed cowardice when confronted with opposition in the air and on the ground, and with the intent of killing and wounding innocent civilians and wreaking havoc on residences and other living quarters of no military significance whatsoever, together with other planes, did carry on indiscriminate bombing and strafing, thereby causing the death and injury of approximately ten civilians and the destruction of numerous residences. The foregoing facts are based on the depositions made by the eight defendants and the copy of the acknowledgment made by the Shanghai Military Police unit in response to the request of Military Police Headquarters. Having signed confessions stating the same, the defendants have been found guilty as charged and are hereby sentenced to death by firing squad."* The judge hammered his gavel, waking Jake from his foggy thoughts.

Jake leaned to the interpreter. "What did he just say?"

"I'm sorry," the interpreter said, "the judge ordered you not be told."

Jake's mouth fell open, and he turned to Bill on his left. After enduring the farce of a sham trial he felt the least they could do was to tell them their verdict. Instead, the shackled men were silently shuffled outside by soldiers and into another structure where they were each shoved into separate six by five-foot wooden cells. Defeated, Jake stood and watched the door close him into near total darkness, listened to the crossbar clunk into place, heard the key turn, the metal bolt slide, and the final clank of the lock. The guard momentarily peered back through the narrow slot looking him directly in the eyes, then walked away. The last meaningful thing Jake still had was finally taken away—his friends.

Chapter 70

October 15, 1942. Kiangwan Military Prison, Shanghai, China.

In a grass clearing beside a Chinese cemetery, Captain Tatsuta, the warden and commanding officer of the Kiangwan Military Prison, looked over the three condemned men, each with his hands tied behind his back: Lieutenant Bill Farrow, pilot of the *Bat out of Hell*; Sargent Harry Spatz, gunner; and Lieutenant Dean "Jungle Jim" Hallmark, pilot of *The Green Hornet*.

As the warden, he knew it was his duty, yet at the same time had come to know and even respect the men he was now ordered to execute. He struggled with how best to put their minds at ease before they breathed their

Interior courtyard of the Kiangwan Prison (photo taken after the war).

last.

The sound of soldiers hammering echoed in the otherwise silent yard. Soldiers tapped three small, newly constructed wooden crosses into the ground behind the prisoners. Six rifled soldiers stood at attention beside a small table burning incense. Three medical officers stood off to the side while three other soldiers stood guard. A late afternoon breeze ruffled the untucked shirt tails of the three prisoners.

The emperor informed Tatsuta that, in a gesture of mercy, only three of the eight captive fliers were to be shot. The others were to be kept in solitary confinement until a final decision was made on what to do with them, pending the development of the war.

The day before, Tatsuta gave each of the three men pens and paper to write out their final words, good-byes, and last requests to those they loved. Perhaps most excruciating were the words of Bill Farrow to his fiancé, Lib Sims, a girl he promised to marry as soon as he was home again, which they both expected would be a month or two after his brief mission.

An officer read off the charges in Japanese followed by an interpreter who summarized the charges in English. When complete, they both bowed and stepped to the side.

Tatsuta walked up to the three men and spoke in English, first looking them one by one, eye to eye. "I feel sorry for you. Your lives were short, but your names will be remembered forever."

Bill stood uprightly and fully raised his head. "Tell the folks back home we died bravely. Will you?"

Captain Tatsuta nodded. He gathered his courage and gave to his prisoners the best he had to offer. "Christ died on a cross and you on your part must die on a cross as well, but when you are executed, when you die on your cross, you will be honored as gods." He hoped, in some way, to give them the most honorable deaths according to their beliefs, to the best of his understanding. "When you are bound to the cross, your faith and the cross will be united. Therefore, have faith." Perhaps this would give them some hope in death, he thought. "Do you have anything else to say?"

Bill, Harry, and Dean looked at each other. Bill shook his head.

Captain Tatsuta bowed deeply to the airmen, stood upright, then nodded to the soldiers who guided each man to his cross, pushed him down into a kneeling position, and tied his arms to the horizontal crossbar with another loop of rope to hold up his head to the center post. Each man was blindfolded with a white strip of cloth. Another soldier daubed a round, black dot in the center of the blindfold over the center each man's forehead.

When the soldiers returned to their positions, Tatsuta waited, then called out in Japanese, "Attention! Face the target!"

The soldiers in two rows of three each turned ninety degrees toward the prisoners.

With a clean motion, Tatsuta drew his sword from its scabbard with his right hand and thrust it into the air as the afternoon sun gleamed faded from the sky. This was his duty, and he wouldn't hesitate.

"Prepare!"

The first row of three drew their rifles to their shoulders, cocked the steel bolts in unison, and aimed at the black marks on the blindfolds. The second row of gunners was prepared in the event the first marksman's weapon misfired, or he missed.

With his sword still raised in his right hand, Tatsuta raised his left hand into the air and held it stationary for several seconds. He looked away from the men to the horizon, then dropped his left hand. "Fire!"

A cluster of three shots reverberated through the cemetery grounds as the three, limp bodies slumped forward and the blood trickled down their faces, dripping onto the dust below. The medical officers walked toward the victims.

Their letters were never mailed.

Chapter 71

The following morning.

Jake found himself handcuffed and escorted to a common courtyard by impeccably dressed armed soldiers. He saw others carrying new shovels. It didn't look good. Guards ordered him and the other four prisoners to wash in a trough. Although forbidden to speak to his fellow prisoners, one look of the eyes told him they were all thinking the same thing. This was the end. Jake casually measured the height of the walls glancing bottom to top—too high to climb over.

Soon, guards prompted them to line up and escorted them back into the same, tiny military courtroom they stood in almost two months earlier, standing before the same judges with their same ridiculous wigs. Fifteen armed soldiers surrounded the five gaunt, bearded prisoners. Everything in Jake wanted to believe that their three missing buddies had been transferred somewhere else, but he knew better. Now it was his turn to hear why, when, and how he and the others would be executed. Shot? Beheaded? Japs are scum.

The center judge nodded to a heavyset officer holding several sheets of paper in trembling hands, sweating profusely. He blotted his face with a handkerchief, then began in English, *"It has been proven beyond all doubt that the defendants, motivated by a false sense of glory, carried on indiscriminate bombing of schools and hospitals and machine gunned innocent civilians with complete disregard for the rules of war . . ."*

Jake seethed, hearing the trumped-up charges for the first time in the kangaroo court. The Japanese knew full well they'd hit military targets. It didn't really matter what he was saying anymore. They had their verdict and only wanted to find some reasons to prop it up. It was all whitewashed propaganda now.

Great beads of sweat dripped down the side of the reader's face. *"The tribunal, acting under the law, hereby sentences the defendants to death!"*

"You sons of bitches!" Chase Nielson shouted as a bayoneted rifle quickly guided him back in line.

Jake clenched his teeth. Soldiers gripped their rifles more firmly.

"But, through the graciousness of His Majesty, the emperor, your sentences are hereby commuted to life imprisonment with special treatment." The officer exhaled deeply and once again wiped the perspiration from his face.

Jake had spent the last two months in solitary confinement, twenty-three and a half hours each day eating rotten fish heads and maggot infested rice and picking lice from his hair, yet a strange sense of joy breezed over him. Moments earlier, he'd been totally resigned to immediate death.

The soldiers marched the prisoners back to their cells and closed them back in, one at a time. Jake's eyes penetrated the wooden walls that had become his only friend. The idea of freedom was a million miles away. But even if he hoped to survive to the end of the war, he knew he'd be executed before he'd ever be turned over to the Americans. His life sentence seemed more of a delayed death penalty, but at least he was still alive, for now.

A Raider's cell at Kiangwan.
Notice the slit in the door.

Chapter 72

December 1942. Madras, Oregon.

"Oh my!" Mrs. Andrus admiringly lifted up a certificate to the light as she sat at the kitchen table with Glen, his three sisters, and Mr. Andrus huddled around her. "Jake's been awarded the Distinguished Flying Cross!"

Mr. Andrus smiled. He knew he didn't mean it, but he wished he did.

"Look at that!" Helen said.

"Who would've ever believed it?" Glen asked. "My big brother!"

"Well, I'm going to put this right next to his picture on my dresser." Mrs. Andrus turned to her husband. "Hiram, you find us a nice frame, will you?"

Mr. Andrus reached out his farm-worn hand and gently grasped the sheet of paper. "I'll do it tomorrow." He smiled at his wife, then looked at the children, who glanced at each other, carefully trying not to spoil their mother's dream that somehow Jake was still alive. There had been no word about Jake or any of the downed Raiders since the public news about the raid eight months earlier. Nothing. Mr. Andrus knew that no news was bad news. He smiled again. "I'll have it up for you tomorrow."

Jake's portrait following his completion of training.

Chapter 73

December 1942. Hopevale.

Under tall trees in the warm, humid morning air, Jimmy stood before sixty or so people singing together in their open air church, sitting on bench seats of stacked stone rows facing each other beneath overhanging trees. Local Filipinos, students from the college, and some miners all joined the dozen or so missionaries and teachers who made their home in Hopevale and the nearby village of Katipunan. At times, they hosted over 100 in their tiny Chapel in the Glen. Francis played away on the foot-pumped reed organ while Jimmy led into the final stanza at the front beside a rock altar with a makeshift cross adorned with large bouquets of wildflowers across the base. He proclaimed every word with honesty:

"In Christ now meet both east and west,
in him meet south and north;
all Christ-like souls are one in him
throughout the whole wide earth."

The final notes of the organ held, then stopped and reverberated through the trees. Jimmy patted his face with a rag. The squeals of a family of macaque monkeys from the boughs above broke the silence. "I thank you all for making the hike to be with us this morning. You can visit any time you'd like. God's best to you."

As the meeting broke up, a weathered middle-aged Filipina woman with her daughter carrying a burlap sack approached Jimmy. The twelve-year-old girl held out the bag and spoke in her best English, "Cassava roots, mangoes, and rice. For you and friends."

"Thank you so much," Jimmy said as he leaned in and gave the young

ABHS

*Jennie Adams, on the right, with friends in
the foliage of Panay before she fled to Hopevale.*

girl a gentle hug. "We couldn't survive without the love and help of people like you and your mother."

The woman shook Jimmy's hand and wouldn't let go as she looked around at the encompassing green foliage. "It so strange that most beautiful church I be in has no walls." She looked Jimmy in the eyes. "But isn't that way it should be? Different people, one God, no walls between any?"

Jimmy was humbled by her simple insight. He thought it ironic that it took a brutal war that divided nations to bring their small band of various people in the mountains so close together. He smiled. "No walls. No walls between anyone is good."

Jennie sat on the step in front of her hut under the watchful eyes of a concerned Filipino father as she wrapped a grass strand around a bamboo splint on a young boy's finger. Charma held his palm steady. "Leave this on, OK? Don't take it off. Come back next week and I'll look at it. It's going to be OK." She looked up at his relieved father. "Don't let him take it off for anything and make sure—"

"Hey, hey, HEY!" Charma said just as she glanced over her shoulder in time to catch a macaque dragging off a small bunch of bananas from a hutch. "Come back here, you rascal!"

Jennie put her hands on her hips and smiled as the monkey disappeared into the jungle. "Y'know, that's really impolite! Next time just ask!" she shouted.

Charma brushed some dirt from her arm. "I guess he's hungry, too."

Chapter 74

December 28, 1942, Hopevale.

Jimmy anxiously watched Jack as he dialed in a dented, battery-powered shortwave radio while the entire Hopevale group stood silently in front of Jimmy's place. Half a dozen Filipinos and four other armed guerrillas joined the audience—two white and two Filipino men. Jack and another gold miner-turned-guerrilla helped maintain the radio for the Hopevale people as it was their only connection to the outside world.

Jimmy waited to hear a speech by President Roosevelt. An important one. It had been just over a year since the Japanese attacked Pearl Harbor when he was confident that the war wouldn't last more than six months. He was also certain the Japanese would never attack the Philippines and even *more* certain that they would never take it. Now he wasn't certain of anything, but, like everyone else, he was impatient to hear exactly what the United States was going to do, and even more importantly, *when*. He'd heard a lot of promises of rescue, but he really wanted to hear it from the president himself.

Through a high-frequency hum and crackle of interference, President Roosevelt's voice sounded through the speaker in his halting, deliberate tone: "*As President of the United States, I know that I speak for all our people on this solemn occasion. The resources of the United States, of the British Empire, of the Netherland's East Indies, and of the Chinese Republic have been dedicated by their people to the utter and complete defeat of the Japanese warlords.*"

Charma folded her arms. Jimmy stood motionless with one ear facing the radio, carefully examining the meaning of each word.

"*In this great struggle of the Pacific, the loyal Americans of the*

Philippine Islands are called upon to play a crucial role. They have played, and they are playing tonight, their part with the greatest gallantry. As President, I wish to express to them my feeling of sincere admiration for the fight they are now making."

Jack glanced across at a Filipino guerrilla who gave a slight grin. His dark skin was slick with sweat and his eyes beamed confidence. The loosely banded guerrillas had already introduced themselves to the Japanese by a series of random hit-and-run attacks near the Villar copper mines in Sibalom, about fifteen miles to the southwest, extracting heavy losses and disrupting the Japanese operations.

"The people of the United States will never forget what the people of the Philippine Islands are doing this day and will do in the days to come. I give to the people of the Philippines my solemn pledge that their freedom will be redeemed and their independence established and protected. The entire resources, in men and in material, of the United States stand behind that pledge."

Francis put his hands on his hips and glanced at Jimmy with a nod of confident hope.

"It is not for me or for the people of this country to tell you where your duty lies. We are engaged in a great and common cause. I count on every Philippine man, woman, and . . ."

A loud, distinct bird call rang out from a tree, from a lookout whistling loudly, a signal Jimmy well knew that meant Japanese forces were somewhere in the area. As the Filipino boy whistled again even louder, Jack shut off the radio and shoved it into the hut under a mat as everyone fled to their designated hideouts.

Charma doused the cooking fire with a bucket of sand as Jimmy threw together a bag of mangoes and a canteen of water and headed out behind Francis and Gertrude into the deep foliage. They never knew how long they'd be hiding and had to be prepared for a long wait. Even though they'd been barefoot for nearly their entire stay, they still had to walk gingerly over the rocks and muddy ground through the woods to their cave. Running wasn't an option without severe consequences.

In a tree above, the boy looked through binoculars down on a group of twenty-two Japanese soldiers about a mile away in the valley below, hacking through bamboo near a path, stopping and pointing, unfolding a map, and pointing again.

Jimmy tripped over a vine but caught himself as the four of them clambered into the small grotto. Charma pulled the vines back over the opening as the others leaned against the cool stone walls and did their best to make as little noise as possible while breathing heavily and listening. Reaching down to his foot, Jimmy plucked a leaf stuck between his toes and noticed a fresh gash on his leg. "I didn't hear FDR say *when* they're coming," Jimmy whispered, "Did you?"

Francis forced a grin. "Whenever it is, it won't be a day too soon. I can tell you that."

This was the second time they'd fled to the cave. The location seemed pretty remote to the locals and certainly to Jimmy, but the guerrillas had stirred up a hornet's nest by their successful attacks and the Japanese weren't willing to wait for the next one. They were determined to take the fight to the guerrillas, once they'd found their center of operations. Jimmy simply hoped that the Americans would take the island before the Japanese found them out. They'd been as close as a half-mile before, but the jungle was so dense it was hard to see a footpath even ten feet away. Jimmy felt they were as safe as they could be.

"Wait," Charma whispered. "Listen."

Each froze as they strained to hear. It was the second bird call, the "all clear" sound from the lookout.

Charma put her hand to her chest and sighed with relief. "This isn't fun anymore. I just want to go back home, to *our* home in Yokohama."

"You know," Jimmy said, "it's possible that we could run into a student we were teaching just a few years ago." As he parted the draped vines, he looked back at the group and paused. "I wonder if he'd shoot me."

Chapter 75

Early April 1943. Rabaul Air Base, the
Australian Territory of New Guinea.

Fuchida looked out through an observation window of a twin-engine Mitsubishi G4M bomber, what the Americans called a "Betty," as it descended toward a grass and dirt runway at the air base. Mountain ridges and a smoldering volcano hemmed in the base against the large, oval bay scattered with cruisers, destroyers, and cargo vessels. The sight of black volcanic soil contrasting with the lush green foliage and the cerulean blue water fascinated Fuchida. Only six years earlier, the eruption of two volcanoes buried the city of Rabaul in ash from volcanic vents on both sides of the bay, itself the caldera of an ancient volcano.

Flying past rows of fighters and bombers, most camouflaged with palm fronds, the plane touched down in a streak of gray dust and came to a rolling stop beside a virtual tent city for over 100,000 Japanese troops.

Engineers work on a Zero fighter on Rabaul, volcanoes in the background.

Rabaul served as the continuous launching point for both air and sea operations in the region.

Previously limited to desk jobs by his healing ankles, Fuchida devoted himself to reviewing past battles and presenting his analyses to the Naval General Headquarters in Tokyo. He'd been out of the field since the battle of Midway nine months earlier and anxiously sought to see and hear the state of operations firsthand– and perhaps, to meet with Admiral Yamamoto.

The round, red Hinomaru on the fuselage side swung out as a door, and the soldiers and officers began disembarking. His casts were off, but his ankles were sometimes a bit weak, and he stepped carefully.

"Welcome, old man," Genda said grinning widely.

"Old man? These are *battle* wounds."

". . . of an old man."

The two companions shook hands and crossed the taxiway. Fuchida looked over at the nearby volcano *Tavurvur* spewing smoke. "Are things as bad down here as they're saying in Tokyo?"

Genda didn't answer as he kept walking. "No." A breeze of dust blew over from a fighter taxiing by. "They're worse."

Fuchida looked back at Genda with concern.

Inside Genda's one-room officer's quarters, Fuchida emptied a glass of beer as Genda bent the cap off another bottle of Asahi lager and sat down. The sound of aircraft taking off and landing droned in the background.

"Yamamoto was bitterly disappointed with Guadalcanal," Genda said. "We thought that twenty-five hundred men could hold the island and control the airfield." Genda refilled both their glasses and set the bottle next to a row of empties. "He truly believed we could win that battle. We *all* did. We threw *everything* into it." Genda took a sip and stared at the wall. "After thirty *thousand* men and five months of fighting we still couldn't retake the airfield, much less the island. The Americans annihilated us."

"But what about the future? What about plans for a decisive battle?" Fuchida said. "When and where will it be?" The past was done, Fuchida thought. Best to get on with the business at hand.

Genda shook his head. "Even though we still have more aircraft carriers than the Americans, for now anyway, we had to send two carriers back home—for lack of skilled pilots."

Upset, but also a bit light-headed, Fuchida pounded his fist. "I *warned* them to stop using our best pilots in battle and to hold some back for *training*, but no one would listen. Now it's almost too late."

"Fuchi," Genda said as he shook his head despondently, "do you realize that over half of the pilots who flew to Pearl Harbor are gone? More than half?"

"Well, we're producing enough aircraft. I know. I see the reports. I just wish they'd send more planes to the navy and fewer to the army in China. We'll have more pilots, but it'll take some time."

Genda took a long drink and smacked his lips. "Yamamoto wants to see things as well. He'll be here in two days and will make an assessment. He'll know what to do."

Genda raised his half-empty beer glass to Fuchida who did likewise. "To victory under Yamamoto."

Fuchida put on his best face but could read the doubt in Genda's eyes. "To victory." They downed their beer.

The following day Fuchida and Genda made the rounds touring the hangars, conversing with the pilots and listening to their adventures as they pointed to bullet holes in their wings and complained about low octane fuel and faulty radio equipment. Fuchida knew what the reports were, but now he wanted to know the truth, and the truth was bad. Still, he believed they could regroup, resupply, and make a strong showing to at least stop the American advance—somewhere.

A few days later, after Yamamoto had met with the base commanders and was briefed on operations, Yamamoto called Fuchida to his quarters on Residency Hill, as it was called, a white stucco house overlooking the bay.

The two of them met in his front room tiled with red terracotta flooring. Fuchida sat on a wicker sofa and Yamamoto on a wicker chair, both in their summer white uniforms. The admiral's presence boosted morale, but Fuchida also knew it was a risk for him to be so close to the action.

"Before we began to fight the Americans," Yamamoto said, "I remember when the navy would say that one Zero fighter could take on ten American aircraft. Even now they still say that one Zero can take on two

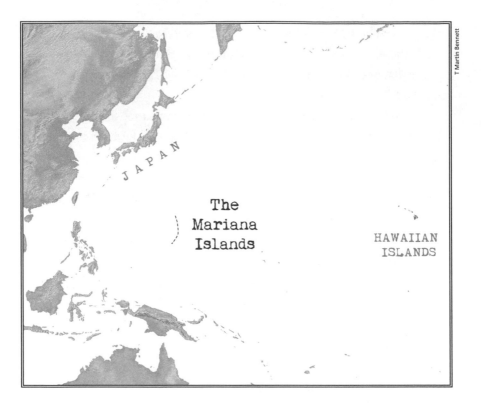

enemy planes. What do you think?"

Fuchida sensed the master strategist testing him. "Sir, our men have shown tremendous fighting spirit and skill, but we might have been wiser overestimating our enemy and underestimating our own strength."

Yamamoto nodded once, looked out across the bay, snapped shut his cigarette case, and tapped a cigarette against it a couple of times before putting it to his mouth. "The Third Fleet now has fewer than one hundred fighters, sixty dive bombers, and a handful of torpedo planes." He lit the cigarette, blew out the match, and turned back to Fuchida. "The fleet's been gutted."

It was a surprise for Fuchida to hear Yamamoto speak so freely and to cast doubts about the future, a future that was clouding for Fuchida, too. Yet he knew Yamamoto understood that nothing other than brutal honesty would do and hunted for ideas. Fuchida got up and moved to a sweeping wall map. Yamamoto twisted to watch. Fuchida traced his finger along a vertical string of islands in the open ocean 700 miles south of Japan and 700 west of the Philippines.

"Here." Fuchida looked back at Yamamoto. "I suggest we establish a firm line of air and surface defense along the Mariana Islands, one which the Americans can never cross."

"The Americans have two dozen heavy carriers nearly completed," Yamamoto said. "Battleships, cruisers, destroyers, and submarines as well." He took a slow drag from his cigarette and blew a cloud of smoke up toward the ceiling. "Eventually, they will come."

"What we lack in carriers we can strengthen with island air bases." Fuchida wanted to recapture the confidence he once had, but the wind simply wasn't in his sails. "I strongly believe that we must not allow the Americans to occupy Saipan and the islands, which would put them within striking distance of our homeland, a situation that is simply unacceptable."

"I've come to the same conclusion. We must make a stand there and control the skies over the Marianas. If we can concentrate our forces and draw out the Americans, we have a chance for a significant victory." Yamamoto stood up. "I'll see that you have what you need to establish more bases." As he shook his hand, Yamamoto's face looked somber. "The enemy

University of Pittsburgh

Admiral Yamamoto sends off an attack fighter on Rabaul, 1943.

has been quicker to learn from their failures than we've been to learn from our successes. We mustn't make the same mistake again."

He escorted Fuchida to the open double doors at the entryway and looked out to the mountains. "At Guadalcanal, we were mistaken about the Americans and found ourselves completely unprepared for their fighting spirit. Now that we know who they are, we must let them know who *we* are."

Chapter 76

April 19, 1943. Yokosuka Naval Base, Tokyo Bay.

Staring at several stacks of paper on his desk, Fuchida, back in Japan, sighed, slid one stack to the side and pulled another toward him, and began leafing through the top sheets. Hearing fast, heavy footsteps, he looked up, waiting to see who would appear. Genda arrived breathing heavily, his face rather pale. Fuchida knew it was bad news. *Very* bad news.

"They got him," Genda stated plainly. "Yamamoto. He's dead."

Fuchida's ears tingled as a wave shot through him head to toe. "How? What happened?" The Imperial Navy had lost its greatest living commander, a giant to all who knew him. The respect he commanded had gone with him to his grave—forever.

"Yesterday, near Bougainville." Genda motioned for Fuchida to follow him. Fuchida jumped up from his desk and rushed out behind him through

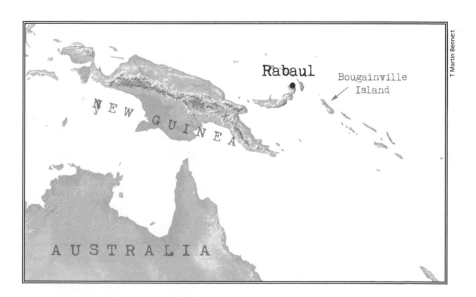

a hallway into another room featuring a large map.

Genda put his finger on Rabaul on the northeastern tip of New Britain and dragged it southeast below the island of Bougainville. "He and commander Ugaki left in two medium attack bombers escorted by six fighters to tour bases to encourage the men before he returned to Tokyo, but about ninety minutes after take-off, a group of American P-38 twin-engine fighters attacked them."

"High-speed long-range aircraft." Fuchida was puzzled. "That doesn't look like a place for a routine American patrol. How many P-38s?"

"The information is still coming in, but the fighter escorts reported twelve P-38s."

"Twelve?!"

Genda looked at Fuchida. They both thought the same thing.

"An ambush," Fuchida breathed out.

"We can't be sure at this point, but it looks like the Americans may have been waiting."

Fuchida shook his head. "The Americans will know our every move if our codes have been broken."

"Something the Naval General Staff refuses to believe possible. They

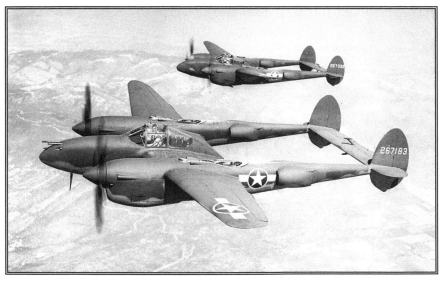

The aptly named P-38 Lightning had a top speed of 414 mph and was the aircraft of America's top ace, Richard Bong, having shot down no fewer than 40 enemy aircraft.

Yamamoto's downed Mitsubishi G4M "Betty"
bomber in the jungle of Bougainville Island, 1943.

believe the code is unbreakable."

Fuchida stared without expression. He'd seen what the overconfidence of the naval command had led them into at Midway. Even he'd been infected by the same "victory disease" from their string of sweeping conquests throughout Southeast Asia and the Pacific. But heavy doses of reality had brought him around, and he feared those who still clung to wishful dreams of invincibility. "Didn't anyone try to dissuade the admiral?"

"Vice Admiral Ozawa begged him not to go, but Yamamoto was determined to visit his men."

"Perhaps," Fuchida said, "it's fitting for the admiral to end his days beside those he led."

"Perhaps," Genda acknowledged, "but who can take his place now?"

Chapter 77

April 21, 1943. Madras, Oregon.

Standing at the kitchen table with his arm around his younger sister's neck, Glen rubbed his whiskers and soberly stared down at the newspaper from Albany, Oregon with the screaming headline announcing the death of the "Tokyo Raiders," but without giving specific names. Like lightning, the news shot across the Pacific Ocean to every home in America and to the White House itself, provoking outrage in newspapers and over the radio, denunciations of savagery and vows for revenge. But to Jake's family, it was a stab to the heart. Helen fell onto Glen's shoulder in sobs.

Outside, Mr. and Mrs. Andrus stood before a sea of anxious reporters crowding for position pinning them to a fence. Mr. Andrus kept protectively close to his wife as she fielded another question from an eager reporter.

"I heard it on the radio today," she said, "when President Roosevelt made the announcement."

The Japanese officially disclosed that the Doolittle Raiders had been "*severely punished*," that all had been put on trial, found guilty of killing innocent civilians, had been justly sentenced to death, and that some had been executed. But without saying exactly who, though mixed reports had trickled out, it left an air of confusion. To the frustration of the American government, Japan also refused to allow neutral Swiss representatives to visit the men, insisting that they weren't prisoners at all, but rather war criminals. The Japanese gave a warning over the airwaves to all Americans to "*Make sure every flier that comes here has a special pass to hell, and rest assured it's strictly a one-way ticket!*"

President Roosevelt immediately pledged that the "*warlords*" of "*these diabolical crimes*" would be brought to justice, further stating that the United States government would hold personally and officially responsible, all officers of the Japanese government who have participated in this "*act of barbarity.*" An American official tersely stated that "*revenge will come in due course.*"

Waving his pencil for attention, another reporter blurted out, "Ma'am, Ma'am, what do you think of the reports listing your son as one of those who've been executed?"

Mrs. Andrus glanced at her husband who put his arm around her. "Well, until last night we didn't worry much about Jacob. He's always been able to take care of himself. But since we heard the latest news . . ." She was doing her best to keep her emotions in check, but began to succumb. "Well, I'm afraid . . . I'm afraid he . . . he may be dead now."

As the reporters unleashed a new flurry of questions, Mr. Andrus saw the toll it was taking, raised his hand and leaned forward with the authority of a trainer pulling his fighter from a match, "That's it, fellas. I'm sorry, but's that's all for now. No more questions. Thanks. Thanks very much."

Carol Aiko DeShazer Dixon

*The last picture of Jake before he left
on the Doolitte Raid. Glen on the left.*

The sweltering, dusty day melted into a deep orange sunset, then descended into night. Late in the evening, the starry sky and near-full moon washed the silhouettes of the house, barns, and fences in a cold blue. A soft yellow glow filtered through the curtains of a single window of the Andrus farmhouse. All was still. All was quiet, but for the lonely sound of crickets and the muffled, distant sound of the uncontrolled sobbing of a bereaved mother.

Early the next morning, the sun broke through the sky over the distant eastern mountain ridge and glazed the front porch in gold. Mr. Andrus carried two blue-speckled enameled cups of steaming coffee out through the screen door. Mrs. Andrus sat rocking in her high-back chair staring at the distant horizon, creaking the wooden deck with each rock. As he held the cup to his wife, she looked up with a smile and an unusual appearance of contentment.

"Thank you, dear." She blew across her cup, took the slightest sip, and sat back and slowly rocked some more, still with a peaceful grin.

Mr. Andrus gently set his cup on the table between them and sat down, keeping his eye on his wife, mystified by her demeanor, even wondering about her sanity.

"Jake's not dead," she stated calmly, then slowly sipped again.

Sunlight flooded the master bedroom as well, illuminating their oak dresser and faded yellow and green flowered wallpaper, marred and stained by time. On the lace runner draped over the top stood a framed black and

white photo of Jake as a boy holding two
puppies in front of a picket fence. Beside it
stood a picture of Jake and Glen in a field
with their arms behind their backs,
squinting into the sun. It was the last photo
Mrs. Andrus had of Jake, taken the last
time he was home in April 1941. Next was
a smaller framed shot of Jake's high school
portrait—a serious picture of Jake in a
herringbone-patterned coat and a dark tie.
Then there was Jake's black-and-gold-
framed certificate of the Distinguished
Flying Cross for his "heroism or

extraordinary achievement while participating in an aerial flight." Below it,
the medal itself, laying on the lace, always in plain view.

Pinned with thumbtacks, a collection of newspaper clippings adorned
the wall with titles of *"Jake's a Hero in His Home Town"* and *"Local Boy*

Helps Bomb Tokyo" with his same military portrait repeated in article after article. Another clipping read, *"Corporal DeShazer Identified in Picture"* showing him in China cowering on the steps among his fellow captured comrades.

But at the bottom far right of the compilation pinned to the wall with silver thumbtacks was a newly added scrap of torn paper with handwritten words in blue ink:

> *This is what the Lord says: 'Refrain your voice from weeping and your eyes from tears. They will return from the land of the enemy. So there is hope for your future,' declares the Lord. 'Your children will return to their own land.' Jeremiah 31:16.*

Below that in larger letters were the bold words,

> *Praise the dear Lord! April 23, 1943.*

On the front porch, Mrs. Andrus stopped rocking and stared at the horizon. "Isn't the sky just lovely this morning?"

Chapter 78

Early July 1943. Tama Reien Cemetery, Tokyo.

Fuchida cupped his hands around a smoldering bundle of sticks of incense and gently blew on the glowing embers. For a moment the breeze calmed, letting the smoke rise before the eight-foot-tall speckled-gray granite column engraved with the name "*Isoroku Yamamoto.*" He slowly stood and eyed the stately stone from top to bottom as if he were venerating the admiral himself, his gaze finally resting on the bouquets of white chrysanthemums he had placed in the stone vases on either side. He stood before the monument with two other officers, the three deciding to pay their respects to their fallen leader.

The fact that Americans had downed Yamamoto's plane on April 18th, exactly one year to the day of the Doolittle Raid on Japan, was a troublesome omen to him. Perhaps it was fate. So long as Yamamoto commanded the Combined Fleet, Fuchida believed that victory was within reach. He was now convinced that all was lost, words he could *never* speak to anyone. Yet he gathered his strength, clasped his hands before him, closed his eyes, and bowed his head to Yamamoto's spirit. He fully vowed to devote himself to the destruction of the American forces and to the protection of the homeland of Japan, the nation he loved and lived for—and for which he was equally willing to die.

The preceding day Fuchida had stood beside Vice Admiral Kakuji Kakuta before Emperor Hirohito as Kakuta was installed as the new commander in chief of the First Air Fleet. Fuchida had been appointed as Kakuta's senior staff officer. With his greater authority, Fuchida felt an even greater responsibility. As he stood upright, opened his eyes, and studied the motionless pillar, a sense of finality swept over him. If the new First Air Fleet failed, then all of Yamamoto's achievements, all of Fuchida's

*The grave of Admiral Isoroku Yamamoto in
the Tama Reien Cemetery, Fuchu City, Tokyo, Japan.*

efforts, and all the work and suffering and death of the *entire* forces of Japan would have been *completely* in vain—a crushing thought. His eyes blurred with tears clinging to his eyelashes.

At the state funeral, the motto had been, "Follow Yamamoto!" He'd wanted *nothing* more than to follow Yamamoto into a new era of Japan. But now, this stone monument over a silent grave made clear the destination of those who would follow him.

Admiral Yamamoto saluting pilots at
Rabaul shortly before his death on April 18, 1943.

Chapter 79

July 1943. Hopevale.

Among a small garden of waist-high corn stalks, Jimmy yanked out a few more weeds, rested his hands on his back, and winced as he stood upright in the muddy row under a blazing sun, then heard someone coming his way. Jack strode up with loads of goods slung over both shoulders. Jimmy headed for the shade of a mahogany tree and sat his aching body down.

"Good afternoon!"

"And a good day to you, my friend," Jimmy replied, fanning his face with his hat.

Jack came into the shadow of the great tree and swung two drab green canvas bags off one shoulder and three brand new M1 Garand rifles and a well-worn machine gun off the other. Most men would have had a hard time lifting the eighty pounds of goods that Jack seemed to carry with ease.

He squatted down and dug a the bag. "Think quick," he said as he threw things into the air for Jimmy to catch: a roll of cotton gauze, a package of disinfectant, and a box of razor blades. He held up a pack of cigarettes and shook them. "Cigarettes? Don't think you want these." He slid them into his pocket, then reached back in and tossed out a package of tetanus antitoxin, and paused. "Ahh, here we go." Pulling out a handful of five small bars he reached out to Jimmy and dropped them into his hand. Jack smiled. "Chocolate. All this stuff came in by submarine on the north shore last night." Jack pulled out another chocolate bar and held it up to Jimmy's face. "Look at this."

Jimmy leaned forward, adjusted his streaked glasses, and read the imprinted label out loud, "I shall return. General Douglas MacArthur." Below the general's hand-written signature in smaller letters, "General

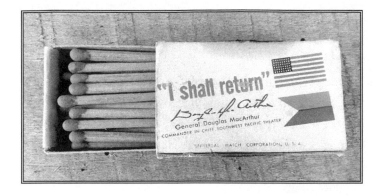

Douglas MacArthur, Commander in Chief Southwest Pacific Theater."
Beside it two, tiny colored flags crossed over, of the United States and the
Philippines. He looked off into the distance. "I shall return. I like that. I like
that a *lot*." He turned up to Jack's sweat-drenched face. "Thanks." His
months of fading hope seemed to resuscitate.

Jack held up two other items with similar emblems. "Matches and
cigarettes, too. I'll take this medical stuff to Fred and Jennie. Just thought
you'd like to see it first." Jack picked up a rifle, sat beside Jimmy and
carefully dusted it with his hand. "You want some weapons?"

Jimmy smiled as he gently shook his head and tucked one of the bars
into his pocket.

"I really think you could use 'em up here. All by yourself, y'know. Just
might buy you some time when you need it most."

"The Good Book says that those who take up the sword will die by the
sword."

Pausing for a second, Jack said, "Or maybe those without swords just
get killed." Jack waited for some response, but there was only silence. "So,
you don't fight?"

Years before in Japan, Jimmy had explored the many aspects of war
and peace. He'd heard every argument for and against, and had come to his
conviction that violence just wasn't the right path, but he sometimes had a
hard time clearly communicating his reckoning. He also felt conflicted at
times because, of all people, he certainly wanted *someone* to come and drive
the Japanese off the island.

Jimmy took the rifle from Jack and ran his hand over it. Still examining the weapon, he said, "We fight, all right . . . but our weapons don't kill people." He handed the rifle back to Jack and looked him in the eyes. "Love brings dead people back to life."

Jack nodded and grinned. They both understood each other, liked each other, and respected each other, but they both knew neither would change the mind of the other. Jack stood back up, collected the rifles and bags and heaved them back onto his sturdy shoulders. "Well, I'll keep using mine until I learn how to use yours," he said with a cheerful wink.

Jimmy looked up. "Jack, you're a strong man, a powerful man, but one day you may find yourself in a position where all your strength just isn't enough. Then you'll know how weak you really are. How weak we *all* are."

"Me and the boys'll be staying the night here, then we'll head out tomorrow morning."

Jimmy gave a casual salute with a smile. "Thanks for taking care of us up here."

"My pleasure."

"Listen, Jack, can you get some letters out if I get them to you? You know, by submarine?"

"Sure. No problem."

Chapter 80

July 1943. Japanese Headquarters. Iloilo City, Panay.

General Tanaka, the incoming leader on the island, meticulously adjusted the fingers of his white gloves as he stood beside a glistening black 1941 four-door Chrysler Imperial, a rare luxury car featuring elegant "coach doors" which opened one to the right and one to the left on each side. A prominent physician formerly owned the car which the Japanese had appropriated along with his estate, which they converted into a headquarters. A soldier opened the passenger door for the general and waited.

The commander's party stood next to a small detachment of soldiers on a circular gravel driveway of the estate just outside the city under the scattered shade of mature palm trees. Japanese colors flew on flagstaffs on either side of the brick-stepped entryway into the manor house.

The new commander, General Shizuichi Tanaka, with his WWI-era mustache, had earned a degree in English literature at Oxford.

"Commander," the base officer said to the general, "you may want to consider an armored personnel carrier for your initial tour." He bowed and held out a hand toward an ugly, behemoth of a machine—a six-and-a-half-ton Type 1 *Ho-Ha* half-track: eighteen feet of camouflage-painted heavy metal with room for three in the cab featuring small, hinged plates for windows. Outfitted with three machine guns, the

Chrysler's top of the line 1941 Imperial.

vehicle accommodated another twelve soldiers in the back. "Some areas of the city can be dangerous. Especially the outlying areas."

The Japanese army had sent General Tanaka specifically to this island to end the guerrilla resistance. They had effectively subdued the fighters on the other Philippine islands, more or less, but the preceding commander on Panay had failed to complete the job. It was rumored that there could be as many as 15,000 guerrillas scattered through the island, and the dynamiting of railroads and the constant ambushing of troops supported the claim. But General Tanaka viewed the guerrillas as little more than pests who were interfering with the establishment of Japanese rule and was fiercely committed to carrying out his orders. For now, he first simply wanted to get a feel for the island. As a master with the sword and bayonet, he had a matching reputation for impatient ruthlessness and cold efficiency.

Tanaka gave a quick look at the rusty half-track and brushed a speck of lint off his breast pocket. "That won't be necessary."

The base officer glanced cautiously at the squad of soldiers. No one would dare venture to contradict the general, especially in the presence of the assistants he'd brought with him, who sat

The Ho-Ha half-track armored personnel carrier.

impatiently waiting in the back seat of the idling sedan, looking forward to an afternoon of touring.

Tanaka ducked his head and sat down in the passenger seat as a soldier closed the door behind him with a crisp clunk. The driver shifted into gear and pulled out over the crackling gravel driveway under the gaze of the officer and his detachment of soldiers.

After an hour or so of exploring in the city proper, Tanaka directed his driver to the west side of the city. Observing street vendors holding out mangoes and coconuts to his vehicle as they navigated the streets, the city was getting along—business as usual.

The windshield shattered with a blast as gunshots rang out and the vehicle careened into a newspaper stand sending papers flying and halting into a wall. Screaming civilians cleared as more shots pocked and pinged the car. Tanaka's passengers dropped to the floor of the car, but his driver fell forward onto the steering wheel—dead. Tanaka threw open his door and tumbled to the safety of the ground behind the wheel well. More shots echoed and ricocheted past him.

Patting the right side of his face, Tanaka pulled his hand away. His white glove was painted with his own, brilliant red blood.

"I've had *enough* of this!"

At the estate headquarters, the base officer blew cigarette smoke into the air as he watched a forest rat shoot across the lawn. The sound of a heavy vehicle slowly faded in, calling the rest of the soldiers to grab their weapons as they looked toward the end of the extended driveway. As the sound grew, the officer dropped his cigarette to the ground and crushed it under his heel while his eyes curiously followed the armored personnel carrier lumbering toward them in a chorus of whining clanks and squeaks, finally coming to a grinding halt near the front steps in a cloud of diesel smoke.

The passenger door flung open with a bang against the steel siding. General Tanaka emerged from the beast pressing a blood-soaked handkerchief to his face.

The officer and soldiers immediately snapped to a salute but were ignored as a scowling Tanaka, disheveled and splattered with mud, quickly stormed past the soldiers with his head down, clumped up the steps, jerked open the front door and furiously slammed it behind him, shattering the glass panes into a wall of shards that jangled onto the brick entryway.

The base commander stared at the door a moment as his saluting hand drifted downward, looked over at the closest soldier, cocked his head, and shrugged.

Captain Kengo Watanabe, a stout man in his thirties with glaring eyes, stood at attention before the desk of General Tanaka. An able and experienced veteran of the Sino-Japanese War, Watanabe had also led battles against the Americans in Bataan on the northern island.

Wearing a white headband of gauze covering his left eye, the general paced behind his desk. He paused and looked at Captain Watanabe with his one, open eye. "Wipe them out! Wipe them *all* out! *Especially* the Americans!" He began pacing again. "We control *all* of the islands except for *this* one. It's a *disgrace!* Begin from the coastal cities and work your way in toward the mountains. We know the guerrillas have hideouts and command posts, and we've picked up radio communications. They're giving our troop movements and shipping information to MacArthur, and now he's starting to supply them. This must be stopped. *Immediately!* I want this island to be *completely* subdued! Do you understand?!"

"Yes, sir!" Watanabe replied with a respectful bow of his head.

"I don't care how you do it. Just get it done!"

Watanabe nodded. Among all of the Imperial Japanese Army commanders in the Philippines, perhaps in the entire Empire, there was none better for this job than Captain Watanabe—and no one worse for the people of the Philippines.

Ten miles northwest of Iloilo City, Japanese soldiers corralled over 700 townspeople into the barrio center as unwilling spectators. Watanabe's reputation had preceded his arrival. They'd heard of "The Butcher of Panay," but they'd never seen him before. When he found suspects, he and his men beat them with bats, pumped their stomachs with water, and had them stomped to death. Others were burned alive. Women were raped in public. Children beheaded. A villager once stumbled upon over 100 dead bodies in a swamp.

He eyed the terrified people. His katana dripped red as more blood oozed under the walls of a nearby hut, soaking into the dirt street. A limp arm dangled out through the doorway. Twenty-two severed Filipino heads rested in a heap near the front door, some of them of children. A Japanese soldier shadowed Watanabe shouting the translation for the crowd.

"You think you can harbor guerrillas?!" Watanabe screamed. He pointed to the pile of bodies. Droplets of red speckled Watanabe's face and shirt. He swung his sword in wild gesticulations. "You think you can be a safe haven for people murdering our soldiers?! Tell your friends!" he yelled as he slowly paced from inside the circle. "Tell your neighbors: You help any guerrilla in *any* way, we will kill you! We will kill your family! And we will kill *all* of your friends! Maybe by sword this time, maybe by fire the next!"

He stepped closer to the paralyzed people and eyed them one by one as he strode around the circle. "Do you hear me?!"

An ordinary barrio in the Philippines in the late 1930s.

Chapter 81

August 1943. Nanking, China.

"Special treatment" is what the Japanese told Jake he was to receive. Now he understood as he sat motionless—staring at the corner of his new cell in near-total darkness. Without explanation, earlier that spring, officers had handcuffed, blindfolded, and flown Jake and the four others to a new location. By peeking out of his blindfold and asking a few questions, he deduced that they'd been taken to Nanking, about 150 miles west of Shanghai.

Hoping for perhaps a little more freedom, disappointment prevailed. The only really new thing was that he was given a name: "Go"—Japanese for "five." As the shortest prisoner, he went into the last cell. Now he had a name: Number Five. But he and his fellow prisoners found names for their captors as well, like "Einstein," "Four Eyes," or "Cyclops."

Twenty-three and a half hours a day he sat in his nine-foot by five-foot wooden cell, unable to talk or communicate with the others, except for the few minutes each day when they came out to brush their teeth and mop their cells. Even then, talking wasn't allowed, although sometimes the guards tolerated a few words.

His treatment meant no books, no radio, no work, no play, no Red Cross packages, no letters in, and no letters out. Nothing. Anything would have been better than nothing, he thought. Then again . . . some things could be worse. At least he wasn't being tortured. He did his best to keep his sanity by playing mental number games or recalling books in fine detail.

Although relieved at escaping death, or at least postponing it, his relief was gradually replaced by a numbing boredom: hour after hour, day after day, week after week, month after month. All was becoming a monotonous blur.

The "Welcome Committee" at Jake's new home . . .

For months he and the others sought to eke out what bits of information they could from the guards on what had happened to their buddies. The officers told them a number of conflicting things. Then one day a smiling guard told them offhandedly, "They were all shot." Upon seeing the look of fear on their faces, he quickly changed his story saying they were transferred. As far as Jake was concerned, his best hopes were trampled, his worst fears realized.

The main source of light in Jake's cell came in through an air vent, a wide slot at the top, twelve feet up. One day it crossed his mind that if he reached out his hands and feet, he might be able to place them on opposite sides of his cell across the narrow width and shimmy up the wall. He did just that and found he could inch up the wall, so up he went, inch by inch. If he got caught, he could face a beating. He also knew if he fell in his weakened condition from twelve feet, he could seriously injure himself.

But the idea of seeing something, *anything* other than his four walls urged him on, so up he went, inching up to the very top where he finally peered out. To his left, he could see the yard, but to the right, well, to the right were hills and trees and sky. Jake took in a smell of fresh air just like back in the hills of home, almost closing his eyes when his left foot slipped a fraction and jolted him back to reality. It was enough. He shimmied the twelve feet back to the bottom and sat down, a little sore and a little tired, and smiled. Just to catch a glimpse of freedom—it was worth it. It was just outside his walls.

Jake stood at his door with his face pressed against the small peep-hole looking at his guard.

"No hope for America," the guard said in English with a smile. "Everything go Japan's way. Only one Japanese plane sink many American ships. America start war, we finish. Power of Japan unshakable. Our emperor, he is a god. We do not lose!"

"Is that so?" Jake replied. Even the guards sometimes longed for conversation and looked for opportunities to practice their English. Any discussion was welcomed, but Jake wasn't buying into the propaganda. "And ah, what if Japan *loses* and *America* wins? *Then* what?"

The guard's face turned more serious. "If Japan lose and America win, then prisoners *not* set free." He stared at Jake's eyes. "We cut off heads!" The guard chuckled as he gleefully threw back his head and laughed again as he strode off.

Jake wasn't amused. Of all the things the guard had told him, it was probably the only thing he said that was actually true.

Under the watchful eye of roughly ten guards at a time, the prisoners walked laps around their square courtyard. Jake paired up with George Barr, the red-haired navigator from Brooklyn.

"So, Jake," George whispered, "How's that diet plan coming along?"

Barely moving his mouth, Jake soberly whispered back, "The pounds are just melting away."

On the opposite side of the yard, Chase Neilson strode beside his crew member, Bob Meder, who wasn't looking good.

"Hey, pal, you OK?" Chase asked.

Jake looked over with concern at Bob, who was nearly dragging his feet. The men felt a keen responsibility to take care of each other. The slightest infection in a degraded condition could easily mean death under these circumstances, and they all knew it.

Bob squinted. "Yeah, yeah. Don't slow down for me. You go on."

A guard zeroed in on Chase and leaned out from the other guards against the wall and shouted in Japanese, "Shut up! No talking!"

Chase glanced over his shoulder as if to say he got the message, then leaned toward Bob again as they shuffled around the yard, whispering more quietly. "I'll set aside a little of my bread for you. We'll all pitch in a little to—"

"I said shut up! No talking!"

Jake and the others stopped and watched with fear as the guard briskly strode toward Chase and came to a halt in the center of the yard. Jake knew that the only rule among the Japanese guards was that there weren't any rules. Anything could happen.

Chase picked up his bucket and mop and started back for his cell, walking near the guard who unexpectedly slapped him across the face. Shocked, Chase stopped.

Jake's pulse pounded. Everyone stared. The other guards began to gather around.

Showing no anger, Chase cleared his throat, gently set down his mop and bucket, then violently slapped the guard across the face, nearly knocking him to the ground.

The other guards sucked air through their teeth and took a few steps closer, but didn't intervene.

Jake panicked. As far as he was concerned, Chase's life was as good as over. He'd seen prisoners beaten to a bloody pulp for lesser offenses, but he knew full well that Chase had simply had it. He wasn't putting up with the insults and humiliation any longer. If they wanted to kill him, he was willing for that, so long as he kept his self-respect. Jake often felt this way, but never acted on it.

The enraged guard struggled to unhook his scabbard and began flailing it with furious swipes at Chase, who shuffled and darted to evade each stroke. The other guards and prisoners gathered into a loose circle, each silently rooting for "their" man. Amazingly, no matter how hard or how fiercely the guard swung his scabbard, he simply couldn't connect with the nimble American. Finally, another guard reached out and grabbed the scabbard, only to have his hand whacked in the process, and the melee ended just as quickly as it had begun.

Jake felt like his heart was going to pound out of his chest.

Breathing heavily, Chase picked up his mop and bucket under a crowd of intensely staring eyes and sauntered back to his cell as if nothing had happened.

Everyone drifted back to their business. Jake was shocked. It seemed that Chase's defense of his buddy and standing up for himself despite the possibly horrendous consequences had earned him the respect of the guards. One even nodded with a grin. They never mentioned the matter again.

Chapter 82

August 1943. The Andrus Farm. Madras, Oregon.

The six family members unfolded their hands having just given thanks for their food in prayer before a lavish display of corn on the cob, steaming mashed potatoes and gravy, and meatloaf—all served on their traditional blue and white porcelain on a faded red and white checkered tablecloth. A basket of oven-warmed rolls and a plate of green beans sat beside a pitcher of milk. The chatter and clinking of tableware began.

Maybe they weren't rich, Mrs. Andrus thought with a smile, but they had all they needed. She passed a basket of rolls to Helen, her youngest

In June 1943, the photo the Japanese took of the Raiders shortly after their capture appeared in TIME *magazine and in other publications.*

beside her, who looked up and said, "I wonder what Jake's eating tonight."

The room went silent. Ruth looked down at her empty plate. Mr. Andrus glanced at his wife and lowered his eyes.

After a few moments, Ruth folded her red and white napkin and laid it across her plate. "I'm . . . I'm just not too hungry tonight. I need to do some paperwork." She slid her chair back and excused herself, covering her mouth with her hand as she hurried away.

Mrs. Andrus nodded with understanding and gazed around the table. Jake's absence and uncertainty left a huge hole in their family, and in her heart.

After a few more seconds of silence, Glen pushed away as well. "I can't eat."

One at a time, each one left without touching their food.

Mrs. Andrus nodded as she felt the same way and tried to hold back the water that stood in her eyes and wondered herself, would Jake be eating tonight?

Chapter 83

Fall 1943. Keuka College, New York.

P eggy peered up at the double-string of Canadian Geese in a "V"
formation flying over and followed them across the southern sky as
they honked and flapped through the autumn air. As she meandered
past students lying on the grass to her favorite bench near the lake, she
unfolded a worn letter—worn from the number of hands it had passed
through before finally reaching her. She couldn't wait as she walked and
read.

"*My dear children,*" the letter began.

She could hear her mother's voice in every hand-written word.

"*We are living in the jungle with the monkeys. We have just finished re-
thatching our roof because the old one was leaking like a sieve. We have lots
to eat, thanks to the Filipinos. We even drink milk from our water buffalo.
We live just like the locals: every day we eat rice and vegetables. We often
have our meals with Signe, Dorothy and the Round family. Mr. & Mrs. Meyer
and the Adams live nearby, but everyone else was captured, and they're being
held in Iloilo and in Manila. I think they're treated OK.*"

Finding her bench and sitting down overlooking the lake, she grimaced
at the thought of her friends in prison and wondered what it must be like.
She wondered if they would survive.

"*The Japanese soldiers came near here three times. Mr. Rose even heard
their voices. The last time they came near our house, your father was at the
Meyer's place. I grabbed a few of our belongings and hid. I was so frightened I
almost thought I was done for.*"

Peggy watched a canoe paddled by two student couples gently slosh
past her. She'd never seen her parents be anything but strong. She just

The Keuka College YWCA in 1943. Peggy third from the left.

couldn't picture either of them being afraid. Of course, if she'd been there, she thought, she'd have been terrified.

"In order to buy food, we sold our tablecloths, sheets, and some clothing. The university chapel hall and the staff residences were burned down and many of the other buildings were destroyed or looted. We heard that the mission hospital in Iloilo City is being used by the Japanese Army. Ida's four girls came to visit us walking 11 kilometers. We heard that they have moved twenty-three times. Their father is an American and Virginia was caught by the Japanese Army because her father was in the communication unit."

She shuffled to the next sheet and glanced at some students on another bench, wondering if anyone she knew could understand what was going on in the war. It all seemed so far away to everyone, just headlines in newspapers with no faces.

"I always pray for you. I just wonder what you're doing right now. I wish I could see you. However I don't want to travel until there is peace again. With lots of love, Mother."

Peggy wondered what her mother and father were doing right then. She so wished for the whole war to be over and folded the letter, slid it back into the envelope, and wiped her coat sleeve across her eyes hoping no one would notice.

Chapter 84

September 1943. Yokosuka Naval Base, Tokyo Bay.

In front of Vice Admiral Kakuta's desk, Fuchida, still on crutches, felt like a patron intruding on a salesman exasperated by customers.

Kakuta flipped sheets of paper then dropped a set into a file cabinet. He never looked up as he quickly signed papers. "By the end of the year, I expect we'll be sending over a thousand planes to the Philippine Islands. Bases need to be prepared." Collapsing papers into a folder, he finally looked up at Fuchida and held the heavy portfolio toward him. "We're sending you to locate abandoned US bases we can rebuild and to locate sites for new ones."

Fuchida welcomed the assignment and was anxious to get back into the field and away from a desk, but even more, he'd become alarmed at the expansion of Japanese installations without the adequate buildup of air support. His pilots needed to fly to their maximum limit to protect their soldiers on the ground and badly needed more bases. He took the folder and swung it under his arm.

"Can you fly?" Kakuta said bluntly.

Fuchida grinned as he looked down and lifted one foot in the air. "Yes, sir. No problem there."

"Good. Get to work." The vice admiral spun around and dialed out on the phone as if Fuchida had already left.

During his five-and-half-hour flight to the Philippines high above the ocean in his B5N bomber he piloted alone, Fuchida reflected on the present circumstances. The Americans could never be defeated. This was now an overwhelming fact, but he was sure they could at least be stopped. The only geography that Japan had given up were some relatively unimportant islands on the outer edges of their expanse. He unconsciously shook his head—it seemed a shame to him that half of the more than 1,000 aircraft being manufactured each month were being diverted to the war in China. But if Japan's Pacific forces pulled back into a defendable posture, doubled up their perimeter divisions, and exacted enough casualties, the American public would soon tire of the bloodletting and call their men back home. What were the Americans fighting for, anyway? They had nothing to gain. Their country was safe. Japan was fighting for its very survival. America should know this, he thought.

He gazed down as he passed over Okinawa. Clouds like sheets of cotton floated against mountains of green.

Fuchida believed the Americans were in for a surprise. When the Japanese took over the Philippines, the people had been liberated as well— liberated from the colonization of Western powers. Japan took captive the American soldiers on the island but set free the Filipino soldiers. Tens of thousands of them. Now, he was convinced, they would taste life under the

Commander Fuchida (bottom right) in June 1943 as senior operations officer. In the center sits Vice Admiral Kakuji Kakuta, commander in chief of the First Air Fleet.

Greater East Asia Co-Prosperity Sphere, free from the white race. More and more, the people of the Philippines would see themselves in a new light and cast in their lots with the Japanese against the Americans. Fuchida grinned. Why wouldn't they?

Cebu City, The Philippine Islands.

There's beer in the ice box," the base commander said as Fuchida sat down on a green stuffed couch and put his hands behind his head. He wasn't expecting such nice accommodations.

"I don't think the locals will ever consider themselves a part of Greater East Asia," Fuchida said.

The host gave a single chuckle. "They hate us."

Fuchida's two-week mission had taken him first to Manila where he discussed his plans for fifteen air bases with the regional commander of Japan's naval forces. Over the course of a few days he selected locations for five bases in the area, then headed about sixty miles south to Batangas where he found locations for two more bases.

From there he flew to Legazpi City on the southeastern end of the main island of Luzon where he had a chance to walk the streets with his flying companions and mix with the locals. He smiled at passersby with a friendly touch to his hat only to receive cold stares. Strange. Picking up a mango at a vendor's stand to smell the fresh scent, he sensed the steely glare of the people. Others across the street stood still. Even with the temperature a sweltering 101 degrees, he felt like he'd been doused in ice water. It was the same in every city he visited. Why?

After establishing two more air bases in Legazpi City the day before, Fuchida's plane touched down on a dirt strip beside a base at the last location to scout—Cebu City on the large island of Cebu. Base officers escorted him and his weary crew to a white guest house with black shutters and white porch railings where they could finally kick off their boots.

Fuchida sat on a couch and leaned forward to examine the magazines on the table, booklets really, all picturing General MacArthur on the cover with bold, block letters stating, "I Shall Return!" He leafed through the pages

of articles and photographs of American landing parties, Japanese ships exploding in the ocean, and dead Japanese half-buried on sandy beaches. "Where did these come from?"

The host handed a newly opened bottle of cold beer to Fuchida's pilot. "From the guerrillas. The booklets are all over the islands." The pilot poured himself a short glass and threw back a swig.

Fuchida winced. "How are these coming in? Air drops?"

The commander shook his head. "Submarines."

Fuchida sighed. If they could smuggle in booklets, they were certainly smuggling in weapons. He let the magazine close to the cover of MacArthur with his look of determination. "MacArthur . . ." Fuchida muttered.

The commander walked to the window and pulled back the white, lace curtain, muffling a belch. "There's nothing to worry about from him. He's a coward. He left his men to die alone."

Fuchida stood up with the magazine in hand and tapped the photo. "He didn't say his *army* would return. He said, '*I* shall return.' MacArthur gives people the will to keep on fighting."

The commander turned from the window and smiled folding his arms and bending his neck a bit. "He's happy eating bacon and eggs in Australia. He'd just as soon—"

"He put his own *honor* at stake!" The room went quiet. Fuchida dropped the magazine to the table with a slap. He spoke more quietly, but with greater conviction, "He will *certainly* return." Fuchida knew that the most dangerous thing the Americans were smuggling in—was hope.

The next day they flew back north to Manila to report to the area commander. His journey high above the lush islands and glittering blue ocean was a pleasant reprieve from the concerns of war. Looking down onto the island of Panay, Fuchida reflected on the overwhelming beauty he'd seen in the past few days, beauty like he'd never seen before. The flourishing vegetation seemed engulfed by brilliant flowers of yellow, white, and pink. He was tiring of war and looked forward to the day the war would be over.

In the jungle mountains below, Jimmy hacked away with a machete at the base of a thick stalk of bamboo when the distant drone of a lone airplane caught his attention in the sky above. Seeing the bright red Hinomaru on the wings of the bomber, he turned back to hacking angrily, longing for the day the war would be over.

Chapter 85

October 15, 1943. New York.

Friday, October 15, 1943   T H E   K E U K O N I A N

Social-Lite

All Saints Episcopal Church in Johnson City was the setting October 7 for the marriage of Miss Margaret Covell, daughter of Mr. and Mrs. James H. Covell, prisoners of war in the Philippines, to Private First Class William T. Struble, U. S. A., son of Mr. and Mrs. William A. Struble, of Johnson City. The Rev. Burke Rivers performed the double-ring ceremony at 7:30 P. M.

Given in marriage by her uncle, Albert H. Covell, the bride was gowned in ivory satin with sweetheart neckline and long sleeves with points over the hands. She wore her mother's veil of ivory tulle which was held in place by a tiara of orange blossoms. She carried red roses and white pompoms.

Bridal attendants were the bride's sister, Alice Covell, of Granville, Ohio, who was maid of honor and Janet Covell, of Oneida, cousin of the bride. Lunette Bryant, Helen Cole and Marva Davis, college friends of the bride were bridesmaids.

The maid of honor was attired in an ice blue dress fashioned with a brocaded top and net skirt and carried a colonial nosegay of pink pompoms.

Lunette was dressed in pink chiffon, Helen in blue chiffon, Janet in yellow marquisette and Marva in pale green marquisette. All bridesmaids wore ivory satin caps fastened with pink and white pompoms.

Pfc. William Young, of Princeton, was best man.

Mrs. Albert Covell, the bride's aunt, chose a gown of blue chiffon and lace and wore a corsage of pink gladioli while the bridegroom's mother selected blue and white taffeta with a corsage of yellow gladioli.

Preceding the ceremony, Mrs. Struble gave a buffet supper for the wedding party in honor of Peggy's twentieth birthday.

After a brief wedding trip, Peggy returned to Keuka while Bill went back to his foreign language studies at Yale.

The student nurses marched into

Chapter 86

October 1943. Hopevale, the Philippines.

A sweaty, wounded Filipino fighter with a rag tied to his head for a hat, the top of his shirt peeled down to his waist, sat biting a cigarette as Jennie, the camp nurse, finished wrapping his shoulder in gauze.

She pulled aside some strands of her hair stuck to her perspiring face. "Not a whole lot of sense in anyone fixin' you up," she said, "if you're planning on killing yourself with that coffin nail in your mouth." She glanced up at his smiling face then tore the end of the gauze strip with her teeth and tied it into a knot.

"It's all right, missy. Cigarettes don't kill you until the end of your life."

She nodded without smiling. "I'll be sure to have them put that on your gravestone." She took a last look at his shoulder. "Come back in two days and we'll have a look." The guerrilla shrugged his shirt back on and started buttoning up as an American fighter stepped up and displayed an ugly gash on his hip with a smile.

In the open-air church under the outstretched wings of the forest canopy, Jimmy read to a gathering of expectant brown and white faces sprinkled with sunlight. The people focused on every word.

"*You have heard that it was said, 'Love your neighbor and hate your enemy,'*" Jimmy said. Everything he lived for seemed wrapped up in these words that had become his life. "*But I tell you: Love your enemies and pray for those who persecute you, that you may be sons of your Father in heaven. For he causes his sun to rise on the evil . . .*"

Jimmy suddenly looked to the back woods that rustled and parted revealing an armed Japanese officer and soldier.

"*. . . and on the good.*" Jimmy closed his Bible.

The entire congregation of sixty-five people turned and fixed their eyes on the uninvited visitors.

Jimmy was petrified, but didn't show it. His heart raced. They'd seen Japanese in the distance, but never inside their camp. Just like everyone else in the area, he'd heard the terrifying rumors of the new Japanese leader on the island, and how he and his men tortured and killed just to put people into a state of fear. It was working.

"We have guests. You are all dismissed." He couldn't imagine what would happen next. The penalty for not turning yourself into the camps was death. Period.

The people cautiously began to rise, but the Japanese officer headed toward the front and held both hands up as he walked, leaving his pistol in its holster. "Suware!" he said, then again in English: "Sit down!"

The snap of fallen twigs beneath the officer's boots seemed deafening to Jimmy as the officer made his way to where he stood at the front. The other soldier remained at the rear, his rifle drawn. Every head followed the officer with a mixture of fear and amazement. He carefully looked Jimmy in the face, then turned to the people and walked to those in the front row: Charma, Jennie, Francis, Gertrude, and the others. The officer reached into a breast pocket.

Jimmy watched—prepared to see anything, but was unprepared to *do* anything. They'd been caught flat-footed. There was nothing to do but to watch and wait.

The officer withdrew a tied roll of paper, loosened the string and, with a look of apologetic humility, proceeded to peel off ten-centavo notes, passing them out freely, walking among the rows silently and nodding to the patrons. The people graciously accepted the currency almost as if they were receiving communion wafers from a priest, each nodding with thanks and a fearful smile.

Reaching the back of the chapel, he turned to face Jimmy and stood stationary for what seemed like a very long time, but was only a few moments. His eyes connected with Jimmy's, then turned downward for a second.

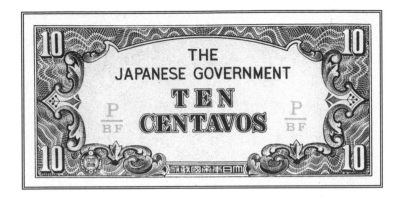

Even though Jimmy knew many were swept up in nationalistic pride, he'd met others in Japan who simply felt pushed into the war. He could see in this young officer's face the shame of the association with his military and what they were doing. He felt sorry for him.

The officer bowed, stood upright, and just as he began to turn, Jimmy shouted out in Japanese, "We're all one blood!"

The officer was shocked to hear a white person speak perfect Japanese.

"We're all brothers!" Jimmy said, again in Japanese.

His eyes smiled back as he replied in Japanese, "We didn't see anything here today." Then, just as abruptly as he had appeared, the foliage enveloped him and the other soldier, and they vanished.

Chapter 87

November 1943. The island of Panay. The Philippines.

Howling and sobbing uncontrollably on their knees in the muddy street, two Filipina women and seven children, begged for mercy as two Japanese soldiers propped up the bloody mess of a Filipino man between them. Beyond, soldiers tossed belongings out through the window of a hovel into the street. Petrified townspeople gaped from a distance as watchful, armed infantrymen stood around Captain Watanabe. Several headless bodies lay in a heap against a blood-spattered wall.

Watanabe grabbed the Filipino's hair and jerked his head up.

"I swear I don't know where their hideout is!" the man blurted out in

An ordinary village in pre-war Philippines.

Ilonggo. "They forced me to help them. I swear I don't know."

Watanabe turned to a Filipino translator who spat out the words in Japanese.

"Liar!" Watanabe threw the man's head back down.

Everywhere, the pattern was the same wherever Watanabe went—they tied up random people, beat them, and stabbed them with bayonets to extract information. Not getting what they wanted, soldiers selected others, perhaps family members, or friends, or children. Soldiers hung some upside down and set them on fire to instill terror. Culminating in Watanabe's total frustration, he sought to execute everyone in the area. In the prior two weeks Captain Watanabe and his men had slaughtered over 2,000 civilians.

"I'll teach them not to lie to me! Blindfold him!" Watanabe's eyes flared with fury.

A soldier wrapped a rag for a blindfold around the man's head as another soldier pushed him to his knees as the victim continued his vain pleadings for mercy.

The women convulsed in shrieks as Watanabe unsheathed his sword and took his stance, slowly raising his katana above his head, completely deaf to the wailing of the horrified women. The Butcher of Panay had transformed the paradise island of Panay into the island of mud and blood.

Chapter 88

Early December 1943. Nanking, China.

Alerted by the echo of hammers pounding nails in the courtyard, Jake braced his hands and feet on opposite walls of his wooden cell and, as was his habit, shimmied his way, inch by inch, to the top of his cell where he strained to peer through the slit to investigate. The guards were completing work on some kind of wooden box. To Jake, it pretty much looked like a coffin. He braced his arms and legs extra hard as he felt a weakness shoot through his bones. Confused, fearful, and angry, he carefully shimmied his way back down.

He slumped to the floor, letting his head fall into his hands in a daze. If someone wasn't dead already, he soon would be. Whatever was going on, it was very, very bad.

The next day, his latch clicked and the wooden cell door creaked open. Jake narrowed his eyes into the light. Two guards and the camp warden stood tall, dressed in new uniforms, something he hadn't seen before. Jake got to his feet and they escorted him toward the cell of Bob Meder, only a few feet down the corridor. Jake glanced at the guards who wouldn't look him in the eye. It was always a bad sign when the guards wouldn't look him in the eye.

They stopped near the entrance of Bob's cell and let Jake walk forward on his own. He took a few tentative steps and leaned to peer into the dark chamber. The room gave off the odd scent of a sawmill, a latrine, and a flower shop. Stepping inside, he gazed down on the gaunt, peaceful body of Bob lying in the raw wooden coffin, a wreath of white flowers on his chest. It wasn't a total surprise, as Jake had seen his life slowly ebb away. Still, to see his friend dead was shocking. On the other side of the floor laid the lid of the coffin with a Bible squarely placed in the center.

Jake studied Bob's peaceful face. To him, Bob was a true gentleman, a prince of a man. When his plane went down in the water on the coast of China, he nearly drowned trying to save the lives of two of his of crewmates. That was Bob. He could have just looked out for himself, but he wasn't that kind of a guy. He deserved better than to be treated like a piece of rotting meat by half-human captors for the past year and a half. His death was meaningless.

As Jake wiped the water from the edge of his eye, a cloud of silent rage descended on him. His head trembled as he breathed more deeply and the vessels in his neck began to pound. One last time, he looked at Bob's face, leaned down, and whispered through clenched teeth, "I hope every damn Jap is wiped off the face of the earth."

He turned toward the door and shuffled out into the hallway, glaring at the guards one at a time who seemed to stare at the horizon, then he looked down at the floor breathing hard, trying to restrain himself from any show of the burning hatred within.

That night, back in his cell with the evening stars providing only the barest hint of dark blue light, Jake sat against the wall under a tattered blanket, hyperventilating and trembling violently—from the biting cold and from the boiling fury that raged in his heart and coursed through his veins. Pure, distilled hatred. Bob was gone for good.

Tokyo, Japan.

Emperor Hirohito spun around from his office window. "Dead?! How could you let him die?!"

The commander remained in a deep bow. "Your Majesty, it couldn't be helped. We have spoken to the prison leaders in order to see that— "

"Don't *dare* let another Doolittle prisoner die! We may need them later. We can't afford to lose another." The emperor looked away angrily. "Do whatever you need to do!"

"Yes, Your Majesty, we will."

One week later, Nanking, China.

Jake proudly puffed on a rare cigarette as he walked the yard and eyed George, who sat on a bench opposite the prison warden, who nodded and rapidly took notes.

George kept blabbing on with his Brooklyn accent. "Bread, butter, jam, steak, eggs, potatoes, milk, ice cream—you got this?"

"Eggs," the warden repeated back, "milk - and - ice - cream."

"And we need to eat three times a day, not two times. No more of that."

"Meals - three - times."

"And we're going crazy in here, too. We need something to read. You know, books, magazines, newspapers. I know you can't give us newspapers, but how about some books?"

"Books," the commander repeated as he wrote.

"And what about letters? And Red Cross packages?"

George knew this short turn of events wouldn't last, but figured it wouldn't hurt to ask for the moon, even if he and the boys only ended up with a few extra scraps.

"Letters," the warden said as he scribbled, then flipped his pad closed and slid it into his pocket. "We will look into these things and let you know what we can do. We will do everything we can to take care of you properly."

As the warden stood and walked away, Jake shook his head in disbelief and exhaled a cloud of smoke in front of his face. George looked back at Jake and shrugged. It was worth a shot.

Jake sat hunched on the floor of his cell under his blanket, devouring a dog-eared copy of a well-worn book. There were no steak and eggs, or letters, or ice cream, but the four surviving Raiders started to get some bread, and for the first time received three meals a day instead of two. A few old books were scrounged from who knows where and circulated among the men.

Stamped on the worn cover of the burgundy volume Jake was reading were the words: *The Pleasures of Hope, by Thomas Campbell*—an epic poem

first published in 1799. For the first time in many months, Jake drifted away
to a better place:

> Primeval Hope, the Aonian[31] Muses say,
> When Man and Nature mourned their first decay;
> When every form of death, and every woe,
> Shot from malignant stars to earth below;
> When Murder bared her arm, and rampant War
> Yoked the red dragons of her iron car;
> When Peace and Mercy, banished from the plain,
> Sprung on the viewless winds to Heaven again,
> All, all forsook the friendless, guilty mind,
> But Hope, the charmer, lingered still behind.

Hope. It was the one thing that kept Jake hanging on.

---

[31] Greek.

Chapter 89

Charma handed Jimmy another section of woven mat to repair an outside window shade. "Yeah, that fits pretty good." Jimmy tied the mat in with a strand of banban, blinking hard as the sweat dripped from the band of his hat into his eyes. As he reached up, he noticed how thin his arms had gotten and realized how pronounced the veins and sinews had become. He was aging quickly.

"Mr. Covell?"

Jimmy and Charma turned to three Filipina ladies standing behind them holding a handmade banner of woven palm strands.

"For your home. For Christmas."

The ladies stepped apart and hung out the full dangling banner with the woven words: "PEACE ON EARTH GOODWILL TO ALL MEN."

Jimmy looked at Charma with a beaming smile, then to the ladies. "Why that's outstanding!" He reached out and examined the brilliant handiwork of the women who blushed with pride. "How did you do that?"

"It's beautiful," Charma said.

"A gift, for all you've given to us," a woman said with a smile.

He looked into the ladies' faces with sincerity. "Thank you. *Thank* you! Here, let's put it up."

He led the ladies to the front of their stilted hut and motioned to a place on their porch railing. "What do you say? I think it'd be perfect right here."

The rain showers that evening fell steadily for hours, cascading off the grass roof of the Covell home and joining a soothing hiss of a million pats on the jungle leaves. A single kerosene lamp illuminated their nipa hut with gold as Jimmy held Charma in his arms in a slow dance to *White Christmas*, crackling in over their radio, Charma's new favorite song by Bing Crosby. Maybe they didn't have much, Jimmy thought, but they had each other, and he loved his wife. They continued their dance while trying to avoid the random leaks dripping through the roof. Charma looked Jimmy in the face for a moment, smiled, put her head back on his shoulder—and wept.

December 14, 1943. Twenty-eight miles north of Hopevale.

Two hundred sixty Japanese soldiers and one hundred fifteen local Filipinos forced into the search by the army spread across a clearing in the mountains. Behind them, clouds of smoke churned into the sky from a torched village. With his hands on his hips, Captain Watanabe squinted and scanned the hilly horizon from one end to the other. He uncapped his canteen and turned to his translator. "Ask him if we go this way to the American camp."

A soldier swung the bayonet of his rifle toward an American slung between two Filipinos, placed the blade under his bearded chin caked in dried blood, and lifted his head. The translator leaned toward the American.

The man was Lieutenant Albert King. Wounded and separated from his men, soldiers had captured him near a tributary of the Aklan River, a river that started high in the mountains and opened to the sea on the north side of the island. He was only half-conscious. Japanese soldiers had torn out his toenails and fingernails.

Despite the fact that General MacArthur had sent communications to the guerrillas in the Philippines to cease attacks and to lay low for the time being to prevent reprisals by the Japanese, and that the guerrillas had complied, the Japanese command had issued a special order to seek and kill all Americans on the island. The past random hit-and-run tactics of the guerrillas had been highly effective and maddeningly frustrating to the Japanese. But now, Watanabe could smell his hunted prey.

"We head south which way?" the translator said in English. "More to the mountains, or toward the southeast?"

Shigeru Suzuki, the officer who had been to Hopevale and passed out currency, looked at the translator, then at the American, hoping he was too confused to know the way.

King blinked slowly and swallowed. His eyes turned toward the lush, jade ridges of the south and barely raised his head in that direction.

Watanabe stood erect, glanced back at his men, and waved them toward the southeast.

December 19, Hopevale.

The warm, damp night air brought its own earthy scent and the familiar chorus of insects. The congregation of nearly eighty people sat quietly in the outdoor sanctuary under the glow of wicker lanterns scattered around the outside and down the center aisle of the open church hidden beneath the luan trees that vaulted into a cathedral ceiling.

The stone seats all taken for this yuletide event, many stood along the sides, local Filipino husbands with their wives and children, working men, farmers, and guerrilla fighters, who had left their guns beside a tree out of respect. Jack stood with folded arms toward the back.

Christmas being only a few days away, the community had decided to have one service in Hopevale that evening. There was never a sense of ownership or sectarianism among the people. It never crossed their minds.

"This Christmas, it would be fitting to read from the prophet Isaiah," Jimmy said as he stood at the front. A small, stone altar displaying three candles beside him brought out the creases in his worn face. "*The people who walk in darkness will see a great light; those who live in a dark land, the light will shine on them. For you shall break the yoke of their burden and the rod of their oppressors, for every boot of the warrior in the battle, and the coat covered in blood will be for burning, fuel for the fire. For a child will be born to us, a son will be given to us, and the government will rest on his shoulders; And his name will be called Wonderful Counselor, Mighty God, Eternal Father, the Prince . . .*'"

Jimmy glanced up. "And this Prince won't be the kind who brings war or bloodshed, death or destruction."

He held the book up before him and continued reading, *"He will be called . . . the 'Prince of* Peace. *And there will be no end to the increase of his government or of peace from then on and forevermore.'"* He nodded with a smile. "Amen."

The next day.

High in the branches of a tropical tree, a Filipino teenager fixed his gaze through his binoculars in the afternoon heat. His friend below looked up anxiously, pacing and rubbing his hands. The lookout jerked the binoculars down, swung them over his shoulder, put his fingers to his mouth and gave the familiar whistle of warning to all that Japanese troops were nearby—three times. He shimmied down toward his friend at the base of the tree. "They're coming from the north!" he said in Ilonggo as he struggled and leaped to the ground in a thud. "They're spreading out on both sides. Hundreds!"

The other boy nodded, and the two of them sprinted in opposite directions into the underbrush.

Jack raced through the camp holding his submachine gun tightly over his shoulder. He pounded his hand along the outside of Jimmy's hut as he ran. "Go, go, go! We gotta get outa here! *Now!*"

Other guerrillas and the lookout called out as people sprinted and stumbled in various directions. Even the monkeys fled from the trees above, infants clinging to their mothers.

Jimmy limped to the doorway. "Yeah, OK. We're coming. Charma, let's go!"

Jack looked at their weathered faces and torn clothes with a sense of foreboding. "Get in your cave. You'll be safe there. Go!"

Francis and his wife trotted up, panting. "Ready?"

Jimmy and Charma stepped down from their hut and began their practiced routine, again heading into the woods barefooted, pushing the foliage aside as they ran, yet with far less energy than in the past. Jimmy could hear the soldiers calling to each other in Japanese and could make out words here and there.

As Jimmy pushed through the leaves, he remembered that a few weeks earlier, Reverend Dianala encouraged him and the others at Hopevale to split up, to seek higher ground and to head deeper into the woods as he felt it was becoming less safe in the area, but Jimmy knew he was simply getting too weak. Francis Rose was nearly sixty, and there were children in the camp as well. Huge ferns brushed across his face as he wondered if they should have tried to move.

Charma tripped over a vine and fell to her knees. Jimmy reached back, took her muddy hand and pulled her up, and they started again.

A single rifle shot cracked behind them echoing through the jungle canopy sending birds into flight. "Tomare! Tomaranto utsuzo!"[32] Violently gasping for breath, Jimmy, Charma, Francis, and Gertrude stood with their sweat-soaked backs and slowly turned to five angry soldiers with their rifles trained on them. They could run no more.

---

[32] "Stop or we'll shoot!"

Chapter 90

Early February 1944. Saipan.

"I nside headquarters on the island, Fuchida stood beside his old commander, Vice Admiral Nagumo, as they both looked out the window watching two Japanese fighters roar off the end of a dirt runway, lifting up over a tropical green cliff, then lofting above a turquoise sea.

In a few months," Nagumo said to Fuchida, "they're going to put me in charge of the Middle Pacific Fleet and the Fourteenth Air Fleet. But with only anti-submarine craft and a few combat planes, my forces are completely inadequate to protect Saipan and the Marianas."

Fuchida sensed the concern on Nagumo's face.

Vice Admiral Nagumo, in the center in white, with his staff on Saipan, 1944.

"I've been promised troop transfers from Manchukuo, but they won't be under my command." Nagumo turned to Fuchida with penetrating eyes. "I need the First Air Fleet under my own command, but they won't give it to me. How can I *possibly* defend all these islands without it?"

Nagumo was right, Fuchida thought. He had been given an impossible task, and he knew it. Saipan, the largest of the Northern Mariana Islands, had become the center of a defensive line against the steady American advances—the *last* line of defense. If Saipan fell, the Japanese supply lines would be cut off, and the homeland would be within range of a new breed of long-range American bombers they'd been hearing rumors about and fearing.

Fuchida wanted nothing more than to put Nagumo's fears to rest. As senior staff officer of the First Air Fleet, he knew exactly what their resources were, where they were, and most importantly at this moment, where they were heading next. "Sir, the First Air Fleet can move to any location they're needed as a single unit," he said.

"But it can only be at one place at a time. What if it's needed somewhere else when I need it here? *Then* what?" Nagumo glanced uncomfortably at Fuchida, then back to the beach where sun-darkened, bare-chested soldiers poured cement for a gun emplacement. The low, rounded structure with horizontal slits for machine guns was one of many defenses rising around the edges of the tiny island.

"Sir, if you will permit me." Fuchida stepped to an oversized wall map and slid his finger from island to island in the Philippines, then to the Mariana chain. "I expect approval of fifteen more bases in the Philippines, and I have orders to establish at least ten air bases to accommodate hundreds more aircraft here, here, here, and here. With your cooperation in completing the airstrips, we can *fully* support you." He had little confidence all would take place as planned, but desperately wanted to assuage his former commander's deepest fears.

Nagumo's eyes surveyed the map, but Fuchida could see that his mind was a thousand miles away. The days of triumph and glory at Pearl Harbor had been swallowed up by days of fear and doubt; the retreating empire of Japan was now under the growing shadow of a specter that loomed larger every day; and the last flame of hope had finally flickered out of Nagumo's eyes. The Americans were coming with overwhelming fury.

He looked over at Fuchida's face as if he'd been given a death sentence, slowly stepped to the window again, clasped his hands behind his back, and gazed out at the exquisite aquamarine surf breaking onto the white-sand beach.

*His best days behind him and near-certain disaster ahead, Fuchida had
little to smile about, even with a bowl full of pineapples. Saipan, February 1944.*

Chapter 91

Clutching a clipboard, Fuchida strode briskly down the taxiway beside Genda past rows of Nakajima B6N bombers straight from the factory, many being prepped by maintenance crews in white coveralls.

Fuchida shouted to Genda, "I have to leave tomorrow." Planes droned overhead as a cargo truck rolled past in a breeze of exhaust fumes and dust. "I'm off to Tinian Island, even though they're just beginning to prepare the ten airfields in the Marianas. But . . . those are the orders." Fuchida shook his head and held out his hand toward a new plane. "Brand new aircraft, but with brand new pilots?" He came to a halt. "Eighteen years old? I feel like I'm training school boys. We need more time." Rushed and overwhelmed, Fuchida knew that his best friend would understand.

"We expected the Americans to attack Truk Lagoon," Genda said. "That was no surprise. We just didn't expect it so soon, just two weeks ago. It was a catastrophe that's shaken the high command and forced their hand. The Americans have simply moved faster and more aggressively than we expected."

It was a painful truth Fuchida *hated* to hear. The Americans! He warned his commanders and begged them to confront them before time ran out. "Preparations *have* to be made for a decisive battle," Fuchida said. "If we don't confront the Americans now, while we still have the strength to do so and before they can consolidate their power, we'll *never* be able to."

They began walking again.

"First they want me to train pilots without aircraft," Fuchida said, "then, when I finally have aircraft, they want me to send new pilots into

Fuchida at Naval Headquarters with Admiral
Soemu Toyada, commander in chief of the Combined Fleet.

battle without training. And with the bases in the Marianas incomplete, I have nowhere to send the aircraft." Fuchida stopped again next to workers unpacking a pair of aircraft wings from a crate. "We need at least two more months for vital training!" He pounded his clipboard with his fist. "In a few months, we can send out a devastating— "

"Fuchi!" Genda waited until he had his attention and spoke softly but directly, "There's no more sand in the hourglass."

A chill spread over his arms and back. Fuchida knew Genda was right, but couldn't bring himself to admit it. It was sickening to think about. He looked off, far away, and spoke as if to himself, "And why do the Americans insult us with their demand for unconditional surrender? How stupid." He looked back at Genda. "Surrender? They should know that this is a word we don't recognize."

Genda nodded. "After Pearl Harbor, it seems 'negotiate' is a word the *Americans* don't recognize."

The next day. Tinian Island. The Mariana Islands.

Two bulldozers and two graders spread out a ribbon of dirt through the low scrub as 150 soldiers dumped wheelbarrows of gravel and raked the edges down. Fuchida pulled up to the side of the airstrip in a *Kurogane* with the top down, the Japanese 4WD equivalent of an American jeep, with Vice Admiral Kakuta in the passenger seat. Coming to a stop, a cloud of dust rolled over them.

Kakuta took hold of the metal frame of the windshield and pulled himself up to survey the project. Workers glanced up at the admiral, then seemed to rake even faster. "This should have been completed a *week* ago!" He glared impatiently. "And the third strip hasn't even been started!"

Fuchida stretched his neck as if he were searching. "Where are the fuel tanks? The sheet metal arrived here last week, but I don't see the welders." Fuchida opened his door and stepped out. This wasn't what he'd hoped to see, but instead was what he had feared most.

Another Kurogane approached from a distance at a high rate of speed, bouncing and jerking right and left over the dirt shoulder until the vehicle came to a squealing halt beside them. Earlier that day, just before Fuchida and his group of aircraft arrived at Tinian, Kakuta had sent out reconnaissance aircraft 300 miles to the east and south. Lacking radar, it was their only hope for accurate intelligence on the whereabouts of the American fleet.

A messenger leaped out and ran to Kakuta with a paper in his outstretched hand. "Admiral, sir! Enemy sighted! Force includes carriers!"

Kakuta nodded, took the sheet and began reading as Fuchida got back in, slammed his door, and started the engine.

The admiral dropped back down into his seat. "The enemy will attack soon," he said as Fuchida turned his Kurogane around and started back for headquarters.

"Most likely tomorrow," Fuchida replied. He knew what Kakuta's impulse would be—*immediate* attack. But Fuchida knew that *his* immediate battle wasn't with the Americans, it was with his direct commander—Kakuta. "Admiral, excuse me, but I don't believe we should risk our forces unnecessarily. We have *no* fighters for cover. Just fly all the bombers back to Japan while they can still escape." They bounced erratically over the dirt road racing back to headquarters.

"Your caution sounds like *cowardice!* We have the advantage of surprise and can attack under cover of night. That's the job you were sent here to do!"

Fuchida restrained himself. "Sir, the pilots aren't sufficiently rested for an all-out battle with the Americans. We *must* have fighter escorts. Sending them out now . . ."

"Sending them *home* now will leave the enemy unscathed! I won't pass up the opportunity to attack the enemy and let them slip by. We will send out our aircraft *tonight!*"

The following afternoon.

On the rooftop of the two-story headquarters, a utilitarian concrete structure streaked with rust, three soldiers silently peered through long-range binoculars on tripods as seagulls squawked above. Kakuta, Fuchida, and communication officers stood beside each other in the salty breeze, searching the empty, silent horizon. The muscles on the side of Fuchida's face flexed as he contemplated the mission of the previous night when Kakuta sent out twenty-seven of his bombers armed with torpedoes against the American fleet of unknown strength. Nine unarmed reconnaissance aircraft escorted them to help locate the target. Only three of these scout planes returned with unclear reports. None of Fuchida's men returned. He swallowed his anger.

An aide stepped up the stairs and approached Kakuta. "Admiral, no radio communications received." The admiral nodded without emotion.

Fuchida fumed. He had vigorously argued with Kakuta that morning, but the admiral insisted on sending off *another* group of fifty-four dive bombers, again, with no fighter protection. It had been hours since they'd left, and if nothing else, they should have received radio communication from at least *one* plane. The sky remained empty. Nothing.

Kakuta abruptly headed down the concrete stairs directly followed by

Fuchida as he looked for an opportunity to speak with some measure of privacy. Kakuta knew Fuchida was on his heels and headed for his office where Fuchida followed and slammed the door behind them.

"I'm going to contact Iwo Jima," Kakuta said, reaching for the phone, "and have them send to us as *many* First Air Fleet fighters as they have, *immediately!*"

"*Are you crazy?!*" Fuchida yelled, pushing aside all military decorum. "It's absolutely *stupid* to bring down planes from Iwo! They only have twenty-seven fighters right now, anyway. They'll arrive here exhausted, be thrown into the ring, and then be pounded to the mat by the Americans— all for nothing!" Fuchida could see the pain and humiliation on Kakuta's face, and respected his willingness to engage the enemy, but this total lack of restraint in the face of appalling odds *had* to be confronted before any more lives were wasted. Fuchida did his best to regain his composure. "Admiral, I believe we'll have our chance. Soon, but not now."

Kakuta stood motionless with his hand on the phone.

Chapter 92

March 1944. Keuka College. New York.

Peggy's senior yearbook photo, 1944.

P eggy anxiously walked down the linoleum hallway of her dorm, clutching her books in front of her with a letter propped in one hand. The year was almost over. Her whole *education* was almost over. There was a feeling of relief in the air. She wasn't going to miss the musty smell of that building. The future for her was wide open.

But the letter addressed to her from the Marshall General, Army Service Forces in Washington, DC left her uneasy. Would it be good news or bad?

She unloaded her books onto the desk and wiped her perspiring forehead with the back of her hand. She was certainly looking forward to not having to carry *those* around again. College turned out to be more work than she thought but she was finally going to get her Bachelor's degree in Religious Studies—but it was bittersweet. She'd wished and really *hoped* her parents could have come to her graduation, but knew it wasn't possible. The school YWCA[33] made her president; she had received the Ruby Lyman Award for the student who, "through four years

---

[33] The Young Women's Christian Association was founded in 1855 as a social and spiritual support system for young English women.

has most perfectly exemplified in conduct and character a life motivated by the spirit of Christ;" and she'd also received the Edith Gurley Estey Memorial Prize for "The student who made the greatest contribution to international understanding and goodwill on campus." Yet it seemed so hollow without Mom and Dad around to see her . . .

She sat on the edge of her bed and ripped open the letter, hoping for the best, but fearing the worst.

As she began reading, her eyebrows came down, she clinched the paper harder. Flipping it over, her eyes darted across the page faster and faster as tears began rolling down her cheeks. Her hands trembling, the paper fell to the floor, and she collapsed onto her bed and wept uncontrollably. "Why? Why? Why?!"

Jean appeared in the doorway with her own stack of books. "Peggy?"

COLLEGE GIRL LEFT AN ORPHAN

PENN YAN. N. Y., March 29.— Peggy Covell Struble, Keuka college senior, has received notification of the death of her parents, Rev. and Mrs. J. H. Covell, Baptist educational missionaries in a Japanese internment camp.

They were the victims of barbarous Jap starvation, cruelty, unsanity and uncivilized treatment.

The message to the young student came from the office of the Provost Marshall General, Army Service Forces, Washington, D. C., and reads as follows: "Information believed to be reliable states that they (Rev. and Mrs. Covell) died in Japanese custody on the Island Nanay, Phillippines, Dec. 19, 1943."

The Keuka College student who was born in Karuizawa, Japan, states that the latest word received from her missionary parents was March 4, 1944, but the letter was dated May, 1943, and contained the information that they had been evacuated into the hills of Panay. Mrs. Struble is a graduate of Bordner high school, Manilla, P. I., and spent her life in the Orient until coming to Keuka in 1940. She has crossed the Pacific 6 times and has traveled in Panama, China, Hawaii, Japan. She is majoring in Christian leadership at Keuka. In October, 1943, she was married to Pfc. William Struble, of Johnson City, who now is stationed overseas.

Rev. and Mrs. Covell originally from Leroy and were associated with the American Baptist Foreign Missionary Society, they had served with the Bavble Memorial School, Yokohama, Japan, and Central Philippine College, Slolio, P. I., Rev. Covell taught English and Christian education and Mrs. Covell, sociology and homemaking.

Besides Mrs. Struble, Rev. and Mrs. Covell are survived by a son, Pfc. David A. Covell, U. S. Marine Corps, in the Pacific Area; daughters, Miss Alice E. Covell, Granville, Ohio; Rev. Covell's mother, Mrs. F. E. B. Covell, Leroy; brother, A. H. Covell, superintendent of schools at Oneida.

The Canisteo Times, Steuben County, N.Y., March 30, 1944.

Part V

No Damn Hypocrite

Chapter 93

May 1944. Nanking, China.

Jake wrung the mop strings with his bare hands into a wooden bucket. He took a morsel of happiness to have some work, *anything* other than to just sit on his cell floor, so he took as much time as possible simply to be occupied as he mopped.

The guard looked in through the door slot. "Hurry up number five!" he shouted in Japanese.

"Keep your shirt on, jackass!" Jake yelled back in Japanese—at least, that's what he *thought* he was saying, as he slowly picked up the language.

The keys jangled, the bolt unclicked, and the door swung open. The guard's posture told Jake everything he needed to know: get ready for a beating. Before Jake could dodge it, the guard smacked him on the side of the head, and Jake reflexively kicked the guard in the gut with his bare foot, shoving him into the corner. Snorting, the guard scampered to his feet, unlatched his scabbard, and landed alternating blows against Jake's back as he cowered in the corner. Jake stared down at his mop and bucket, then grabbed it and pitched the whole thing at the guard, hitting him right in the face with the mop. Stunned, the guard let out a string of what Jake presumed to be Japanese curses, then snatched Jake's mop and bucket, stormed out, and slammed and locked the door.

Jake's head throbbed. The angry footsteps faded down the hallway. Jake stood silently panting, staring at the streaks of water dribbling down the wooden wall. He grinned as he rubbed his aching shoulder. "Well," he said, "at least it wasn't another boring day."

As his empty days dissolved one into the other, books the guards passed around provided the only source of mental stimulation.

Late that May, a guard knocked on his door. "Book!"

Jake grabbed his copy of *David Copperfield* and slid it under the door to the guard. A few seconds later, the guard shoved another worn, dog-eared book back to him. It was a Bible.

"Keep book three weeks," the guard said in English, then walked to the next cell.

He never had much interest in this book. The only thing he really remembered from Sunday school was when the teacher talked about how he punched a hole in his muffler to make it louder. Jake always wanted to try that. Never did.

Now, though, under entirely different circumstances, he was intrigued and a spiritual hunger gnawed within. He admired his mother's inner strength and gentle courage and knew she drew this water from an extraordinarily deep well. He knew it was genuine. When he heard a Bible was being passed around, he jumped for a chance to get ahold of it, too.

As long as there was enough light in his cell, he read, and read, and read. The hardest thing was finding a new position that didn't make his bones hurt. He lay on his back, on his side, and on his stomach as he went through every page.

He kept asking questions, sometimes repeating them out loud, "C'mon! How could this be true? What's the proof?"

After two weeks, having read through every page cover to cover at least twice, he focused in on the prophets, amazed by what they seemed to know. But he wondered how they could possibly know the future. "How could that be?" he said. "How could that be if God didn't tell them?" Lying on his stomach, he let the book fall flat. "So, you still talk to people?" Jake looked around but heard nothing. "I said, 'So, you still talk to people?'" He waited. Nothing. "I didn't think so."

But the prophets apparently knew a lot about the future and it seemed to happen—at least, according to the book. Things about the Messiah. A *lot* of little things about the Messiah. Jake started flipping back and forth between the prophets of old and the stories from Matthew, Mark, Luke, and John. The same things they said hundreds of years earlier *would* happen, *did* happen. Born in Bethlehem, betrayed by his friends, pierced in his hands and feet, given vinegar to drink—a *lot* of things. How could this have been predicted if there wasn't a God to tell them ahead of time? How could it all be true? Or how could it all just be a big lie? Maybe people just concocted all this stuff. He didn't know.

When he read the part where soldiers nailed this man Jesus to a cross, he thought he would have said the same kind of things the people said: "If he's really God, why doesn't he just save himself and get off the cross?" It didn't make any sense.

Time passed, and it neared the end of the three weeks for him to have the book. He came across the words of Isaiah the prophet who spoke about a man of sorrows, suffering, rejected, and despised. "Yeah, I know all about that," Jake said. But this time, he noticed the words, "*... our griefs he himself bore, and our sorrows he carried ... he was wounded for our rebellion ...*"

Jake felt a twinge of guilt as a chill ran over his skin. There were parts of his life he wasn't proud of. He still lied all the time to the guards. He was a liar. Genuine hatred of the darkest kind constantly smoldered in his heart toward the Japanese. But the idea that love was the most powerful thing in the world impressed him. That's what it was all about, he decided. Love. He thought it would make the world a better place if he could love people. If this God was real, he felt he had to listen to him and he made up his mind he had to at least *try*. He decided he would do what God wanted *if* God made the way clear for him.

Jake had one, final request. He closed the book for the last time, stood up and stretched. "All right, all right . . . just don't let me be one of those *damn* hypocrites! I *hate* those guys!"

Chapter 94

Morning, June 19, 1944. The aircraft carrier
Taihō. The Pacific Ocean between the Philippines
and the Mariana Islands.

On the flight deck of the carrier, as the wind swirled around him, Fuchida stood and watched another torpedo bomber flagged off to thunder into the brilliant sky. The Imperial Japanese Navy had recently promoted him to air operations officer of the entire Combined Fleet. Looking to his left, another idling torpedo bomber inched into position in front of a group of five more rumbling aircraft. Another bomber mystically rose to the deck on the rear elevator.

The day had come. The Imperial Japanese Navy finally had their "decisive battle." The Japanese and the Americans were to lock horns in the biggest naval air battle the world had ever seen. Nine Japanese aircraft carriers in three battle groups carrying 450 aircraft scattered the sea. Five battleships and more than forty other support vessels filled out the attack force. Since they believed the Americans to have thirteen or fourteen carriers and the Japanese were limited to what aircraft they could launch from the sea, Kakuta had arranged for 500 more attack planes to launch from Guam to join the battle, giving the Japanese nearly 1,000 aircraft to throw into the fight. But this wasn't the battle they had chosen; it was a battle that had chosen them.

To see and feel the power of these aircraft exhilarated Fuchida, especially on the deck of the newest carrier and flagship of Vice Admiral Ozawa—the *Taihō*. Unlike the *Akagi*, which had been converted from a battleship under construction, the *Taihō* was a new generation of Japanese carriers, built from the ground up to withstand torpedo and bomb attacks while still carrying on in battle.

But a dark cloud spoiled his excitement as Fuchida caught eyes with the bombardier in the middle seat who enthusiastically smiled and nodded to him. Fuchida knew the feeling, but this was a young, inexperienced flier, completely ignorant of the prowess of the American forces they faced. Fuchida smiled back, giving no hint of his fear that he'd very likely never see this young man again.

As he opened the door and headed to the command center, his smile immediately faded into a scowl while he trudged down the freshly painted gray passageway. Troubling thoughts dogged him. What had led to the beginning of the war was now leading to the end of the war—*oil*. They waged war to get it, but without more of it, they couldn't continue the war, either.

Now they had less than ever. Three thousand five hundred miles was a *long* way to haul oil from Indonesia to Japan, and there was no way to provide protection to their tankers from American submarines, which were biting off more and more of their supplies. Their navy couldn't train new pilots and they couldn't move ships—all for lack of fuel.

The American strategy had finally come into focus—to attack along two prongs: to the southwest, General MacArthur would lead his troops through New Guinea up toward the Philippines; to the northeast, Admiral Nimitz would lead the American armada toward the Mariana Islands, most likely to establish air bases for the new B-29 long-range bombers to rain hell on the homeland of Japan. But the Japanese had been uncertain where Nimitz was going to strike next.

Three days earlier, they had their answer when fifteen American battleships began hurling thousands of two-ton shells day and night onto

The Taihō *was commissioned only three months before the Battle of the Philippine Sea.*

Saipan.

Fuchida entered the smoke-filled command center, glanced at the blackboard "scoreboard," then looked at a wall map as radio traffic sounded out from speaker boxes. Communication men with headsets scribbled notes, as some marked tallies on blackboards and others pushed models on the sprawling map table. A wall clock showed 0905.

As Fuchida studied the Marianas Islands on the map of the world, his eyes drifted across to France. Two weeks earlier, the Allied forces turned loose a breathtaking assault on the coast of France involving 360,000 men and 5,000 warships. His eyes drifted over to Russia. That spring, the Russians had leaped onto the Germans with bloody vengeance, rolling over them with thousands of T-34 tanks. Japan's hopes had always presumed a German victory—now a discarded dream.

In the previous 26 months, Japan had lost a full third of its entire air fleet, over 26,000 aircraft. Not only that, when Fuchida had recently sent for a hundred of his best pilots from Halmahera in Indonesia to fly to the Marianas, fewer than ten arrived. Malaria immobilized the rest. *Ten!* Fuchida shook his head in anger. Fuchida's eyes wandered to the floor, and he mumbled under his breath, "The gods are *not* on our side."

He proceeded to the blackboard beside the commander in chief of the carrier forces, Vice Admiral Jisaburo Ozawa, who stood six feet seven inches, the tallest man on the ship. Privately among the shipmates, his less than stellar looks had earned him the ignominious nickname of "the Gargoyle." Fuchida gave a quick glance. He didn't think he was that ugly.

Examining the numbers of airborne fighters and bombers on the board, Fuchida lit up a cigarette. This was their best chance to seriously

Vice Admiral Jisaburo Ozawa.

damage the American fleet, bring them to a halt, and allow an opportunity for a compromise for peace—a thought on the minds of all, but spoken by none. If the Marianas fell, it was all over. The Americans would load the islands with long-range bombers and pound their homeland into the sea.

"Admiral," Fuchida said over the din of the room, "what have we heard from Vice Admiral Kakuta on Tinian?"

An officer on a headset turned and shouted, "Second attack wave of one hundred ten aircraft en route to the American task force. All aircraft airborne."

"He's already sent out two waves with excellent results," Ozawa replied. "Early reports are several carriers on fire, perhaps two sunk. Severe damage to cruisers and other vessels."

"Good!" The news relieved and amazed Fuchida. Their only ace in the hole was Kakuta's planes, the second prong of their own frontal attack, giving them an advantage. Without him, it would be a one-sided battle. Scouting reports indicated that the Americans had three or four battle groups of carriers with perhaps four or five more carriers than the Japanese.

Taking another long drag, Fuchida examined the board. Their three battle groups had launched the first wave of sixty-nine aircraft at 0745 that morning, and they should be shortly arriving at the American fleet. The second wave of 110 planes had just been sent off. Kakuta was engaging the enemy. Hundreds more aircraft were being readied for the third and fourth waves, and there'd been no sign of American detection of their fleet.

As Fuchida took a puff of the last of his cigarette, he raised his eyebrows and gave a slight grin as a ridiculous thought crossed his mind— *We might even win this battle.* He folded his arms, nodded, and blew the smoke out through his nostrils.

A massive shockwave thundered from below, dimming the lights for a second and ending all chatter. The bridge radio blared out, "Torpedo hit. Fore starboard!"

Ozawa looked grimly at Fuchida. He didn't have to say the words. Fuchida knew the commander wanted a damage report he could trust, so he nodded to Ozawa and made his way down the passageway to the upper hangar, dodging through the maze of dive bombers and engineers to the forward elevator. The platform for lifting aircraft to the deck was jammed about at the bottom of the shaft—leaving a gaping hole at the top at the front of the runway. Hurrying down ladders to the lower level, he saw seawater mixed with aviation fuel bubbling up. After further investigation, he learned that the fuel tanks were ruptured, but the steel plates leaking seawater showed minimal damage. The hit seemed survivable. The new, heavy plating had done its job. American torpedoes, Fuchida thought, were no match for Japan's Type 93, the best in the war. Many of the enemy torpedoes failed to explode and, on one occasion, a Japanese sailor survived in the water by clinging to an American dud torpedo.

He located the nearest phone and rang the command center. "Admiral, no serious damage. I advise we immediately board over the forward elevator and direct all aircraft to the aft elevator and continue flight operations." The admiral agreed. Within thirty minutes, carpenters had dismantled galley tables and benches, covered the hole in the flight deck, and the ship resumed flight operations.

Returning to the command center, Fuchida continued to study the blackboard and monitor air reports. At 1000 that morning, forty-seven more aircraft sortied as the fourth wave of eighty-two planes prepared to launch by 1130. But the information being radioed back troubled Fuchida along with everyone within earshot of the radio speakers.

Fuchida watched as white chalk marked out the growing tallies of

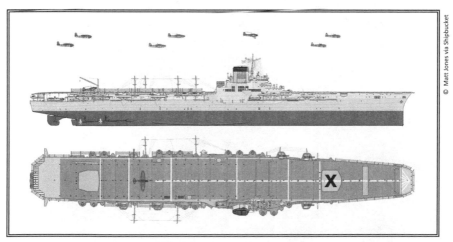

The Taiho *with an "X" marking the location of the collapsed forward elevator.*

downed Japanese aircraft. Of the first wave of sixty-nine aircraft, Americans shot down forty-two. Of the second wave of one hundred ten planes, only thirteen survived. Few were even getting past the outer defense perimeters of the American battle groups, and fewer still had actually landed a hit on any ship—none of significance. The new American Grumman F6F Hellcat fighters were shredding every wave of inexperienced Japanese fliers. Japanese blood soaked the Pacific Ocean.

Even though the Japanese fleet was yet to be attacked by enemy aircraft, flames engulfed the carrier *Shokaku* after taking four torpedoes from a submarine.

Fuchida went to a phone and called down to the engineer in charge of stemming the ruptured fuel tanks. "What's the status of the tanks?"

"Commander," the engineer responded, "we've been able to stop the entrance of further seawater, but we've been unable to seal the fuel storage tanks. When we tried to transfer fuel to the rear tanks, we discovered the lines were ruptured. We're operating all ventilators to disperse the fumes

The Japanese fleet under full assault by the Americans.

the best we can."

"Very well," Fuchida said. "Keep me posted on developments."

Over the ocean near the American fleet, Hellcats continued to decimate the Japanese fighters and bombers, streaking the sky with countless smoke trails ending in the water below. The elite aircraft and pilots the Japanese possessed at the start of the war had now been eclipsed in both areas by the Americans, and in numbers as well. Hundreds of aircraft filled the sky, dancing in fierce combat, and, one at the time, the ocean below swallowed hundreds of planes, nearly all Japanese. Fuchida scanned the table map as officers swept Japanese flight groups off the board like table scraps to the dogs.

All at once, a tremendous blast and a deep *whoosh* sucked the air from the room, roared through the ship, smashed open the doors of their control room, and sent papers flying. Ozawa grabbed a support pole and looked at Fuchida.

"Fuel vapors!" Fuchida yelled. The entire ship had turned into a bomb when the vapors found a source of ignition. He rushed out and up to the flight deck. Opening the door, clouds of acrid, jet-black smoke blew over him, billowing from flames sweeping out both sides of the front runway and up from the elevator shaft. He froze. The Americans were shredding the remains of their rebuilt air power in a humiliating one-sided battle. While the rumbling thunder of the gas-fueled fire raged, Fuchida looked up and behind him as the sky filled with clouds of smoke and the hangars below his feet crackled and popped in the inferno. He'd finally been promoted to the position of air operations officer of the Combined Fleet. He hung his head. What fleet?

Vice Admiral Ozawa and Fuchida stood on the deck of the heavy cruiser *Haguro* as she powered away from the conflagration of what was once part of the hopes for a victorious Japan, the *Taihō*. Forced to transfer his flag, Ozawa and evacuees packed the deck.

"She was our newest, most powerful carrier," Ozawa said with bitterness. Multiple, small explosions burst and rumbled through the flaming wreck. "The best!"

The Haguro—*a Myōkō-class heavy cruiser of the Imperial Japanese Navy.*

The sadly familiar sight likewise mesmerized Fuchida, but he knew that the battle was still very much under way. "Admiral, we must immediately proceed to command quarters."

Ozawa adjusted his hat, nodded, and turned to walk with Fuchida when a distant rumble of thunder exploded into a horrific shockwave that shot across the water as a colossal fireball mushroomed into in the sky above the *Taihō* reflecting in the ocean below. Ozawa looked at Fuchida ominously. As another dying carrier sank lower in the waves, so did the hopes of the Imperial Navy.

Chapter 95

`Two weeks later. Saipan.`

Vice Admiral Nagumo, in his filthy, torn uniform with unbuttoned collar, leaned against the wall of his concrete-reinforced command cave. He stared . . . out beyond the heaps of dead soldiers piled beside a smoldering machine gun into the open sky. Clouds of smoke drifted inside the stale air. Echoing guns rattled and pounded away in the distance as the faint calls of American officers urged their men forward. He wiped the sooty sweat of his face onto his sleeve and let out a slow sigh. The heroic commander of the Pearl Harbor attack had become little more than a cornered animal.

After days and nights of earsplitting bombardment from battleships and from the air, the Americans had overwhelmed the Japanese on Saipan, pouring 70,000 marines and infantry onto the island from a seemingly

Another wave of Marines floods the beach of Saipan.

endless supply of ships. American fighters pulverized the 150 aircraft Nagumo possessed on the ground before ever having a chance to get them into the air. His 32,000 men fought ferociously, yet hopelessly, to the death. Fewer than 2,000 soldiers scattered across the tropical wonderland turned to hell—some in bunkers, others firing their last rounds from behind the dead bodies of their fallen comrades.

While gazing into the daylight, Nagumo mindlessly opened the leather flap of his holster and drew his Colt 1903 .32 pistol to his waist and racked it. His story would not even have the dignified ending of the defeated noble samurai of old, dressed in white and surrounded by his peers as he committed *seppuku*.[34] The children of future generations would never be told his humiliating story. He gently brought the steel barrel to his temple. As the endless chatter of machine gun fire and mortar rounds churned outside, a single shot cracked from within the cave.

---

[34] Literally "stomach cutting." Ritual suicide whereby a samurai warrior accepts responsibility both for his own failure or shame and for his carrying out his own punishment. Often performed in a formal ceremony.

Chapter 96

July 14, 1944. Northern Honshu, Japan.

A black sedan rolled through a countryside of flooded fields, green with rice shoots as the morning sun broke over the horizon on the big island of Japan. Fuchida, in his green uniform, sorted papers in the back seat beside another officer while his aide drove toward the airfields of Misawa.

"I was tired of my desk job," Fuchida said without looking up, "so I decided to lead the mission myself." He glanced up at the officer beside him. "Our navy is all but gone, our carriers have no planes or pilots, and what attack planes we have left on the ground are fueled by vodka and wood alcohol." Fuchida shrugged with resignation. He'd been in and out of meetings for days as plans were made, remade, and made again. Circumstances changing for the worse perpetually whittled down their options.

"You said the mission is for twenty-five attack planes and two hundred fifty men? Is that enough?" the officer asked.

Fuchida nodded. "It has to be. It's all I could get."

"And you're confident of this plan?" the officer said while drawing out a cigarette from a gold case.

"No, but I know we can't stop the American bombers in the air. We've given Genda the newest fighters and best pilots for home defense, but it's still not enough. We need to destroy them on the ground, so I've ordered a night attack to land on the American airstrips in Saipan and attach explosives to the B-29 bombers by hand."

"And escape?" The officer lit his cigarette and blew the smoke out the top of the slightly rolled-down window.

Fuchida looked back down and shuffled his papers together and shoved them into a slot of the folder. "The objective is the destruction of the B-29s and the protection of our homeland."

Passing the entry gates of the air base, the driver came to a squealing halt and looked over his shoulder back toward Fuchida. "Lieutenant?"

Fuchida glanced up to see fire trucks and workers directing arcing streams of water over the smoldering carcasses of aircraft. Every plane had been blown to pieces on the ground by an American raid that morning. Deeply disappointed, he lowered his eyes.

Chapter 97

Fall 1944. Nanking, China.

"Hayaku! Hayaku!"[35] the guard impatiently shouted from behind Jake as he headed for his cell. Jake couldn't understand what the big rush was. All anyone did every day was sit around, from the prisoners to the guards. "Hayaku shiro!" he yelled again and whacked Jake across the back of his head. Jake stumbled forward as he cringed from the stinging pain.

Opening the cell door, the guard shoved Jake and slammed the door on his heel, wedging it between the door and frame. Jake grunted in pain as he tried to pull his foot in, but the guard only leaned against the door tighter and started kicking Jake's bare heel with his boot. In desperation, Jake hammered his shoulder against the door, releasing enough pressure for him to scrape his heel free, and collapsed onto the floor clenching his bleeding foot.

The guard bolted and locked the door with an extra cold *clank*, and clumped away down the hallway.

Jake's head and heel throbbed. After getting the courage to look at his foot, he wiped off some of the blood. His flesh was torn, but it seemed like it would heal. He clenched his teeth in anguish and panted. He'd come to *hate* this Jap guard. *Hated* him!

While seething, words rolling through his mind interrupting his thoughts: "*Love your enemies and do good to those who hate you.*" "Hah!" he mumbled as he massaged his foot. "Friends? Yeah. Strangers?" He cocked his head. "Maybe. Enemies? *No - possible - way!*" Jake looked up at the peephole in his cell door and shouted, "I'll be *damned* if I'm gonna . . ." He

---

[35] "Hurry up!"

stopped mid-sentence. His eyes drifted back down to his aching, bleeding foot.

The next morning, Jake stood in his cell peering through the slot in his door as the same guard made his rounds. A single shaft of sunlight from the vent above lit his dark cell. Jake waited until the guard came near his cell, then smiled and said, "Ohayo gozaimasu!"[36] Bewildered, the guard stopped and blinked, then turned around and walked away briskly, glancing one last time back at Jake's cell.

The following morning, as the same guard approached, Jake cheerfully said in Japanese, "How are you today?"

The guard stoically walked past Jake's cell.

This went on each day, until the sixth day. He waited for the guard to approach in the morning, smiled, and in Japanese said, "Good day, sir!" The guard didn't reply, but at least looked at Jake through the opening for a moment, pausing to catch Jake's eyes, then moved on.

Toward afternoon, as Jake daydreamed about his mom's cooking, fried chicken with biscuits and gravy, he heard the sound of a tin plate slide in the food slot at the bottom of his door. It was a whole, freshly cooked sweet potato. He'd never seen one the whole time he was in prison. Peering down on him through the door was the same guard who looked at Jake without emotion and walked on.

Jake sat and stared at the potato, unable to reach for it. He began to nod as if he just solved a puzzle and whispered under his breath, "This is the way to go." He kept nodding. "Love. This is *really* the way to go."

A few days later, the guard stood near Jake's door, like a cautious bird perched on a railing, wondering if it was safe. Jake didn't know much Japanese, but he'd been forced to learn enough in the past two and half years to stumble through basic communication.

"You have brothers?" Jake said in Japanese.

The guard waited a long moment. "Two."

---

[36] "Good morning!"

Jake allowed himself the smallest smile. "Sisters?"

The guard walked up to the wooden door and looked at Jake's face, dimly lit by the opening against his dark cell. "One sister." He paused again. "She's the oldest one."

"I have three sisters. One is half-sister. When I two, my father dead. So my mother got new husband."

The guard nodded and paused again. "Brothers?"

"One," Jake said, then smiled a bit broader. "But I number one son."

The guard studied Jake's face and for the first time let the edges of his mouth slightly turn up. "So am I." He glanced down at the floor with embarrassment.

"My name not 'number five.' My name is Jake." He gathered his courage and reached out to the cautious bird. "What's your name?"

The guard glanced around for fear of being accused of fraternizing with the enemy and gave out a nervous sigh. He looked back at Jake and moved his face close to the opening and spoke softly, "Aota Takeji."[37]

Jake was ecstatic but controlled his enthusiasm. "Aota?" he asked, just to be sure.

Aota nodded. "I've got to go . . . Jake." Aota gave a slight smile, then walked off to his business.

Jake's eyes followed him until he disappeared from view. He whispered to himself, "Aota . . ." He wasn't sure, but it appeared that Aota had a slight spring to his step.

---

[37] Japanese traditionally say their family name before their given name and often prefer it in conversation, although sometimes will use their given name. "Aota" was his family name.

Chapter 98

Fall 1944. Downtown Rochester, New York.

Peggy hoped she looked her best in her soft yellow dress, white gloves, and white hat adorned with a chiffon scarf tied in a bow at the back. As people walked past her on the sidewalk, she stood reading address numbers of the two and three-story, ornate stone storefronts decked with vertical signs. Among cars and smoking buses, a streetcar bell clanged to part the river of pedestrians crossing the street.

This was the right place. She nodded and tucked the sheet of paper back into her purse, snapped it shut, and headed two doors down to the Federal Services building. She loved adventure but was apprehensive of the unknown before her. With her husband in the service, she wasn't going to worry about what she couldn't change but determined to make herself useful until they could be together again.

Upon arriving at the right office, she waited beside an assortment of young men and women in a row of wooden chairs against a hallway wall. Light streamed in from a tall window at the end of the hall illuminating the musty building. Clicking typewriters, ringing phones, and muffled conversations filled the air.

As she sat quietly, she studied the war posters on the walls, one after another, each shouting their message:

"When you ride ALONE, you ride with Hitler! Join a Car-Sharing Club TODAY!";

"Buy War Bonds!" pictured Uncle Sam mystically standing in the clouds with a huge American flag, silhouettes of bombers above him and hundreds of soldiers below his feet;

"Wings Over America— Air Corps US Army," with an eagle soaring among fighter planes in a blue sky with clouds;

Uncle Sam rolling up his sleeve revealing a muscular arm holding a huge wrench, *"JAP . . . You're Next! We'll Finish the Job!"*;

And at the end of the row, a poster displayed a photo of a blindfolded American strong-armed by a pair of Japanese soldiers with lettering across the top of the poster that blared out, *"The Jap way—COLD-BLOODED MURDER"*

"Mrs. Struble?" a lady's voice called out. Peggy remained lost in thought. "Mrs. Struble? He can see you now."

"Oh. Oh, I'm sorry. Thank you." Peggy clutched her purse, stood up giving her hat one last adjustment, and followed the assistant to a balding officer wearing glasses flipping through papers at his desk. She sat down waiting for some acknowledgment, but she understood she was only one of many the officer needed to interview that day.

"Religious Studies major," he said, looking over the top of his glasses. "Very good grades." He licked his finger, flipped the page, "Awards," and paused and cocked his head. "Japanese? You speak Japanese?"

"Hai, I mean, yes." Peggy smiled politely.

The officer kept reading a while, then dropped the papers on his desk, tossed his glasses on top, and leaned back in his chair. "Listen. You seem like a nice girl, and we'd love to have you, but you need to understand what you're getting yourself into. Some of the Japs are good people, but a lot of 'em just plain hate our guts, understand?"

Peggy gave a nod. She felt it impolite to interrupt his speech with some of her background.

"I mean, there can be social implications for a young lady like you, you know, working with the Japs. Like what would your neighbors say, or what would your *parents* think?" He leaned forward and raised his eyebrows. "Have you thought about that?"

She glanced down at the rough ridges of the worn wooden floor. How could he possibly begin to understand? She didn't want to show any emotion that might keep her from getting the job. She looked up with a confident smile and a slight nod.

"You *sure* this is something you want to do? It's a *hell* of a journey."

Peggy looked straight into his eyes and took a breath like someone about to scale a mountain, and with equal determination. "Yes, I'm sure."

The Santa Fe Express locomotive rumbled across the northeastern plains of Colorado heading west hauling a dozen passenger cars, its coal-fired engine painting a fading river of black smoke across the canvas of a light-blue sky. Jostled by the endless click-clacking of the tracks, Peggy gazed out the window at the monotonous landscape of the prairie plains, decorated with barbed wire and the occasional western windmill. Stiff from the 1,300 miles she'd already traveled from Buffalo, New York, she breathed a sigh knowing it would only be another 150 more miles until she'd arrive in Denver. Her journey began three days earlier, taking her through Chicago and Omaha, Nebraska. Family friends would meet her in Denver and drive her another 200 miles across the state to the town of Lamar, about fifteen miles from the camp in Granada.

Her mind drifted to what she'd read in a letter from her brother, as she'd done a hundred times before. She could hear the angry Japanese soldiers surrounding her mom and dad, see the teachers and the missionaries in the mountains of Panay gathering together, getting on their

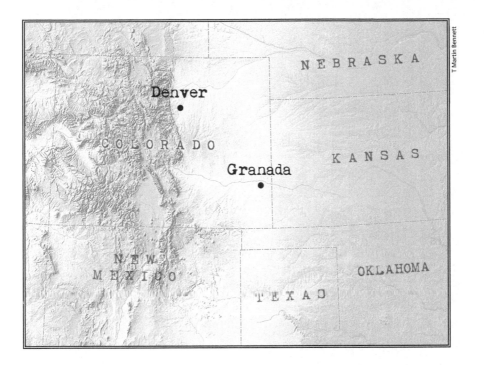

knees into a circle to hold hands. Among the chaos of shouting soldiers and weeping children, she listened to the voice of her father in a humble voice praying, *"Dear Lord, where there is hatred, may we sow love; Where there is doubt, bring faith; Where there is despair, may we bring hope; Where there is darkness, light; And where there is sadness, may we bring joy."* Now, this prayer had become her own and a part of her very being.

The shrill sound of the train whistle startled her, bringing her back to the present. She looked down at a worn, creased photo of her parents clutched in her fingers, blurred from the mist in her eyes.

The Granada War Relocation Center, also known as Camp Amache, one of many internment camps where Japanese Americans were housed after the start of the war.

Chapter 99

October 1944. Tokyo, Japan.

"They were all *lies!*" Fuchida fumed to Haruko as they sat together on their back porch. His German Shepherd, Lilly, lying beside him looked up in alarm. "Filthy lies!" Fuchida ran both hands over his head in frustration.

Sitting beside her husband in his civilian clothes, Haruko reached over and gently rubbed his back. "Well," she said, "at least in most other places, things are going well for Japan. Just this morning, the papers said that—"

"*Haruko!* This is what I'm trying to explain to you. You can't trust anyone. *No one* is telling the truth about the entire war. *Everything* you read and hear about the war is *false*. It's propaganda! We're on the verge of total defeat!"

She stopped rubbing his back and looked puzzled.

Fuchida turned more toward her and sighed with exasperation. "Off the Marianas, in the battle of the Philippine Sea, half of our entire strength for the battle was with Vice Admiral Kakuta and his five hundred aircraft on Guam, Rota, and Saipan. He kept sending us reports of what his planes had done and were doing all through the battle, engaging the enemy and sinking ships, but American attacks from the air destroyed *every* plane he had on the ground days before." Fuchida looked as if he could hardly believe his own words. "He never sent a *single* aircraft into the battle. He was lying to his *own* commanders about *everything!*"

In the yard, Yoshiya, now eleven, and Miyako, seven, threw a knotted rag for their Lilly to retrieve. They laughed and giggled, oblivious to the plight of their nation, and of their father.

Fuchida twisted a small, dead branch in his hands and leaned forward in resignation. "In the end, we lost over six hundred planes, three aircraft carriers . . ." His eyes seemed to glaze as he looked into the distance and continued to snap the sprig into ever smaller pieces. ". . . thirty thousand men on Saipan alone. Nagumo. He killed himself. And the papers continue to print preposterous lists of triumphs. Even the *emperor* thinks we sank two battleships and eleven American carriers." He turned back to Haruko's pained face. "*Eleven!* We didn't even *hit* one!" He looked away in disgust.

He tossed the broken pieces of the twigs into the air, letting them sprinkle onto the steps and grass. "I never thought I'd see the day when Germany was in retreat." He paused longer between each statement as if being forced to confess against his will. "It won't be long . . . They have complete control of the Marianas . . . The American bombers will come . . . So many of our nation's best . . . so many of my own friends sacrificed . . ."

He stared at Haruko's sympathetic face. "For what?"

Chapter 100

October 1944. Yokosuka Naval Base, Tokyo Bay.

The shoulders of both Fuchida and Genda displayed their new rank of captain, another gold stripe on their epaulets, as they stood on astride of a wall map of East Asia and the Pacific. Officers and teachers of the Naval Staff College sat along the sides of a long table and listened attentively while blowing cigarette smoke into the air.

Genda swept his hand over the archipelago of the Philippine Islands. "We believe the next strike of the Americans will be in the Philippines in order to come between us and our supply of oil."

Fuchida continued. "There's no point in wasting more planes in hopeless duels with the Americans. We understand we cannot defeat the US Navy, so the agreed plan is to make the war as expensive as possible in the way of American casualties, to concentrate on attacking troop transports, and to extract such a painful price that Americas will shift against their government to pressure them to end their needless sacrifices."

Genda paused to scan the faces of the officers. "We believe we can kill one hundred thousand of their soldiers."

Heads nodded among the officers.

Stepping closer to the table, Fuchida gave his final pitch and leaned on the table with both arms. "By exacting the heaviest possible toll on the enemy, we believe that public opinion in the United States will pressure their government to stop the bloodletting. At some point, it will simply be too much to bear, and they'll be forced to look for a way to negotiate an end to the war." He stood upright. "As we speak, the Shikishima Unit of the first Kamikaze Special Attack Corps[38] are preparing in the Philippines for their

---

[38] "Kamikaze" means "divine wind" and this unit specialized in suicide aerial attacks.

first wave of assaults against the expected American invasion. A single plane filled with twenty-five hundred pounds of explosives can sink a capital ship. We will send thousands more. The Americans have yet to experience the devastation we will inflict through the courage and determination of our warriors."

The light carrier USS Belleau Wood *suffering from a kamikaze attack. In the background, the carrier* USS Franklin *burns from another kamikaze hit, Oct. 30, 1944.*

Chapter 101

November 1944. Nanking, China.

Jake pulled his tattered blanket around himself tighter in the blue darkness of the chilly evening air. He looked up at the vent and saw only a few stars through the slit, but he was familiar enough with the pattern that he knew they were approaching the middle of winter.

Hearing a slow pace of footsteps in the hallway, he got up and went to his door and peered out through the peephole. Aota paced with his hands clasped in front of him, mouthing words silently as he walked, sometimes closing his eyes.

Seeing the light glimmer off of Jake's eyes behind his door, Aota walked over to him in the quiet of the night. "I was praying to my mother," he said softly in Japanese. "I know she hears me."

Jake nodded soberly. "When she die?"

Aota looked away for a moment. "When I was a young boy." He looked back at Jake.

"I'm sorry." Jake wanted to speak but had no words to say that he felt could ease the pain he saw.

"Sometimes at night . . ." he trailed off a bit, "I think I can hear her voice." He sighed as if to gather strength. "I thought I heard her last night."

The two looked at each other briefly, both knowing that they shared the loss of a parent and the anguish that others would never understand.

Aota bowed his head toward Jake, who likewise bowed in return, then he turned and slowly faded into the darkness of the arched brick hallway.

Chapter 102

November 1944. Granada, Colorado.

In a darkened, small-town theater, Peggy sat off to the side by herself, her hand to her mouth, listening to every word of the narrator. Her whole being studied the shaky black and white newsreel images and thunderous sounds of an American battleship firing a full broadside of sixteen-inch guns, American fighter planes tearing into Japanese aircraft, ships blown to pieces, and waves of soldiers wading ashore onto white-sand beaches under a hail of bullets and bombs.

The high-strung narrator continued: "Our boys are giving hell to the

General Douglas MacArthur returns to the Philippines on Leyte, October 20, 1944.

Japs in the Philippines with sweet revenge. Most battleships sunk at Pearl Harbor have been raised and sent back into this colossal battle in Leyte, both on land and at sea, sending Jap carriers and battleships to the bottom, and Jap soldiers to their graves."

Film shot from the decks of American ships showed Japanese planes diving toward vessels and disintegrating into the sea while another exploded into an aircraft carrier.

"In an act of hopeless desperation and blind devotion to their emperor, whom they call a god, the Japs have begun the practice of crashing dozens of their planes into Allied warships in suicide attacks they call 'kamikaze'— 'The divine wind.' We call it insanity. Only a few get through."

Higgins landing crafts dropped their ramps into the shallow surf and unloaded soldiers in the knee-deep water as General MacArthur and officers stepped from the craft through the surf onto the shore.

"And much to the dismay of the Japanese occupying forces, General Douglas MacArthur kept his promise and returned once again, bringing along a couple hundred thousand soldiers to liberate the Philippine Islands."

Peggy leaned forward, engrossed in the stories as MacArthur's face filled the screen with his iconic pipe.

"Next stop, Tokyo!"

The screen suddenly displayed the close-up of a rotting Japanese corpse; the flesh half melted off the skull.

Chapter 103

November 1944. Nanking, China.

The wind howled in a driving rainstorm outside Jake's cell as he sat in the corner, bundled as best he could. He searched for the right words, then whispered, "Lord, I . . . I want to follow you in the right way. You know, be on the team all the way. Make a stand. Be baptized, just like it says in . . ."

He looked up as a gust of wind blew a spray of water through the upper slot against the wall high above him. Jake grinned and nodded, and started his ritual of climbing the wall to the very top where he put his smiling face into the wind which promptly doused him in a spray of freezing rainwater. "Whoa! That's cold!" He shook his face with joy. "I sure won't forget this day! *Ever!*"

Early December 1944.

Dirty snow hemmed in the edges of the prison courtyard as the four remaining prisoners took their daily exercise laps. Under the eyes of a half dozen, warmly-dressed guards, Jake, Bob, George, and Chase hugged themselves and exhaled clouds of vapor while jogging through the slushy mud in bare feet.

"Where are your sandals?" a guard called out in Japanese. "I told you to keep your sandals on!"

Jake understood the words but kept jogging. The men agreed beforehand to ditch their sandals, which only got sucked off their feet in the muck, anyway.

"Stop! Everyone! Now!"

The men stopped, picked up their sandals and headed for the water spigot to rinse off their feet.

"No!" The guard decided to make them pay a price for their insolence. "Use snow instead!"

Jake looked at the other three. The mud was cold enough. Washing in the freezing snow? It wasn't worth the fight, so he headed off with the others to a snow pile to clean off his feet. But George, the Brooklyn red head, had had enough bossing around for the day and headed back to his cell, muddy feet and all.

Wiggling the mud off their feet into the numbing snow, Jake and the other two anxiously watched George from the sides of their eyes.

As George, at six feet two, walked past, the perturbed five-foot-two-inch guard grabbed his scabbard and flailed it across George's calves.

A streak of fear shot through Jake's veins as he, Bob and Chase stared in dread.

George swung around and belted the guard in the face, knocking him to the muddy ground as the rest of the guards converged from all directions, shouting.

Aota motioned for Jake and the other three to head to their cells. As Jake walked past him, he caught Aota's eyes, which darted to the ground.

The guards laid into George, beating him mercilessly.

Trembling from the cold that night, Jake cinched his blanket tightly around himself while he sat in his cell, watched his ghostly breath swirl before him, and unwillingly listened to the muffled shrieks of George Barr echoing through their compound as guards beat him again and again. Then they hung him in the air by his wrists tied behind his back. This time, George surrendered to all his feelings and filled the air with nightmarish howls of pain. Jake hoped George would make it. He hoped they'd all survive, but even his own health was deteriorating, and no one knew how long they could last—physically or mentally. It was a painfully cold winter. George's piercing screams made it painful to the bone.

December 25, 1944.

Jake opened his eyes with a start that morning. He leaned up on his elbow and listened to the sounds. He could hardly believe it. Cheers emanated from the cells of his three other partners. He *didn't* believe it and quickly shimmied up the sides of his cell until he reached the top and peered out through the narrow slit. American P-51 Mustang fighters roared over at low level, one after another—at least two dozen of them. He heard their machine guns firing in strafing runs in the distance and thrilled to see black clouds ascend into the sky.

"Now *that's* music. That's *real* music." For months, for years, the guards had been bragging of Japanese victories on land and at sea, of Japanese invasions in California, that they'd conquered San Francisco and

P-51 "My Girl" takes off from the American air base on Iwo Jima.

New York City, how American citizens were taking orders from Japanese officers, that the Americans had little hope, and that the entire war was *all* going the way of Japan. Jake and the men never bought into their braggadocio, but, then again, they always wondered what actually *was* going on. Where were the Americans? Why weren't they in China? Now he knew.

He shimmied back down, dropped to the floor, and stood by his door staring out through the slot waiting for a guard to walk past. From the commotion and arguing between the soldiers in the yard, it was clear that none of them were prepared to see anything like American planes flying directly over the prison. It seemed to Jake that even *they* had bought into their own propaganda.

Eventually, a guard walked nearby, and Jake spoke out in English, "So . . . those planes seemed like they're an *awful* long ways from home, wouldn't you say?"

The guard stopped for a moment. "They kill a few fish in river. So what?" Agitated, he walked on.

Jake's eyes followed the guard until he left his sight, then he smiled. "Merrrrrry Christmas."

Chapter 104

March 9, 1945. Zushi Prefecture, twenty-five
miles southwest of Tokyo, Japan.

In the middle of the night, Fuchida's wife, Haruko, lay on her side under the covers on her matted floor, her eyes wide open, kept awake by the endless drone of wave after wave of B-29 Superfortress bombers. In the past three weeks, the bombers had come four times. They lived far enough away from the downtown section of the city and the docks that she didn't fear their home being bombed.

Listening to the children whispering in the other room, she threw aside her covers, donned her kimono, and crept out to see what was going on. Slowly walking up behind the two of her children, just outside the back door, she, too, stared out into the mesmerizing, glowing red smoke filling the entire sky in the distance and the rumbling inferno of the city below.

Hundreds of heavy bombers released thousands of napalm-filled incendiaries onto Tokyo, and the winds whipped the flames into a fire-breathing dragon of death, a beast with an unquenchable appetite.

Miyako felt her mother against her back, looked up at her, and took her hand. "Mommy, when's the war going to be over? When's it going to stop?"

The foul odor of smoke scented the dry evening air. She ran her hand over her daughter's hair but had no reply. She wished it had never started. It was a ghastly dream that never left.

March 18, 1945. Tokyo, Japan.

Emperor Hirohito impatiently peered out of his vehicle window, having become increasingly weary of his advisors and their empty words of impending victory. An unannounced motorcade of three, highly polished, burgundy and black 1935 Mercedes-Benz 770K limousines escorted by soldiers on six motorcycles with sidecars rolled down the street of downtown Tokyo, a scorched wasteland of blackened brick walls, burned trees, and rusted shells of automobiles—an endless horizon of charred debris.

Each of the super-luxury cars with dinner-plate-sized headlights, long swept front fenders, and flat windshields displayed a stylized gold chrysanthemum in front of the radiator and on each of the rear doors—the imperial seal of the emperor. The royal burgundy of his automobile was forbidden for use on any other vehicle in the nation.

A week earlier he had witnessed the walls of flames stretching a hundred feet into the sky beside his palace, heard the air raid sirens, and had received the official reports of tens of thousands of people suffocated or burned to death, perhaps over one hundred thousand citizens, trapped in the flames and consumed along with every combustible object in an area of over sixteen square miles. In the conflagration, asphalt streets boiled, glass

Emperor Hirohito's Mercedes-Benz beside his mechanic and possibly his driver.

For the first time, the emperor examined
with his own eyes, the cost of the war upon his people.

melted, and the rivers had filled with corpses of people seeking protection
from the all-consuming fire, in vain. Air raid shelters became oven tombs.

He had made up his mind against the counsel of his advisors to see for
himself what had become of the capital of Japan. As he stoically stared out
of his walnut-paneled, calfskin-upholstered coach compartment and
observed the soot-covered poor carting off charred debris, the hideous
reality of a people enduring unimaginable suffering tore away the veil of the
elegant theories of war.

Upon seeing the imperial vehicles, those digging through rubble
quickly bowed, turning their eyes to the ground, yet a few were defiantly
willing to look up, barely hiding their resentful glare.

Leaning forward, the emperor rapped on the dividing glass with his
white-gloved knuckles. The driver looked back, nodded, and brought the
Mercedes to a halt over the charcoal-covered street. The aide exited and
came to the emperor's door with a look that asked if the emperor, indeed,
wanted to get out. Hirohito nodded firmly and the aide swung the door
open for him with a deferential bow.

Hirohito disembarked in his riding boots, sword, and military
uniform, as did the officers in the following two matching limousines. A

woman picked through the ashes of what was once her home. She lifted an earthenware teapot and shook the soot from it.

The emperor walked uprightly, turning his head from side to side attempting to take in as much as possible, then came to a halt as the other officers strode up beside him. The group of them stood and examined the horrific devastation in a long gaze from one end of the horizon to the other.

"Your Majesty," the officer nearest the emperor said in a low voice, "we must be patient. Soon, the people will accept the bombing and in time our resolve will become stronger and stronger. Then our diplomats will have room to devise a more advantageous situation for Japan. We must resist surrender no matter what the cost."

The emperor nodded, then, out of curiosity, walked to an overturned steel bowl, scorched and rusted. He squatted down and picked it up, but quickly realized it was a helmet as it revealed a bleached skull covered in white ash. The words of his late commander, Yamamoto, echoed in his mind, "Tokyo will be burnt to the ground three times before it's over." Yet, this was the eighth time his city had been firebombed. Pausing, he looked back at the officer who had just spoken, then carefully replaced the helmet over the fallen soldier, stood, and bowed with reverence.

The day following the March 9, 1945 firebombing of Tokyo.

Chapter 105

April 1945. Nanking, China.

Spring brought a relief from the biting cold of winter, but as Jake took his walk in the yard that morning with his comrades, he winced in pain. His body had erupted with painful boils in several places, even on the bottoms of his feet. He tried to put his mind on something other than the searing pain of his flesh when a guard came alongside of him and the three others.

"So, your leader, Roosevelt, he dead now. You have no leader," The guard said, smiling broadly.

Jake didn't look back at him. He did his best not to wince from his pain. "Yeah, we heard," Jake said. He raised his eyebrows and looked over at Bob, beside him. "Well . . . looks like General MacArthur's gonna be in charge now." Still walking, he turned to the guard. "What do you think about that?"

The guard scowled. "No more talk!"

June 15, 1945.

Once again, without announcement, guards hauled Jake, Bob, George and Chase from their cells early in the morning, had them clean up, lined them up, dressed them in large, green canvas raincoats, and unceremoniously hand-cuffed and put them in leg irons. Jake knew this routine well. They were taking another trip. Why or where, as usual, he had no idea. He eyed his companions without a word, and he knew they felt like he did: the known, bad as it was, was always better than the unknown.

Aota checked Jake's shackles around his wrists, then dropped his arms and stood in front of him. Although born in different countries from opposite sides of the world fighting on opposite sides of a world war, Jake felt strangely connected to his captor, who was equally captive of the same prison. The other three prisoners exchanged a few words of small talk with the guards.

In spite of the harsh treatment, the fights, and the dire circumstances, there was an inexplicable camaraderie between them all.

Instead of the traditional eastern bow, Aota put out his hand in a western-styled handshake. Jake gave a slight smile, lifted his cuffed wrists and shook his hand.

"Good . . . luck, Jake," Aota said.

Jake stopped shaking his hand for a second and held it steady. He knew Aota had to have practiced saying that over and over to be able to say "luck" instead of the typical "ruck" he was more used to. Aota wanted to say it right, one last time, and it produced the desired effect.

And Jake wanted to leave just a hint of cowboy culture behind. "Take care of yourself, partner." He wasn't prepared for the lump in his throat and his feelings of sorrow in leaving a place of such isolation and pain. Both were conscious that neither of them would forget these twenty-six months they had spent together, years they could never explain to anyone, years no one else would ever understand, and that they would never see each other again. They gave each other one last, long look.

Appearing uncomfortable, even somewhat ashamed, Aota sighed heavily, shook out a green hood with two eyeholes and yanked it down over Jake's head. As Jake peered out through the two holes, he could see Aota look downward and wipe the edge of his eye.

The coal-fired train chugged through villages and towns that seemed to repeat themselves endlessly. Sitting beside his guards with a rope around his waist, Jake and the three other hooded Doolittle Raiders traveled north across the flat, open farmlands of China. Through his canvas mask, Jake observed people of all kinds board and exit their coach. He found his heart moved for the uncounted masses of people in the world living lives of near poverty, poverty like he'd never seen before.

In the summer heat, sweat dripped down over his face under his hood, and he tried not to hyperventilate, as he feared he might pass out. The escorting soldiers decided to withhold water from the prisoners to minimize "bathroom breaks." It nearly killed them.

The only thing Jake could do on this journey was to observe the other people around him. He studied each person, one at a time and became as uncomfortable in his mind as he was in his flesh. It seemed oddly rude to him for the women to be forced to sit on the floor while the men took the seats. Officers routinely slapped subordinates in the face for trifling offenses, or perhaps for none at all. Jake cringed as he watched a soldier slap an old woman on both sides of her face for not moving her heavy baggage quickly enough.

Though he hadn't memorized much from the Bible, some words drifted into his mind: *Treat others the way you want to be treated; the one who is least among all of you, this is the one who is great;* and *The greatest of these is love.* If they only knew a better way, he thought, they could lead much happier lives. All of them.

After the train had come to a stop in another tiny village, a young mother with an unwieldy bundle strapped to her back boarded their coach with two young children who were instantly captivated by the strange, hooded men. As the little girl and boy cautiously ventured closer to examine Jake under the watchful eye of the guards, the mother looked at the guarding soldiers and gave a sly smile, put her finger to her mouth, and backed away from the children, leaving them "alone" in front of Jake.

He stared down at the awestruck children whose mouths hung open. Jake leaned down toward them, his dark eyes wide behind his hood. "Boo!"

Shrieking in terror, the children fled, running for their mother. The passengers broke out in a few, rare chuckles. Even the guards smiled. All over the world, Jake thought, people were people. Just the same.

Toward the end of the third day, after over 600 brutal miles of travel, guards disembarked the hooded Raiders and loaded them into a military cargo truck and told them they were in Peking.[39] Jake settled on the floor

---

[39] Modern Beijing, China.

beside the guards and his fellow prisoners and looked up at the canvas-covered ribs above him. If escape to free China was a long-shot in Nanking, it was now beyond impossible in Peking, even further inside the continent.

The hooded mystery guests, Jake, Bob, George, and Chase, arrived inside a walled structure, and soldiers escorted them into another hell-hole of a prison. Worse than what they'd been in before, 1,000 hollow-eyed Chinese souls stared at them—men who looked like they'd gladly welcome their own death. After being unshackled, a guard shoved Jake into an even smaller, darker cell than he'd had before.

"Sit on stool!" the guard shouted in his broken English. "Face wall! No move!"

Jake settled down on his wooden stool—a four-by-eight-inch seat about eight inches off the floor—and faced the rear wall as the heavy wooden door clunked behind him and latched closed. The constant, muffled sound of beatings and wailing let him know they meant business. The days of walks in the prison yard were over. Now he was only let out once a week to wash. Sitting and staring at the wall, Jake felt sure that this would be the road to his insanity.

The boils under his skin had come back and had spread over his entire body. Each one ached with continuous pain, yet there was no relief in the darkness. After collapsing several times and blacking out, the guards finally permitted him to lie on a filthy straw mat. Jake sensed his body beginning to shut down and his life ebbing away. He drifted in and out of consciousness. The screaming, the darkness, the pain, all combined to drew him to the edge of delirium. As much as he may have wanted to, he had little strength to even scream.

One morning he felt his heart laboring in his chest, each beat feeling like a struggle. He remembered Bob Meder telling him that his heart was hurting not long before he died. Jake felt he was coming to his end. His heart couldn't hold out much longer. He was ready to die. He'd made peace with God and even looked forward to the relief of death, to death and new life—life free from the filth and pain and loneliness of his existence.

Yet, something inside told him to ask for help. He remembered the verses he'd read, that if he had the faith of just a tiny mustard seed, he could speak to a mountain and make it move. He thought, maybe he should take what little faith he had, go to God, and ask for healing and for life, and he believed that God would answer.

Jake gathered all of his strength, strained up onto one elbow, then onto his side, struggled up from his mat, and settled his aching bones onto his stool facing the back wall. He leaned forward and began to pray. He decided he'd just keep praying until he got an answer—or simply passed out and collapsed onto the floor.

Unexpectedly, he thought he heard a voice tell him that he was free. He smiled. *You're free.* He somehow had a sense that he would know what to eat and what not to eat and that God would, in fact, save his life. For the next two days, he ate no food, clearly sensing he shouldn't eat it. Then, each day, he asked God if he should eat the food served him or not, and he knew when to eat it, and when to not eat it. Although extremely weak, his health gradually returned ever so slightly.

Some days afterwards on his stool facing the wall, he whispered a prayer, "What should I do now?" Jake nodded, then got down on his knees and faced his door. He'd never faced the door before and knew it could easily lead to a brutal beating, but he followed the clear leading and got down on the floor onto his hands and knees, folded his hands, and began to pray silently.

In time, when the guard checked, he rapped on the door with his scabbard and yelled in English, "Get off floor! Get on bench and face wall!"

Jake remained unmoved.

"Face wall or I come in!"

Jake didn't move. He was certain he should just stay put.

The guard left and Jake could hear that he'd returned with more people. The lock jangled with keys. Jake was pretty sure he should stay where he was, but he still feared the worst. His jaw tightened.

The bolt cocked back and the guard flung the door open and stared down at Jake. Three guards and a doctor in a white coat stood motionless examining Jake, then looked at each other in concern. Two guards reached down and turned him over onto his mat as the doctor rolled up Jake's sleeve and gave him an injection of vitamins. By the time the sun was about to set,

Jake was eating soup, bread, boiled eggs and fresh milk.

That night as Jake lay on his back in the darkness, in the stench, surrounded by the echoed cries of unknown men—he smiled as he took a bite of bread. "You keep your promises, God," he said with tear-filled eyes. Jake had taken his half mustard seed of faith and come to God with one request, and God heard him, told him what to do, and rescued him. He tore off another piece from the chunk of bread, placed it in his mouth and chewed it slowly, savoring the sweet taste. "You keep them all."

From that day on, Jake received the same kinds of food each day. His health returned.

Chapter 106

August 5, 1945. Southern Naval Headquarters.
Hiroshima, Japan.

Fuchida rubbed his eyes, loosened his collar and, with his elbow on the table, rested his head on his hand—another endless meeting of officers discussing *Ketsugō Sakusen,* the extensive preparations for the defense of Japan against the inevitable American invasion. Hiroshima was home to the headquarters of the Japanese Fifth Division as well as the Second Army. This would be a joint operation between the army, navy, and air forces.

Trying to pay attention to the speaker, Fuchida sighed unconsciously as he reflected on the once powerful navy that had been pared down to only

After being struck by no fewer than eleven torpedoes and six aerial bombs, while sinking,
one of the powder magazines of the Yamato *exploded into a massive mushroom cloud.*

eleven major ships, with little to fuel them. The naval command had sent the majestic battleship *Yamato* on a suicide mission to defend Okinawa four months earlier. American bombers annihilated the battleship, sinking her on the open seas before ever reaching her destination. An estimated 3,000 of her crew went down with the ship, including Vice-Admiral Seiichi Itō, the fleet commander—a successful mission according to the Japanese press.

The naval command handed rifles to the remaining members of the navy and sent them to the southernmost island of Kyushu as marines to be part of the 900,000 troops assembling for the battle. Only a month earlier, the intense fighting for the island of Okinawa ended, resulting in the deaths of over 100,000 Japanese soldiers. Fuchida had heard that an equal number of civilians had died—maybe even more. It was an ominous portent of what lay ahead for mainland Japan.

Through a PA that echoed through the hall, the commander boasted from the platform, "Our plans for suicide attacks against troop ships and landing crafts will be unlike *anything* the Americans have experienced! We *can* and we *will* repel *any* attack they can send. Carrying out the objectives we've outlined, we will crush their invasion forces while they're still at sea with over ten thousand of our aircraft. On land, we are ready to sacrifice a *million* men while inflicting the same casualties on US troops. The American public will give them *no* choice but to negotiate for peace with terms favorable to Japan. The sooner the Americans come, the better!" Applause filled the hall.

Stifling a yawn, Fuchida looked at his watch, which seemed to be running *extraordinarily* slowly, then took a puff of his cigarette. This was all nonsense.

A rather square-faced communication officer strode up to Fuchida. Lieutenant Hashimoto whispered as he bent down beside Fuchida. "Captain? Admiral Yano needs you at Yamato immediately for Army-Navy coordination planning. Can I tell him you're on your way?"

"They certainly don't need me here." He took a last puff and snubbed his cigarette. "Tell him I'll fly up and be there by this evening."

"Yes, sir."

As he passed through the entry area of his hotel, Fuchida touched a finger to his hat with an informal salute to his navy men sitting around having drinks and smokes. "Business up in Yamato," Fuchida said with a grin as he stepped between chairs sitting on a Persian rug. "See you in a day or so." A couple of men lifted their glasses in a goodbye gesture as he left the Hotel Yamato.

Fuchida slid down into the front pilot's seat of the familiar B5N2 bomber. He'd be flying alone this time, about a two-hour flight, a welcome break. His aviator clock hung around his neck read 1745—still plenty of daylight. Flipping switches and checking gauges, the engineer gave him the "clear" signal. Another ground crewman used a crank to wind up the engine, which faithfully stuttered and rumbled into a familiar roar.

During the meeting, Fuchida's mind kept wandering off to his own plans for putting together another *Operation Tsurugi*[40]—sending troop planes to the Marianas to land and deploy soldiers who would attach bombs by hand to B-29s sitting on the ground. He signed up to participate himself believing it was Japan's best chance to stall the Americans.

He wound his Nakajima B5N up to full throttle and tore down the runway taking to the sky, banking to the right, and headed northeast. Although he knew if *Operation Ken* was successful it would be the last deed of his life, he still felt content if it kept a single B-29 from dropping its payload on Japan. It was merely his duty as a soldier.

---

[40] "Tsurugi" means "sword."

Part VI

*The Light of
A Thousand Suns*

On July 16, 1945, at 5:29 a.m. in the desert of
New Mexico, the United States successfully detonated
the world's first atomic bomb. The blast was the
culmination of the work of over 130,000 people for
3 years at a cost of $2 billion ($26 billion today).
Immediately upon witnessing the brilliant blast, the
project head, J. Robert Oppenheimer, recalled
these words from the *Bhagavad Gita*:

If the radiance of a thousand suns were
to burst at once into the sky, that would be
like the splendor of the mighty one . . .
Now I am become Death,
the destroyer of worlds.

Chapter 107

Jake lay on his straw mat staring at the raw wood ceiling as the faint morning light began to illuminate his shadowy cell. Hearing bits and pieces about the war, and simply having American planes bomb nearby, Jake was sure the Allies were making inroads and certainly turning the tide, but his heart went out to the Japanese people, whom he knew would be devastated by the prospect of defeat.

Rolling to his side, he asked, "What would you like me to pray for?" Just as quickly, he sensed a reply to pray for peace, and to pray without stopping. It seemed like a ridiculously generic prayer, but it also seemed just as obvious as one he should request. He'd never prayed for peace before as it seemed useless. Yet he felt compelled to do so this day, that God wanted his cooperation, his participation in what he was doing on earth. Jake figured God could do anything he wanted to do, with or *without* him, but he *clearly* sensed he wanted to do things *with* him, right then and there.

He got up onto his aching knees and asked for God to put a desire for peace in the hearts of the Japanese leaders and for the Allies to treat the Japanese with mercy after the war. His heart and mind ranged over a myriad of hopes and wishes and requests for the people of Japan and for America.

Having lost track of time, he felt he heard the Lord tell him that he didn't need to pray any longer, that the war was over.

"It's over?" Jake whispered out loud. The sound of the words rolling off of his tongue amazed him. "The war's over?" he said again, a bit louder. He leaned back, sat upright and looked around with a smile and chuckled to himself. "The war's over." He finally said it. He was getting news faster and better than anyone with a newspaper or a radio!

He slid the wooden cover from his benjo hole, leaned in, and whispered loudly, "Bobby! Hey, Bob?"

Bob uncovered his benjo hole and tried not to breathe too much, "Yeah?"

"I was praying this morning . . . and the war's gonna be over today. It was revealed to me. It's over!"

Hearing footsteps, Jake shoved the cover back on, got to his feet, and brought his face against the small grate as a guard came by. "Pssst!"

The guard stopped and looked quizzically at Jake. Since Jake's brush with death, they'd let up on him having to stay on the bench.

In his best Japanese, Jake said, "The war's over. It's over."

The guard stared, shook his head as if a child had told him he'd just seen Santa Claus, and walked on out of sight.

"It's over," Jake whispered to himself.

Chapter 108

L ieutenant Hashimoto, the officer who informed Fuchida he was needed at the Yamato base, stood beside two other men in the underground restroom of the Hiroshima train station drying his hands. As he stared at his face in the mirror, a violent shockwave ripped through the building, showering him with cinders from the concrete ceiling and dousing the lights. He'd experienced earthquakes before, but this was much more abrupt and far more powerful. Unquestionably a bomb of some sort.

In the darkness, he pushed through the door and stumbled up the dark steps into the dust-filled light of the station where hundreds of people were lying or crawling on the floor, littered with debris. The explosion blew out all the windows of the train cars. He looked up at the huge trussed roof over the rail lines and parked coaches, caved in and leaning, but still standing. Despite the nearby detonation, the station remained eerily quiet.

Looking through the wide, concrete arches to the outdoors, he saw a huge, black column of rumbling smoke, about a mile away. He hadn't heard any air raid sirens, so the sky should have been clear of any enemy aircraft. Maybe a weapons depot had discharged, and the shockwave knocked the people down, he thought.

He made his way to the entrance, dodging between people struggling to get up and into another world. The entire landscape blazed. The explosion seemed have collapsed every wooden structure to the ground and set them into raging flames. Only a few concrete and stone structures stood, like gravestones in a flaming prairie.

A woman beside him stood with her arms stretched out, her clothes hanging in shreds from her arms. Confused, he looked at her face. It wasn't her clothes that were shredded, it was her skin, revealing her raw, glistening flesh. Half her hair was burned to her skull.

Panicking, Hashimoto stared at the people around him on the sidewalk, posing like scarecrows, standing or sitting in shock, no one making a sound. It seemed as if half of each of their bodies had been burned in a fire, and the other half left unscathed.

A man bumped into him, his eyes shut, shards of glass protruding from his face and arms with blood pouring from his flesh and dripping onto the sidewalk. Hashimoto realized that anyone much nearer to the blast was certainly dead. Tens of thousands of people.

Fear gripped him and he bolted away from the blast column, running through waves of smoke, down the train tracks, then to a road, strewn with debris and tangled power lines. Hundreds of people walked in all directions—some perfectly fine, others completely naked with burns on their bodies, still others covered in blood. He heard no screaming, only voices from the rubble of fallen structures, women calling for their children, or husbands for their wives. It was so strange.

Overwhelmed with the need to escape whatever had just happened, or was *still* happening, he wanted to get away. Maybe this was some kind of new death ray he'd heard about. He ran. After a few minutes, he slowed from his frenzied jog, gasping for air, then stopped to look back at the city. A huge umbrella of smoke near the ground was being pulled into a vertical super cloud. The wind rushed past him as the roaring furnace inhaled the air of the entire city. The overarching black column climbed higher and higher, flashing with lightning and spreading out at the top, like a giant mushroom. A growing black sky followed him and overtook the sun, reaching over him like a terrifying creature in a nightmare that couldn't be outrun.

He began running again, yet the cloud even reached out ahead of him. Along with the crackling flames of burning homes, the sky thundered right above him. Then he felt a drop of rain on his hand and saw several more fall on the street. As he panted and ran, huge drops of oily, black rain fell from the sky. Then it began to pour black rain all around. The liquid ashes of ten thousand souls were raining on his head. He ran faster.

In a surreal world of strange death, Hashimoto's mind slowly began to clear as the black droplets abated. This was certainly a powerful, new bomb, a *devil* bomb, he thought. Exhausted, he came to a stop, leaned over with his hands on his knees, and panted violently. He was ashamed. Ashamed for being a coward. Ashamed for having run away. He looked around at the buildings and up at the power lines and wondered if the phones were working at this distance. Surely there was a phone nearby. *Someone* needed to call the base to tell Fuchida what had happened. He needed to tell them *now* so they could send help.

9:05 a.m., Yamato Naval Base.

In a conference room of a dozen officers, all eyes were riveted on a clearly shaken Fuchida as he slowly set the receiver back down onto the telephone.

"The entire city?!" an officer exclaimed.

Fuchida nodded while contemplating. "A single explosion," he said, drifting in thought. A picture of the city he had just walked the streets of the day before flashed through his mind—filled with merchants, vendors, streetcars, families with children—now incinerated. His friends at the Hotel Yamato—cremated alive.

"How could that be?!" another said. "What was it?"

"It can only be an atomic bomb," Fuchida said softly.

The first officer grunted, "Impossible! They don't have the technology or the resources to build such a weapon! The Americans aren't that advanced!"

Fuchida raised his eyes from the table to the officer. "Apparently, they are."

Heads turned to the senior commander who cleared his throat. "Fuchida, we need a full report of *exactly* what happened. Return to Hiroshima immediately. I'll send a team from Tokyo to meet you at your headquarters tomorrow morning."

One thought was indelibly stamped into Fuchida's mind—the war was over.

Chapter 109

August 6, 1945. 1:40 p.m. The skies above Japan.

The brilliant sun shone through Fuchida's canopy as he flew in the skies above lush, green plains of rice. He held the control stick of his plane as he navigated southwest, back toward Hiroshima and reflected on the leaflet he'd read, one of millions that had fluttered down from American bombers eleven days earlier over Japanese cities, leaflets explaining the terms of the Potsdam Declaration, terms for surrender:

"The prodigious land, sea and air forces of the United States, the British Empire and of China, many times reinforced by the armies and air fleets from the Western Powers, are poised to strike the final blows upon Japan . . . This military power is sustained and inspired by the determination of all the Allied Nations to prosecute the war against Japan until she ceases to resist . . . The full application of our military power, backed by our resolve, will mean the inevitable and complete destruction of the Japanese armed forces and just as inevitably the utter devastation of the Japanese homeland . . . We call upon the government of Japan to proclaim now the unconditional surrender of all Japanese armed forces . . . The alternative for Japan is prompt and utter destruction."

The Japanese government acknowledged the Allied offer and even printed the declaration in the papers, but Prime Minister Suzuki told reporters he didn't attach any importance to the declaration at all, that the only thing to do was to "kill it with silence."[41]

Fuchida grunted angrily. Kill it with silence? Now the Japanese were being silenced by being killed. The bitter medicine stuck in the back of his throat: "*. . . the utter devastation of the Japanese homeland . . . unconditional*

---

[41] "Mokusatsu."

surrender or prompt and utter destruction."

He scanned his gauges—fuel, airspeed, altitude—then looked toward Hiroshima in the far distance beyond the green mountains that hemmed it in. There was certainly a great deal of smoke over the city, some of it much higher than his aircraft. He decided to drop down and circle the area to take a look from above before landing at the base.

Before leaving the Yamato airfield, he had spoken with Admiral Yano over the phone, the admiral who had called him up to Yamato in the first place. He urged the admiral that Japan should sue for peace—*quickly*. Yano listened, but many of the die-hard commanders would have none of it— *Death before surrender . . . we will win the final battle . . . the Americans will lose their taste for war*—now all foolishness to Fuchida. Old men and schoolgirls were practicing with bamboo spears to defend the nation from the inevitable onslaught. Fuchida shook his head—*bamboo spears!*

As the city came into view, and he made a wide, arcing turn to his left, tilting down to give himself a good look. There was no question in his mind that the devastation was from a single blast. The completeness of the

In addition to incendiary bombs, B-29s dropped tens of millions of warning leaflets, naming cities to be targeted, urging civilians to flee, and warning of total destruction. The Japanese government punished anyone found in possession of these leaflets.

destruction amazed him. The explosion left few structures standing. He anticipated what they would discover for themselves.

The following day.

Fuchida stood in the middle of the street with a team of eight officers, some with cameras, others with notebooks and leather portfolios, but in vain. What they were seeing was not possible to record. Through a constant breeze of smoke permeated with the smell of charred flesh, he saw thousands upon thousands of bodies stacked along the roadsides like railroad ties. Scorched hulls of overturned automobiles lined the roads. He somberly pulled down his soiled white mask and gazed at the smoldering city of endless rubble, from one side to the other. It seemed that the blast had reduced everything, *everything*, to smoking ash as far as the eye could see in all directions, except for the few, obstinate concrete structures which defied the concussion and the consuming flames that followed.

People rode past on bicycles. An adolescent boy walked by carrying a baby on his back whose face and forehead were burned. Four men loaded blackened bodies onto the flatbed of a delivery truck. The charred remains of a horse lay on its side under the debris of a cart, its legs stiff, its skull laid bare. A hundred yards beyond, masked civilians threw charred remains onto a makeshift funeral pyre.

Earlier he'd seen a streetcar with the carbon remnants of passengers still seated or standing in their places. Those who survived the immediate blast sought relief from the fires and their unquenchable thirst in the many rivers of the city and perished in the waters. One could walk from one riverbank to the other side on the densely-packed corpses.

The stench of rotting, burning flesh was nauseating. Fuchida had never been this close to the effects of war on a city. Dropping a bomb from hundreds of feet above a target couldn't compare to standing beside the smoldering body of another human being. He came as an officer and as a representative of the military, but he saw with the eyes of a husband and the father of two children he loved.

Continuing further down the road, he passed a long, makeshift bulletin board plastered with photographs and desperate notes seeking lost family members studied by an anxious crowd of survivors. Having previously crossed the hypocenter of the explosion, he'd been surprised that he found no bodies there at all. They were simply vaporized into little more than ash.

The officer beside him jolted from his thoughts.

"How could they use such a weapon against us?" he said in near disbelief.

Without averting his eyes from the catastrophe, Fuchida replied, "If Japan had a bomb like this, we would have used it on the United States, wouldn't we?" Fuchida thought he would have been proud to strike such a devastating blow for Japan. "This is war," Fuchida said plainly.

The party moved forward again, the debris crackling under their boots. Fuchida stooped down to pick up a piece of clay roofing tile, melted from the extreme heat. He shook his head at the thought that intense heat was used to *bake* tile, yet this bomb was hot enough to *melt* tile. He dropped it into the ashes, creating a puff of gray smoke. "Everything's gone. It's all just . . . rubble and ash."

Another officer replied, "Not everything." He motioned with his eyes for Fuchida to look over his left shoulder.

There it was. The roof and windows were gone, but the scorched stone walls and steeple of the Nagarekawa Church still stood tall, the church he and Genda stood in front of twenty-one years earlier. The church he had insultingly flung his cigarette butt toward.

An old woman in a filthy kimono pulling a cart with rusted bicycle rims approached. She stopped and glared at the officers, incredulous that they had the gall to take a sight-seeing tour among the wasted ruins and human suffering. "That's right," she said boldly, nodding her head. She gazed around at the ruined land, then back at the officers, who were now curious. "That's right. Take a good look around you. And there are many more cities just like this one." All the while staring at them, she lowered the cart handles and walked closer to Fuchida. "This is where you have led us." She sarcastically held her arms wide. "This is your great - Yamato - empire!"

"How *dare* you disrespect an officer!" one of the men said as he stepped forward.

She turned to the man and spoke with authority, "What can you *possibly* take from me that I haven't already lost?" She looked again into Fuchida's eyes as she stepped even closer and spoke with quiet fury. "You lied to us about everything. You betrayed us. My husband is dead. My sons are dead. My daughters are dead." Without looking back, she stiffly swung her arm toward her cart full of charred belongings. "This is all I have left!"

He recognized they weren't just the words of a hopeless old woman, they were the words of an enraged nation, furious for having been led into a war that had devastated their country, a land they loved, a nation that had been ground into the dirt in humiliating defeat. She was the voice that was never heard by the military commanders when they passionately argued for war, and she was the voice of the millions who would never speak again.

She stepped still closer to Fuchida, her voice beginning softly, "I never wanted this filthy war. Everything is *lost*. Gone! *Destroyed!*" With her sooty hands, she seized Fuchida's lapels, to the amazement of the other officers.

The Nagarekawa Church in Hiroshima among the charred landscape.

"*Now* where will you lead us?! Where do we go *now?*" Her words exhausted, her composure broke, and she began to weep and tremble, slowly sliding down to Fuchida's feet, her hands streaking his uniform with soot as she wept.

As the speechless officers stared, the woman moaned on the ground before Fuchida, his eyes fixed on the smoke-shrouded horizon.

Chapter 110

11:01 a.m., August 9, 1945. Nagasaki, Japan.

A spectacular brilliant blue-white flash of light illuminated the city for a fraction of a second followed by a thunderous shockwave; wicked, billowing flames; and another fireball within a rumbling column of smoke rising into a churning mushroom cloud high above Nagasaki.

Among the over 60,000 people instantly killed by the explosion, the sprawling Mitsubishi-Urakami Ordnance Works lay in twisted, smoldering ruins. Constructed on the east bank of the Urakami River, the atomic bomb brought an end to the factory that manufactured the Type 91 torpedoes— the torpedoes launched against the US fleet in Pearl Harbor—the torpedoes that began the war with America.

1:30 a.m., August 10, 1945. Tokyo, Japan.

Alone, dressed in his khaki military uniform, Emperor Hirohito sat in a stuffed burgundy leather chair in his living room in the Imperial Palace, his head resting on his hand, his eyes closed, his other hand clutching two sheets of paper. A single lampstand beside him lit the deathly silent room.

Opening his eyes, he sat upright and looked down at the pages which he had read through a dozen times—a translation of a White House press release from President Harry S. Truman. His eyes stopped at three penetrating sections:

"We are now prepared to obliterate more rapidly and completely every productive enterprise the Japanese have above ground in any city. We shall destroy their docks, their factories, and their communications. Let there be no

mistake; we shall completely destroy Japan's power to make war."

"It was to spare the Japanese people from utter destruction that the ultimatum of July 26 was issued at Potsdam. Their leaders promptly rejected that ultimatum. If they do not now accept our terms they may expect a rain of ruin from the air, the like of which has never been seen on this earth."

"It is an atomic bomb. It is a harnessing of the basic power of the universe. The force from which the sun draws its power has been loosed against those who brought war to the Far East."

The words hovered over him—scavenging birds awaiting death. The power of the sun had been turned against the land of the rising sun. Sighing deeply, he looked through the exquisitely draped window into the hollow night of the future.

Chapter 111

August 12, 1945. OSS Headquarters, Kunming, China.

"We've gotten word from Washington that the Japs are going to surrender soon," said Colonel Bill Peers, the six-foot-two OSS[42] officer to his band of seven volunteers, some standing while others sat on tables and chairs.

Dick Hamada, a twenty-three-year-old bilingual sergeant, eyed the map behind Colonel Peers as he listened attentively. The open windows of the clapboard building gave him little relief from the sweltering heat.

"Your team is going to be dropped into the area of Peking to get as many American POW's out of the hands of the Japanese before they can do anything to them in retaliation. You know, one last act of revenge for the emperor."

"Yeah, yeah," Major Ray Nichols said. "You told us fifty times." Nichols, a fearless bear of a man from Alabama, headed the team. He had no patience for stupidity. Also attached were a doctor, two Chinese interpreters, a radio operator, and another officer. "General Wedemeyer's given us carte blanche to do *whatever's* necessary to get our boys out."

Dick Hamada of OSS Detachment 202 in China.

---

[42] "Office of Strategic Services." This Allied espionage agency was a precursor to the Central Intelligence Agency of the US government.

The multi-purpose Douglas C-47 Skytrain served as a backbone for troop transports and paratroop drops from the coast of Normandy to China.

Located in far south-central China 150 miles north of the border with French Indochina, the Allies made the city of Kunming a major hub of activity and cooperated with the Chinese military for operations of all kinds in China and Burma. During 1941 and 1942 the famed American Volunteer Group, *The Flying Tigers,* made the airfield their home to two of their squadrons.

Dick examined the scattered black pins on the map dotting China, Korea, and parts of Southeast Asia—all identified prison camps. Born in Hawaii, the third of four children of Japanese immigrants from Hiroshima, he served as an interpreter for the OSS. He was livid when the Japanese attacked Pearl Harbor as it gave him and his family the impossible task of proving they were loyal Americans. Subject to false accusations and suspicions, he volunteered for an OSS combat team. Like the other members beside him, he'd written off his life when he began working behind enemy lines. He felt this next job would be his last one, live or die. The risk was well worth the chance to him, to see any of the starved, tortured Americans make it back home again—alive.

"Some months back," Colonel Peers continued, "we inserted a three-man team of Chinese into Peking." He turned and pointed to the city on the map behind him. "For a long time, we didn't hear a word. A few weeks ago they sent a message. They'd located a large POW camp in Fengtai, about four miles southwest of the city of Peking. And they've got details of another military jail inside the city they believe has some of our men—prison number 1407."

He pointed down to their city of Kunming and followed a red tape marker across the map. "A C-47 will fly you from where we are here in Kunming, to Chongqing, to Xi'An, and then to Peking: 1,300 miles in all." The Colonel looked back at them soberly. "It'll take a couple of days to get there. Your assignment is to check out the rumors about our boys in Peking and see how many you can spring from the camps before they get shot or have their heads chopped off, and bring 'em home."

Colonel Peers lifted two, drab green duffle bags, dropped them on a table, and zipped open one of them. "You'll have three pistols each," he said as he held up a pair of M1911 .45s in one hand. "Enough to get you out of a pinch, but that's about it." In the other hand, he displayed a carton of *Lucky Strike* cigarettes. "We'll give you whatever you need to negotiate and get the job done." Then he dumped onto the table two handfuls of banded packs of

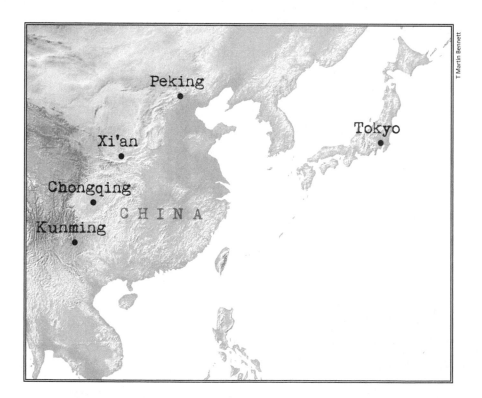

twenty-dollar bills.

Dick had seen a lot of crazy stuff before, but this made his eyes pop.

"Work real carefully and diplomatically, but be strong and forceful."

"Well, what do you want," Nichols said, "strong and forceful, or careful and diplomatic?"

"Never mind. Just play it by ear . . . and be strong . . . and diplomatic."

"You'll each get $10,000[43] cash, except for Major Nichols here, who's heading the team. He'll have fifty grand[44]. Don't spend it all in one place."

Dick smiled with the small break of levity in the otherwise serious room.

"It'll be a daytime parachute drop onto an airfield outside the city. The Japs are well armed and may very well ignore any orders they may get from Tokyo to quit fighting." Colonel Peers put both hands on his hips as the men huddled close and inspected their bags. "Listen, fellas, the big thing is, these are our boys who fought at Wake, Bataan, and Malaya. Even some Doolittle Raiders. They're starving, they've been tortured, and the Japs have been threatening to kill 'em rather than let 'em go. So do your best to get 'em home."

Major Nichols rubbed his cheek. "When do we leave?"

"Tomorrow morning," Peers replied. "Early."

Dick nodded. The sooner, the better.

---

[43] Equivalent to about $130,000 USD in today's dollars.
[44] Equivalent to about $670,000 USD in today's dollars.

Chapter 112

12:00 p.m. noon, August 15, 1945. Yokosuka, Japan.

Fuchida stood crisply at attention among the perfectly ordered rank and file of officers at the Combined Fleet Headquarters on the courtyard behind the main building. Their commanding officer faced the men between two loudspeakers on stands at opposite corners.

Only three days earlier, Fuchida had thrown in his lot to join a coup d'état to overthrow the emperor and force a military rule to avoid surrender to the Americans, something worse than death to him and to most of the military. Yet, when confronted and taken aside in person by Prince Takamatsu, a younger brother of Emperor Hirohito and, coincidentally, a fellow classmate of his from Etajima, Fuchida relented upon hearing that the emperor earnestly desired surrender to secure peace for the nation. That morning, the leader of the coup committed suicide, as did many other leaders when they learned that the emperor would accept defeat by the Allies.

Fuchida resigned himself to the idea that in the same way he had fought in loyalty to the emperor, he would accept surrender in the same spirit of loyalty, however painful and humiliating it might be.

The speakers crackled as they broadcast the announcement being heard by the entire nation:

"To my good and loyal subjects: . . ."

Every officer immediately snapped into a salute and held throughout the speech.

"After deeply pondering the general trends of the world and the current

conditions of our Empire, I intend to effect a conclusion to the present situation by resorting to an extraordinary measure. My subjects, I have ordered the Imperial Government to inform the four governments of the United States, Great Britain, China and the Soviet Union that our empire is willing to accept the provisions of their Joint Declaration."

Kneeling beside a radio with her and Fuchida's two children, Haruko's ashen face bowed to the floor as she quietly wept.

"Despite the gallantry of our naval and land military forces the diligence and the public devotion and service of our one hundred million people . . ."

In a public square, hundreds of people stood with heads hung low, some stared blankly, others knelt and wept openly as the broadcast echoed over the crowds.

". . . the situation of the war has developed not necessarily to Japan's advantage while the general trends of the world have all turned against her interest."

The people of Japan hear their emperor's voice for the first time.

Inside a meeting room, Genda and officers stood at attention around a long table staring at each other as a radio sounded out the somber message.

"Moreover, the enemy has begun to employ a new and most cruel bomb, the power of which to do damage is, indeed, incalculable . . ."

A chef stood still behind the counter as shocked patrons sat listening, their faces in fallen grief—many unable to control their emotions.

"Should we continue fighting in the war, it would cause not only the complete annihilation of our nation, but also the destruction of human civilization."

Without emotion, Tomiko sat kneeling in her bedroom listening to a small radio, staring out her window.

"The thought of our Imperial subjects dying on battlefields, sacrificing themselves in the line of duty, of those who died in vain, pains my heart and

body night and day. The hardships and sufferings to which our nation is to be subjected hereafter will be certainly great."

As the emperor completed his words, Fuchida and the officers struggled to maintain their composure.

"I am keenly aware of the feelings of my subjects, but in accordance to the dictates of fate, I am willing to endure the unendurable and tolerate the intolerable to establish peace to last a thousand generations."

The commanding officer signaled the men to end their salute. *A thousand generations?* Fuchida wondered. He shook his head. No. There will *always* be war.

*Subjects of the emperor bow, listen,
and weep outside of the Imperial Palace.*

Chapter 113

August 15, 1945. Madras, Oregon.

The morning sunlight illuminated the clouds of dust that billowing behind a black Chevy coupe as the bouncing car barreled up the dirt road to the farmhouse. At the wheel, Glen waved a newspaper outside the window and skidded to a turning stop in front of the house.

He leaped out of the car, slammed the door, and held up the newspaper to his stepfather, sitting on the front porch. "You heard?! The Japs surrendered! It's over! The war's *over!* We beat the Japs!"

Mr. Andrus stood up just as the screen door swung open and Glen's mom stepped out. "We heard on the radio this morning," he said, calmly smiling.

Glen bounded up the steps and reached his arms around his mom. "Isn't it great?!"

"Why, it's *wonderful,* son!" she replied.

He looked at his mom's face and realized she couldn't completely celebrate. He glanced over at his stepfather who raised his eyebrows, then to his mom whose eyes drifted to the ground as she tried to hide her tears. For her, the war *wasn't* over.

Chapter 114

August 17, 1945. Kure Naval Hospital, 15 miles from Hiroshima.

Fuchida tried to keep up with a doctor carrying an armful of files as they dodged nurses and patients down a hallway filled with gurneys of countless sick and bandaged people. Fuchida curiously rubbed his chin and wondered what all the fuss was about and why he was nearly commanded to fly down to the hospital.

"And you were walking around at the blast site for three days?" the doctor queried while glancing at his watch.

"Yes, but what was the urgency of me coming down here right away?"

The doctor stopped at the doorway of a room and looked at Fuchida, almost in disbelief. "Not just those who survived the blast, but many who were in Hiroshima directly after the blast are dying from some strange disease. We don't really understand it, but we're calling it radiation sickness." The doctor led Fuchida into a room with some of the men who accompanied him in Hiroshima on the day after the blast. The doctor looked at Fuchida's face for his reaction as he spoke. "All these men were with you. They're all dying. Others who were with you are already dead."

Fuchida was speechless.

"Have you noticed any of your hair coming out? Have you felt sick in any way? Nausea? Red spots on your skin? Anything?"

Fuchida slowly shook his head as he painfully studied each of his stricken teammates who stared back in hopelessness. Splotches of red marked many of their faces, hands, and arms. What looked like tumors protruded from some of their faces. Others were completely bald or had only a few, odd clumps of hair left. Others wore bandages soaked with blood.

"We'll have to keep you here for observation," the doctor said, again glancing at his watch and making a final note in his book.

In the last few years, Fuchida knew he could have or should have died on many occasions. At times, he even felt guilty for still being alive. He should have been in Hiroshima on the day of the blast and died with his men at the hotel. Even though everyone else in his search party was affected, he suffered none of the ill effects any of his fellow officers experienced. Nothing. For the first time, he sensed that somehow his life was being preserved, preserved by something beyond himself.

Chapter 115

August 17, 1945. Peking, China.

Dick Hamada sat in the rumbling plane watching airmen pitch handfuls of printed flyers down through a large, round hole in the floor of their B-24 Liberator as it circled and made passes over an airfield outside the city. Engineers had removed the belly turret from the four-engine heavy bomber for the literature drop and for the men to jump through. The fact that their plane hadn't been intercepted by fighters or even shot at from the ground by anti-aircraft fire surprised him, but the idea of blanketing their drop zone with leaflets in Japanese telling the soldiers that the war was over, that they shouldn't kill the Americans, and that they should surrender was little comfort. On the ground below, he saw hundreds of armed soldiers scurrying and appearing to take positions. Once they'd opened their parachutes, they could be carnival targets in a shooting gallery.

With the last heave of leaflets fluttering to the ground, an airman gave the thumbs up to the rescue team. They'd jump during the next pass over the field.

Getting to his feet and holding onto the frame, Dick tightened his harness and checked his gear. As he stood waiting for the timing for their jump, he thought about the letter each man carried—personally signed

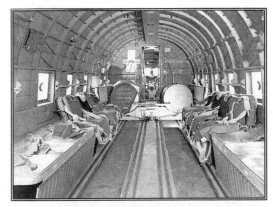

The inside compartment of a C-47 equipped for paratroopers, similar to the B-24.

Paratroopers drop from a B-24 Liberator.

on official letterhead from General Wedemeyer, the commanding general of all US forces in China. It firmly commanded that this team represented him and that no harm should come to the men. But one thing concerned Dick—it was only written in English.

"Fifteen seconds!" an airman yelled over the drone of the four engines.

On cue, one at a time, each man dropped through the opening and pulled his ripcord and cascaded into a line of seven blossoming parachutes swinging slowly in the sky. Looking down from his harness, Dick realized that the fields, moments ago swarming with armed men, were now vacant, yet he felt a thousand eyes staring at him. At least no one was shooting . . . yet.

After tumbling to the ground, he unhooked his harness and began rolling up the yards of his silk parachute when the plane made a final pass and dropped several more packages by parachute containing their gear.

Major Nichols headed toward what looked like some sort of an administration building near the end of the airfield. As Dick jogged to catch up, gunshots rang out from distant bushes, sending bullets whizzing past his head. He ignored them. What else could he do? There wasn't anywhere to run or hide. If they wanted to kill him, they could easily do it, so Dick figured it was just a warning. Just as suddenly, the rifle fire stopped.

He picked up his pace despite with his heavy pack, knowing he had to catch up to the major as quickly as possible where he'd be needed.

From the opposite direction, he heard the whining of a truck's shifting gears accelerating. Keeping his pace, he looked over his shoulder to see an old troop truck with soldiers standing in the back holding a huge white flag.

The truck arrived, circling in front of the men and came to a halt as a dozen Japanese soldiers with bayoneted rifles poured out along with a lieutenant in his traditional black boots who blurted out in English, "The war is *not* over! You must give up your weapons at once!" The soldiers pointed their rifles at the group.

Dick looked at Major Nichols. Apparently, the Japanese hadn't heard the speech of their emperor or hadn't received commands to surrender from headquarters, or they'd simply chosen to ignore it all and had decided to continue to fight on.

The major gave a confident nod and replied in his deep drawl, "I'm Major Nichols of the United States Army. We are *not* giving up our weapons, and we *demand* to be taken to your commanding officer, *immediately.*"

Dick understood that any sign of weakness could mean the end of the mission and their lives. The two commanders locked eyes.

Both the American major and the Japanese lieutenant held strong and weak cards in their hands. For the Japanese lieutenant, he could kill all the Americans, and that would be the end of it. He had the upper hand in strength, and there would be no favorable witnesses to the event. For the American major, he knew that they *both* knew the war was over and, sooner or later, the place would be overrun with Chinese and American soldiers who would demand an account of what happened to the team. The Japanese lieutenant would most likely be found out and could face the death penalty.

The Japanese lieutenant stared up at the hulking major. He blinked a few times, inhaled deeply, then turned to his men and said in Japanese, "Load their equipment into the truck." Then he looked into Major Nichols' face again and said in English, "I will take you to General Takahashi."

August 20, 1945.

A strange, brilliant light seemed to shine on Jake's face that morning as he lay on this mat, so bright, he couldn't open his eyes. Just as clearly, deep in his spirit, he heard the Lord speaking to him, that his anguish was over, that he'd soon be free and rejoined with his family, and that he was going to be sent back to Japan to help teach people, to teach them a better way to live.

He knew it was true. Everything in his being confirmed it. Jake sat up and opened his eyes to his dark cell, surprised at how much his health had been restored. He felt like a little boy on Christmas morning.

Later, the guards led him to a bath area to wash up. As he splashed his face with water under the eyes of a guard, he couldn't help hearing a commotion some ways away and saw men carrying boxes of documents off behind a concrete wall where a bonfire sent up plumes of smoke and flakes of ash. He also noticed the guards had broken out clean, new uniforms. Jake's heart beat with anticipation.

His feelings of hatred toward his captors had dissolved away. Waves of love seemed to have swept over him in the preceding days. He couldn't be angry if he wanted to be. Patting his face dry, his joy of release was tempered by a sadness he felt for the Japanese people. He feared that despair could overwhelm the nation.

Major Nichols' OSS team of seven squeezed into a room with fifteen Japanese officers and soldiers. He sat at a small table opposite General Takahashi. The record-breaking scorching heat wasn't the only thing creating a profusion of sweat sopping the shirts of all.

"Don't tell me that!" Major Nichols bellowed at the petrified Japanese officer standing near the table. He continued in his Alabama drawl with all the authority of a mother grabbing a child by the scruff of the neck. "I know that in fact, you're *not* an officer in the Army, you're an *interrogator* for the *police!*" The major waited for the officer being scolded to give the translation to his commander, even though words seemed almost unnecessary.

Dick understood this was an extremely high stakes game where no one could predict the breaking point. He only knew that someone and something was going to snap soon.

As the Japanese general nodded, the translator began to sit when Major Nichols glared and shouted so loudly, everyone in the room jumped. "You will *not* sit down! You will interpret only, and you may *not* volunteer *any* information either. Is that understood?" The Japanese officer's arms trembled in fear as he nodded and haltingly gave the translation to his general.

Major Nichols leaned back and fanned himself with a soiled folding paper fan, the only air conditioning system in what felt like a sauna as the sweat trickled down his face, soaking his collar.

The general leaned forward seeking to gain some high ground. "You shouldn't even be here as the war is *not* officially over. *Nothing* has been signed, yet."

As Dick translated to the major, he nodded and also leaned forward, still fluttering his fan. His six-foot-two-inch bulky mass was intimidation enough without his speaking a word to the five-foot-one-inch general. "Tell the general that we're not asking him to surrender—*yet*. And let him know that we know about prison 1407, where the prisoners are in the city, how many he has, and that we *demand* their *immediate* release!"

When the officer gave the translation to Takahashi, Dick watched the eyebrows of the general go up and the eyes of the Japanese officers dart back and forth. It was clear they had all believed that the whereabouts of the Doolittle Raiders was still a secret.

Lifting his head, General Takahashi said in Japanese, "Tell the major that he has put himself in *extreme* danger by coming here like this!"

As soon as Dick completed his English translation, Major Nichols instantly responded, "And tell the *general*, that if he doesn't turn over our prisoners *now,* he'll be putting *himself* in extreme danger! He'll be court-martialed and executed, just like Tojo and those rascals in Tokyo are gonna be!" Even as the Japanese translator was finishing, Major Nichols continued, his voice seeming to shake the walls. "And tell him we've been waiting for three days, now, and if I don't get some action real soon I'm gonna belt him in the mouth so hard his teeth are gonna come out the back of his head!"

But Dick noticed that the officer mistranslated the last bit to the general, saying, "He says he is beginning to tire of waiting and is concerned about the health of the prisoners." Dick spoke directly in Japanese to the translator for the first time. "Tell him *exactly* what he said, or I'll do it for you!"

The translator swallowed hard, looked at both Dick and the major, then gave the correct translation to the general, who then leaned back, unbuttoned his collar, and wiped his brow with a handkerchief.

Major Nichols' eyes drilled into the general as he fanned himself. Then, while keeping his eyes fixed on General Takahashi, Nichols snapped the paper fan shut and slid it to the general, who picked it up, snapped it open, and began fanning himself.

Lt. Robert Hite, Corporal Jacob DeShazer, and Lt. Chase Nielsen as they appeared directly after being released from prison. Lt. George Barr was too ill to stand for the photo.

Jake heard swift footsteps in the hallway, then, with a clanking of keys, the metal latch clicked crisply. Sitting on his mat, Jake looked up at the dim light coming from the tiny grate in his door as it creaked open and daylight broke in. General Takahashi and Major Nichols stood behind a guard who bowed to Jake. The guard said in English, "War over. Go home now."

Chapter 116

August 21, 1945. Madras, Oregon.

Mrs. Andrus gave a rinse to the last plate and stacked it in the dish drain while her husband oiled a horse halter on the breakfast table as the news sounded over their radio. She'd heard the night before that an American team had found four of the eight Doolittle Raiders in China, but the report gave no information on their names. As she wiped out a frying pan with a red and white checkered towel, she and her husband stopped as the radio announced:

"... *and from China, we have just received news of the four surviving Doolittle Raiders who were found and rescued, having endured forty months of brutal captivity under the Japanese. We now have their names.*"

She felt as though her heart stopped beating and her hands began to tremble.

Mr. Andrus sat motionless staring at the radio.

"*Their names are: Lieutenant Robert Hite . . . Lieutenant George Barr . . . Lieutenant Chase Nielson . . . and Sergeant Jacob DeShazer. The men are doing fine and are enjoying . . .*"

The pan dropped from her hands onto the counter with a clang and Mr. Andrus jumped up from the table. She embraced her husband in tears of joy and began dancing in euphoria. "I *knew* it! Jakie's coming home!"

Mr. Andrus stood with a relieved smile as his wife raised her hands and head toward the heavens.

"Oh, thank the good Lord in heaven above! My boy is coming home! I *knew* it!"

Chapter 117

August 31, 1945. Tateyama Naval Base, Tokyo Bay.

F uchida stood with his hands behind his back beside another officer on the concrete docks of the Tateyama Naval Base watching two American destroyers unload marines into rubber rafts offshore. Headquarters informed him they would be turning over the base to the Americans that day. The two men wore white bands on their left upper arms signifying their submission to Allied rule, as all Japanese military had been instructed. Any man without an armband would be suspect for being in a state of war against the Allies.

"Has the base been fully evacuated?" Fuchida said to the officer beside him.

"Yes, sir. All but for a few clerks."

Since the emperor's speech two weeks prior, it had been an exhausting and harrowing time for Fuchida. He'd hastily written a pamphlet entitled "We Believe This," explaining to those tempted to continue the fight that they'd done their best and had nothing to be ashamed of, but that now surrender was the will of the emperor. Fuchida had it printed and distributed by the thousands. To help smooth the transition, even members of the imperial family traveled the nation, personally encouraging compliance.

Yet, pockets of die-hard officers, soldiers, and airmen refused to lay down their arms, still reeling from the crushing decision to surrender to their sworn enemies. Rumors persisted that the Americans would behead all Japanese officers. Aircraft were stolen. Militarists took over bases and set buildings ablaze. Well-known leaders of the military committed suicide rather than living in defeat. Talk of overthrowing the emperor, installing a new government, and rejecting surrender persisted. On one occasion,

Propellers and weapons removed, Mitsubishi
A6M Zeroes await scrapping at Atsugi Naval Air Base.

Fuchida, armed with a pistol and sword, confronted a close friend leading a small insurrection, knowing full well that if the friend resisted, he would have to kill him. Fortunately, the man was drunk and delirious. With the help of a few officers, Fuchida tied him up and sent him to a psychiatric hospital.

The formal surrender ceremonies on *USS Missouri* in the bay were two days away, and Fuchida's primary responsibilities were now to ensure that all air bases in the greater Tokyo area were cleared of military personnel, that all aircraft were disarmed and disabled, and that the air would be free of threats. Others saw to the disarming of all soldiers.

The officer beside Fuchida leaned toward him with a quizzical look. "What, exactly, are they doing out there?"

Likewise, perplexed, Fuchida slowly shook his head, "I don't quite understand." He'd expected the ships to pull up to the pier and disembark their men, but instead, he watched heavily armed marines row two dozen rafts to shore.

Coming into shallower water, the men jumped into the chest-deep water, held their rifles over their heads, and waded in. Finally, the commanding officer climbed up the ladder onto the pier and trudged toward Fuchida, who exercised all of his self-control to keep from laughing out loud. The sopping wet officer, somewhat embarrassed wrapped in hand grenades and ammo clips, walked up to Fuchida as his boots squeaked from the sloshing water.

Fuchida asked with a straight face, "Is this a practice maneuver, sir?"

"No, this is a genuine operation!" the officer said in frustration.

Fuchida couldn't entirely blame him. The Americans didn't know quite what to expect from a nation of kamikaze soldiers willing to die rather than surrender, and Japan was still in a state of disarray. Fuchida watched the other drenched marines clamber onto shore. "We have hot baths for your men while their clothes dry off." Like a hotel concierge, he swung his arm toward the barracks. "Let me take you."

The marine commander sighed. "Yeah. I think that'd be great."

Officers surrender their swords at Kuala Lampur, Malaya.

Chapter 118

The battleship *USS Missouri* rested proudly in Tokyo Bay surrounded by five other battleships and nearly two hundred American warships of every kind—powerful imagery to the world of total victory. While patrol planes flew overhead, a resourceful photographer positioned his launch to snap a picture of the bow of the *Missouri* arching high over the iconic Mount Fuji in the distance, exactly what every American delighted to see on the front page of their newspapers.

On board, hundreds of sailors in khaki or white, marines, journalists, and photographers from around the world cascaded over gun turrets, railings, and filled every conceivable place to sit, stand, climb, or perch for this once-in-a-lifetime historic event. Packed beside Japanese and American reporters on an upper deck, Fuchida looked down on the admirals, generals, colonels, and marshals representing the Allied Powers who stood in a tightly packed group on the area below referred to as the "surrender deck."

USS Missouri, *September 2, 1945.*

Earlier that morning, Fuchida made arrangements for a boat to transport the official Japanese delegation to the ceremony, but the Americans provided a destroyer instead. He and a party of liaison officers came separately shortly after 7:30 a.m. at the same time the many international correspondents and cameramen boarded.

Just before 9:00 a.m., the Japanese delegation—comprising eleven men and representing the Imperial General Staff, the civil government of Japan, the Imperial Army, and the Imperial Navy—soberly formed into three rows before a table bearing two huge, open books: the formal Japanese instrument of surrender.

The sun just began to break through the overcast skies when General Douglas MacArthur, supreme commander of the Allied Powers, approached the microphone stand. The eyes of all were riveted on his well-known image.

In the previous four years, Fuchida had experienced excitement, frustration, anger, pride, joy, disgust, fear, despair, sadness, and a thousand

other emotions, yet now he felt strangely detached as he observed this almost mystical event.

MacArthur began in slow, deliberate words that echoed from the ship's speakers across the water: "As I look back on the long tortuous trail from those grim days of Bataan and Corregidor, when an entire world lived in fear, when democracy was on the defensive everywhere, when modern civilization trembled in the balance, I thank a merciful God that He has given us the faith, the courage, and the power from which to mold victory."

Fuchida was surprised, as he was expecting triumphant arrogance from the general. He could have bragged of America's power and victory, but he didn't.

"We have known the bitterness of defeat and the exultation of triumph," MacArthur said, "and from both we have learned there can be no turning back. We must go forward to preserve in peace what we have won in war." He looked up momentarily from his written speech at the concerned eyes of the military leaders of the war.

"Men since the beginning of time have sought peace. Various methods through the ages have attempted to devise an international process to prevent or settle disputes between nations, but military alliances, balances of power, and leagues of nations have all failed, leaving the only path to be by way of the crucible of war. We have had our last chance. If we do not now devise some greater and more equitable system, Armageddon will be at our door."

University of Pittsburgh

Unconsciously, Fuchida nodded in agreement.

"The problem, basically, is spiritual and therefore requires a spiritual renewal and improvement of human character that will harmonize with our almost matchless advance in science, art, literature, and with all the material and cultural developments of the past two thousand years. It must be of the spirit if we are to save the flesh. Let us pray that peace be now restored to the world and that God will preserve it always."

Fuchida looked down at his feet, stunned. He was entirely unprepared to hear such humble words from the victorious supreme commander of the Allied Forces. He knew if the Japanese had won, they would never have spoken to the Americans with such magnanimity. He moved to get a better view of MacArthur.

"It is my earnest hope," the general slowly said into the microphone, "and indeed the hope of all mankind, that from this solemn occasion a better world shall emerge out of the blood and carnage of the past—a world dedicated to the dignity of man and the fulfillment of his most cherished wish for freedom, tolerance, and justice."

Justice? Fuchida wondered as the formal signing began. *Whose* justice?

To him it wasn't *justice* that had prevailed; it was simply superior *power* that had prevailed. The emperor spoke of "everlasting peace" and now General MacArthur spoke of "peace" for God to preserve. He didn't buy it. Peace wasn't coming. More trouble was coming. It was the nature of the world. It was the nature of man himself. He was convinced—there would *never* be peace.

Mamoru Shigemitsu as plenipotentiary for Japan
signs the Surrender Instrument, thus ending the Pacific War.

Chapter 119

`September 1945. Madras, Oregon.`

Jake sat in his army khakis and tie at the table biting into a thick drumstick, but not chewing or moving. His mom, beaming with joy, stood pouring coffee for him over a table piled high with potato salad, fried chicken, coleslaw, cornbread, and blueberry pie.

"That's good," the photographer said. "Hold it just like that. That's perfect." A barrage of flashbulbs popped and the crowd of cameramen hurriedly wound their cameras to the next frame to get off another shot.

Jake mumbled with the chicken in his teeth, "Is it OK if I eat this now? I'm sure hungry." Upon hearing chuckles, he took a huge bite and looked up at his proud mom and the rest of his family applauding with cheers. He could hardly believe that a month earlier he was in solitary confinement facing death by starvation. Life had gone from a nightmare to a dream. He was back from the dead.

Doolittle Hero Eats Fried Chicken, First Home Meal

SALEM, Sept. 13 (AP)—Staff Sgt. Jacob DeShazer slept late this morning at the little white home on Oak street where he came home shortly before midnight last night.

The underweight Doolittle raider who arose from the dead so far as the western world at large was concerned 24 days ago when liberated from a Japanese prison camp, ate his favorite food—fried chicken—before his first night in his Salem home.

DeShazer entered the army from Madras.

Jacob DeShazer's homecoming is something his mother, Mrs. Hulda Andrus, has been looking forward to for years. Even after she had learned that her son was with the Doolittle fliers, after notification that men on that raid had been condemned to death in Japan, Mrs. Andrus lived in hope.

Ate Fried Chicken

The fried chicken her "boy" ate last night she had prepared with loving care to go with the cakes brought in by the neighbors as their tribute to the sergeant. There were flowers on the table, too, gift from a neighbor's garden, although late summer blossoms bloom in profusion in the Andrus home yard.

Morning Celebration

Hiram Andrus, who married the sergeant's mother 3½ years ago after the death of the little boy's father, was in the early morning celebration as was Hel-

en Andrus, the sergeant's sister.

Even while he ate the good American home cooking, DeShazer declared he would again eat rice.

And the Free Methodist parents told reporters they thought Jacob's decision to return to the Orient as a missionary "fine."

DEATH PROBED

MEDFORD, Sept. 13 (AP)—Deputy Coroner Carlos Morris said today he was conducting an investigation into the death of Oral W. Pollard, manager of the Forester Jewelry store here, who was found in his hotel room. Pollard, who worked at the Forester store in Eugene before coming here, was found yesterday.

S-T-R-E-T-C-H!

S-T-R-E-T-C-H your supply of this home-grown sugar. Don't waste a single spoonful of this scarce food energy.

SPRECKELS SUGAR

HONEY DEW

HOME SWEET HOME looks good to S/Sgt. Jacob D. DeShazer after nearly three years in a Jap prison camp from where he was rescued 24 days ago. He arrived at his Salem home Wednesday midnight, and his first task was to devour a platter of fried chicken, prepared only as his mother, Mrs. H. M. Andrus, could prepare it. DeShazer was one of Doolittle Tokyo fliers captured in 1942.

As he drove his 1940 Pontiac Torpedo Coupe down the road, the events of the last few weeks seemed a frenetic blur to him: military interviews, hospital examinations, days of air travel from China to India to Europe to New York and Chicago, press conferences, and arriving home. *Home.* It felt good to say that word and to actually *be* where he'd longed to be for so many, many days. He was truly, finally *home!*

But he had business to take care of, business he knew would be first on his list. Turning up the dirt driveway that ran alongside a post and barbed wire fence, he crackled up the road toward the home of Henry Wheeler, who happened to be outside his barn directing men hauling hay into a loft.

Henry turned toward the stopping car and wiped the sweat from his forehead with a handkerchief as Jake, back in civilian clothes, got out and made his way toward him.

"Jake!" Henry said.

"Great to see you, Henry!"

The two shook hands vigorously, both with painfully big smiles. The rest of the farmhands stopped to admire the local hero.

"You're a celebrity now! And to think you once worked for me!"

"Well, you see, Mr. Wheeler, that's what I wanted to talk to you about."

Mr. Wheeler winced. "Jake, don't tell me you need a job! I just put on two—"

"No, sir. The government's treated me real good. I got all my back pay and just bought me a car, and a newspaper company paid me way too much for my story. But, back when I was working for you, I, well, I wanted to apologize to you for taking, well, for *stealing* some of your tools, and I'd like to make it right." Jake pulled an envelope from his pocket and held it out.

Embarrassed, Henry looked down at the envelope and held up his hand. "Aw, Jake, you've been through so much, you don't need to—"

"Yeah, I do. That'll cover getting new tools and more. I'm real sorry."

Sighing, Henry slowly grasped the envelope and paused. "They say you're gonna go back to Japan. Is that true, Jake?"

"Yes, sir. When I'm ready."

Henry patted the envelope onto his palm a few times while staring at Jake's face, then gave a series of gentle nods.

Jake knew that Henry got it. His job here was done, and it felt good.

A few weeks later.

In the Andrus' master bedroom, soft, blue moonlight beamed in from a window and blended with the yellow light flooding in through the open door lighting the collection of press clippings. In the other room, the sounds of family, laughter, and the lingering aroma of food warmed the home with a joy only those who've experienced it can ever comprehend.

The wall of newspaper articles graduated from the headlines of *"Mother Fears Son Executed By Japs"* and *"Mrs. Andrus Has Faith, Says Son Is Still Alive"* to the newly posted entries of *"Four Doolittle Tokyo Raiders Found by Chute Team in China,"* *"Oregon Doolittle Flier Comes Home to Mom,"* and many others.

At the table crowded with all four siblings and their families, his stepfather, and neighbors, Jake spoke while holding a half-eaten cob of corn. "So there I was in New York City at some radio station, and I said, 'You gotta be kidding me! For one sentence?'" Enraptured family members gobbled biscuits and chicken as Mrs. Andrus delivered a dish of baked beans while Jake spouted on. "So I read the sentence over the radio and they paid me four hundred dollars! *Four hundred!*"

Hoots and hollers rang out with cheers.

After the guests had had their fill of ice cream, pie, and tales from Jake's world adventures and the last pair of red taillights coursed away down the driveway, Jake and his mom sat in rockers on the porch in the cool evening air. They quietly swayed under a vast sky of stars and moonlight, the gold-lit windows highlighting their backs.

"I thought, maybe I could serve in Japan," Jake said, "by being a janitor in a church or something. But I felt like the Lord told me to get in and work for all I'm worth."

Mrs. Andrus smiled and rocked.

"I don't quite know what that means or what I could do," he continued, "but I'm gonna go back to school, Ma, *really* learn Japanese, get a degree . . ."

Her chuckles interrupted his little speech. "My, my, *my!* At thirty-three you'll be the oldest boy in school!"

Jake hung his head and grinned. "Well, I'm kinda short anyway, so I don't think too many folks'll notice." He looked across the expanse of stars in the sky. "When I was on those planes coming home, I had a lot of time to think, think about where I've been, what I've done, where I'm going, and where I want to be heading. I told God I'd never smoke another cigarette or drink another drop of alcohol. It's not like I felt I had to, or that it was some big deal, I just want to live clean, you know, shoot for the best."

His mom took it all in. She was still in a state of disbelief. Not only had her son come home alive, he was also alive inside.

Jake gave a single chuckle. "Huh. To think, all those years me and the boys just wanted to get back home. Now all I can think about is getting back to Japan." He looked his mom in the eyes. "Strange, isn't it?"

"It is. And all those years *we* waited, and hoped and prayed for you to come home, and now?" Her eyes sparkled as she reached over and put her hand on top of his. "I'm with you all the way, son. I'm with you all the way."

Chapter 120

Early December 1945. Tokyo.

Kneeling beside a charcoal fire heating an iron pot, Haruko folded clothes with Yoshiya and Miyako. Haruko glanced at her son's face as he grudgingly folded a shirt. She saw a sadness that a boy of twelve wasn't allowed to talk about. "What's the matter, Yoshiya?"

His little sister stopped and looked at him.

With his head down, he waited a few seconds. "When's Dad coming back home? Is he working somewhere?"

Haruko forced a smile and finished folding the shirt in front of Yoshiya. "Your father needs time to be by himself. He'll be back."

Yoshiya looked up through his furrowed brow and folded his arms. "When?"

The mountains of Chichibu, 50 miles northwest of Tokyo.

The cold crimson sky closed into night over the dense groves of tall Japanese cedar, cypress, and red pines clinging to the rocky mountainsides. A waterfall hissed in the distance. Fuchida, his hair and beard untrimmed since September, sat warming his soiled hands over a fire. The wounded tiger had withdrawn into the darkened recesses of the forest. Beside him lay his only source of consolation—his loyal German Shepherd, Lilly.

He once clearly knew everything he believed in and where he was going. Now, holed up in an abandoned shack, he wrestled with the voices of the past and echoing questions about the future for which he had no answers. He cinched his overcoat tighter around his neck and exhaled a cloud of vapor as the cold bore down on him.

Everything he'd lived for and led others to die for had come to nothing. *Worse* than nothing. He no longer knew what he believed.

Picking up a stick, he stoked the burning logs, sending crackling embers into the night sky. As he stared, he saw the smiling faces at the air base after his raid on Pearl Harbor chanting his name, *"Fuchida! Fuchida! Fuchida!"* Hero? Now he was the villain, the leader of the attack on a day that will live in infamy. *Infamy!* The things on which he'd spent his complete life had only ruined the nation he loved and helped destroy an entire generation, not to mention people of other nations.

Lilly muzzled her cold nose against Fuchida's leg. Looking down at her glimmering brown eyes, he gently ran his hand over her head. "What have I done?" he whispered.

The words of the emperor came to him, *". . . to establish a peace to last a thousand generations."* But all Fuchida had seen was war and more war. What did the emperor know of peace?

MacArthur, despite his proud posture and reputation, surprised Fuchida with his humble, penetrating words, which now lingered in his mind, *"... methods for peace have all failed . . . We have had our last chance . . . Armageddon will be at our door . . . The problem is spiritual . . ."* The problem seemed clear, but what was the solution?

Yamamoto died a noble warrior's death, and Nagumo took his life, as many of Fuchida's fellow officers had done. Gazing distantly into the flaming embers, he almost felt abandoned in life by those who had entered into death, left behind to face the lifelong shame and torment of defeat. Perhaps, he thought, it would be best if he followed them . . .

Fuchida lay back against the ground with his hands behind his head. He looked up into the sky, watching the smoke drift upwards lit by the flickering flames below, and the impassioned plea of the old woman from Hiroshima came to his mind, *"Now where will you lead us?! Where do we go now?"* He sighed in angry frustration. For the first time in his life, he was a ship without a rudder on the open seas. Lilly pressed her muzzle against him and licked his hand.

Chapter 121

March 1946. Seattle Pacific College, Seattle, Washington.

Lugging more than a few books under an arm, Jake bit into an apple as he trotted down the steps of a brick building in his overcoat and hat in the chilly morning. Still in a state of wonder, he paused for a moment to look up at the tall, leafless trees. His every need was met as the government was paying his tuition, and every desire he had was being fulfilled. He was swept from the doorstep of death into a hallway of life.

Back in September, he stopped by to see his sister, Helen, who happened to work for the president of Seattle Pacific College. Free Methodists established the school shortly before the turn of the twentieth century to help train missionaries for the field, but the school was also fully accredited in the liberal arts.

Carol Aiko DeShazer Dixon

Since she encouraged him to consider the college, he ended up meeting the president, who was only too happy to meet the "Doolittle Raider" featured in papers across the city. Jake wasn't sure if he was up for all the mental stress of college, having been out of school for some years and still recovering at the time, both physically and mentally. When the president offered him a spot and asked when he could start, Jake told him he thought he'd be ready by the winter. Instead, the president persuaded Jake to start the very next day.

"Hi, Jake!" a student said with a wave.

"Oh, hi. How ya doing?" Jake responded, trying not to spit out chunks of apple as he spoke. It seemed like everyone on campus knew him, and he did his best to remember their names, but still couldn't keep up.

Two girls with matching blue scarves smiled as they came closer. "Hellooooo, Jake."

Jake politely put his hand to the brim of his fedora. "Good morning, ladies." The girls whispered as soon as they passed by. He hadn't really thought about attention from women when considering school, but now that he'd landed there, he didn't mind it a bit.

He ran up the steps into Anderson Hall, a four-story brick building with twin octagonal towers capped with pointed turrets. Administrators approved putting him on a fast track to get his degree in three years' time, as he was anxious to get back to Japan. A bit weary from his relentless speaking engagements around town, often several times a week, he was excited to get to his next class, among his favorites.

Anderson Hall

Coming into the classroom of students, Jake attempted his best Japanese, "Good morning Professor Tsuchiyama. How are you today?"

With a smile, the professor kept writing kanji on the blackboard, then turned with a bow to Jake and said in Japanese, "I am very well in the good care of the Lord. Thank you. Please take your seat."

It was his favorite class, all right, especially getting to sit next to

Carol Aiko DeShazer Dixon

Miss Florence Matheny.

Florence, a blue-eyed brunette. Jake had become "the" man on campus and was ready to settle down, with the right girl, that is. He still had his good looks, a new car, and back pay.

But to Florence, he was someone she admired. She gave a coy glance, then pretended not to notice him.

Professor Tsuchiyama came up to Jake and laid a set of type-written pages on his desk, marked with red ink. In English, he said, "It looks good, Jake, but we need to cut it down more if we're going to print this onto a single piece of paper, then we can start to work on the Japanese translation. Why don't you go over it and give me a new version in two days, OK?"

Jake nodded. "Yes, sir, I mean, sure. I'll get on it." Having told his story countless times in the preceding months, more and more people wanted a copy of it, and an organization offered to print it up and distribute it for free. On top of that, people wanted a book as well, a daunting task he wasn't quite up to, but the school president volunteered to help.

"It's a good title, too. I think it'll intrigue people," the professor said as he turned and walked away.

Florence leaned over to see: *I Was a Prisoner of Japan. By Jake DeShazer, the Doolittle Bomber.*

Chapter 122

Summer 1946. The village of Unebi.[45]

Fuchida knelt before a sheet of paper while holding a calligraphy brush in his hand, studying what he had just written.

"Are you going out to the property tonight?" Haruko said as she entered the bedroom stacked with belongings against walls. Realizing he was deep in thought, she gently knelt beside him.

Shaking his head, he laid down his brush and sighed in frustration.

Haruko's eyes scanned the sheet: *"Mankind must escape from this cycle of hatred generating hatred, of resentment breeding resentment. Only by translating destructive emotions into brotherly love can humanity be saved."*

Their family of four crowded into the home of Haruko's sister and brother-in-law who operated a drugstore in Kashihara, about twelve miles from where Fuchida grew up. The military was no more, and he had taken what little money he had saved to purchase a small plot of land to grow rice, barley, fruits, and vegetables, and hopefully, to raise egg-laying chickens, too. But for now, they had no home of their own. When the gardens were complete, he would start to build a home for his family.

For the moment, Fuchida's struggle was with thoughts and words. Watching his friends in the hospital die a slow, horrid death from the atomic bomb prompted him to shout in his mind, *No more Pearl Harbors! No more Hiroshimas! No more Nagasakis! The atomic bomb must never be used again!* So he vowed to write a book on the way of peace, yet he discovered it a profoundly difficult undertaking.

"Look at me," he quietly said to Haruko. "I should be dead." He looked

---

[45] After the war, Unebi was incorporated into Kashihara proper.

down at his half-written page. "A part of me feels I should be with my fallen comrades at Yasukuni,[46] yet I somehow feel I need to say something about how we can live in peace. There must be a way. There must never again be another Pearl Harbor or Hiroshima." He gazed back into Haruko's face. "But I . . ." He turned and looked back down.

She tried to smile, but she didn't know how to ease the pain on his face.

Stars punctured the velvet-blue night sky. Fuchida positioned his son's hands on a ten-foot wooden pole and then looked straight up from the pole into the sky. He had tapped multiple stakes into the ground with strings tied between them laying out their new home.

"You see it? You see it right there? That's the North Star—Polaris."

Yoshiya seemed lost as he searched the sky.

"My book says that the house should face fifteen degrees southeast for maximum sunlight during the winter."

Miyako stood a little ways away from her big brother so Fuchida could use the two of them as a kind of sextant. "But the sun's not out, Daddy," she said.

"No, we use the stars. If you follow the two stars on the edge of the Big Dipper," Fuchida continued, swinging his arm across the sky, "they point straight to the North Star. Right there." That steady star he'd come to trust and love through the years stood out among the rest.

"Oh, I see it!" Miyako shouted.

"Me, too!" Yoshiya said.

"I've done this a hundred times on the ocean. You can find your direction anywhere in the world with just the stars."

"Daddy?" Miyako said. "Who put the North Star there?"

He looked at her innocent face, then turned his eyes up into the starry sky. His eyes drifted to infinity. It had never dawned on him how useful that star had always been and that it seemed to have a purpose. It was so steady, so useful, and so beautiful. He, likewise, wondered who put it there. Still gazing at the sky, he said, "I don't know. I don't know who put it there,

---

[46] The Shinto shrine in Tokyo where it is believed that the spirits (kami) of soldiers and those who have given their lives for the Emperor of Japan reside.

Miyako." For the first time, he sensed a starting point that might give him some sense of direction to find his bearings once again.

A few weeks later, with a hoe over his shoulder, Fuchida stood beside his small, flooded rice paddy and examined a grasshopper perched on his finger. It was beautiful to him. So perfectly formed and designed. As it leaped off his finger and flew to the ground, he looked up and around at the trees, the birds, and the sky. Everything in nature seemed to fit together in such harmony, in a way that only God could do it. Yet it all remained a mystery.

Haruko sat further away on the porch of their half-built home, smiling as Yoshiya held a chicken and chased Miyako who screamed and laughed with Lilly barking at their heels.

Fuchida reached down and pulled up a single rice shoot and carefully studied it as the wet mud dribbled through his fingers. He could plant seeds and water them, but he couldn't make them grow. The more he took in the world around him, the more he could see that it was good, and could only have been made by a good God.

He squatted down and pressed the shoot back into the mud under the water. The more he felt that God must be good, the more he realized that man was not, that *he* was not good. He cringed as he remembered hearing the neighborhood boys jeer at his son, "Your father lost the war!" His son was innocent, and he had caused him to suffer. And what about the countless thousands of sons lost in the war? He shuddered to think of the pain he caused so many others. But these were things he could only reflect on in the

Miyako Fuchida Overturf

Fuchida and Miyako at their farm house.

recesses of his own mind. Never could he or would he dare mention a whisper of this to anyone else. It was his burden to bear—alone.

Turning toward his framed house without a roof, he walked down the pathway. He had been so proud and self-confident for so many years and was only now beginning to see that, like the plants and animals, he, too, must depend on the Creator for life. Everything that lives, lives because of him, he thought.

Chapter 123

August 29, 1946. Gresham, Oregon.

Mrs. Andrus, in her Sunday best, sat in the front pew of the church with her arm through her husband's arm. Beside her sat all her grown children: Julie, Ruth, Glen, and Helen. All her children but one.

Jake stood at the front, beside Florence in her floor-length white gown and lace veil. He looked at his bride's glowing face, then to his mom, who wiped a tear from her eye. It turned out college was a mighty good decision. For Jake, life seemed like it couldn't possibly get any better.

Mr. & Mrs. Jacob and Florence DeShazer—day one!

Part VII

Why Are You Here?

Chapter 124

Early June 1947. Yokosuka Naval Base, Tokyo Bay.

Cleaned up and back in the office, Fuchida dressed in civilian clothes since the military was now disbanded. He vigorously made notes on a pad at his desk behind large glass windows separating him from a roomful of desks and clerks at typewriters, all men.

A fellow ex-officer stepped into Fuchida's office, dropped a packet of folders on the corner of his desk, pulled a cigarette from his mouth, and eased into a chair. "Another war crimes trial?"

Fuchida didn't look up. "More like a mockery of justice. This one's about Rear Admiral Okada Tametsugu[47]." Fuchida laid his pencil down and glanced up. "He captained the heavy cruiser *Tone* when we went to Pearl Harbor. Then he commanded the aircraft carriers *Junyo* and *Shokaku*. And later, he commanded of our naval base at Ambon, which included a prisoner-of-war camp." Fuchida angrily tore the page off the pad and inserted it into a folder.

Testifying at war crimes trials in Tokyo.

The ex-officer blew smoke and snubbed the butt of his cigarette waiting for the rest of the story.

"He's been charged with being responsible for the deaths of some prisoners, even though he had nothing to do with it."

---

[47] Okada was his last name.

"And you're being called to testify?"

Fuchida opened another folder. "I don't know. I might. I have to be there, though, because I know him well."

A strikingly beautiful woman appeared in the doorway with a tray of handmade confections, startling both of them.

"Manju? Wagashi?" she said with a smile.

Fuchida raised his hand to wave off the gift pretending not to be interested. "Oh, I couldn't."

She responded with a silly frown. "But I made them myself for the office."

Glancing to the other ex-officer, Fuchida nodded. "One of each, then. Thank you so much."

The other man, likewise, nodded and helped himself to one of each. "Thank you."

"You let me know if you want some more. Don't be shy, OK?" She said with a smile.

The two men nodded like boys to their mother as they each took bites and allowed their eyes to follow her outside the office to the desk of another staff member where she bent over and offered her treats once again.

Fuchida whispered, "Wow!"

"Yeah," the other man replied, still staring. "That's what her fiancé said when *he* first saw her."

Abruptly shaking his head, Fuchida looked at his watch, then at the ex-officer. "My plane leaves in two days for Rabaul. I need to get back to work."

The ex-officer stood up. "Sure."

As Fuchida ran his hand over a sheet in his folder, he looked up again through the glass window at the woman, who glanced back with a smile.

Rabaul, New Britain. The Australian Territory of New Guinea.

A squad of military police cordoned off a weathered, schoolhouse flying an Australian flag under a cloudless, burning sky.

Only 300 miles south of the equator, the school room overflowed with perspiring Australian soldiers at the perimeter, and seated and standing reporters, civilians, witnesses from Japan, journalists, photographers, and diplomats—all present for the trial of Fuchida's friend, Rear Admiral Okada, now in full swing.

Dressed in a white civilian suit and tie in the front row of the gallery, Fuchida sat waving a fan to ward off the stifling heat and humidity, but unable to cool the intensity of the trial. He came both as an observer and as a possible witness and shook his head with disapproval as he studied the judges. At the head of the makeshift courtroom on a raised platform sat the head judge, or president, a lieutenant colonel in his military uniform with salt and pepper hair and a waxed mustache. Two majors flanked him. All wore headphones to hear translators interpret the trial. A British Royal Coat of Arms banner draped the wall behind them, crossed by two Australian flags on poles. Fuchida expected no sympathy from them.

The Australian prosecutor paced before the Japanese witness, Captain Shirozu, seated with folded arms behind a wide table stacked with folders and papers. The prosecutor spoke in respectable Japanese. "And the four listed prisoners were guilty of stealing rations and the fifth prisoner of attempting escape, is that correct?"

Shirozu nodded. "That's right."

The head judge adjusted his headphones.

The prosecutor leaned on the table with both hands. "And ordered to be executed for these offenses, is that correct?"

"Those were the orders."

"How were those orders carried out?"

Shirozu paused looking at the floor, then looked up. "Four of the prisoners were bayoneted, the fifth was decapitated."

The prosecutor glanced to see the expression on the judge's faces.

"Were those orders given to you in official papers?"

"No, I received them by telephone from Captain Kawasaki."

Fuchida looked to the ceiling with impatient eyes. Kawasaki was dead and surely couldn't defend himself.

Standing upright, the prosecutor continued. "Did you know that under Japanese law prisoners of war had to be court-martialed before being executed?"

"Yes, I knew that," Shirozu said matter-of-factly.

"Wasn't it your duty to send these prisoners to be court-martialed first?"

"It was *not* my duty."

"Then, whose duty was it?"

Shirozu turned his head toward a man in a khaki jumpsuit with a large letter "P" stenciled on his shoulders and knees: "P" standing for "prisoner." "I believe that was the duty of the commander of the Twenty-Five Naval Base Force." He looked back to the prosecutor. "Rear Admiral Okada Tametsugu."

All eyes in the room turned toward Okada.

Fuchida fanned harder. He'd seen this before. Both Shirozu and Kawasaki were clearly involved, had conflicts of interest, and were doing little more than shifting blame upwards until there was nowhere else to shift it. The last man in line got the axe.

The prosecutor studied papers in his hand, then let his arm swing to his side as he addressed Okada, now seated behind the table. "Do you think the execution of a prisoner of war who has committed a crime, without a due trial, is a lawful homicide?"

"No," Okada said plainly in Japanese. "It is absolutely *not* lawful."

"And you agree that all lawful orders from the headquarters originated from you?"

"That is correct."

"And you always maintained strict discipline and order of the forces under your command?"

"Yes, I maintained a strict chain of command."

Fuchida was engrossed. Regardless of being in the role of a defeated enemy, he'd seen Japan receive at least an attempt at some form of justice from the military courts, although it always seemed slanted against the Japanese. The Australian authorities had given Okada a capable defense attorney and was allowed to submit a sixteen-page plea of innocence to the judge—fully translated and typed in English. Fuchida held out hope that *somehow* Okada would be vindicated, however distant it seemed.

Nearly 6,000 former members of the Japanese military were put on trial for war crimes under the auspices of the International Military Tribunal for the Far East and by each of the nations of the Allied Powers. A total of 920 were ultimately executed.

"Captain Shirozu testified that orders from headquarters were given for the execution of the prisoners through Captain Kawasaki, who is now deceased. Did you give these orders or did you delegate that authority to Captain Shirozu?"

"Neither. I was not consulted on the matter."

Fuchida sucked air through his teeth. This was the critical point of the trial. Okada swore to him that he *never* gave an order for the prisoners to be killed, so either someone in the courtroom was lying or Kawasaki lied. Fuchida believed in his friend, granting the fact that it would be extraordinary for Okada to be that far removed from an order for execution.

"So," the prosecutor said, allowing himself a sarcastic grin, "we are to believe that you knew *nothing* about a matter of this importance, that you gave *no* orders, and that subordinates acted on their own, *completely* contradicting your testimony of strict discipline and chain of command?"

Okada looked directly into the prosecutor's eyes and thought for a moment. "I should have been consulted, but I was not."

After a short break in the trial, the judge tapped his gavel as people took their seats and a hush quickly spread across the broiling courtroom. He cleared his throat and peered through his reading glasses at the sheet of paper in his aged hands. Journalists grabbed their pads. Hand-held fans fluttered throughout the room.

Sitting on the edge of his seat, Fuchida leaned forward. He was convinced that no civilian court of law would convict anyone on such insignificant and sometimes contradictory circumstantial evidence. But this was a military court that ruled in the eyes of an angry world who wanted justice for the untold bloodshed among thousands of prisoners who were grossly mistreated, left to die, or killed. Justice or maybe revenge. Sympathy for the defeated foe simply wasn't a consideration.

The judge spoke in his Australian English as Okada listened to a translation via headphones, "In regards to the Australian War Crimes trial number twenty-nine-sixty-three, Rear Admiral Okada Tametsugu and the cases of the five named Australian prisoners of war, this court finds the accused guilty of all charges, of committing war crimes, that is to say murder, and is hereby sentenced to suffer death by shooting." The judge slammed his gavel and the room burst into chatter and a barrage of camera flashes.

Okada listened over his headphones as the interpreter completed his translation and nodded, showing no emotion as he stared at the floor. He raised his head, pulled off his headset, and glanced across the murmuring room at his old friend.

Fuchida felt the pain in his eyes. His blood boiled.

DPW(AG13(2a))SS/CF. AUSTRALIAN MILITARY FORCES AAF A117(a)
(Introduced Jan 46)
HQ AMF Use Only

RECORD OF MILITARY COURT

(JAPANESE WAR CRIMINALS)

AWC No. _2963_

Accused: Rear Adm OKADA Tametsugu

Aust W.C. List Ser No..............

Court, Place, Rabaul
Date and 23 & 24 Jun 47
Formation: 8th Military District.

Charge(s)	Plea	Finding
First charge.		
1. Committing a war crime, that is to say MURDER, in that he at AMBON on or about 26 Apr 45 murdered VX39756 Pte WADHAM T.F.J. of 2/21 Aust Inf Bn, QX10714 Spr MORRISON J. of 2/11 Aust Fd Coy, NX7039 Dvr SIMPSON R.A. of A.A.S.C. and NX2116 Cpl SOLOMON J. of A.A.S.C. Australian prisoners of war.	Not guilty	Guilty
2. Committing a war crime that is to say MURDER in that he at AMBON on or about 30 Apr 45 murdered VX19415 Pte SCHAEFER F.N. of 2/21 Aust Inf Bn.	Not guilty	Guilty

Precis of Evidence: The evidence for the prosecution was mainly documentary whilst verbal evidence was given by Capt SHIROZU Wadami and Capt KAWASAKI Matsuhei. The documentary evidence was contained in a number of statements made by members of the accused's command.
First Charge : The prosecution produced evidence to the effect that the accused was Commander of 25 Naval Base Force, and that as such he issued orders for the execution of the Prisoners of War named in the charge sheet. It was alleged by the prosecution that the prisoners of war named in the charge were suspected of having stolen rations and were interrogated at the direction of Capt SHIROZU Wadami. A report of this interrogation was submitted to HQ 25 Naval Base Force, and on or about 25 Apr 46 Capt SHIROZU Wadami received orders from that HQ, which were alleged to have originated from the accused, to execute the prisoners of war mentioned in the charge sheet. This execution was carried out by members of Capt SHIROZU's command. Three of the prisoners were executed by beheading and the other by bayonetting.

(PTO)

Sentence and Date: To suffer death by shooting.   24 Jun 47.

Confirmation and by Whom: Maj Gen W.M ANDERSON Adjutant General AMF 7/8/47

Promulgation: Confirmation of finding and sentence promulgated to accused on 2 Sept 47. Accused executed 3 Sept 47.

Petition: Lodged by the accused against finding and sentence on 7 Jul 47.

J.A.G.'s Report on Petition: First charge : should not be confirmed.
Second charge: confirm finding & dismiss the petition.
Consideration should be given to the appropriate sentence in view of the
Action on Petition: advised non confirmation of the first charge.
↓ Dismissed 7/8/47

Filed in Attorney-General's Department and Numbered.......81209

H.Q. A.M.F. Press—2022—1/46—5m.

Chapter 125

June 1947. Osaka.

Leaning his head back, Fuchida finished off another glass of beer and slammed it onto the bar table. "Victor's justice! That's all it is!" he yelled to Genda over the din of music and patrons in the dark drinking hole.

Genda smiled with amusement at his tipsy friend and took a cool puff of his cigarette.

"Justice?" Fuchida's eyes grew wide. "What the hell . . . the hell does *MacArthur* know about *justice?!*" Without waiting for an answer, he pointed his finger at his friend. "I've testified at war crimes trials in Yokohama . . . Yokohama three times; in Manila; in Rabaul; and in . . ." Catching the bartender's eyes, Fuchida motioned for a refill. "Genda, you know, you *know*, if we had won, we'd be putting the *Americans* on trial for how they treated *our* prisoners because *they're* guilty of the same things. *The very same things!*"

Genda sipped his foamy beer and smacked his lips. "How do you know that? How do you know that, Fuchi?"

Fuchida smiled confidently and pulled a folded newspaper out of the breast pocket of his coat, then started tapping on the paper. "You see that? One hundred fifty prisoners to be returned at Yokosuka from America."

Genda picked up the paper and read the headline.

"You know what I'm going to do?"

"No," Genda said with a patronizing voice. "Tell me. What are you going to do?"

He leaned toward Genda. "I'm going to go down to those docks when they come in; I'm going to talk to them and get *proof* about American . . .

about American torture and starvation and *death*, and the next time I'm at a war crimes trial . . . I'm going to *fling* it in the judge's face and tell him if he convicts us, he'll have to convict the *Americans* of the very same crimes they committed against us!" Fuchida focused his attention on grasping his refilled glass on the first try, took it, and gulped it down.

Uraga Harbor, SE of the Yokosuka Naval Base.

With folded arms, Fuchida stood in his tan suit and fedora, impatiently tapping his foot. His eyes followed a string of ex-prisoners disembarking down the gangplanks from an American troop transport ship out onto the dock. It looked to him like the first group off were sick or on crutches. Some were clearly amputees. He scanned the men for a likely candidate.

With his thoughts clearer than a few nights before with Genda, he gravitated to a subject he'd long turned over in his mind. Each nation in a war feels it's justified in its actions. Victory is no guarantee of being right any more than a large rock is right in crushing a smaller rock. All military victories are victories of power. The Americans had no right to judge the Japanese.

He stretched his neck looking for the right person. Who could possibly judge another person, anyway? To judge others, you must know every intention of a person's heart and mind, every action of his life; you'd have to possess perfect knowledge, and you'd have to have complete virtue as well to judge fairly. No man on earth could ever do that. No human had such knowledge, virtue or power. Only God can judge. The Americans should leave the Japanese alone.

Suddenly, he saw a face he thought he recognized. He stood taller than the rest. He couldn't believe his eyes. He mumbled out loud, "Kanegasaki?" Could it be? His old engineer still alive? As he came more into sight, it was true! He yelled and waved his hat, "Kanegasaki! *Kanegasaki!*"

Lugging a bag over his shoulder, Kanegasaki's face lit up and he waved back and broke into a trot. "Fuchida!"

Coming together, they grasped each other's hands and arms, both somewhat in disbelief in finding the other, but certainly Fuchida more.

Burns scarred the left side of his face and neck, and Fuchida couldn't help but see his prosthetic hook for a left hand.

"We all thought you were *dead!*" Fuchida exclaimed. "There's even a grave marker in your hometown with your name on it. What happened? Your name wasn't on any of the lists of prisoners from the Americans."

"I can assure you, I'm not a ghost!" They chuckled in their mutual discovery, and the two joined the stream of men coursing away from the docks.

"I made it into the water after our ship sank at Midway," Kanegasaki said, "and a few of us found a life raft. We were on the ocean for two weeks when an American seaplane rescued us." Kanegasaki shrugged and hung his head. "I was ashamed to be a prisoner, so I gave a false name."

Fuchida smiled and nodded, still in a state of awe. He understood. All men vowed death over imprisonment as a matter of personal honor and dignity. It was drilled into them from the time they were young boys.

"I wanted to kill myself and even tried to starve myself rather than face the shame of being captured, but some Japanese ladies from a church visited me in jail and brought me tuna maki rolls and tempted me to eat. I couldn't resist. They saved my life."

Seeing a noodle shop, which he knew would fill fast, Fuchida grabbed his friend's arm and pulled him ahead. "Let's hurry to get a table. We have a *lot* to talk about!"

Kanegasaki steadied the bowl with his hooked left arm, tipped the bowl to his face and slurped his noodles voraciously as Fuchida exhaled the smoke of his cigarette. They were lucky to get a seat in the overflowing restaurant, now with a growing line of ex-prisoners waiting outside.

With his mouth full of food, Kanegasaki looked into Fuchida's eyes. "I think I missed Japanese food more than anything, besides my wife, that is. But, no, they didn't torture us or put us in cells or anything like that. It wasn't like a vacation, but we had decent rooms in a prison camp outside a hospital. We even bathed in nearby hot springs."

"They didn't mistreat you in any way?"

Reaching into his rice bowl with his chopsticks, Kanegasaki paused and looked up for a moment. "If you consider bad food mistreatment, yes!

They don't have *real* rice over there, but otherwise, not really."

Fuchida's face fell. He certainly wasn't hoping that his friend was tortured, but neither was he expecting to hear no tales of suffering and deprivation.

After stuffing his mouth again with rice, Kanegasaki set his bowl down. After a big swallow, he said, "But I need to tell you," pointing at Fuchida with his chopsticks, "there was this American girl who was there at the hospital."

Fuchida raised his eyebrows.

"After the Americans rescued us, they took us to San Diego, later transferred us to Montana, then sent us to a hospital near Salt Lake City. It was big. There were beds for hundreds of patients. To the east were beautiful, rounded mountains. Our prison camp was fenced in with barbed wire and guard towers, but we spent most of our time in the hospital." Kanegasaki sipped his tea.

"Most of the prisoners were Germans, but there was a group of Japanese, and, of course, we stayed together. All of us were amputees of

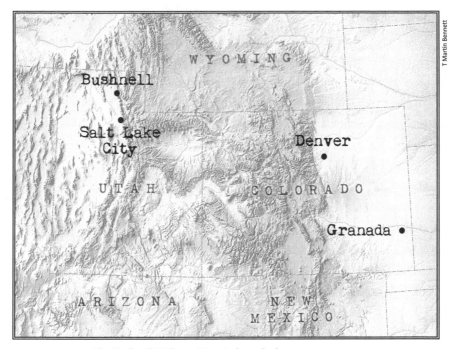

The Bushnell Military Hospital regularly sent out requests
for volunteers to help with patient care. The facility specialized in
amputees and had facilities for prisoners of war from both Germany and
Japan. In early 1945, when Peggy heard of the need, since she spoke fluent
Japanese and was Red Cross certified, she responded and volunteered.

some sort," he held up his left hook "as the hospital specialized in that kind of thing."

Wondering where this was going, Fuchida leaned forward on his elbows.

"But I need to tell you; there was this American girl on our floor in the hospital who spoke excellent Japanese and she always asked if there was anything we needed, if we had any problems. She brought us books and magazines in Japanese, she got us gum and, well, whatever we needed. She helped us with sending letters and worked very, very hard and we were all so impressed with her kindness, especially when we found out that she traveled so far from her home to come there to work. She was like an angel from heaven . . . and it seemed like she had a great debt or obligation to pay to the Japanese people, as if some Japanese had done her a great favor."

Fuchida refilled his cup with tea.

"We wondered why a Yankee girl would be so thoughtful to us and we kept asking her why she was there, but she would never give us an answer. So, one day when she was tending to us in our beds, she brought us all a big tray of rice cakes, and as we were all enjoying the treat, I smiled and asked her again in front of everyone, 'So tell us, *really*, why are you here? Why are you so kind to us?' We all stared at her with curiosity."

Kanegasaki had Fuchida's full attention.

"She said, 'Because my parents were killed by Japanese soldiers.'"

"What?!" Fuchida's mind crackled with confusion as he strained to comprehend the astonishing words he had just heard. He looked away, then back at Kanegasaki. "The murderer of one's parents should be a sworn enemy for life!" His mind raced. "She didn't vindicate the honor of her parents? She traveled far and didn't take revenge?!" Fuchida leaned back with disgust. "She had no self-respect. She must have been weak."

"No!" Kanegasaki shot back. "She was very strong."

Nothing was making sense to Fuchida. He felt dizzy and bewildered as he lowered his head and rubbed his neck.

Kanegasaki grinned. "I know the feeling." He, likewise, hung his head. "We were horrified when we learned who she really was. Her name was Peggy."

Fuchida continued to shake his head while contemplating. He sighed deeply and, with his head down, looked up at Kanegasaki. He spoke softer. "What happened to her parents?"

"She told us her parents were teachers in Japan, but fled to the island of Panay in the Philippines thinking they could hide in the mountains until the war was over, but our soldiers eventually found them."

Jimmy, Charma, Francis and Gertrude stood panting in the jungle, their soiled, torn clothes soaked in sweat. Slowly they turned toward the Japanese soldiers rigidly pointing their bayoneted rifles at them. The four raised their hands in surrender as the soldiers surrounded them and herded them back to the camp.

Arriving at the clearing, they saw over 400 soldiers and Filipinos who were pressed into service for the hunt. The lead soldier waved to Captain Watanabe near the center. "We got them! They didn't get away!"

As Jimmy shuffled to the center of the group, he scanned the frightened eyes of the rest of the captured members of Hopevale standing there—Jennie, Dorothy, Fred and Ruth Meyer, and eleven-year-old Earl Rounds with his parents behind him, their hands on his shoulders. He looked at Mr. Clardy, a miner with his wife and two children. The Japanese captured a total of seventeen people at Hopevale—everyone. Since Jimmy spoke Japanese, he knew that the group looked to him for some kind of leadership, and somehow, to find a way out.

Watanabe stood with his arms crossed, leaning back triumphantly and said to his men with a grin, "Just as I thought. Building an American city in the hills!" His soldiers smiled in victory.

"We're missionaries," Jimmy said in perfect Japanese. "We want no part of this war or *any* war!"

Watanabe and the soldiers were stunned. "How did you learn Japanese?!" he demanded.

Charma stepped forward and also spoke in Japanese, "My husband and I spent our lives in the service of the Japanese people." A strand of dirty hair fell across her face. "We only came here to get away from all the fighting."

The Japanese were only further confounded by this woman, likewise fluently speaking their language. Watanabe's eyes narrowed with suspicion.

Jimmy continued, "If you have to take us as prisoners, we'll all come with you peacefully. We won't resist."

"Liars!" a soldier exclaimed. "You aren't missionaries, you're *spies*, giving information to the guerrillas! We have orders for all Americans to be killed!"

Watanabe grinned. "We have people who say you're helping the guerrillas. Admit it!"

The confusion of the other Hopevale captives deepened on their pained faces as they witnessed an argument they couldn't understand.

Shigeru, the Japanese officer who surreptitiously visited Hopevale, stood close by, just as anxious, but never giving a hint of his feelings. His eyes darted from Watanabe to Jimmy as they lunged and parried with words.

Holding his arms wide, Jimmy countered. "We don't have any guns, but if a wounded guerrilla comes here, *yes*, we help him, but we'd help a Japanese soldier just the same."

"So, you're collaborating with the guerrillas!" Watanabe snarled.

"No! We're *not* collaborating!"

As Jimmy dropped his arms, Watanabe proudly produced a crumpled chocolate wrapper imprinted with the words *"I Shall Return!"*

"*Liar!*" he fumed. "Americans are bringing supplies in through this camp and you *know* it!"

Jimmy's face went blank. The other Hopevale members now clearly understood what was happening. Jennie and Dorothy grasped each other's hands.

Looking more helpless than ever, Jimmy gathered his courage and shouted back pointing his hand to the ground, "We can't stop them from coming through here any more than we can stop you!"

A soldier pushed into the crowd. "Captain! Look what we found!" He held up a pair of binoculars splashed with mud. Jimmy's face fell.

Another Japanese officer spoke up. "The guerrillas meet here to make plans to attack! They're all spies!"

"*No!*" Charma replied. "We're teachers and professors!" Pointing with authority, she continued, "She's a music teacher, she's a French and math teacher, and he's a surgeon for the children's hospital. We're no threat to *anyone!*"

Captain Watanabe stood staring, huge drops of dust-laden sweat trickling down the sides of his face, his bulging eyes glaring with intensity at Jimmy as they both came to the visceral realization that each of them was everything the other was not—despising each other for their beliefs, yet admiring each other for their tenacity.

Shigeru briefly bowed his head to Watanabe and spoke softly, "Captain, excuse me for suggesting, but perhaps we should leave them alone. They're unarmed civilians."

Still staring at Jimmy and Charma, Watanabe paused a moment, sighed heavily, then, without looking away from them, shouted, "Get me the radio! Call headquarters! *Do it now!*"

A soldier bolted off through the crowd to another soldier with a small leather-bound box, knelt on one knee, opened it, and quickly grabbed the receiver. He turned the crank three times and waited for a reply.

Watanabe gave a last, angry glance at Jimmy, Charma, and the group of captives, then turned and briskly marched away toward the radio where the soldier held out the receiver.

Other soldiers began dismissing the Filipinos, unneeded now that the Japanese had their quarry in hand. Lieutenant King, the tortured American who ultimately led the Japanese to Hopevale, sat slouched against a tree under guard, exhausted, breathing deeply, nearly unconscious.

Jimmy ran both hands through his sweaty hair, exhaled, and looked into the faces of his people. He saw they were desperate to know something, *anything*, about what was going on and swallowed hard. "He's calling headquarters because the orders are to execute all Americans. We're Americans, but we're not guerrilla fighters. They have to know that."

In his headquarters in Iloilo, General Tanaka stood at his desk with the phone to his ear, trembling with anger. "They're *Americans!* They're spying on our movements and reporting it to our enemies by radio! Execute them all *immediately* before I come up there and do it myself . . . and *you* with them! *Now!*"

The soldiers parted as Captain Watanabe strode back into the center of the circle with one hand on his sword. He walked up to Jimmy's face. "We came here for one purpose and one purpose only! *Nothing* has changed! The decision is final!"

Jimmy half expected the answer and considered his response. Bowing and holding his bow he replied, "Please allow us thirty minutes to pray together, then you may fulfill your duty however you wish."

Watanabe squinted, glanced at Shigeru, and then back at Jimmy's bowed frame. "Thirty minutes. Go!"

Jimmy rose, looked Watanabe directly in the eyes and said, "Thank you very much" in a tone of such sincerity that it shamed the soldiers. Looking at the members of his group he motioned with his head for them to follow as he led them through the soldiers while being escorted by several guards.

Francis sidled up to Jimmy. "What'd he say?!" The group pressed in around Jimmy and Charma.

Jimmy only looked forward as he answered. "They're going to execute us, but they gave us time to pray." He put his arm around Charma. "So let's worship the Lord together."

Francis nodded in acquiescence and likewise put his arm around Gertrude. Fred Meyer grasped his wife's hand as they all headed to the open chapel they had built under the trees—for one final meeting. Charma held a rag to her face wiping her eyes and nose.

Shigeru came up beside Jimmy as they walked. He said in English, "So . . . your story ends here."

Jimmy stopped and looked at him as the rest of the group continued towards the Cathedral in the Glen, as they called it. "Can you read English?"

Shigeru nodded.

Charma gazed at Jimmy in curiosity as he reached into his shoulder bag, pulled out a ratty, dog-eared book, and flipped to a certain page with various parts underlined. He spun the book around to Shigeru, confidently put his finger on the page, and looked Shigeru in the eyes. "Please. Read the underlined words out loud."

Shigeru looked around hesitatingly, then peered down at the page and read: "*In your great pride you claim, "I am a god. I sit on a divine throne in the heart of the sea." But you are only a man and not a god, though you boast that you are a god.*"

Startled, Shigeru glanced up at Jimmy, who stared into his face. Shigeru continued. "*Therefore, this is what the Sovereign Lord says, "Because you think you are as wise as a god, I will now bring against you a foreign army, the terror of the nations. They will draw their swords against your marvelous wisdom and defile your splendor! They will bring you down to the pit, and you will die in the heart of the sea, pierced with many wounds. Will you then boast, 'I am a god!' to those who kill you? To them, you will be no god but merely a man. I, the Sovereign Lord, have spoken.*"[48]

---

[48] Excerpts from Ezekiel 28:1-10

Jimmy lowered the book, all the while looking into Shigeru's eyes. "It's *your* story that's coming to an end, my friend." He paused. "Mine's just beginning."

The hair rose on the back of Shigeru's neck. "What is this book?"

Closing it, Jimmy held the spine up so he could see the faded words: *Holy Bible.* "The world's worst-kept secret," he said.

Charma impatiently tugged at Jimmy's sleeve, desperately trying not to disintegrate into uncontrolled weeping. He patted her hand and started off again following the last of the group to their private sanctuary.

Walking again beside Jimmy, Shigeru ventured his final question. "You're not afraid?"

As he held Charma closer to him, Jimmy said without looking, "I gave my life away a *long* time ago." He gave a parting glance at Shigeru and said with a smile, "No one can take it now."

Shigeru stopped and observed the members gather and kneel into a circle, some hugging, some weeping.

Hiding in the nearby woods under heavy foliage, Jack the miner crouched with three other guerrillas witnessing the spectacle while grasping their weapons, useless against the overwhelming force of the Japanese presence. Through clenched teeth, he whispered in a muffled shout to himself, "It's *me* you're looking for, not *them!*"

A Japanese soldier leaning against a porch post next to a cogon grass Christmas tree took a long puff of his cigarette and watched the hundreds of flying insects highlighted by the orange setting sun. Others lay on the forest floor for a brief nap, their caps over their faces. Kneeling on the dirt and gripping the handle of his katana with one hand and the sharp end with a folded cloth in his other, Watanabe meticulously drew his sword across a water stone again and again as his sweat fell to the ground.

Children clung tightly to their parents in the circle as they offered up prayers from the greatest depths of heart. Francis Rose kindled a small fire on the stone altar he'd constructed, which sat lower and in front of the cross, the smoke rising upwards with the prayers of the saints. Soldiers stood off to the side, pretending not to hear or see anything. High above, macaque monkeys watched, seemingly concerned about the events below.

The last rays of burnt orange sunlight glimmered off the gold rim of Watanabe's watch as he turned it to his face. He nodded to the officer beside him. The rest of the soldiers roused themselves and slung their rifles over their shoulders.

An officer approached the condemned prisoners who were finishing a hymn. "Let's go!" he said in Japanese. "Now!"

Jimmy nodded and helped Charma up, her face smeared with grime and tears.

The other soldiers closed in and walked them back to the center of the camp where Captain Watanabe motioned for Charma to be blindfolded first. Shigeru followed at a distance. He couldn't bear to watch, nor could he bear to leave.

Dumbfounded, Jimmy looked at Watanabe as if to ask why a woman would be the first to be killed.

Watanabe could see his question. "She speaks the best Japanese. She's the guiltiest." He looked at one of his officers. "Take the children to one of the huts." Two soldiers grabbed Earl and the two other young boys and tore them from their parents.

"Mom! Dad!" Earl screamed out.

The Chapel in the Glen where the Hopevale group held their final meeting.

His horrified mother wept silent tears.

With a black blindfold around her head, a soldier pushed Charma to her knees in front of them all.

She moaned loudly in English as she bent her head forward, "Why are you killing us? We're *missionaries!*"

Watanabe took his stance beside her, then, in one motion, drew his sword high above his head. Jimmy looked away and closed his eyes. With a shout and brisk swing, Watanabe swung it downward, spattering his khaki pants with fresh blood.

The birds in the branches above burst into flight.

Two soldiers prodded the three howling children with bayoneted rifles, forcing them up the stairs and into a hut. Earl screamed out again, "Mom! Dad! Jack! *Jack, help me!!*"

Jack watched, immobile, the strength draining from his body as the blood-curdling screams of children pierced his heart. A feeling of weakness swept over him, a powerlessness he'd never known before. When the screams ceased and the soldiers exited the hut wiping fresh blood from their bayonets, his knees nearly buckled beneath him. One of the guerrillas beside him looked at Jack and raised his rifle. Jack shook his head, then fixed his eyes again on the cruel spectacle, the surreal images blurred by the water standing in his eyes. He knew that, while they might be able to kill a few of the Japanese soldiers, it wouldn't save Jimmy and the others, and it would only result in their own deaths as well.

"No!" Lieutenant King yelled as two soldiers lunged at him with their bayoneted rifles. "You *promised* me if I . . . *Nooo!*" Their bayonets ran clear through his torso into the tree behind him.

In the clearing, Jimmy and Watanabe caught each other's eyes one final time as a soldier was about to tie a blindfold tied onto Jimmy. Although he should have appeared as the vanquished, Jimmy's eyes proclaimed him the victor, exuding authority and confidence before they were concealed beneath the black cloth. He got down onto his knees as he had many, many times before in prayer, for the last time.

Soldiers giggled while firing rounds into the pump organ, splintering the wood into the air, then kicked it over and crushed it with the butts of their rifles.

Captain Watanabe's sword fell again, again, and again, until he completely fulfilled his responsibility to his commanding officer. Pulling a clean handkerchief from his pocket and carefully wiping the length of his blade, he said, "Throw the bodies into the huts." He folded the handkerchief and wiped his blade again. "And torch them."

Pairs of soldiers began dragging the bloody, headless corpses into the two closest huts.

Watanabe walked up and eyed one of the huts from top to bottom and pulled out a small matchbox. He struck a match and lit his cigarette, chuckling to himself as he silently read the cover, *"I Shall Return. General Douglas MacArthur."* He touched the burning match to the edge of the cogon grass roof and smiled as the flames crackled and crawled up the roof.

Soon, all of the huts were rumbling blazes of fire, sending smoke and embers drifting up into the twilight sky. Their mission complete, the soldiers grouped and moved toward the path back down the mountain— some weary, others joking with each other.

Shigeru stood opposite the front porch of one of the huts as the rippling orange flames engulfed the home and reflected off his stoic face. He had been swept away in a raging river of war, a torrent that had become a river of blood. His lips pursed while his eyes followed the flames inching across a hanging banner, "PEACE ON EARTH, GOODWILL TO ALL MEN."

"What did her father pray?" Fuchida said as he squashed his cigarette into an ashtray overflowing with butts.

"What?" Kanegasaki said just before he took a sip of tea. "How would I know? What difference does it make?"

"What good was it to pray to a god who couldn't save them?" Fuchida said as he looked out the window into the dark street, dimly lit by signage and passing cars.

"I don't know. But I do know this." Kanegasaki set his cup down and leaned in. "That girl loved us like we were her own brothers. Even *better* than brothers."

Perplexed, Fuchida looked down at the table, confronted by a strange force he'd never encountered before. He couldn't imagine why a girl would do such a thing after what her family had suffered. It was a long-held tradition of the samurai to uphold the honor of their family through revenge killings, or "*katakiuchi,*" a staple of kabuki stage plays and countless stories of folklore for generations. It was noble. It was right. It was true justice. What she had done simply made no sense at all.

But Fuchida couldn't stop wondering what her father could have possibly prayed. He *had* to know.

Chapter 126

June 1948. Seattle, Washington.

"Susan Decker," the school president said into the microphone that echoed through the graduation hall. A young lady in her black cap and gown strode to receive her diploma among pleasant applause. "Congratulations, Susan."

Jake's family anxiously shifted to get a good view of the next name coming up. Mr. Andrus grimaced as his wife carefully ripped the page of yet

Airman Who Found God

Tokyo Bomber and Wife Get Seattle-Pacific Diplomas

DOOLITTLE RAIDER GRADUATED — Jacob De Shazer, bombardier on Gen. James Doolittle's first air raid on Japan, is shown with his wife, Florence, and their son, Paul Edward. Mr. and Mrs. De Shazer were graduated from Seattle Pacific College yesterday. They will become missionaries to Japan. — Post-Intelligencer Photo.

another newspaper, this one with the title: *Ex-Air Force Man Will Return to Japan.*

"Jacob and Florence DeShazer," announced the speaker, "Bachelor of Arts."

The hall exploded into cheers and a standing ovation as Jake, arm in arm with his new wife and their baby, Paul, walked across the stage. Florence stopped and shyly turned to the adoring crowd and nodded in thanks. The president didn't even try to quell the commotion. Jake and Florence looked at each other, embarrassed by the attention but celebrating in the moment, and looked across the auditorium smiling and nodding in thanks.

Mrs. Andrus stood with the crowd, clapping furiously as she smiled, tears of joy streaming down her face. Life seemed like it couldn't possibly get any better.

Chapter 127

December 3, 1948. Tokyo. Shibuya Train Station.

Fuchida glanced down at his watch as he exited the overflowing train car in his long, black overcoat and hat, and worked his way through the crowds toward the exit. He had plenty of time to get to his meeting with the head of the historical department in General MacArthur's headquarters for another set of post-war interviews that would last a full week. It was another ordinary day, but it was also his birthday. He was forty-six years old. He shrugged.

Things were going well, or at least moving in the right direction. His farm was producing, he had completed his home, his hens were laying, and

The Shibuya area as it was shortly after the war. The opening of the Tokyu Toyoko Train Line in 1932 made Shibuya into a major train station.

the cold stares of the local people were slowly replaced by nods and an occasional wave. He lived in near poverty, but then, his cares were few. The trials of Japanese officers by the Allied tribunal still consumed some of his time and remained a sore spot.

Getting to the top of the stairs, he looked over a nearby news rack, bought a newspaper, and tucked it under his arm.

After his time with Kanegasaki a year earlier, he interviewed others who were with him at the same hospital in Utah to learn more about the girl who served them, Peggy, and they all confirmed the same story. Fuchida was convinced she had a kind of genuine love that had stopped the cycle of revenge, but he couldn't understand where it came from. Certainly, no one could love like this on his own. There had to be a secret.

"Read about the Doolittle Raider who was a prisoner of war!" a man yelled out in Japanese over the crowd. "Free pamphlet on the Doolittle Raider!"

Fuchida looked for the source of the voice and saw a hand in the air holding up a piece of literature next to the bronze statue of Hachiko, the dearly loved Akita memorialized at the Shibuya station, a well-known large dog breed from the mountains of northern Japan.

As he made his way toward the sculpture, he saw a Westerner handing out the leaflets, smiling.

From the day he first heard of the Doolittle Raid, Fuchida held a respect for the fellow airmen who risked their lives to carry out the daring raid. He walked up and nonchalantly took the paper and read the Japanese title, *"I Was a Prisoner of Japan."*[49] He was curious.

Stepping to a nearby low, stone wall, he found an open spot to sit and read the brief story of Jacob DeShazer.

Later, grasping a ring suspended from the ceiling in a streetcar, he wondered if what had happened to Jacob was the same thing that had happened to Peggy. Jostled with the other passengers as the trolley took a sharp turn, he mindlessly scanned the row of ads posted above the windows across the ceiling: ads for beer, women's clothing, cigarettes, and an ad for a new book, *I Was a Prisoner of Japan.*

---

[49] "Watashi wa Nippon no Horyo Dearimashita."

At his stop, he made a beeline for the nearest bookstore and was relieved to see the book displayed in the window. He would have never considered reading it if it were by just any American, but this was a man whose exploits he admired. Maybe this birthday would be something special after all, he wondered.

"I Was A Prisoner of Japan"
is the vertical title in the center.

Fuchida pushed his wooden wheelbarrow beside the rows of tall barley in his field and came to a stop, his German Shepherd faithfully by his side. He glanced back at his house, then sat beside a tree on a simple bench, pulled the DeShazer book from his bag, and found his bookmark.

By the end of the week, he had followed Jake on his journey from his anger after Pearl Harbor through his time as a prisoner in China. It was an engrossing and unusual story. What had happened to Jake seemed very much of a mystery to him, but Fuchida felt that Jake seemed to have much in common with the girl at the hospital that Kanegasaki talked about.

He scratched his dog under the chin and thought that someday he'd like to get a Bible and see what it was all about, but not now. He had no interest in religion, per se—just a curiosity about what turns a person from a mind of war to a mind of peace. The emperor's desire to establish peace to last a thousand generations and MacArthur's dream of peace, these were just dreams. But Jake's story—well, that was *real*.

Chapter 128

December 28, 1948. Tokyo.

In an overcast mist, Jake clutched his year-old son, Paul, as he stepped down the gangway along with Florence toward the dock from *USS General M. C. Meigs*, a twin-smoke-stack decommissioned troop transport. Seeing the crowds pressing in, calling out his name, and flashbulbs popping, he turned to Florence with the expression of a little kid, "Gee, I wasn't quite expecting *this*."

Their voyage began at San Francisco; the very port he had once departed from on a mission to kill Japanese in revenge. The ocean crossing gave him time to contemplate about what may lie ahead for him. Six years earlier he came in the name of war; now he came in peace. The war was over, yet another had begun—a war of ideas. He wondered how the Japanese people would view him, and how his wife would adapt to this completely different culture. At least for now, things seemed good.

"Mr. DeShazer! Welcome!" a Japanese man and his wife said in English. "We loved your book! It was wonderful!" Jake nodded shyly. "Well, thank you. I'm glad you got something out of it." Others crowded in to shake his hand. Jake hadn't given much thought to the little pamphlet he wrote that was translated into Japanese, but he learned that over a million copies had been printed and distributed all over Japan. Everyone was curious about the man who loved his enemies and had now become their friend.

Out from under the drizzle in a part of the covered area of the dock, Jake stood behind a small podium clustered with oversized microphones and surrounded by over forty reporters, pressing in for a good view. He'd taken off his hat, but still lovingly held his little boy, who was mesmerized

Carol Aiko DeShazer Dixon

by the event. Jake gave his attention to another question from a journalist who spoke in English. "What happened to you? Didn't your captors spit on you and beat you?" he said from the front. "So, why would you want to come back here?"

Other journalists quickly nodded in agreement, pads and pencils fully prepared for the reply.

"I don't have any bitterness toward the people who mistreated us," Jake said plainly. "I feel sorry for them. They didn't know any better way to live. At first, I thought God would help me love good people, but wouldn't expect me to love the mean ones." He looked down and stroked his son's hair. "But that didn't sound right, and I remembered what I read, that Jesus said to love your enemies and to do good to those who mistreat you. God was patient with me and forgave me, so, I'm just doing the same for others. Pretty simple, really."

Reporters shook their heads while furiously scrawling notes.

Three months later.

Jake threw his coat over the back of the sofa and slumped into a kitchen chair while Florence fed Paul. A dangle of hair stuck to his sweaty forehead. "Do you realize that in the last three months I've spoken at over two hundred places? *Two hundred?*"

Florence gave a brief grin without looking.

"I'm happy for the opportunities, but . . . sometimes I feel like I'm just not getting anywhere. I don't know if I'm getting *through* to people. Most just listen and smile and nod. I can't tell what's really going on inside their heads, in their hearts."

Taking advantage of every opportunity to tell his story to packed, curious crowds, Jake enthusiastically spoke at department stores and community centers, constantly traveling to churches, to public schools and Buddhist centers, telling his story to everyone and anyone who would give him the chance to speak.

Florence wiped a washcloth across Paul's face and glanced at Jake. "I know you're tired, but I'm so proud of you, honey." She got up and pulled

Carol Aiko DeShazer Dixon

A sign outside a building announces Jake DeShazer as the guest speaker.

out an envelope from between some books on the shelf and removed two sheets of folded paper. "Listen to this. I had to get it translated for you."

Jake stoically held out the crust of a piece of toast to little Paul, who grabbed it and began sucking on it.

"This is from a young lady. 'Thank you very much for coming to our town. While you were talking, I cried very much. The Japanese were cruel in their treatment of you, and I saw you had a great deal of hatred for them. They were ignorant and unreasonable in the way they treated you. I have no words to apologize to you. Please forgive us.'"

Florence looked up for a moment. Jake still had no expression on his tired face. She kept reading. "'But you have already forgiven us and came to Japan to help us. I could not keep my tears from falling when I saw the love that God had put into your heart. I had been a very evil girl. I told many lies, but now I am sorry.'"

Florence flipped the sheet over and glanced at Jake gazing at the floor.

"'I had been working at a factory to support my three brothers and my parents who were sick and I was very discouraged. I tried to kill myself three or four times, but I couldn't go through with it. I didn't care about myself or my country, and soon I was becoming sick.'"

"'I had always hated God, but through you, I was born as a child in the heavenly kingdom. Now the Lord is my light and my shield, and I'm not afraid anymore. I'm full of hope for the future, and I even started taking classes at the university. Thank you very much for what you have done. I hope that I can hear you again. Please give my kindest regards to Mrs. DeShazer. May God bless you.'"

Florence wiped her cheek with the back of her wrist and sat down beside Jake. "So you see? All those thousands of seeds you're scattering?" She put her hand under his chin and looked into his eyes. "Some are starting to grow."

Chapter 129

Spring 1949. Tokyo.

Inside a small store with shelves packed to the ceiling with books, a gray-haired vendor behind the counter shook his head at Fuchida, standing on the other side along with a growing line of impatient people behind him.

"No Bibles, sorry," the vendor said peering through his glasses. "If you're looking for Christians, I think there's a church –"

"No, no, no. I'm not interested in that." Fuchida scratched his head in frustration. This was the third store he'd visited with no luck. "I just want to understand how Christians think, why they act like they –"

"Sorry, no Bibles. Next?"

Since he was not far from the Shibuya train station, he decided to go by the Hachiko statue with the distant hope that perhaps the man he saw might be there again and be able to help direct him. As he approached the area of the statue, he saw a Japanese man in a black suit with a gentle smile beside several boxes stacked up, holding a small, black book in each hand.

"Man shall not live by bread alone!" he called out. "Get your Bible— food for your soul! No book in the world can compare with it. Read it for yourself, thirty pages anywhere, and you will find something that will touch your heart."

Fuchida walked nearer to the man. He was interested, but something inside him felt like testing him. "You speak of a God we can't see."

The man let his arms drift down. "Yes, and we wait patiently for him to return again."

Fuchida gave a cynical grin.

"Like Hachiko," he said gesturing to the bronze casting, "who waited faithfully and loyally for his master every day for eleven years at this very station, we, too, wait for our master."

Fuchida, and all Japan, for that matter, knew the story of Hachiko well. The beloved dog of a university professor, the Akita had waited daily at the station to greet him when he came home from his job at school. One day the professor died, but Hachiko continued to come to the station, daily waiting for his master for the following nine years. Children and adults who came to know him loved and admired him equally as a living example of faithfulness and devotion and regularly fed him. Newspaper articles spread his fame and moved the hearts of people everywhere.

When Hachiko died on March 8, 1935, the entire nation felt the loss. Yaeko Ueno (bottom, second from right) the owner's wife, mourning over Hachiko.

"But his master never returned," Fuchida replied, "How do you know yours will?"

The man leaned forward with a kind glint in his eye and said, "You don't know him, do you?"

Feeling uncomfortable, Fuchida dug into his pocket. "How much?"

"Three yen."

Fuchida was surprised and even suspicious. "Why so cheap?" He found the right coins, dropped them in the man's outstretched hand, and reached for the book.

"It doesn't cost much to purchase," he said as Fuchida grasped the book. But the vendor kept his grip on it and looked Fuchida in the eyes. "The true cost is in following." They both held still for a moment, then the vendor released his grip with another disarming smile, reached into his box and grabbed another Bible, and held both hands up again. "Read any thirty pages of this book, and you'll know it's true. Test it and see for yourself!"

A woman cleans the tile walkway of the statue of the beloved Hachiko, April 1949. In 1934, a bronze statue was cast and installed in Shibuya, but was later melted down for the war effort. Despite the poverty of the community after the war, people generously donated to have a new statue cast, which was installed in the fall of 1948.

Chapter 130

Spring 1949. Nagoya.

Tomiko sat finishing lunch with a female friend on a warm afternoon. It had been eight years since her fiancé was killed at the refinery. The war had left few eligible men, and she felt she was no competition for some of the more beautiful, younger women, so she remained alone. They ate together on a matted area of an open-walled restaurant, a café featuring a traditional thatched roof that lay beside a luscious garden of rocks, ferns, and an array of flowers. Alongside, a tiny, bubbling creek poured into a koi pond.

"But they gave the promotion to another girl because she flirted with the boss," her friend complained. "So did I, but they didn't give it to me!"

Tomiko shook her head in disgust. "My boss is a pig. I would never even *want* to flirt with him."

As Tomiko refilled her teacup, her friend drew out a newspaper and carefully unfolded it in front of her, observing her reaction. "Tomiko—have you seen this?"

She looked down at the paper. "What?"

"A man from America will be speaking at the garment factory this Friday. He's one of the Doolittle Raiders . . . who bombed Nagoya."

Her eyebrows furrowed as she seized the paper and intently read the headline and skimmed the article.

"He was the bombardier . . . the man who actually dropped the bombs on our city that day." The friend waited as Tomiko contemplated the photograph of Jake DeShazer, the first she had ever seen the assailant.

"He's the man who killed Kenji."

Tomiko looked up as the blood rushed to her face. The muscles in her jaw tensed as her eyes filled with tears and she turned, looking out at the water cascading over the rocks. She breathed harder. Every day for years she had awoken thinking only of Kenji and went to sleep longing for him. She felt robbed of her future, of her family, of all her hopes and dreams. What she loved most had been stolen.

Her friend broke into her thoughts. "It's the chance you've waited for."

Tomiko's face slowly darkened. The love she'd lost was forever gone, but justice had finally come within her reach. After a long pause, she spoke quietly as if only to herself. "At last." She gazed across at lavender wisteria in full bloom, cascading from the leafy branches of a nearby tree and whispered. "I will have this one, last pleasure." She looked back with piercing eyes. "I *swear* it!"

Candles her only light, Tomiko knelt in a white silk kimono at her closet door and slid it open. From a dark recess, with trembling hands she drew out an inlaid wooden box and gently carried it to a three-mirror vanity that sat on the floor, and knelt down before the mirrors.

Her face expressionless, she stared at herself in the flickering gold of the candlelight, then picked up a tiny cut-glass bottle of perfume, removed the stopper, inverted it onto her finger and touched behind both ears and once again looked at herself.

Her eyes fell to a framed portrait of her and Kenji. Closing her eyes, she breathed deeply and leaned her head back in one, last, imaginary embrace, drifting to a world that could never be.

Opening her eyes again in the near darkness, her eyes rested again on the photograph. A worn, red origami crane leaned against the frame with her faded name written on it by Kenji years ago. She reached out as she had done a thousand times before and lovingly stroked it with a single finger. There were no more tears to cry. She was left only with pain.

Tomiko sat uprightly and looked down at the wooden box between her and the mirror. With both hands on the lid, she swallowed hard and calmly opened it revealing a white cloth, which she unfolded exposing a bone-handled knife. After studying the carved handle and pointed blade, she lifted it before her face and twisted it, observing the candlelight as it glanced off the polished metal into her blurry eyes.

Looking past the blade, she caught her face in the mirror—hard, emotionless, determined. She continued to stare at herself and gently lowered the blade, and whispered, "For you, Kenji," unable to hold back two tears from making their course down her cheeks.

The next morning, she walked along the city roadway toward the garment factory, dressed in a simple kimono of blue and white, eyeing only the walkway a few feet in front of her as a streetcar rumbled past.

Up ahead, people gathered at the doorway of a building up ahead, chosen because of its large warehouse area that could be used as a makeshift auditorium.

As she continued along a fence line, the song of a blue-and-white flycatcher caught her attention, bringing her to a stop to admire the black-faced glistening bluebird as he sang his song. The bird seemed unafraid and turned toward Tomiko and sang his song again in a long series of chirps.

What were the faint beginnings of an unconscious smile quickly turned into a hard countenance. "I've made up my mind," she breathed out. "I'm not turning back." She started off toward the meeting leaving the bird to sing out his appeal one last time and flutter away.

"Welcome!" the woman at the doorway said with a broad smile. "Please come in!" Tomiko stoically nodded as others directed her down a hallway among guests heading into a back warehouse. She hunted for a seat near the front, on the end of a row where she knew she could quickly lunge without being stopped by anyone. Though the seats were filling fast, she found what she was seeking in the second row in an aisle seat, very close to the center and the microphone stand.

Though it was a cool, spring day, she wiped her forehead with a folded handkerchief and looked around behind her at the growing audience. Then she saw him. Her heart began to pound. He was standing there, shaking someone's hand, smiling. She shuddered, detesting him from head to toe. Beside him, she saw some American woman with a baby. Tomiko unconsciously nodded. Soon, this woman would taste what she had been forced to drink for so many years.

Glancing around surreptitiously, she reached into her *obi*, the wide belt of her kimono, and wrapped her fingers around the knife handle to assure her it was in the best position, then withdrew her hand.

The meeting came to order and, after introductions, Jake was soon into his story.

". . . and things didn't turn out like I had hoped. I had to accept the cards I was dealt."

Tomiko had no concern or interest in what he had to say. His Japanese wasn't very good, but she could understand him.

"In one of the jail cells, we were packed in like animals, and I remember watching the guards beat a Chinese woman. She hadn't done anything wrong. They beat her badly and I had to ask myself, why were the Japanese so full of evil and hatred?"

Of all the people in the world to say such a thing, Tomiko thought. Who was he to judge others, after what *he'd* done? He was a murderer. She tried to hide her scowl as she, once again, squeezed the knife tightly in her fist inside her belt.

Jake put his hand onto the microphone stand. "I attacked Japan for revenge. That's what I wanted. That's what *every* American wanted. I hated the Japanese for what they did at Pearl Harbor. And when I was tortured, and when one of my best friends died because of the Japanese, I was *filled* with hatred, *crazy* with hatred. All I wanted was the chance to kill. I wanted revenge!"

Tomiko looked down at the floor, somewhat shocked. She didn't like the idea of being anything like this disgusting man.

"But as I thought, I faced a harder question: why was *I* so full of evil and hatred?"

Tomiko briefly glanced up at his face as he paused, but was quickly deflected down by his expression of humble honesty.

"Even when I made up my mind not to shoot at civilians from my plane, I was so angry—I did it anyway. I knew right from wrong; I just didn't have the power to do it. As I sat in prison, I knew there *had* to be more to life than hatred and revenge and killing. Where does it end? *Where?!*"

He finished his sentence looking straight into Tomiko's eyes. Fear shot through her as she looked away. Did he know why she was there? How could he? Although tense, she was becoming curiously captivated.

"They passed around books to read in prison. One day a guard gave me a Bible. I read and read, looking for some answers from God. I read about another man who was insulted and tortured and no one cared. People thought he was getting what he deserved. They didn't realize who he really was. But it turned out that he *chose* to be tortured and killed so we could have a chance to be free from the power of hatred. I wanted that. I knew I needed that. It wasn't the evil *around* me I needed to be rescued from; it was from the evil *inside* me."

Tomiko's face softened as her eyes looked past Jake to the bolts of fabric on the racks behind him. She didn't understand how, but she knew Jake was speaking directly to her.

"He made this great sacrifice because of a great love— for me, for you."

She looked up at Jake as his eyes scanned the audience.

"In that dark jail cell, I was set free from the prison of hatred, and a deep love for the Japanese people began to grow in my heart. I found that with my new heart, God was giving me new eyes. I looked at the guards who had treated my friends and me with such cruelty, and I found my hatred for them had turned into love . . . a *real* love that brings me here to you today. That's why I've come to Japan and have chosen to live here with my family. I come in the name of peace and in the name of love."

Tears formed in Tomiko's eyes as she stared at the floor. As they rolled down her cheeks, she made no effort to wipe them away.

Chapter 131

Fuchida tapped a branch to the backside of the last of four goats. "C'mon. Let's go, get in there." He stared with disgust at his German Shepherd, Lilly, as he closed the gate behind the goats. "You're a shepherd." He held out his arms. "You're supposed to help me do this." Lilly looked back with a dumb smile and let her tongue hang out. He scratched her head. "You're a good girl anyway."

As Haruko poured water into a small trough for the goats, Fuchida tossed a rake and shovel into his cart and wheeled off down the path away from the house to a tree beside his garden rows of vegetables. Lilly faithfully trotted behind him. He rubbed his upper lip, which felt so odd to him since he shaved his mustache off. It was time for it to go, though.

Getting to the tree, he looked back at the house to see if Haruko was watching him. She wasn't. He ducked behind some bushes to his little bench beside the tree, sat down, and drew from his pocket the small black Bible he had gotten months earlier.

He had the book many months before he ever opened it. Needing to work from morning until nightfall to keep his little family afloat in the fragile economic times following the war kept him occupied. But an article he read in the newspaper once again piqued his curiosity to crack open the book. The writer said if he were sentenced to live on a deserted island and could only take one book with him, it would be the Bible, as it was the most amazing book in the world.

The Bible he had purchased was the New Testament, the four stories of Jesus' life and the letters to the churches. Despite things he'd never heard or seen before in these pages, he was determined to keep an open mind, as he believed this book might contain secrets, secrets that DeShazer and Peggy had discovered, if only he would continue to dig. In the months he had already been reading, he found answers to some questions about life that took shape in his mind, yet didn't quite feel he could put it all together.

This day, he came to the end of the account of the life of Christ, a story he had never heard before. Here was a truly good man who only gave to others, yet treated horribly by those who hated him, killed for no good reason. In the fall breeze, he whispered as he continued to read aloud with deep interest and curiosity. *"When they came to the place called the Skull, there they crucified him, along with the criminals, one on his right, the other on his left. Jesus said, 'Father, forgive them, for they do not know what they are doing.'"*

In a flash, Fuchida saw the jungle mountains of Panay and the circle of grieving people holding hands in prayer surrounded by soldiers. He saw the face of Peggy's father, and he knew what he had prayed. He *knew* it, and could hear the words fall from his mouth, *"Father forgive them. They don't know what they are doing."*

This was the source of their deep love! Overcome, he fell with his face into his hands and let himself weep freely. He was finally home. His long wandering journey was over.

That night, Fuchida went through drawer after drawer, sifting through old papers and books. He knew it was somewhere. He yanked out the bottom drawer of his desk and pushed through papers. There it was.

He grabbed the wrinkled pamphlet with the title *"Watashi wa Nippon no Horyo Dearimashita."*[50] and flipped it over. Just as he remembered— there was a rubber-stamped name and address of the man who had given it to him beside the statue of Hachiko. Fuchida nodded with satisfaction, sat down at his desk, and pulled out a fresh sheet of stationery.

---

[50] "I Was a Prisoner of Japan."

Chapter 132

Early Spring 1950. Nagoya.

A young Japanese man in a coat and tie led Jake to a pair of double doors inside the community center. "Everyone's ready now," he said with a smile as he opened the door for Jake. "We're so excited."

Jake wasn't quite sure what was in store and was surprised to see more men and women greeting him at the door, quite dressed up before a group of about fifty men, women, and older children seated in rows in preparation

Jake and Tomiko.

for a photo.

A smiling young lady in a red kimono patterned with white and gold bowed to Jake, who bowed in return.

"Tomiko, so good to see you again! What's going on here?"

"Well, all of us decided we wanted to have a picture with you so we could remember our times together. We'll miss you until you return."

"You know I'll be back again for some of your *daifuku*.[51] Where would you like me to sit?"

Tomiko led Jake to the center where a smiling young girl handed a bouquet of yellow and pink flowers to Tomiko, who held out the arrangement to Jake. "As a token of our love for you, Mr. DeShazer, from all the people of Nagoya."

Jake felt he was in a dream, yet the sweet smell of the bouquet and the tears forming in Tomiko's eyes told him it was all real. He and Tomiko took their seats next to each other in the front.

The photographer motioned for people to look at him. Sitting beside Jake, Tomiko's face beamed with joy as the room was filled with a flash of a brilliant light.

---

[51] A confection consisting of a sweet rice cake with a filling.

Chapter 133

April 14, 1950. Osaka, Japan.

As he stood on a downtown street corner, a streetcar filled with passengers rattled past Fuchida. He searched to find a particular address among the buildings plastered with advertising. Glancing around, he headed toward a hotel through a sidewalk teeming with people. He'd thought about doing this for many months. Now, after he and another fellow had exchanged a number of letters, he was finally at the place. He paused when he looked at the glass doors of the hotel, then strode forward.

Fuchida sat nervously among four other men in the lobby: Tim Pietsch, the American who gave him the pamphlet about Jake DeShazer by the statue of Hachiko; Kinichi Sato, the Japanese man who sold him his little Bible; and another Japanese and an American man.

The four worked with an organization founded in 1893 by a young lady in England, Helen Cadbury, the granddaughter of the founder of Cadbury Chocolate. At an early age, this heiress to a fortune decided to dedicate her life to helping others in less fortunate circumstances and to reading the Bible each day, but found the old books too large to carry. She and a group of young ladies agreed to sew a small pocket into their skirts for a compact Bible and started the Pocket Testament League.

Years later, the organization flourished in many nations. Responding to a direct request from General Douglas MacArthur for ten million Bibles, the league met the challenge. Fuchida received one of the over eleven million Bibles that were eventually distributed to the people of Japan following the end of hostilities.

All the men sat on the edges of their seats, trying not to appear as intensely interested as they were. Fuchida was many things, but one thing he was not, was ordinary.

"Yes, I read the Bible often," Fuchida said. "I feel like I'm learning something new every day."

"And you're taking time to talk to God each day? You know, pray?" Tim said in Japanese.

"Yes, yes, all the time. I've been doing these things for months now," Fuchida responded with a bit of impatience. "I understand the importance." He had been slowly piecing together everything he'd read with everything he'd experienced along with everything he was thinking. He believed he had it right about what it meant to really believe, as he knew he did, but he felt he had to meet with some others who were more solid in their faith. He feared that perhaps he might have come up with something that wasn't quite right. He wanted assurance.

"Then, as a Christian," Kinichi said leaning back with a smile, "you should tell others what God has done for you."

Fuchida recoiled in puzzlement and with offense. "*What?* I haven't even spoken to my *wife* about this. This is a completely private matter!" Fuchida glanced around the room, surprised that none of them seemed surprised. Kinichi even smiled a bit. "Do you know what people would say? People would consider me a *traitor*—to embrace the God of my enemies?!" Fuchida shot his arm out. "The God of the *Americans?!* No, this is something I will *not* do!"

The group in the lobby went silent. Kinichi responded softly, "Just for you to know, Jesus is not from America."

Everyone smiled except Fuchida. He was serious and let his eyes fall to the floor in contemplation.

Kinichi leaned in toward the captain, as Fuchida was now known. "Listen . . . you do what you want, but remember this . . ."

Fuchida looked up into Kinichi's eyes that spoke of a deep wisdom.

"Christ said that if you're ashamed of him before men, he'll be ashamed of you before your Father in heaven. A true samurai maintains unflinching loyalty to his lord. If Christ is now your lord, he has made you his retainer. Your life belongs to him, now."

Fuchida's gaze again drifted downward.

"But you must decide what you will do."

He wasn't prepared for this. His posture fell. All Fuchida wanted was advice to help confirm some ideas about what it really meant to be a true follower of Christ. He liked living his life as a nobody on a farm with his family. Life was simple. He was happy to be left alone. Now it was becoming complicated again, and he chafed at the idea—but inside, he knew he was a coward. In many ways, he was the same man he had always been, but inside, he felt he was being renewed. Certainly, he thought, this must be seen in the outer man, too. It dawned on him that perhaps this was part of the cost of following, but he didn't like it.

Tim spoke up. "Fuchida, your nation is at a crossroads. They need hope. A new beginning. We're going downtown to the business district today. Why don't you come with us and watch?" Tim raised his eyebrows.

The team parked their black panel van on a lot beside a bridge spanning the Yodo River in a busy part of Osaka. Tim stood on a small platform beside their van painted with lettering in Japanese and English saying, "*Pocket Testament League.*" They'd mounted loudspeakers on the roof and a tiny crowd of fifteen or so stopped from their sidewalk journey to listen to the odd American who could speak their language.

"There is good news for everyone. The God of heaven cares about you and wants to help you." He paused to let a truck pass by, draped with a banner promoting a brand of socialism, filled with people in the back throwing handbills into the air, blaring propaganda over speakers.

Fuchida listened to the competing loudspeakers of the van and felt the country was turning into a circus of ideas in the vacuum after the war. No one knew what the nation would become a decade later, so everyone with an idea seemed motivated to get out there and get known. Tim's voice was simply one of many. No one cared. Few listened.

"There's a better way to live," Tim continued as the truck rolled out of sight.

As he spoke, Fuchida saw the disappointment in Kinichi's face, like a man with a key watching people unable to open a locked door. Most people walked by on the sidewalk pretending they didn't see or hear anything. They were more interested in survival than propaganda. Some listened for a sentence or two, then walked on.

Fuchida wondered what would become of his country. Glad that his life was somehow spared, he was also coming into understanding and freedom, but felt torn: either he would have to be willing to suffer the shame of those of his friends who would never understand his change of heart, or suffer the shame of a Lord who trusted him to speak on his behalf.

As Fuchida wiped the sweat from his forehead, he caught Kinichi glancing at him.

Tim was running out of steam. "If only you could . . . if you could see . . . you'd have purpose and direction in your lives in every way."

A middle-aged woman listening with a blank, hopeless face caught Fuchida's eye. His heart went out to her. If for no one else, he would speak for her. He stepped up onto the platform, and to Tim and Kinichi's surprise, stood behind the microphone.

"My name is Mitsuo Fuchida!" he proclaimed loudly. "I served our emperor with devotion and loyalty as if he were my very father. I was proud to lead the attack on Pearl Harbor!"

Electricity shot through the air. Bystanders on the sidewalk came to a standstill and turned to look.

Fuchida's heart pounded. "Yes, that's right. I am Fuchida. I sent the message, 'Tora, tora, tora!'[52] I believed in the war, that we were on a righteous path, that we were superior to other nations and races, and that we had a great destiny to fulfill."

People cautiously moved toward the platform, almost in disbelief. Whispers trickled through the growing crowd as others pointed.

"For years we were told over and over that we stood high above all the nations of the world, but where did this proud idea lead us? Doesn't Yamato mean great harmony? Yet, what harmony did we produce? In seeking honor for ourselves, instead, we reaped disgrace."

Kinichi was mesmerized. He never imagined Fuchida possessed such eloquence. Then he nodded to himself with realization. This was the same determined warrior, only in a new battle—a majestic and powerful tiger

---

[52] "Tiger, tiger, tiger!"

flexing his newfound strength from within.

"After the war, our emperor said he wanted to establish a peace that would last a thousand generations. I reflected on this over and over. How could we *possibly* do this? How could *anyone* establish a peace that could last a *thousand* generations?"

His eyes moved from face to face, each one waiting in anticipation for his next words.

"Some say if we get rid of weapons we'll get rid of war . . ."

Several people in the audience nodded with affirmation.

". . . but this isn't true. War comes from the heart. Therefore, peace must begin in the heart as well."

Tim strained his neck to get a view of the growing crowd, now filling the lot and almost blocking the sidewalk. He looked over at Kinichi who shook his head in astonishment.

"I've seen the effects of the most powerful bomb ever created by mankind. I walked in the rubble . . . among the tens of thousands of dead in Hiroshima the day after the blast of the devil bomb . . . but I have seen something *much* more powerful, a power even able to overcome hatred, the most destructive force of all."

Fuchida's posture seemed to relax.

"I heard of a girl whose parents were killed by Japanese soldiers. But, instead of seeking revenge against them, she offered forgiveness. She traveled very far and served the soldiers of Japan. I couldn't understand why she would do this. At first, I thought she must have been crazy, that she should have taken revenge. But deep inside I was ashamed—ashamed because I knew she had a sincere love. As surely as the sun rises, *katakiuchi*[53] is wrong, and this young lady was right. She had stopped the wheel of hatred. I asked myself, 'Where does this love come from?'"

The swelling crowd remained perfectly quiet, sensing they were witnessing something extraordinary.

"And I heard of an American prisoner who also found this secret, who was tortured by our soldiers, whose friends were executed, and who

---

[53] Revenge killing.

somehow came to love his enemies, so I decided to study the book they studied, the Bible. And as I read, I began to understand."

As the people standing in the streets began to block traffic, police proceeded to route cars around them, but they, too, found themselves captivated by what they heard echoing from the speakers.

"We were mistaken about God. The respect and honor that belongs to him, we had given to a mere man, like us. Even our emperor must take his proper place among men. And we were mistaken about ourselves. There is no favored race. Yes, stronger animals dominate weaker animals, but people are made in God's image. Those who believe they are no more than animals will live like animals, fight like animals . . . and end up dying like animals."

The late afternoon rush hour near the bridge came to a standstill. Tim turned the volume up as loud as it would go.

"Slowly I began to understand how these people could love like they did. They simply gave to others the love they received from their Father in heaven. And they could freely forgive because they had been freely forgiven through his Son."

A few bystanders nodded with understanding.

"I thought about how I waged war with hatred and revenge in my own heart, a war that led to the deaths of *millions* of people. *Millions* from many nations!" He paused to control his own, unexpected emotions and rubbed his eyes against his sleeve. "I would give *anything* to take back my actions at Pearl Harbor . . . but this is impossible. What can I possibly say to the God above, but to ask forgiveness? I didn't know what I was doing."

Listeners remained unmoving and silent, weighing each new thought they heard.

"We hate, and are hated in return, and then we hate even more. But when we love, we are likely to be loved in return, which begins the cycle of love. I have participated in the cycle of hatred for much of my life. But now, I want to begin the cycle of love as often as I can in as many places as I can."

The fire in Fuchida's heart seemed to blaze through his eyes.

"Our nation wasn't destroyed by the Allied Powers. No, we destroyed ourselves . . . by reaping the results of our own pride. We are all children of the same God . . ." He lifted his hands and brought them closer together.

"And, therefore, all brothers of the same blood—*hakko-ichiu*—all people under one roof, one family."

His eyes gazed across the crowd. He felt they were part of his own family. "Japan still has a great destiny to fulfill in bringing harmony, but not through war. Now I finally understand." He looked out with absolute conviction. "There can be no brotherhood of man . . . without the fatherhood of God."

Chapter 134

Early May 1950. Southeast of Tokyo.

From his first memories of seeing the ocean, Fuchida had always loved it. The salty gusts blew his hair while he sat on the mountainside overlooking the bay listening to the churning surf below and the calls of seagulls above. The beaches of Hayama lay on the opposite side of the peninsula from the Yokosuka Naval Base. Fuchida leaned back in the late afternoon by himself as the sun slowly descended on the far side of the ocean bay.

It was so calm, unlike the stormy waves crashing within his mind. He picked up a pebble and hurled it toward the ocean and sighed with exasperation. It wasn't hard for him to see how he had gotten himself into this predicament, but it was exceedingly difficult to find a way out.

He knew what he should do. That wasn't the problem. The problem was *doing* it and the pain it would cause the people he loved. The pain it would cause himself.

A pair of red-crowned cranes entered the sky from his left, and he followed them as they gracefully flapped beneath the clouds until they left his vision in the west. Perhaps it was a sign, he thought, as the birds have been long-believed to be a sign of luck and fidelity. Cranes partner for life.

Fuchida ran his hands over his head several times, then headed down the rocky hillside. There was so much he was uncertain of now, but there was one thing he *was* certain of—he had to do this one thing.

Sitting in a streetcar, he gazed out through the windows to the lighted businesses in the fading sky, yet he saw nothing. His mind was far away.

He climbed the steps of the dark wood apartment building with heavy feet, opened the door, and entered a long hallway. A man and wife walked past him carrying bags of food from the market.

After an unhurried walk down the corridor, he came to a pale green door with cracked, peeling paint, and stood before it without knocking. He could only stare at the door number, which he had seen many times before.

Sighing deeply again, he knocked three times and waited.

Quick, small steps came into hearing and the door creaked open revealing an adorable four-year-old Japanese girl, who immediately broke into a smile.

"Daddy! Daddy!" The door swung open, and she latched onto his leg. "You're back!"

Fuchida struggled to smile down at his daughter and entered, quietly closing the door behind him.

An attractive woman sat brushing her hair in front of a mirror, the woman who had served him confections in the office five years earlier. "You're an hour late," she said without looking.

He crouched down and hugged his daughter, wrapping his arms fully around her tiny body as tears formed in his eyes.

"I want to try that new restaurant," the woman said, "that just opened two blocks down," She made a few touches to her hair, checking it from both angles in the mirror. "Finally, they're rebuilding some of the shops."

Fuchida silently released his daughter and stood upright, motionless.

As she gave a last brushing to the back of her hair, her head faced Fuchida for the first time since he entered. She saw his eyes. "No. Oh no you don't! You *promised* me!" Fury swept over her face as she stood and ran from the room, beginning to sob.

The little girl looked up with fear at her mother, then at her father, who followed her into the next room.

"You said you would *leave* her!" she screamed holding a handkerchief to her face. "You promised you would divorce her and marry me! You *promised!*"

He reached out to put his hand on her shoulder, but she batted it away.

"Don't you *dare* touch me! Don't you *dare* try to take our daughter, either! She stays with *me!* You'll never see her again if you do this! Do you hear me! *Never!*" She broke down into uncontrolled weeping. "You *liar!*

You *promised* me!"

He returned to the front room realizing there was nothing more to say or do where he saw his daughter's trembling body and tear-stained face. He knew she couldn't understand what was happening, but he could clearly see she knew it was terrible. Muffled sobs from the other room filled the air.

Approaching her, she spoke with a trembling voice. "Daddy, where are you going? Daddy don't go! Daddy!" She fell into tears.

Fuchida squatted down to her and wiped her tears with his hands. Then he grasped both of her hands in his. "Daddy will write you letters. I'm so sorry. I am so, so sorry." It required all of his strength to control his own emotions as he looked into his daughter's eyes. "I have made a terrible mistake. I have to go now. I will always love you. Forever."

He released his daughter and reached for the door handle.

"I'll never let you see her again! *Never!* Do you hear me?!" the woman screamed. "*Never!*"

His daughter ran to the other room in tears.

Turning the handle, Fuchida opened the door, quietly exited, and closed the door of a room he knew he would never enter again. And he knew she was right. Japanese law gave all rights to the mother.

The following evening in his little farmhouse, Fuchida stood silently across the room from Haruko in their kitchen. The courage that propelled him to wage war and seek victory in national pride, now implored him to sue for peace in personal humility.

She wiped the same part of the counter repeatedly.

Staring without emotion, he spoke with a small voice, "Haruko, I . . . I need to talk with you."

He could tell that she knew. She'd known all along. It was a pain she'd learned to live with and had hidden just like he had, only she had no choice in the matter. She glared back at him, threw the dishrag down, turned and left the room.

His head lowered, Fuchida followed her.

Chapter 135

February 1950. Tokyo.

U nder a dusty hotel chandelier, Jake leaned on a lectern mounted with an assortment of microphones. He listened to one of the seated reporters in the meeting room. Flashbulbs popped sporadically from different angles.

"No, I'm not saying they're not guilty," Jake said in English, showing some frustration, "I'm saying that if Emperor Hirohito showed mercy to me and to some of the others who bombed Japan and let us live even though we were guilty, and if the US Government showed mercy to the emperor and didn't prosecute him, then I think that the people of America can take a stand and encourage our government to be a world leader and offer mercy to the forty Japanese men convicted of war crimes, to extend Christian mercy and forgiveness to these men."

Jake looked confidently at the reporters and finished forcefully. "The world knows America has great power." His face softened. "I'd like the world to know we have great kindness as well."

2 Part II—SATURDAY, FEB. 11, 1950 ★Los Angeles Times

Ex-Airman Pleads for War Guilty

Bombardier, Now Minister, Asks Forgiveness for Condemned Japs

BY WILLIAM A. MOSES Times Religion Editor

The former bombardier who forgave his Japanese tormentors after He spent years in a solitary prison cell now asks his fellow Americans to forgive the nearly 40 condemned Jap war criminals.

The Rev. Jacob De Shazer, shot down on the Doolittle raid of Tokyo, went to Japan as a Free Methodist Church missionary in early January of 1949. His message to more than two

comparable service records at their ease while recruits relieved them of potato peeling and pot-scouring chores.

As presented by Dr. Bryon S. Lamson, general missionary secretary for the Free Methodist

Seated in a restaurant booth, Jake glanced over at Florence with their newborn, John, on her lap, and little Paul sitting between them, then back down at a bowl being set on his plate. He stared at the brown saucy mix and carefully probed it with his chopsticks.

The Japanese couple across the table tried to contain their amusement as they observed Jake. "It's called ika no shiokara," the man said.

"Well, I'll give it a try," Jake said before swallowing hard and bringing it to his mouth, closing his eyes, and taking a bite.

Watching him wince, the friend said, "Fermented squid guts."

Jake shook his recoiling head with one eye closed and reached for his glass of water. "That's not right."

"Oh dear," Florence said, covering her mouth as she suppressed her giggle.

As Jake upended the glass trying to wash the nasty taste from his mouth, the silhouette of a man standing in the restaurant aisle caught his attention. Finishing the whole glass, Jake gave a sigh of relief to Florence, then looked back at this man who stood with his hat in his hands. Jake stared for a moment, then put his hand on Florence's shoulder. "Hey, honey, just a second."

Jake wiped his mouth with a linen, stood up, and curiously walked toward the stranger who soberly stared back at him. Jake couldn't believe his eyes and raised both hands, palms up. "Aota?" It was his old Japanese guard from his days in China.

Aota nodded as Jake came closer. "I heard you speak in the big meeting a few nights ago."

"Aota-san! How are you?" Jake said in Japanese as he reached to grab his hand and shook it vigorously. "Let me introduce you to my family!" Jake enthusiastically escorted Aota to his table.

Jake put his arm around him. "Florence, this is an old friend."

Florence smiled with a nod, but Aota looked at Jake in amazement.

Turning to the other guests in this booth, he said, "Masashi-san, this is Aota-san. We were in China together. Can you believe that?" Jake turned to Aota. "Do you live here in town?"

Aota motioned to Jake that he wanted privacy, so the two of them walked to the side of the restaurant beside some dark windows.

"I want to know more . . . about what you said. I've starting reading, you know, *the book*."

Jake gave a slow nod and couldn't help but smile. "God's kingdom is like a buried treasure—you have to dig a while, but in time, you'll find what you've been searching for. I *know* you will."

Aota hung his head and started wiping his eyes. "I'm . . . so sorry . . ."

Grabbing his shoulders with both arms, Jake looked at his friend, "The past is past. *All* is forgiven. It's time for new things, a day to celebrate. Come. Please eat with us."

After a moment, Aota looked up at Jake, gave into a smile, and nodded.

Late May 1950. Tokyo.

Holding their six-month-old second child, John, on her lap, Florence sat beside Jake slowly swinging on a hanging bench in their small backyard garden. Paul, now three years old, curiously investigated orchids.

"I don't want you to hurt your health, honey," Florence said, playfully bobbling their son.

"No, I'll be all right. I really need to do this." Jake said.

Florence looked worried. "Fasting for forty days? That's a long time,

and your body's been through so much already."

Jake looked at his wife. "Don't get me wrong. We've seen some good things happen, I'm just not getting through." He took his tea, blew over the surface and took a sip as Paul carefully disassembled a flower blossom.

"I'm a gaijin, a foreigner. Sometimes I feel welcome, but sometimes I feel kind of like . . . like I've been invited to dinner, with no place to sit. They want to hear from one of their own. Maybe someday it'll change."

Stopping the swing from rocking, Jake turned toward Florence. "But I'll tell ya, if the Japanese people ever show the same kind of zeal and devotion to God, the *real* God, that they've shown to their emperor, wow. They could do *great* things in this world for others. *Great* things."

Florence stopped rocking the baby in her arms. "Forty days on only water? Are you sure?"

Jake smiled as he enjoyed the garden, then looked at Florence. "Yeah. I'm sure."

Chapter 136

Village of Unebi.

The joyful farmer—
at rest and at peace.

The vegetable gardens in good order, Fuchida and Haruko took time to dress up the front of their little house with the planting of a few bushes and budding irises. Yoshiya and Miyako dutifully unloaded each plant beside their parents as Lilly tried to stay out of their way chasing chickens behind them.

In a wide straw hat tied with a ribbon under her chin, Haruko knelt while carefully hollowing out another hole between her and Fuchida. He delicately seated the iris with its bright purple blossoms just beginning to show as Haruko pushed the dark soil around it with her bare hands and patted it down.

Fuchida gently placed his hand on hers. "In time . . . in time, this will grow into something beautiful."

She was afraid to look into his eyes, but couldn't resist.

"I know it will," he said.

For the first time in a long while, Haruko smiled.

Inside their home, Fuchida wiped off his hands, scanned his little library, and pulled out a book on flowers and flipped through the pages.

"Honey?" Haruko called from the front porch. "Another visitor is here to see you!"

"Send him in!" Fuchida shouted back, still poring over his book.

As time went on, more and more of his old friends had found out where he lived and came by to visit and catch up. All of those who'd been in the war shared a common experience and relished each other's company.

A young man in his late twenties arrived in Fuchida's study using a single crutch, poorly dressed in worn clothes and missing one leg. He smiled and reached out his hand. "Mr. Fuchida, I'm Noboru Nakamura. It's an honor to meet you."

Fuchida smiled and glanced down at his one leg as they shook hands.

"Okinawa," Noboru said. "I was a second lieutenant."

"I'm sorry," Fuchida replied, viewing the man somewhat askance. He wasn't sure who he was or why he was there but was willing to give him an opportunity to explain.

Noboru held out a pack of cigarettes and shook one toward Fuchida.

"Thank you, but I don't smoke anymore."

He smiled and put the pack into his pocket. "I'm the president of an organization for disabled veterans, but no one will hire veterans, though, all because of *MacArthur*."

Fuchida nodded in sympathy. He, too, was disappointed in many of the new rules put in place by MacArthur, including the closing of military hospitals making crippled soldiers into street beggars. The policy of denying pensions to all former members of the military, even those from before the war especially angered him.

Noboru shuffled closer to Fuchida. "Is it true, what the newspapers say about you? I've always respected and admired you, but I can't believe that you, *you*, would become a Christian. Christianity is just the camouflage of America's occupation policy!"

"I am a Christian," Fuchida stated flatly. "This is true."

Noboru's eyebrows lowered. He nodded as if his suspicions had been confirmed. "You were once brave when you served our emperor. But now, now you've become a weak coward and a traitor." He looked at Fuchida with disgust. "You've betrayed our people. You led thousands to their deaths, men who *trusted* you and *followed* you! Now you're following the Yankee demon bastards!" He suddenly drew a knife and swung it to Fuchida's throat pushing him backward against the bookcase. "How could you turn your back on your own people, your own ancestors, and become a *Christian*, of all things?!" His eyes drilled into Fuchida's, yet Fuchida showed no fear. "What is your answer?!" His crutch fell to the floor as leaned further against Fuchida, whose arm sent a lamp crashing to the floor.

From outside, Haruko called out, "Is everything all right?"

"Everything's fine!" Fuchida yelled back.

Noboru's trembling hand pressed the blade against Fuchida's neck as the two minds wrestled, eye to eye.

"I was a patriot then, and I'm a patriot now," Fuchida responded. "I love my country and our people *deeply!*" He pushed forward against Noboru and the knife. "I was born on December third of the thirty-fifth year of the reign of Emperor Meiji in the Year of the Tiger, and I served as a samurai warrior to our emperor!"

Perspiration dripped down Noboru's face as Fuchida breathed harder.

"A samurai is a servant of a lord and I served our emperor *faithfully*. I was personally commended by the emperor and spoke to him face to face! *Have you done that?!*"

Noboru swallowed hard but held the knife firmly as their eyes remain locked.

"But our emperor himself declared that he is *no* god and *no* master. Therefore, you and I are both *ronin*, samurai without a master. *True?!*"

Their faces were now inches apart, and neither would back away.

"And according to Bushido, how does a samurai remove his dishonor, *hmm?!* There is only one way, by taking his own life—*oibara!*[54] Better to die with honor than to live in shame, right?!

"Of course!" Noboru shot back. Blood began to dampen the blade pressed against Fuchida's neck.

"Tell me," Fuchida said more gently, "what do you know of Christ?"

Noboru's eyes darted back and forth across Fuchida's face. "Nothing," he said loudly. "I don't know anything about him, and I don't care!"

"In battle, it's considered a great honor and privilege for a warrior to lay down his life for his master. But when have you ever heard of a master laying down his life for his servants?" Fuchida let the strange words sink in. "This is the master I now serve!"

Unconsciously, Noboru lowered his knife. "Why? Why would he do something like that?"

"He took our shame so we could share his honor. It was the only way to restore perfect balance and harmony."

They both continued to study each other.

"The living God who made heaven and earth, the sea, and everything in them says, '"A son honors his father, and a servant respects his master. If I am your father *and* master, where are the honor and respect *I* deserve?"'[55]

Noboru listened intently.

Fuchida sighed deeply. "I'm not proud of what I've done or how I've lived, but I will devote the rest of my life to bringing respect to the one who rightly deserves it."

"What about your reputation? Don't you care what people think about you now?"

"On the last day, all the opinions of all the men in all the world will

---

[54] The practice of committing seppuku at the death of one's master.
[55] Malachi 1:6

mean *nothing*. If it will mean nothing then, it means nothing to me now. I'll give an account of my life to God alone, not to anyone else. I'm not interested in saving my own face, but rather in saving the face of the one whose image was marred and *deserves* to be restored."

Noboru's eyes lowered, he wiped the blade on his pant leg, put the knife back into its sheath, and reached down for his fallen crutch. Balancing himself once again, he snapped into a deferential bow, like a swordsman acknowledging being outmatched. "I apologize to you, Captain Fuchida." He held his posture. "I spoke in ignorance."

"Noboru, whether you realize it or not, he is your master as well. He says, 'From the rising of the sun even to its setting, my name will be great among the nations, and in every place incense is going to be offered to my name.'"[56]

Noboru slowly straightened upright. "I accept your explanation, but I don't understand what or who you're talking about. Perhaps someday I will."

The two nodded to each other with the mutual respect of warriors.

---

[56] Malachi 1:11

Chapter 137

Mid-June 1950. Tokyo.

Jake drained the last of the orange juice from his upturned glass and set it hard on the table with a smack. "Ahhh. Now *that* is good." His taut skin and haggard appearance from his long fast were no match for his lively spirit as sunlight lit the breakfast table.

He'd broken fast only two days earlier, and his strength was returning. Although he hadn't sought publicity, the news of what he was doing touched the hearts of many Japanese who had known of Buddhists fasting as part of their discipline before, but who had never heard of someone, especially an American, fasting for their nation and spiritual well-being.

With John on her hip, Florence poured pancake batter onto the griddle.

Jake tore up a piece of toast on Paul's plate when a crisp knock on the door startled the family.

"I'll get that," Florence said, wiping her free hand on her apron.

"No, it's OK. *I'll* get the door, *you* keep working on breakfast," Jake said as he got up. "That's more important to me right now."

He opened the door.

"Hi," the man said in English, "I'm Mitsuo Fuchida."

"Welcome," Jake replied with a sincere smile as he reached out to shake his hand in amazement. "I know very well who you are. Please come in. I guess you know that I'm Jake."

As Fuchida came within view of Florence, she suppressed a gasp.

"I was sent by— "

"I know who sent you," Jake interrupted as he gave a brief, glowing look at Florence. "Please sit and eat with us."

Fuchida gave a slight bow and entered. "Thank you."

Jake closed the door behind him as Fuchida took off his shoes and said, "You're like a ray of sunlight to me. And you've put a smile on the face of God, my friend."

Looking down, Fuchida smiled and shook his head. He glanced into Jake's blue eyes. "No, *he's* put a smile on *my* face."

The formerly sworn enemies could only gaze at each other in wonder at all that had happened to each of them, how they had begun so very far apart as mortal enemies and had now ended as brothers.

Chapter 138

Peggy in a tan overcoat, red knit cap and scarf walked beside her friend down the city sidewalk on a busy Saturday. The trees stood in their fall glory of brilliant oranges, reds, and yellows. Peggy carried a single book, and her friend toted a bag of groceries in her arms.

"Hey, Peg, did you see the paper?" her friend said as she struggled to pull a folded newspaper from her bag. "Look at this." She held the paper so both could see. "It says the fella who attacked Pearl Harbor is sorry. Heard about some girl who lost her parents. Poor kid. Anyways, it's a great story."

Peggy took the paper with interest as they continued in the flow of shoppers down the Main Street sidewalk.

"Listen, I gotta run and get this pot roast in the oven. Got company coming over tonight! See you Sunday!" She cut between two cars, looked both ways, and crossed the street, leaving Peggy reading the paper by herself as she unconsciously continued down the sidewalk.

Coming to a public waste bin, she stopped, smiled, folded the paper and dropped it in the can, whispering in Japanese, "Where there is darkness, may I always bring light and where there is sadness, joy." She breathed in the cool air and enjoyed the view of a long row of trees in blazing color, the handiwork of the Master Artist. Still speaking in Japanese, she said, "Thank-you, dear Lord, for making this happen. Only you could have done this."

EPILOGUE

A man on crutches hobbled down a long, hilly road between two rice fields. Five years after he first confronted Fuchida, Noboru bowed his only knee to the one he, too, could call his Master.

Flames of the burning banner "PEACE ON EARTH" reflected off the face of Shigeru as his sober eyes followed the sparks high into the night sky. After the war, Shigeru finally came to know the same peace as that of his captives.

Reverend Dianala shook hands and smiled to townspeople leaving his little church in the mountains. Following the Hopevale massacre, he and several helpers buried his missionary friends in the mountains. He continued to serve the people of his village to the age of 112.

A terrified Captain Watanabe waved his men backward into the jungle as they fired in retreat. A shell exploded nearby, throwing him into the air. In April 1945 Captain Kengo Watanabe was killed by allied mortar fire on the island of Negros, the Philippines.

In full pilot's gear, Genda climbed into an F-104 jet fighter. Minoru Genda became a member of the new Japanese Air Self-Defense Force and was later elected to four terms in the Upper House of Councilors.

Tomiko smiled broadly as she carried a tray of hand-made daifuku into a room of friends, including Jake and his family. She became known as a woman whose face beamed with joy.

On a grassy bank in front of flowering bushes, Jake, Florence, Paul and John squeezed together beside Aota with his wife and child as a photographer focused his camera. Jake's former guard found the treasure he had long sought, and he and Jake remained friends for life.

After Jake DeShazer had feared his heart might stop in July 1945, and prayed—his heart continued to beat another 1.8 billion times. Jake fulfilled his vision and served the people of Japan for the next thirty years helping establish over twenty new churches.

A young lady in a red knit hat slowly blended into the throng of warmly dressed weekend shoppers on a busy upstate Massachusetts sidewalk. Peggy Covell declined interviews and publicity her entire life. She didn't want the death of her parents to cause others to think badly of the Japanese people, whom she deeply loved.

On their farm, Fuchida and his wife gently placed a rabbit into a wooden cage. Mitsuo Fuchida turned down the offer of the post of the first chief of staff of the air self-defense force, choosing rather to spend the rest of his life traveling the world telling others what God had done for him. Unashamed.

But for you who fear my name, the Sun of
Righteousness will rise with healing in his wings.
And you will go free, leaping with joy like
calves let out to pasture.

—Malachi 4:2

ADDENDUM

The Hachiko statue as it stands today at Shibuya Station.

Plaque on the campus of Central Philippine University in memory of those who lost their lives in Hopevale.

Jimmy Covell during a moment of reflection at the Settlement in Yokohama.

Tsurumai Park in Nagoya where 15,000 people waited to hear Fuchida speak, 1950.

The Hamada Family

Brig. Gen. John Magruder (left), presents Dick Hamada the Soldier's Medal on Jan. 3, 1946 in Washington, DC, for his role in the rescue operation that saved the lives of the Doolittle Raiders in China.

Carol Aiko DeShazer Dixon

Jake DeShazer heading to the Philippines with his friend, Aota Takeji, the guard who gave him a Bible in prison, 1976.

WOUNDED TIGER SPONSORS

I will remain forever grateful to those who lent a hand to me when I needed it most—first, to Tyler and Ian Bennett, my sons, and to Stan and Carolyn Bennett, my parents. Without you, this journey would have been immensely more difficult and prolonged.

As this project came to life through Kickstarter, I am also deeply grateful to those who trusted me enough to back the project in a significant way from the beginning. I am honored to permanently list these names in appreciation:

David R. Barrett	Michael & Anne Marie Morgan
Timothy D. Boyle	Tim Murakami
Junko Nishiguchi Cheng	James & Joy Patton
Jeff Dickerson	The Pieschke family
Steve & Kathy Giske	Howard & Dottie Reeve
Roland Haley	Audrey Rich
Mike & Beverly Hicks	Ric & Shirley Riordon
Frederick Neal Hicks	Hosanna Sillavan
John C. Housefield	Nicholas & Ioanna Sillavan
Scott & Dionne Husted	Maury Scobee
Duke Jackson & Ayami Sakaeda Jackson	Matthew William Shealy
Fred Jennings	Michael Singer
William Frank Kutney	Gregory Smith
Donovan Layton	Gary Sobczak
Patrick J. Maloney	Margaret Sorrells
Robert Francis McMahan III	Ronald & Monica Spooner
Danny & Jan Miller	Karen & Dee Tedone
Darrel & Elizabeth Mills	Linda Thompson
Charlotte Monk Stukenborg	Del & Rose Tucker
David & Karen Moore	Yoshi & Meredith Tsunehara
	Marcus Wall

WOUNDED TIGER
THE MOTION PICTURE

I first penned *Wounded Tiger* as a screenplay for an epic motion picture and it remains a vision I am fully committed to and for which I have made great preparations. Selling or optioning the rights to a studio would result in a total loss of control of the story, so, to produce *Wounded Tiger* as a motion picture I have opted to raise equity capital to partner with a studio while retaining creative control to protect the integrity of the story.

To see a test film trailer (rip-o-matic) of *Wounded Tiger* made from existing footage of other films, go to www.WTTrailer.com.

If you have a vision to see this story as a motion picture and would like to know more about participating financially, please inquire at:

Investors@WoundedTiger.com